SHADOW
OF
REDEMPTION

S.G. HUGHES

Copyright © 2020, Creidyl Publishing

All rights reserved. No part of this publication may be reproduced or transmitted in any form or by any means—electronic or mechanical, including photocopying, recording, or any information storage and retrieval system—without permission in writing from the publisher.

Published by Creidyl Publishing
To contact the publisher, please
email creidylpublishing@gmail.com

Hughes, Samuel (1997), author
Shadows of Redemption

ISBN: 9798525169012

Under a Federal Liberal government, Library and Archives Canada no longer provides Cataloguing in Publication (CIP) data for independently published books.

Technical Credits:

Cover Image: Zoe Webster
Editing & Proofreading: Bobbi Beatty, Silver Scroll Services, Calgary, Alberta
Printed and bound in Canada by Independent Publishing

Table of Contents

Prologue: Fires in the Night 1
Chapter 1: Wounded Soul 23
Chapter 2: Whispered Murmers 39
Chapter 3: Flight! 59
Chapter 4: An Ill-Traveled Path 75
Chapter 5: An Unexpected Encounter 87
Chapter 6: Secrets of the Core 100
Chapter 7: Fresh Air 113
Chapter 8: Caern Vaughn 125
Chapter 9: An Unseen Force 138
Chapter 10: An Ancient Darkness 149
Chapter 11: Over Hill and Dale 160
Chapter 12: The Inn of the Flying Raptor 174
Chapter 13: Resistance 189
Chapter 14: The Battle for Commerel 198
Chapter 15: Fate of the Traitors 212
Chapter 16: The Road to the Capital 227
Chapter 17: The Lines Are Drawn 241
Chapter 18: A Reason to Fight 251
Chapter 19: Traces of the Past 263
Chapter 20: The Rot in the Roots 272
Chapter 21: The Short Way Down 284
Chapter 22: The Council Speaks 295
Chapter 23: To War 313
Chapter 24: The Night Before 324
Chapter 25: Assault Initiation 338
Chapter 26: The Battle of Byrantia 350
Chapter 27: The Debt Comes Due 363
Chapter 28: Trial of the Traitor 371

The Kingdom of Renderive

Timeline of the Continent of Creidyl

The Glory Age

Glory 1: Recorded history begins.

Glory 232: The Selevirn Union develops the first Pralia Core.

Glory 689: The continent of Creidyl is discovered over the Faar Mountains.

The World Age

World 1: The Selevirn Union expands into Creidyl.

World 236: The city of Kelin is founded by the Creidylan Selevirnians on the Kelin Plateau.

World 453: Pralia infrastructure is established throughout Northern Creidyl.

World 453 to 699: Era of Unprecedented Prosperity for the Selevirnian Creidylans.

World 543: The city of Telerian named as the capital of Selevirnian Creidyl in what would become The Wastes.

World 627: The city of Aelser is founded north of the Dolgaard Cluster.

World 654: Caern Vaughn is founded by the native Hillmen of the Llewyn Hills.

The Breaking Age

Breaking 1: An unknown catastrophe occurs. The Selevirn Union collapses. The Wastes and the Faar Desert are formed, and Selevirnian Creidyl is destroyed.

Breaking 2 to ~685: Most records are lost, marking a period of chaos and the disintegration of the Selevirn Union into warring tribes across Creidyl. The city of Jakert is founded in the Galgre Range but soon abandoned. All Pralia technology and resources are burned by angry mobs. Creidyl descends into tribal warfare for several hundred years.

Breaking 686: Legrang the Hero unifies the warring tribes under the reign of the Warlord Grelgaard, who becomes the first Emperor of Legrangia, rebuilding the ruins of the city of Kelin and naming it the Capital of the Legrangian Empire.

Breaking 694: A dissenting Legrangian tribe ventures south where they found the Dominium of Sihleo.

The New Age

New 1: The first Emperor Grelgaard relocates to the ruins of Aelser, rebuilding it as the seat of the empire and renaming it Deregaard.

New 24: Part of the native Hillmen tribe of Caern Vaugh break off and found the city of Galgrenon in the Galgre Range.

New 172: The city of Deirive is founded in the southern region of the Legrangian Empire.

New 175: The Church of the One is founded in Sihleo. The prophet Lekaia is named as the first Speaker of the One.

New 198: The Sihleons declare Theoneria the capital of Sihleo.

New 199: The Sihleons and Legrangians contest the Terrestian War, named for the forests in which most of the conflict occurred.

New 211: The Terrestian War concludes. The Legrangian Empire retreats beyond the Terrestia Forest. Sihleo is formally recognized as a theocracy under the jurisdiction of the Church of the One.

New 222: The prophet Renderive establishes the Holy Church of Renderive in Southern Legrangia, centered in Deirive.

New 389: The mining city of Setogaard is established in the Northern Faar Mountains.

New 432: The Creidyl Conference results in the forging of the Five Holy Weapons in Setogaard.

New 560: The Legrangian Emperor Solrega initiates the religious persecution of the Holy Church of Renderive. Tensions rise in Southern Legrangia.

New 620: The city of Commerel is founded in Southern Legrangia.

New 640: Multiple rebellions are incited in Southern Legrangia. Legrangian forces from the north attack the native Llewyn Hillmen.

New 645: Rebellions in Southern Legrangia are suppressed. Heavy taxation and other cruel practices are applied by the new governor of the region installed by Emperor Gelrog. Peace is maintained by force.

New 699: Southern Legrangia rebels again. Religious leaders of the Holy Church of Renderive are burned as heretics. The hero, Asta, chosen by the Holy Church of Renderive, leads an uprising in the city of Deirive, driving the Northern Legrangians out.

The Schism Age
Schism 1: Asta declares the independence of the Holy Kingdom of Renderive from the Legrangian Empire. The First Schism War begins between the new country of Renderive and the Legrangian Empire.

Schism 31: Asta leads a unified force of Renderiveans and native Hillmen, Highlanders, and Plainsmen against the Legrangian Empire in the Battle of the Felgaard Fields, finally driving the Legrangian Empire out of Renderive and ending the First Schism War.

Schism 32: At the Deirive Conference, The Holy Kingdom of Renderive is formally created by unifying the former Legrangians and the native Hillmen, Plainsmen, and Highlanders. Asta nominates the Chief of the Plainsmen Relstert to be king of the united Renderivean forces.

Schism 45: The Archpriest Halderon of the Holy Church of Renderive establishes the Commandant's Bastion in the mountain pass to guard Deirive from the rest of the continent.

Schism 48: King Relstert establishes the Order of Guardians.

Schism 59: The Church of the One declares the Holy Church of Renderive to be heretics, and the Sihleons march on Renderive.

Schism 60: The Heretic War is initiated between the nations of Sihleo and Renderive, provoked by religious conflict.

Schism 72: The Heretic War ends with the ascension of Delius II to the position of Speaker of the One. Hostilities cease. Sihleo begins a long policy of isolationism from the world. The Politik government is founded to decentralize power away from the Church of the One in Sihleo. Peace is agreed to between the Church of the One and the Holy Church of Renderive.

Schism 74: A new border fortress, named after the hero, Asta, is constructed on the border of Renderive and Sihleo.

Schism 75 to 645: Long period of peace and prosperity between the three nations of Creidyl. Renderive becomes a thriving country.

Schism 323: The Hillmen of the Llewyn Hills formally accede to Renderive.

Schism 545: The Chelian Isles formally accede to Renderive.

Schism 646: The Legrangian Empire initiates the Second Schism War by attacking the border fortress of Caern Porth.

Schism 663: Commerel destroyed by Legrangian forces.

Schism 688: The Second Schism War ends. Renderivean forces drive the Legrangian Empire back to Regigaard but cannot take the fortress. Renderivean forces retreat back to Caern Porth where a peace treaty is established.

Schism 692: Commerel rebuilt after it's destruction in the Second Schism War.

The Rising Age

Rising 243: The City of Byrantia is established in Southern Renderive.

Rising 248: The Holy Church of Renderive removes itself from governance, retaining only a moral and cultural role in Renderivean life.

Rising 249 to 630: Uneasy peace between the Legrangian Empire and Renderive continues. Small skirmishes occur along the Sieth River border, but none erupt into full-blown conflict.

Rising 653: Bleiz Terin is born in Deirive.

Rising 655: Aiden Greshaun is inaugurated as King of Renderive at the age of seventeen after the unexpected death of his father.

Rising 655: The Third Schism War begins with the Legrangian Empire seizing the land to the north of the Llewyn Hills.

Rising 657: The Third Schism War ends when King Greshaun, aided by his companions, Conan Draca, Brynmor Berwyn, and Isaac Glathaous, defeats the Legrangian forces at the Battle of Icaron north of Caern Porth.

Rising 658: Isaac Glathaous is granted lordship and gifted the lands of the forests around the town of Forent, which is renamed Glathaous.

Rising 661: Valthor Tarragon is born in a small village outside Caern Vaughn.

Rising 670: The Marveuz Excavation discovers the remnants of Selevirnian Pralia technology in The Wastes.

Rising 673: Luca Draca is born in Draca.

Rising 674: Alistair Glathaous is born in Glathaous. Calunoth is brought to Glathaous by his mother.

Rising 678: Valthor Tarragon attends The Royal University of Renderivean Akadaemia and subjects himself to Ynia-infusion experiments.

Rising 680: The Legrangians again launch an attack on Renderive: the Sieth Incursion. They are swiftly driven back by the heroics of Felix Draca, son of Conan Draca, and Valthor Tarragon of the Llewyn Hills.

Rising 681: Valthor Tarragon is named the youngest Guardian in Renderivean history at the age of nineteen.

Rising 687: Bleiz Terin resigns his command as Commander of the Wings and becomes an instructor of the Knights of the Wilds.

Rising 692: Isaac Glathaous perfects the Glathaous Core in his laboratory at Glathaous. Calunoth leaves Glathaous with Luca Draca, Bleiz Terin, and Lauren Abraham to begin a realm-changing journey.

Prologue

Fires in the Night

    The bright spring sun cast its glaring gaze throughout the halls of Glathaous Castle. It was approaching midday when the sun would reach its zenith and bathe the ancient stone walls with light through all its many windows. No clouds obscured the light's path as it encroached on the castle and the surrounding forests. The last vestiges of snow had recently vanished from the castle grounds, rendering the ground firm but not frozen and allowing the castle's denizens to erect their banners, flags, and white pavilion tents.

    The castle itself was abuzz with activity; the peasantry of the castle and the town had earnestly begun preparing for the Spring Dawning Day celebrations, of which the castle was to be the staging ground for much of the festivities. Although only a select few townspeople had been invited; everyone nevertheless found themselves in the spirit of the occasion as they adorned the weary old castle with decorations and lanterns to enliven the grounds. While only the highest-ranking members of the town, such as the mayor and the sheriff, would join the castle's residents at the night's feast, the townspeople would be enjoying their own celebrations. Their celebrations would be less grandiose, but far more lively.

    Lord Isaac Glathaous himself was renowned throughout Renderive for his eccentric yet brilliant inventions. He dabbled in matters both arcane and mundane and, more often than not, produced success. Although not noble by birth, Lord Glathaous had distinguished himself fighting alongside King Greshaun with sword and shield in the Fourth Schism War against the Legrangian Empire thirty-five years ago. Lord Glathaous had been granted the lordship and title of the region of Glathaous as a reward for his bravery. Forever a man of the people, he was beloved by his subjects in the small town of Glathaous and by his soldiers for both his intellect and the care he exercised over his people. His men, for their part, could be recognized by their simple iron-plate mail—common for the time—emblazoned with the chipped ax that served as the Glathaous insignia. While the iron plating was inferior to the steel armor worn by the national military, the Holy Knights of Renderive, it was far more economical and better suited to the demands of its wearers.

Isaac Glathaous had once attempted to host the Midsummer Celebrations for the entire town and castle; however, he had been forced to reign in his generosity when the resulting celebration had led to such enormous consumption that a merry band of farmers from an outlying region had accidentally broken the doors to the stables, leading to a stampede of horses escaping into the town. The resulting damage had put the Glathaous treasurer in such a state of shock that he expressly forbade the lord from ever attempting such an endeavor again.

And so, the people of Glathaous were both attentive and jovial in their preparation for the celebration. The packed dirt of the courtyard was further tromped down by the trampling of boots and the nervous shimmying of horses as the people went about their work. As they worked, rumors circulated that the festivities would be attended by a Sihleon minister. Although the Sihleon people were far more refined in their demeanor than the Renderiveans, the townspeople were keen to show off their hosting capabilities. The fine silks and olive skin of the Sihleons would not be outdone by the hearty and boisterous Renderiveans.

The camaraderie between the noble and the lower classes of Glathaous was unique among Renderivean culture. Isolated from the world by the surrounding Terrestia Forest, the enclosed nature of the territory resulted in a casual and familial relationship between the upper and lower classes. Under the stewardship of Isaac Glathaous, even the poor of Glathaous lived comfortably, with the upper classes enjoying a more modest life than their compatriots in other regions of Renderive.

The bustling of people in the courtyard was a source of frustration to the castle's old quartermaster, Keil, who, as manager of the feast's provisions, was in a markedly fouler mood than many of his comrades. So much darker was his mood that he had taken to addressing his soldiers by the first aspect he noticed about them rather than their names.

"Oi, Scarbrow, get those barrels into the hall! Skinny, if you're not strong enough to lift the benches, then why are you trying to lift them? Bignose, if rotten fruit ends up on the table, I'll throw you *and* them over the wall! Princely, stop standing there looking noble! You're supposed to be in charge of these people! Get them organized, or by

Asta, I'll have you polishing the silverware rather than your sodding armor!"

The last command was directed at Oscar, the captain of the guard. Dressed in the iron armor that marked him as a defender of the castle, Oscar maintained the highest standard of appearance and consequently spent a great deal of time ensuring his armor gleamed brighter than those of his colleagues. As a former Knight of the Wings, he was unused to being ordered around by the angry old quartermaster, but he had the sense to understand this was not a fight he would win. Oscar cordially apologized and beckoned to one of the young guards to follow him and assist. Although technically of a higher rank than the quartermaster, the older captain had no qualms about listening to the man, who was widely respected as the caretaker of the castle.

"Calunoth, with me!" Oscar barked at the guard the quartermaster had just branded as "skinny."

The young guard, who had been struggling valiantly to shift the heavy oak benches from a storage alcove, passed his duties on to one of the larger guards and hurried over to his commanding officer.

"Yes, sir?" Calunoth responded, saluting the captain.

"I told you to drop the excessive formalities, lad. I appreciate your zeal, but it makes me feel like I'm back in the Knights again," Oscar responded. "We'd best make ourselves useful away from Keil. He's working hard, but I think the stress is getting to him. I was planning on going into town to pick up the last wagon of ale, but I think it would be best if I stayed here to help organize matters. Not to mention, I'm still expected to administer Alistair's swordplay lessons on top of all this."

"Whatever you say, sir," Calunoth responded, his fern-green eyes shining. "Would you like me to take the delivery for you?"

Oscar regarded the eager young man with a guarded sense of amusement. He was taller than his peers, but his height was counterbalanced by his slight frame. His short crop of jet-black hair highlighted his eyes. In truth, he bore a resemblance to Lord Isaac Glathaous himself, and this naturally caused rumors to sprout among the men, especially since no one knew who Calunoth's father was. The boy's mother had appeared at the steps of Castle Glathaous on a cold winter evening nineteen years ago, injured and with child. Calunoth had been born later that night, but his mother had not survived the ordeal. She had lived only long enough to pass on her wishes for the boy's name, which had been honored.

Lord Glathaous had taken Calunoth in and had him raised among the servants until he was sixteen, and which point he had joined the castle guards. To avoid the stigma of being labeled nameless, Isaac Glathaous had granted the boy the last name, Leiron, and entrusted him to the care of the castle servants.

Now, Calunoth considered the guards his family, a stand-in for the family he'd never had. Generally well liked, the boy owed his life to Lord Glathaous and his fellows at the castle, a fact Calunoth honored with his dedication to his work. He was a man of ascension in the castle, to be sure. If Calunoth maintained his course, he could be the captain of the guard within fifteen years.

"Aye, that's exactly what I was about to suggest. Take one of the horses and go to The Ax and Stable. There should be a wagon there with the ale. Here's the money." Oscar handed him a small bag of coins. "Just be wary that the innkeeper there is a bit … disreputable. Try to talk to one of the serving girls instead. If the innkeeper tries to charge you more than this bag as negotiated, just rattle your sword and glare at him a bit. With men like him, their greed rarely outstrips their cowardice."

"I'll be back as soon as I can, sir," Calunoth said, taking the bag.

"Take your time, lad. We have men enough here as it is, and with Keil screaming at everyone, we're just getting in each other's way. We'll have everything in order soon enough," Oscar replied.

"Oh, and Cal!" Oscar called to Calunoth as he turned to leave. "If you want to bring that stable girl to town with you to help, I'm sure she'd appreciate the time away!"

Calunoth flushed a deep red as Oscar grinned at him. Attempting to maintain his dignity, he merely gave a stiff salute and turned to wade his way through the crowd massing in the courtyard.

***

The stables sat in the northernmost corner of the courtyard, just inside the iron-bound front gates.

Calunoth did not resent the task at all. In fact, he was happy for any opportunity to visit the stables. He was not overly fond of horses, but he was always excited to meet with one lady who worked with the horses. Although he was a relatively handsome young man, he always had some reservations about his own prospects and was prone to severe awkwardness around any female he found becoming.

This was something some of the guards had picked up on when Calunoth had fallen off his horse when returning from a long patrol once and had been assisted by a young stable worker named Willow. His reaction to the woman, namely to stammer, then entangle his bracer in the straps that held the saddle in place, had been the subject of great mirth to the guardsmen around the fire later that evening.

Regardless, Calunoth had eventually gained the courage to go and speak with Willow, and although he had been, according to one of his colleagues, "as red as a steamed pig," he had managed to get through an initial conversation and had thanked her for her assistance. She had been graceful and becoming in Calunoth's eyes, and he had soon found himself thinking about her more and more. As time passed, he had attempted many times to engage with her more formally but never quite managed to get the words out. Calunoth was no coward. He could run unarmed into a group of bandits or tackle a loose boar to the ground without hesitation, yet he could not muster the courage to confess his feelings to the woman. Willow, for her part, always spoke with him but never seemed annoyed by his hesitance.

The two had grown much closer in recent months, and Calunoth had sworn to himself that he would eventually tell her how he felt. He hoped that by midsummer he would find the opportunity to do so, but that was a matter for a later time. When Calunoth appeared at the stables today, he was to appear as a guard, not as a potential suitor.

Calunoth knocked on the door of the stables before entering, careful not to startle anyone. Many of the stable hands were busy cleaning the stalls and restocking the horses' feed. Most of the workers were the young children of the servants or guards who were made to work the stalls as a lesson in hard work. Raising a hand of acknowledgment to the stable crew, Calunoth walked to the last stall to find Willow brushing down one of the guards' horses.

Willow was atypical of the other stable hands. She was older for one, only a year younger than Calunoth. Her long auburn hair was tied back as she worked, revealing her delicate features. She wore short trousers, rather than the typical dress, and was taller than most other women. Willow also had no desire to continue living in the castle or town indefinitely. She spoke often about her keen interest in the magical practices and technologies of Ynia and wanted to apprentice herself to one of the researchers in the castle. Her ultimate goal was to eventually attend the school of Akadaemia in Eastern Renderive. Willful and hard working, Calunoth had no doubt that she would get there eventually.

"Good afternoon, Miss Willow," Calunoth said formally. "I trust you're not finding these preparations too taxing?"

Willow turned away from the horse and looked at him, amusement shining in her eyes. "So, I'm getting guard Cal and not fun Cal today, am I? How disappointing." She shook her head, hiding her smile. "I'm managing. Most of the work is already done. And fortunately, much of the ordinary evening work is being put off until tomorrow. Once the horses are all back, we'll all be heading into the castle for the celebrations." It was standard for the townspeople to celebrate with their families and friends in town while everyone who lived and worked at the castle was rewarded with Isaac Glathaous' generosity.

"I'm glad to hear it," Calunoth replied smiling, loosening up a little. "Captain Oscar has asked me to procure some supplies from town, and I'll need a horse to help tow the cart. I was hoping you could help me."

Willow motioned at the horse she had been brushing with the fine comb. "You can take old Greyhoof. He's a little tired, but he's reliable." Willow smiled her radiant smile at Calunoth, her eyes sparkling mischievously. "He'll probably make it up the hill."

Willow attached the reins to the old mare, Greyhoof, and then handed them to Calunoth with a slight air of expectation.

Picking up on the hint, Calunoth took the reins and hesitantly cleared his throat. "A wild horse like this might cause me some trouble. I don't suppose you'd like to come with me to town? Just to make sure the horse doesn't bolt on me, you understand?" Calunoth offered, a slight tremor in his voice.

Willow smiled at him, sending a pleasant shiver down his spine, and responded with a hint of teasing in her voice. "Of course, good sir. I certainly wouldn't want to see you hurt by the beast." Her tone turned more serious for a moment. "Unfortunately, I don't think he'll manage too well with both of us on him. It would probably be better if we just walked alongside."

"You can ride him if you want. I don't mind walking. It's not too far to town," Calunoth suggested, offering her the reins.

"It's probably best if we save his strength. If you'd have come earlier, we could have taken one of the younger horses, but the rest are being used for the preparations now," Willow responded.

Calunoth nodded and thanked her for her assistance. Willow was a capable woman and did not need to be treated delicately. Regardless, Calunoth had felt required by honor to suggest she ride. So, with the old mare in tow, the couple left through the mighty front gate of the fortress and strode down the hill road toward the smoking chimneys of the town.

***

Glathaous Town was a fair distance from the castle. The castle itself had not been wholly built by Renderiveans. Rather, the ruins of an ancient castle had been reconstructed during the First Schism War and had weathered numerous assaults in the first Legrangian invasion. The castle had then become a military base during the Third Schism War and the center of a great deal of magical and mechanical military research and innovation. The town had risen a full two miles away from the castle for two reasons.

Firstly, as the castle was surrounded by the eastern fringe of the Terrestia Forest, the town had been built around the only road a large armed force could foreseeably traverse. This road had been built by the castle's founders and continued up the steep hill the castle was situated upon. As a result, any invading army would have to travel through the town first, thereby allowing time for the castle's defenders to ready themselves for an attack.

Secondly, the nature of the experiments conducted at Glathaous Castle necessitated the distant location of the town. While the mechanical contraptions Lord Glathaous designed were useful, their capacity to cause damage were significantly less than their magical counterparts, which held the potential for enormous destruction. Using the strange flow of energy known as Ynia, Lord Glathaous and his researchers frequently dabbled with the fringes of the natural world, thereby requiring the town's distance for its own safety.

The researchers' work was a well-kept secret, with not even the captain of the guard made aware of it. What the people did know was that an Ynium experiment gone wrong could cause significant damage not just to the castle, but the surrounding area as well. As a result, the town had been built away from the castle, and the experiments conducted in the laboratories beneath the castle were performed with the greatest possible secrecy.

There were rumors about the experiments, but for most denizens of the castle and the town, it was information that simply didn't interest them. There was food on the table and peace in the land. And that was enough for most.

The town itself was awash with activity when Calunoth and Willow arrived. Children played in the streets. Merchants peddled their wares. The alluring aroma of spiced meats and fine stews wafted from the stalls, many of the best products having been saved for this occasion. All the townsfolk were busily moving about in preparation for their own celebrations. While a few members of the town would enjoy the feast in the castle, most of the townsfolk were staging their own feasts. Families would come together and enjoy the company, hot food, and fine drink.

And then there were always a few who would forestall their own preparations and instead head to the local tavern to enjoy the evening with friends and good company. The only tavern in Glathaous was The Ax and Stable, named for the logging industry of Glathaous that served as the main source of income for the town. The tavern itself had passed under new ownership only in the last year after the previous innkeeper had passed on from old age. With no known family, the tavern had become the property of Lord Glathaous, who had it sold to the highest bidder, an investor named Owen Cacce from the city of Commerel to the east. The new innkeeper was not nearly as well liked as his predecessor as he had increased the price of drink and failed to warm to the people of Glathaous. His patrons likewise had failed to warm to him. Regardless, as the sole tavern in the town, Owen was not denied business, and the tavern was as busy as always.

It was to this tavern in the center of town that Calunoth and Willow led their old mare. The Ax and Stable was designed in much the same way as the other buildings in town. The sturdy lumber that served as the town's main export was on full display, the sanded mahogany trunks, thicker in girth than many men and glistening with the oil that maintained them, standing as mighty sentries for the entranceway. Unique to the tavern was the stained-glass window inset above the door on the third floor. Glass of any kind was rare in Glathaous, saved only for the wealthiest of shopkeepers, so the stained-glass window with its depiction of a rose ax laid across a yellow horseshoe was the pride of the proprietor.

    Calunoth remembered Oscar's advice and resolved to avoid the innkeeper if he could. Fortunately, the staff were beginning to arrive to prepare the tavern for the evening, and Calunoth was able to catch the attention of one of the serving girls sweeping the floor outside the door. "Excuse me, miss!" Calunoth said, walking up to her and handing her the note the captain had given him. "I'm here from the castle to pick up an order for Captain Oscar. It's for a cart of ale."

    The serving girl looked up from her sweeping. Her eyes bore the deep circles of sleepless nights, and her face was etched with lines from years of toil, leaving her face lifeless and vacant. The girl took the note from Calunoth, read it, and nodded.

    "Come this way," she said, leading them around the back of the tavern. "The cart arrived this morning. It's waiting for you here."

    As they set about attaching the cart, Calunoth struck up a conversation with the serving girl.

    "So, are you expecting a busy night tonight?" he asked politely.

    "I'm only here to set up the tavern," she responded, working quickly. "I've been asked to help serve at the castle tonight."

    "We're going back up to the castle after this. If you'd like to join us, you can," Willow offered politely. The serving girl shook her head.

    "Thank you, but there is still much to do here. And Owen will have my head if everything isn't perfect before I leave."

    Willow and Calunoth wished her happy festivities, to which she only grunted in response, and then set upon the road to leave town.

    As they traveled back to the castle, Willow nudged Calunoth's side and whispered, "Hey, Cal. Do you see those black-robed fellows?" she asked, pointing out a pair of travelers wearing exclusively black garb with hoods over their head. "Do you know who they are?"

    Calunoth gazed at the two people she had indicated. They walked quickly, immersed in the shadows. Had it not been for the glint of steel from the swords on their belts, he wouldn't have noticed they were there. He certainly did not recognize them.

    "I have no idea, honestly," Calunoth responded. "Maybe they're just wary travelers."

    "I thought that about the first ones I saw," Willow replied, "but they're the fourth group of people I've seen wearing the same garb so far. It's awfully strange clothing. Do you think we should tell Oscar about them?"

Calunoth glanced at her, catching her gaze, surprised she had noticed them when he hadn't. Realizing he was staring directly into her eyes, Calunoth quickly averted his eyes, a tiny blush appearing on his cheeks.

"They're a bit strange, but perhaps they're just passing through. Perhaps a large group of them came in for the festivities and broke up into smaller groups. Perhaps they're from Kelin. I've heard they dress strangely there," Calunoth responded. "I don't think there's any need to worry Oscar. He has enough to deal with right now."

"You're probably right, but I get a bad feeling from them. I can't really explain it," Willow replied, still looking slightly worried. "I'd feel better if we told him about them."

Calunoth, aware there was no point in arguing the matter, agreed and resolved to talk to Oscar when they returned. Turning to happier topics, Calunoth and Willow talked merrily as they led their charge back to the castle.

The sun was low in the sky by the time Calunoth and Willow arrived at the gates of Glathaous Castle. Ynia lanterns lit the inside arch of the gate, past the portcullis. The lanterns cast an unnatural shadow across the face of the gates. An invention of Isaac Glathaous, the lanterns were unusual in that they were lit by magic rather than flame. Each contained a small crystal imbued with a small amount of Natural Ynia. It generated an eerie white light but no heat, and many of the guards found this unsettling.

The gate had already been partially closed, the guards having anticipated that no further supplies would arrive for the remainder of the evening. So, when Calunoth and Willow arrived, Calunoth had to flag the guardsmen in the gatehouse. "Can you open the gate please? We have more supplies!" Calunoth called loudly.

An elderly guard peeked his head out of the gatehouse and squinted at them. "Is that you, Alistair? What have you been doing outside the castle?" he shouted down at them.

Calunoth recognized the elderly guard as Silas, the eldest member of the guard. Once a ferocious warrior in his day, he had refused to hang up his gambeson as he had aged, insisting he could still fight like a man half his age. And, still viewed favorably after years of service, his attitude was humored. However, though his dedication was never doubted, his senses had quickly begun to deteriorate. He could barely hear if you didn't shout at him, and his eyesight was failing. Combined with his refusal to wear spectacles, Silas was no longer an effective guard. But anyone who suggested otherwise would most likely be challenged to a duel, and the injuries that would result from said bout would not be to anyone's benefit. So, he was kept on, though another guardsman always worked alongside him to ensure the castle's security was not threatened.

At the mention of Alistair, a second guard appeared at the gatehouse window. Alistair was the youngest son of Lord Glathaous and was held in much lower esteem than his elder brother, Julian. Few people ever engaged with Alistair as he kept himself confined almost continually to the castle. He had never ventured into town and was quiet when in public. The idea that he had left was a surprise to anyone with their senses intact, and so the second guard gazed down at the pair.

"That's not Alistair, you daft old man! That's Calunoth. I know they look similar, but you should know by the voice." The second guard called down then. "We'll open the gate for you, Cal. Just give us a minute!"

In just moments, the cast-iron gates slowly ground open. The gates of Glathaous Castle were famous for their strength and resilience. The gates were the originals as they were of such fine construction that the new castle had been built around them. As Calunoth and Willow passed through them, they saw the courtyard was almost empty now. Everyone had either already gone inside the castle or returned to town. The only others in the courtyard were a small entourage of men in white cloaks leaving the castle.

They moved silently, and Cal could hear them speaking in a strange dialect as they approached. The leader had a distinctly rat-like appearance, with a thin, sallow face. He bore a deep scar across the left side of his face, trailing from just below his eye to the tip of his mouth. Calunoth couldn't help but feel unsettled by the man, for despite his ghastly appearance, his voice was like sweet honey. The man glanced at Calunoth as he passed, seeming to pause for a moment, but Calunoth dismissed it as a trick of his imagination. The men swept past them and through the open gate. As they left, the heavy iron doors ground to a close behind them.

"Who was that?" Calunoth wondered out loud.

"That was Lenocius, the Second Minister of Sihleo," Willow answered. "The castle maids were gossiping about him earlier. He's a guest of Lord Glathaous, but apparently he spent the better half of the morning talking to the lord's son."

"What does he want with Julian?" Calunoth queried.

"Not Julian, Alistair. And I have no idea," Willow responded. "But it's not important. The feast will be starting soon, so we'd best hurry."

Calunoth and Willow enjoyed a quiet walk to the back of the kitchens where a couple porters helped them unload the cart. After they were done, Willow took Greyhoof by the reins and turned to Calunoth. "Thanks for inviting me to help you do your job," she said teasingly. "I have to go and prepare myself for the feast. Would you be interested in walking in with me afterwards?"

Calunoth was startled by the invitation and could swear Willow was blushing in the encroaching darkness. He desperately desired to say yes. However, he had to attend to his responsibilities first.

"I'm so sorry," Calunoth said, bowing his head. "I would love to, but I volunteered to take the gate shift tonight. Almost everyone else will be at the feast. I wouldn't be able to meet you until past midnight."

"Oh," Willow said quietly, her smile fading. "That's okay. Maybe I'll still be there at midnight. Will you come and join me after your shift?"

"Absolutely!" Calunoth replied, deeply relieved he hadn't offended her.

"Then I'll wait for you there," Willow said, some of her earlier smile returning.

With that promise made, Willow bade farewell to Calunoth and headed back to the stables with Greyhoof. Calunoth was frustrated. Why had he volunteered to take this shift? He could have spent the night dancing with Willow. Maybe with enough ale he might have found the courage to confess to her.

However, he had promised Captain Oscar that he would take the shift. And it seemed highly unlikely the captain would be able to find anyone else to take it at this late hour. The castle would be practically unguarded tonight as it was. There would only be a skeleton crew of three men, including him, at the front gate. Seven other guards would be dotted around various posts, all to be relieved at midnight, but most of the guards would be inside the castle enjoying the feast.

Though it wasn't likely anyone would threaten Glathaous Castle, the veneer of security had to be maintained.

Realizing that he would have to start his shift soon, Calunoth went searching for Oscar to report that he had completed his task. He found the captain in the training hall in the west wing.

The training hall also doubled as an armory and was where the guards and the nobles practiced their battle craft. The room was large, with long rows of weapons dotting the wall. Wooden blades were kept in chests at the back of the room, and shields adorned racks behind the chests. The entire room was built around the practice floor. On a normal night, there would typically be a dozen pairs of guards training on the floor; however, given the occasion of the evening, the room was deserted but for one lonely pair.

Captain Oscar stood facing Calunoth, his opponent facing away from him. In a flurry of wooden training swords, Oscar handily disarmed his opponent.

"You're getting much better, but you're still too weak," Oscar said, addressing his opponent. "You need to put more passion into it. I know you understand the technical skills, but if you don't *want* to win then you'll always lack the conviction needed to land a heavy blow. I know you don't like fighting, but sometimes you have to." He wiped the sweat off his brow with a forearm. "That's enough for tonight. You may retire."

The opponent merely nodded and callously tossed his weapon into one of the metal chests. As he turned toward Calunoth and made to leave, Calunoth realized the man was Alistair Glathaous, the son of Lord Glathaous. Even with the bustle of the ongoing celebrations, Isaac Glathaous had insisted that his son continue his instruction. Unlike the guards, who trained under the castle's instructor, Alistair received the tutelage of the busy Captain Oscar.

Alistair's jet-black hair hung partly over his face. His eyes were a severe forest green that boasted of an arrogant intelligence, and he glared at Calunoth as he stepped out of the lordling's way. Alistair left with a contemptuous, "Humph!"

Oscar shook his head, his gaze following the young noble, and sighed. "That boy could be as useful as you one day if he could just get out of his own head. Physically, almost identical, but mentally, worlds apart. But I'm sure you haven't come to me to hear me complain. What can I help you with, lad?"

Calunoth reported that he had completed the delivery, then told him of his concerns about the black-garbed men in town. Oscar listened thoughtfully as Calunoth described the men. When he had finished, the captain shook his head.

"I don't know anything about these people, but I'll ask the servants and the guards to see if they've noticed anything amiss. Anything short of an army won't get past the gate, but I'll tell Aaron about it anyway. Maybe he'll conjure something up. We had the Second Minister of Sihleo here as Lord Glathaous' honored guest earlier, but he left a little while ago. You might have even passed him on the way in."

"I did," Calunoth said. "Nasty scar he's got there."

"Aye," said Oscar, nodding. "He's an important man, but if someone's got plans for him outside the castle, there's very little we can do now. If he had stayed here with Lord Glathaous we could have done something, but the lord is our first priority. Anyway, I believe you're supposed to start your shift in a few minutes. Make sure you come inside when you're done. We'll try to leave some food for you."

Calunoth thanked the captain, saluted, and left. As he walked back to the gatehouse, he couldn't help but feel troubled. The black-garbed men and the strange minister weighed heavily on his mind, but he had to dismiss it. He would just have to keep a careful watch tonight.

***

"It's too damn cold up here!" Jovi complained, rubbing his hands by the fire. The guardsman was originally from Chelia and bore the same darker skin and cold intolerance all of his fellow Chelians displayed.

"I don't know why you're here in the first place!" Paul retorted. "You had a beautiful island with constant sunshine, and you leave it to come here to our cold, wet forests. You must be funny in the head."

The two guardsmen continued their argument while Calunoth grimly maintained the lookout. The gatehouse stood almost thirty feet above the gate, and although he was not afeared of heights, the distance made it difficult to detect activity on the road. The road itself was lit for about a hundred feet by the magical lanterns, but any activity off the road would be hard to see.

The fact that those lanterns were there at all was at Oscar's behest. Sharing Cal's discomfort, he had asked the mages to set up lanterns lining the road early in Calunoth's shift. He and the guardsmen had been particularly surprised when Archmage Aaron had emerged in his flowing green robes to do the job himself. Taller than most of the guards and with over thirty years of experience under his belt, the archmage was the chief mage and researcher, working directly with Lord Glathaous on military innovations. As a master battle mage of the Renderivean Upper Circle, he could single-handedly cause more damage to an attacking foe than all of the stationed castle's soldiers combined.

However, he considered himself above such actions and so spent most of his time buried in his research, his piercing eyes—crinkled at each outside edge—darting between complex tomes. Despite his rank, he bore a casual air and rarely raised his voice. The only thing that ever angered him was being distracted from his research. When Jovi had asked why he had come to light the lanterns instead of sending one of his disciples, he had replied candidly. "Because I'm seriously concerned that my people have already drunk so much they couldn't manage a match, never mind an Ynium device."

The guardsmen took that information, along with the sounds of revelry emanating from the castle behind them, as evidence the night was proceeding as expected. Nevertheless, Calunoth couldn't shake the feeling of disquiet he felt.

Paul and Jovi had now ceased arguing as Paul had fallen asleep, and Jovi had devoted himself entirely to the small fire they kept burning in the gatehouse. So Calunoth stood vigil alone, his hand never far away from the hilt of his sword. With the road seemingly quiet, Calunoth's thoughts drifted to the festivities. Every attendee would put on their best attire for the occasion, but if he were to visit afterwards, he would have to do so in his uniform. He thought about Willow, likely dressed radiantly, waiting for him. Maybe she'd have even let her hair down. *If I make her wait too long, she might end up dancing with someone else,* Calunoth thought, and his stomach twisted at the thought. He would ask for her love tonight, he resolved. The longer he waited, the less likely it was she would choose him. After all, she wouldn't have a lack of willing suitors.

So absorbed was he with his thoughts and the noise coming from the castle that he didn't hear the soft tap of boots on the stone stairs behind him. And neither did the other guards.

***

    Oscar was enjoying his evening. Realistically a bit too much. He had arrived late to the feast after speaking with the servants and meeting with the archmage, who had arrived at the high table shortly after him. After Aaron had assured him of the road and castle's security, he had journeyed down to the kitchens where he was told by the matron, in no uncertain terms, that if anyone unauthorized stepped into her kitchen, they would be served as the appetizer. Oscar often thought she and Keil would make a good couple.
    With both the castle and the sole road leading to the castle well secured by the guards above the gate and the lanterns illuminating the path, he had relaxed. Although he'd had the great fortune of missing the lord's usual speech, he had correspondingly had less time to catch up with his guards, who had already worked their way through two casks of ale before he'd arrived. Though he was required as an officer to sit at the high table, Lord Glathaous had hinted that if he were to socialize with his guards, nobody would notice.
    The archmage sat to Lord Glathaous' left with Julian, his eldest son, to his right. Oscar was supposed to have sat next to Alistair, two seats to the left of the lord, but for some reason, the boy was nowhere to be found.
    Oscar scanned the throng of tables and people clustered in the hall. He could see Keil in the corner, appearing distinctly more relaxed than he had been earlier in the day, and some of his guards attempting to begin a chorus of drinking songs, to the obvious chagrin of the castle pastor. No sign of Alistair though. He thought he saw that stable hand Calunoth liked among the servants' tables. Swallow? Was that her name? Whatever her name, she was clearly dressed to impress. And impress she did given the small contingent of young guards clustered around her table. *For Cal's sake, I should probably go and scare them off. If the boy's willing to work on a night like this, it's the least I can do for him,* Oscar thought. Finishing his drink, he put all thoughts of Alistair aside and went to relieve the young lady.

***

    Paul's guttural cry from behind him was the only warning Calunoth received. Drawing his sword, he spun around to see three black-clad figures advancing over Paul's body with their swords drawn. Two had their features obscured by black hoods. One wore no hood, but in the rush of adrenaline, Calunoth didn't take the time to examine his face.

    The men moved swiftly. Jovi managed to draw his sword as he was approached but was caught off balance by the unhooded figure. Reaching desperately into the fire as he fell, Jovi slammed his hand down on the logs, causing one to fly out onto the cold stone floor, brightening the space and giving him the time he needed to recover his footing. Swiftly finding his balance, he engaged the unhooded figure with his sword. The burning log on the floor sent flickering shadows dancing across the walls of the gatehouse as they dueled.

    The other two figures moved toward Calunoth in a pincer movement, coming at him from both sides. Recognizing the maneuver, Calunoth dove and rolled forward into the space the two figures had previously occupied, using his right hand to push himself off the floor while slicing left with his sword. The move had been risky, but effective. His blade had swung true and cut deep into the thigh of one of his assailants, severely reducing his movements. In another brilliant move, Calunoth kicked back into the wounded thigh of the assailant causing him to fall to his knees, at the same time bringing his sword across to the other assailant to block his blow. In one last motion, he whipped his left hand around—still clutching the hilt of his sword—and bashed it into the head of the kneeling man, knocking him out of the fight temporarily.

    The other assailants were now more cautious. By killing Paul first, they had sacrificed their element of surprise for the life of their least dangerous opponent and now had to contend with the more capable guards. Calunoth approached the assailant with razor-sharp focus, aware from the sound of swords clashing behind him that Jovi was still keeping the third assailant busy. Likely realizing that the longer and louder the fight, the more likely they were to be discovered, Calunoth's opponent lunged forward, attempting to end the fight quickly, driving Calunoth toward the wall's precipice.

    Calunoth was having none of it. He parried the blow and replied with a feinted stab at his opponent's stomach, shifting the blade at the last moment to instead cut into his sword arm. His opponent let out a gasp of pain but attacked again, recklessly and ferociously. Calunoth reacted quickly to block the blows, each one sending shockwaves down his arm, as he waited for the opportune moment to strike. After enduring the brutal onslaught for several long moments, he finally saw his opening and deftly sidestepped as the attacker lunged at him, causing the black-clad man to fall to the floor. Then he flipped over onto his back in an attempt to dodge the stab he had expected and was instead surprised to find Calunoth's blade sweeping across his throat, ending his involvement in the fight.

But there was something wrong. Calunoth had been so focused on his opponent, he had failed to notice the lack of noise behind him. He whipped his head around to look for Jovi only to see the Chelian fall to the third hooded figure, the one Calunoth thought he had rendered unconscious. As Calunoth watched the Chelian fall, sliding down the wall, he was suddenly aware of the unhooded man behind him. He instinctively went to jump forward, but he was too close to the edge of the wall and could only turn his head over his shoulder to see the face of his attacker. As he felt the cold steel pierce through his back and out through his chest, so too did cold steel pierce his heart.

The unhooded man who had stabbed him was Alistair Glathaous.

Alistair's face had gone deathly pale, and by the flickering light of the torches and the fire, he looked like a dead man walking. His eyes widened as he saw the life begin to flicker out of Calunoth's eyes, and he kept his hand on his sword instead of pulling it out.

That was all the opportunity Calunoth needed. Flipping his sword in his hand, he stabbed backward as hard as he could, piercing flesh, blood, and bone. In his shock, Alistair's grip tightened, and he pulled his sword free of Calunoth, his face, if possible, turning even whiter as he staggered back, Calunoth's sword embedded in his chest. Calunoth felt his strength ebb as blood poured freely from the wound in his chest. He turned as he fell, staring at the man who had betrayed them. Alistair mirrored Calunoth, staggering back as the grievous wound in his chest freely hemorrhaged blood, as he fell off the back of the wall. As Calunoth fell off the front of the wall, the last sound he heard was the grinding of the gates echoing in his ears, and he thought wistfully of auburn hair. Then his mind went blank with shock and rage at the man who had betrayed them.

***

I am weightless, falling. I'm falling. Where am I falling to? Light blazes all around me. The sun. But it's night, isn't it? Pain. Such incredible pain in my chest, my back. Is this the end?

Noise is exploding all around me. The sounds of battle. The metallic scent of blood thick in the air. And the smoke. Smoke? Is the castle on fire? The cold spring air is reverberating with screams.

Footsteps. Frantic footsteps. And a voice shouting, "Here, sire! But I must protest!"

Now another voice. Filled with urgency. "No time. We must get him to the laboratory while he still lives. This fight is lost."

Weightlessness again. Then back to darkness.

***

Battle. Agony. Chaos. I am not safe here. Where is here?

That's the ceiling. The castle ceiling? Can I speak ... no. Who ... whose voices are those?

"Go, sire! We'll buy you time!"

Another voice. One I recognize. Oscar. And the other, deeper voice. More regal. Lord Glathaous.

Blackness again.

***

Lights. Bright Lights. Unnatural lights. I'm no longer weightless. I'm lying on something. Something hard. And my chest is bare. It's cold. So cold. Why am I so cold?

Shapes of people flash by all around me. I hear noise. Not battle noise, but a strange noise, like a fervent insect needling one's sanity with its clicking, whining, humming.

Screaming voices ring out all around me. I can't understand what they're saying. What are they saying?

Then warmth. A gentle, soothing warmth. A calming warmth.
Blackness.

***

"Into the tunnel! Take him far from here! Under no circumstances can they take it!"

A voice. Lord Glathaous.

"They're almost at the laboratory. Go! Go! *Go!* And never let them find it, Aaron!"

"Yes, sire." The archmage. His voice is breaking. "You two, with me!"

Weightlessness again. Something opens. A door? Am I leaving? Am I done now? I am tired. So tired. I want to rest.

Shifting blackness.

***

"Aaron! We can't outrun them!" the two men cried out, formality abandoned as they rushed through the hidden tunnel.

Aaron turned and yelled back at them. "Buy us time! They cannot lay their hands on the boy!"

The two soldiers grimaced, then looked at each other. "For Lord Glathaous," one said.

"For Lord Glathaous," the other agreed.

They turned as one in the narrow tunnel and moved to slow the enemies' advance, giving Aaron the time he needed to escape. Aaron cursed and kept running. Ending the spell that had kept the body floating next to him, which had, since the beginning of the tunnel, become much more strenuous to maintain, Aaron caught the young man in his arms and continued running. The tunnel angled gradually upward until it terminated at a burrowed hole in the earth in the forest, hidden by a carefully camouflaged panel. Soon he could see the end of the tunnel and the exit into the forest.

Bursting through the wooden trap door, Aaron laid the body among the ferns and collapsed next to him. They were in a grove over a mile to the southwest of the castle. The tunnel that led here from the laboratory had been designed to smuggle the lord out if a battle proved unwinnable. Only the lord wouldn't be making use of it this time. The tunnel would have to be blocked, or the enemy would find them. But how could he do that? At least only the men following them would have found the tunnel. Isaac would see to that. But what would stop others from digging around and finding the tunnel? The men that had found their way to the lab had to be killed and the tunnel destroyed.

But the implantation process he'd just performed had taken an abhorrent amount of his strength from him. With his current energy level, the magic needed to kill the men, and to permanently hide the tunnel, would likely cost him his life.

So be it. Isaac will give his life to protect our work. So too should I. I will pray it's found a worthy soul to bear it. Though given the circumstances, it seems unlikely this soul is worthy, it's the only choice I have, Aaron mused as he gazed in the direction of the castle, which now had large spires of fire raging throughout the keep.

Mustering his strength, Aaron threw his green cloak over the body to help hide the light that now emanated from the boy's chest, then he dove back into the tunnel, sealing the door behind him and leaving the body alone.

Aaron moved as quickly as he could through the tunnel, jogging when he could and walking briskly when he couldn't. The men he had brought with him into the tunnel had been well picked. They'd kept their pursuers busy but still couldn't hold them. Aaron came face to hood with the black-clad assailants. Although only a few of the dozens upon dozens that had poured into the hall during the feast had made it as far as the laboratory tunnel, these few had been the only ones skilled enough to get this far. That same skill made them wary of standing against a powerful archmage, but it was clear how weary Aaron was, so they advanced upon him.

They never came close. Aaron could feel the Ynia rising higher and higher, setting the air tingling. He knew what was about to happen. Isaac was about to destroy the laboratory and everything in the surrounding area with it. The enemy had taken no prisoners in the hall. Servants, guards, women, men, no one had been spared. There was nothing in this place left to save, and Isaac knew that. The town and the body would be far enough away, but nothing within these walls would survive. The tunnel, being so far underground, might. So Aaron knew what he had to do.

As the soldiers approached with their swords brandished, a shockwave sliced through the cave, throwing them off balance. Aaron took that as his signal, and with a cry of defiance, he carved out the last Ynia formulae he would ever cast.

***

Aaron's explosion destroyed the tunnel.

Isaac's explosion seemed to destroy the world.

The ground shook and seemed to split open. An enormous burst of heat and light radiated from the northeast. The man lay under a cloak on a bed of ferns, watching with agony in his soul as the explosion destroyed the castle. His home. His friends. His family. His heart. His soul.

And before he faded into the unyielding darkness, a single name blazed through his mind. The name of the man responsible for this end of days. The man for whom the dead now demanded a debt of blood be paid.

Alistair Glathaous.

Chapter 1

Wounded Soul

    Bleiz Terin breathed a great sigh of relief as the edge of the Terrestia Forest finally crept into focus. The road from Commerel to Glathaous was the most uninspiring journey one could undertake in Renderive. Crossing over two hundred leagues of flat, fertile plains, with none for company but the errant farmer and his charges, the road was neither well traveled nor well maintained. The plains stretched from the Galgre Foothills to the Llewyn Hills in the north and to the Terrestia Forest in the west. Sparsely populated, there was little to interest the despondent traveler traveling northwest beyond the trading capital of Commerel.

    Even the citizens of Commerel themselves hardly looked westwards. All of their trade came from the north, east, or south. Short of the odd transport or a troop of dignitaries from Sihleo, the edge of the world may as well have been the western wall. And such was the incredible flatness of the plains that the most eagle-eyed sentry could reportedly see the border fortress with Sihleo from Commerel's walls.

    Bleiz was no eagle-eyed sentry though. As a man who would soon see his fortieth winter, his eyesight had deteriorated accordingly. Although he could clearly see the crisp and verdant greenery of the grasses that extended through the eastern half of the plains, objects in the distance forced him to squint to verify their existence. This was not something he would ever have admitted to though as he maintained he still had the physical abilities of a man half his age.

    "Are you running out of breath, old man? Do you want stop for a nap?" a chirpy voice chipped in from behind him.

    Bleiz looked over his shoulder to address the brawny young man mocking him. Despite being past his physical prime, decades of service in the military had left him stronger and faster than most men his age, and his experience in combat was expansive enough to disconcert even the most hardened of warriors. He enjoyed the work he did as a Knight of the Wilds, and he was used to traveling for days on end. As a result, he was far more patient with the source of the voice than many other commanding officers would be after a similar journey. But that didn't mean he had to take any cheek from his charges.

"Keep it up, and I'll happily order you to run the rest of the way," Bleiz responded dryly, wiping the sweat away from his forehead. "The forests look much closer than they are. We've still probably got about a day and half of walking before we get there. I'll take a nap when I find you lying exhausted on the ground."

As a captain in the Wilds division of the Holy Knights of Renderive, Bleiz had many responsibilities to attend to. He had to judge distances and terrains, make and read maps, maintain enough stamina to run for a day without stopping, and, most importantly for this mission, had to ensure that the young Draca heir finished his training correctly and on time.

Luca Draca was the youngest of four brothers born to the hero, Lord Conan Draca, and served as the family oddity. As the son of one of the most powerful men in Renderive, second only to the king himself, Luca had been raised to be a master of politics, governance, and warfare. Unlike his elder brothers though, he flaunted the responsibility of his studies, surmising early on that, as the fourth in line to rule Draca Province, he was unlikely to inherit any power or influence from his father. He had, however, inherited his father's bright, sky-blue eyes and messy crop of caramel hair, along with the tanned skin that marked his Chelian ancestry, and this inheritance meant Luca would not have to worry much about finding a suitable mate. With three capable elder brothers to fill the role of statesmen, generals, and leaders, Luca had departed from the serious, somber, and formal lifestyle the rest of his family lived. When he had come of age, rather than proceed with his studies at Akadaemia, he had asked his father to enlist him in the military, his only desire to serve his country and see the world. Unfortunately for Bleiz, noble sons often required greater attention than typical soldiers.

The scouting division, officially termed the Knights of the Wilds, was considered the safest division, so Lord Draca had approved the decision. Bleiz had suffered dealings with the children of lesser nobles before and found them to be universally cowardly, lazy, and more useful to the world as decorations than as functioning human beings. Upon meeting Luca however, he had been pleasantly surprised: the boy had clearly been raised well by his father. Attentive, sharp-eyed, and possessing the ability to learn most skills well and intuitively, he had the potential to be an excellent soldier in time.

Luca responded to the barb with a hearty laugh. "Well, if you say so. But I reckon even if I collapsed from exhaustion, rested, and then got up, I could still make it to Glathaous before you!"

"You might if you had any idea where it was!" Bleiz responded with a laugh of his own. Although any company was better than no company on a long road, having Luca along was almost enjoyable. Luca had inherited the cheerful optimism of his father that had failed to manifest itself in his elder brothers. Bleiz credited that to the freedom of Luca's upbringing, for, having met two of his older brothers, the captain knew that regardless of how capable they were, the elder brothers always seemed moody, reserved, and reticent.

"I'd find it!" Luca retorted. "From what I've heard, I just have to follow the sound of saws and axes. What are we doing escorting a researcher from the edge of the country anyway? Is there some new kind of tree they're researching at Akadaemia that they need samples for?" At Bleiz's raised eyebrow, he innocently put his hands up, fingers splayed wide.

"I suppose you haven't been told about the military importance of Glathaous then?" Bleiz asked, to which Luca shook his head in response. "Castle Glathaous is the military laboratory that services armies in times of war. It's not the main research institute—that's at Akadaemia of course—but its location is highly defensible. It's much closer to both borders, and therefore much closer to where we'll likely need them."

"But wouldn't that make it a prime target for our enemies though? And an easy one as well given it would be difficult to respond quickly to an attack on the other side of the country?" Luca questioned.

"Yes and no," Bleiz responded after a moment. "It's an appealing target for strategic purposes, but attacking it and seizing it are two different efforts. While it may be easy to reach in terms of distance, the forests make it difficult for an army to move effectively. That, combined with the capabilities of the guards at Glathaous, makes it an appealing target but not a smart one. An attacking army would likely lose more men than it was worth to take the castle."

The pair continued walking along the dirt road for several hours until the sun drifted downward below the western mountains, casting long shadows on the plains that continually stretched out to meet the pair yet never quite reached them. They had been on the road for almost six days and expected to rest on the side of the road for at least one more night. When the sun had dipped behind the mountains and the road ahead had grown too dark to see clearly, Bleiz halted their walk and announced they would stop there for the night. Although they could travel through the night, there was no real need to on this mission. They would also make better time during the day if they were rested.

Unable to build a fire for fear of sending embers into the dry grass of the prairie, Bleiz and Luca simply made soft beds out of the flowing grass that had already shaken off the winter chill. While the plains were not particularly dangerous, an open fire risked setting off an uncontrollable wildfire. It posed an even greater threat if the howling winds that frequented the plains during the spring months decided to make an early appearance. So, without a fire, the pair were relegated to eating cold salted meat and bread provisions. Hardly a gourmet affair, but the road required traveling lightly.

"So, what is this researcher doing that requires an escort?" Luca asked Bleiz between mouthfuls of bread.

Bleiz responded between bites. "I don't know specifically what she was supposed to be collecting. All I know is that she was sent from Akadaemia to retrieve some sort of product of an Ynia experiment. King Greshaun wants it delivered to the capital, to the Grand Council. I think it's something important, but I have no idea what it could be. I don't really understand how this Ynia stuff works."

"If it's important, why are they sending us?" Luca asked, then seeing Bleiz glare at him, hastily added, "I mean, why are they sending two people instead of a troop?"

"We're less suspicious. A couple of lone travelers aren't going to attract as much attention as the central army," Bleiz replied, finishing off his bread. "There's still a ways to go, yet. I'm going to bed now. You should sleep too. We'll resume at dawn and should arrive in two day's time."

Luca was still curious about what this Ynia device could be, but he knew asking Bleiz more would be pointless. He was a seasoned and grizzled soldier, with exceptional combat prowess for a man his age. However, he knew virtually nothing about magic beyond how to avoid getting roasted by it. Determining to ask the researcher about it when they met her, Luca followed the lead of his commanding officer and was soon snoring softly atop his bed of grass.

The wind was blowing softly through the plains, gently rustling the blades of grass that carpeted the world. The sky was clear of clouds, allowing the light of the half-moon and the peaceful glow of the stars to fall upon the land. Insects buzzed quietly just above the ground, undisturbed, enjoying the tranquility of the starry plains at night. It was a fine place to rest, untouched by human endeavors.

But just after midnight, there was a shift in the air. The insects abandoned their dancing rituals and swerved away. Deer roaming the plains were suddenly unsettled by a primal urge, an urge that caused them to perk their ears and dart away as they pre-emptively felt a force that had not been felt in ages.

Luca continued to lay undisturbed in a state of peaceful slumber as nature around him bristled, sensing an unnatural occurrence.

Then he was jolted awake, very suddenly, by a clap of thunder and a sudden unnatural breeze pushing against him from the east. Turning toward the source, Luca could see in the dimly lit skies massive plumes of smoke billowing out from the forest, visible for miles around. Bleiz, likewise, was jolted awake and turned to the source of the disturbance. Watching the plume of smoke, Luca felt a terrible sense of foreboding come over him. Adrenaline drove the drowsiness from his eyes, and he felt a real sense of fear, though he could not tell what caused it. All he knew was that something had happened in the forest. Something major.

Something bad.

Luca turned to Bleiz, who looked upon the sight with a furrowed brow and a grim face. He thought for a moment, slowly scratching his graying beard as he did so, before turning to Luca with resolve.

"Are you awake? Good. We're leaving," Bleiz said brusquely, gathering his belongings. "That smoke is coming from somewhere close to Glathaous. We need to get there as soon as possible." Shouldering his pack and replacing his weapons belt, Bleiz trudged off the path, tromping directly across the plains in the direction of the smoke. Not wanting to be left behind, Luca hastily gathered his belongings and followed his captain into the darkness.

Bleiz and Luca moved rapidly as the night ran out and fell victim to the dawn. In the light rising over the forest to the east, the magnitude and origin of the smoke became far more apparent than it had been in the night. Although the pillar was dissipating slowly, the thinning trail of vapor left its mark on the sky.

The smoke, Luca noticed as the light increased, was not the black smoke of a typical fire, but instead rose into the sky as an eerie shade of green, discoloring the sun and leaving an unnatural assortment of colors blotching the dawning sky.

As the light increased, so too did the visibility, and when the light became palpable, Bleiz increased their pace accordingly. As a result, the pair spent most of the day jogging across the plains toward the smoke, running when they could, and taking the most direct route. As a result, they reached the borders of the Terrestia Forest by dusk. They attempted to wade though the deep foliage as darkness descended but found their way blocked by the overhanging trees. Cursing, Bleiz ordered a halt, and he and Luca collapsed against some nearby trees, allowing the stiff trunks of the trees to brace and support their weary muscles, which for Luca, ached terribly. Bleiz, while similarly tired, would likely suffer more in the morning than he did now. With the darkness of the forest impenetrable to the eye, they risked becoming lost in the vast forests that sprawled the border between Renderive and the neighboring country of Sihleo.

Still resting against a tree, Bleiz prepared two days worth of rations to account for not stopping all day and his evident fatigue. With the trees blocking them from view, Luca wearily gathered kindling and started a small fire for warmth. They had barely spoken since the night before when they had first felt the shockwave roll through them, exchanging only the most necessary of words and stifling the deep sense of foreboding that lay in their hearts.

After taking time to eat, Luca asked Bleiz the question that was eating away at them both.

"What do you think happened?" Luca asked quietly, sitting close enough to the orange glow that he could feel the heat radiating on his youthful face as the flames bathed it in warmth.

Bleiz stared into the campfire, the spitting flames casting shadows onto his weathered face, exposing the crinkles in his brow and obscuring the worry in his smoke-gray eyes. "It wasn't a lightning strike. There was no storm. And there isn't a fire that I can see, at least not a normal one. No fire I know emits green smoke."

Bleiz shifted as he spoke, putting his hands on his knees to warm them. Then he sat with his eyes closed. After a short silence, Bleiz opened his eyes and ran his hands through his short graying hair before adding, "I can think of only two possibilities. Whatever is causing that smoke is definitely magic of some kind. So, either there was a major problem at the laboratory or ..." Bleiz trailed off.

"Or?" prompted Luca, trying to recall the magical theory he remembered from his studies.

"Or someone has attempted to assault Glathaous using Ynium technology. If that's the case, then we'll have to proceed with caution. We should avoid the town and scout the area to see what we can discover first. We'll have to go into town eventually as we need supplies, but if it's been taken over by a hostile force, we need to find out as much as we can," Bleiz responded. "We ought to hide our crests as well. If the castle has been taken, we're likely to be taken prisoner if we're seen. If we look like simple travelers, then we could save ourselves some trouble. Also, if we're captured poking around an enemy camp, then they'll think that we're just private citizens, and the rules of war protect us from being killed on the spot. If they know we're soldiers, they'll have every justification to kill us."

Bleiz's military instincts had taken over completely, making Luca feel a bit better. On the journey thus far, the old captain had been relaxed, even engaging. Now he was like a lute string strung taut. Attempting to adopt his captain's disposition, Luca suggested they sleep in shifts, with one of them keeping watch. Bleiz agreed and volunteered to take the first shift. He was clearly uneasy.

The rest of the night passed without incident, and the pair began moving as soon as light was visible above the trees. The dawn revealed their progress, and they were now, according to Bleiz, within three leagues of the town of Glathaous, and slightly closer to Glathaous Castle. The castle was now the obvious source of the smoke. The eerie green vapor had shriveled to barely more than a wisp, but the pair were close enough now to reach the castle in just hours. Rarely speaking, the pair forged north through the lush forest, cutting through offending branches with their swords as they went. Bleiz had chosen this route so that they would marked as traveling mercenaries rather than traveling Knights, which would be advantageous to them if spotted by a hostile force. They had also covered the crests of the winged crown on their shoulders and bracers that marked them as Holy Knights of Renderive on their tooled leather armor with pieces of bark and sap scraped from the trees.

When Luca questioned the need to disguise themselves as mercenaries, Bleiz was blunt in his response. "Mercenaries often camp in forests to save money when they're traveling. The Holy Knights would never seek to hide in their own country during times of peace. So, should we encounter an enemy force, we need to avoid arousing suspicion as much as possible." Bleiz explained, then added irritably, "They should have taught you this at the academy, man." The stress of the situation was beginning to show. There was no sign of a hostile force, but they had to be ready for it just in case.

The two soldiers steadily pushed through the undergrowth of the forest and soon came to a clearing less than a league from the fortress. The clearing was uphill from the rest of the forest and offered a clear vantage point from which they could see the castle. Bleiz stood in the middle of the clearing and gazed in the direction of the smoke.

Bleiz had visited the keep once before, many years earlier, when traveling back home to the capital city of Deirive on the east coast after attaining victory in the Sieth Incursion twelve years earlier. Having fought as a young man at the rear of Lord Draca's forces, he had assisted in driving the Legrangians back over the Sieth River. He had accompanied Lord Draca to Glathaous, and the town was nestled so deep in the forest he would never have visited Glathaous had it not been for the whim of his commander as they had returned from the north. When last he had come here, the castle had been a sight to behold. Standing free and mighty on a hill overlooking the forest, the castle could be seen from miles around. With twenty-foot walls and an even higher central tower, it held a commanding presence as the central tower's spire stood fifty feet above the ground. Or it had.

From his vantage point in the clearing, Bleiz could no longer see the tower that rose above the trees, nor the roofs of any of the buildings inside the walls. The walls themselves were still standing, though there were several gaps in them. The forest was eerily quiet, as though even the insects and animals had deemed this place cursed. Turning, Bleiz started to order Luca, who had been gazing around the clearing, to come with him to the castle—against his better instincts—but he was cut off before he could issue his command.

"Bleiz, look!" Luca cried, pointing to the other side of the clearing where the ferns grew lush. "There's a body here!"

Bleiz put his hand on his sword hilt immediately as he scanned the clearing where Luca was pointing. He was right. A body wrapped in a green cloak was lying among the ferns. The cloak had camouflaged the body and made it almost imperceptible. Had it not been for the body's head sticking out from under the cloak, he could have lain there unnoticed indefinitely. Bleiz relaxed his stance when he realized that the body was no danger, but he had to wonder how it had gotten there. This grove was in the middle of the forest a decent distance from the castle. He moved forward with Luca to examine the body.

Bleiz knelt next to the corpse, examining his features. He was young, about the same age as Luca, with jet-black hair and a thin but muscular frame. He was incredibly pale, but that was likely a result of the length of time he'd been here. At least a day by Bleiz's reckoning. How had a man so young come to meet such a fate? As Bleiz mused over his fate, Luca, a true gentleman at heart and in action, also knelt next to the body and went to remove the cloak, being as careful as he could to not disturb the dead. When he removed the cloak from the body's chest, he suddenly let out a startled gasp that shook Bleiz from his reverie. Following Luca's gaze, the captain's eyes widened.

Embedded deep within the man's bare chest was a shining crystal orb imbued with a strange white light. The orb was surrounded by a strange combination of scarring. Large, deep, and messy scars surrounded the orb while much smaller, more precise marks were engraved nearest the orb. The man himself was covered in dried blood. Motioning for Luca to turn the body over, Bleiz saw a smaller ugly scar between the man's shoulder blades. All of the scarring had healed, yet the blood was freshly dried. What had happened here?

"Bleiz!" Luca said suddenly, looking at the body in bewilderment. "I think he's still alive! He's still warm!"

Bleiz almost laughed until he looked at Luca's face and saw the sincerity in it. Leaning over, he pressed his finger to the man's neck, feeling for a vital sign.

His hand dropped, limp.

"Impossible," Bleiz breathed. He had felt a pulse. Not just a weak and thready pulse, but one that was strong, if a bit slow. "This man's got an orb sticking out of his heart. He should be long dead."

Luca did not allow his astonishment to stall him as he carefully leaned the man up against a tree and covered him with the cloak.

Having recovered his senses from the initial shock of seeing what should have been a dead man live, Bleiz fumbled in his pack and brought out a small flask. Unscrewing the top, he handed it to Luca and said, "Try to feed him some of this. It's Galgre whiskey. If anything will revive the dead, it's that."

Luca accepted the flask, noticing it was nearly full, and carefully poured a few drops down the man's throat. The man suddenly gave a vicious cough as the fiery liquor raced down his throat, jolting him awake. He shuddered as he opened his eyes.

He appeared unaware of his surroundings and looked around in a panicked frenzy. Luca had held his face as he had awoken to steady the delivery of the whiskey, and now the man pierced Luca's cerulean-blue gaze his own wild green one.

Then he screamed. Like a frightened animal awakened by a primal urge to flee, he attempted to jump backward on his hands and rear end, sending the cloak flying as he tried to push himself away from Luca and the tree against which he had lain. His attempt was stymied by the nearness of the tree, so he tried to stand, but his legs buckled beneath him, leaving him to collapse onto the forest floor. He was agitated but still clearly weak.

With Luca paralyzed in surprise, Bleiz stepped into the gap that had opened between him and the man. He clamped a hand down on the man's mouth to muffle the screaming and wrapped his strong arms around him. Holding him tightly, Bleiz spoke slowly and calmly. "Relax! Relax! We're here to help you! We do not want to hurt you. We're here to help you." Bleiz kept repeating the words to the struggling man, slowly and quietly. Finally, he slowly stopped struggling and was quiet.

Once he had calmed down, Bleiz helped him to rest against the tree and tried to speak with him. "My name is Bleiz Terin, Captain of the Knights of the Wilds. And this is Luca, my student and recent Knight Academy graduate." Bleiz spoke slowly and patiently, gesturing to himself and Luca. "We found you in this clearing about a mile away from the castle. Can you tell us what happened here?"

The man looked around fervently again before steadying his green-eyed gaze on Bleiz. He did not answer Bleiz directly. Instead, he just stared at him wide eyed, and with shallow breaths, tried to speak. "I … I … I …" the man stammered slowly, meeting Bleiz's now concerned gaze. "I … I … I don't … I … I can't …" He continued stammering and his shallow breathing quickened to a concerning rate. Reaching back for his flask, Bleiz took it from Luca and pushed it firmly into the boy's hands.

"Here," he said, smiling patiently. "Have some of this. It'll help steady you."

The man looked at the flask, and slowly, with shaking hands, lifted it to his lips. The liquor helped to restore a great deal of color to the man's face, and when he had finished, he was able to offer it back with steadier hands.

"What's wrong with him?" Luca whispered, unsure what to make of the man's actions.

"He's in shock," Bleiz replied, also in a whisper, never letting the patient smile leave his face. "I've seen it before. Men who have seen terrible things are so shaken to the core by them that they lose their mental faculties. They often lose their sanity, and they have visions of what traumatized them. The trauma can be worked out, just like any other mental strife, but it takes the right hand, and not everyone has what it takes."

"So, are we going to be able to learn anything?" Luca asked in response.

Bleiz thought for a moment. "Maybe. I think I can get a few of the basics out of him, but I believe this is the first time he's woken up since the incident. I'll see what I can do."

Turning back to the man, he looked him in the eyes and explained what he was going to do. "Okay, I'm just going ask you a couple of questions. All you have to do is nod or shake your head. Do you understand?"

The man nodded in response.

"Good. If you don't want to answer something, just take a sip of that drink. So, do you live in this area?"

The man nodded.

"Did you live in the castle?"

The man refused to answer, instead drinking from the flask.

"Do you know what happened at the castle?"

The man drank from the flask again.

Luca knelt behind Bleiz, marveling at the know-how of his mentor. This clearly wasn't the first time he had done this, but by asking questions that the stranger tried to avoid, Bleiz could determine the source of the man's distress while also convincing him to drink more of the liquor, which appeared to be steadily reviving him.

"Was there an attack by a foreign force?" Bleiz continued, careful to be as deliberate as possible with his questioning. The liquor was helping, but too much could cause the man to become unreliable.

The man nodded shakily, then drank again, rivulets of the amber liquid leaking unchecked down his face.

"Do you know who they were or where they came from?"

The stranger did not answer and took another sip instead.

"Do you know anything about that crystal in your chest?"

The man shook his head and cast his gaze downward, apparently unwilling to speak any further. He put down the flask and averted his gaze.

Bleiz questioned the man for a few more minutes, then thanked him and turned to Luca. "Well, he lives in the area, in the castle I suspect. I'm going to have to go and investigate."

"But what if the people who attacked him are still there?" Luca asked concerned. "How do we know we won't end up like him?"

It was clear to Bleiz the man's condition had unnerved Luca. But he knew how to deal with it. "We won't end up like him because *we're* not going. I'm going alone. You'll stay here and make sure our friend doesn't disappear anywhere," Bleiz replied, cutting off Luca's protests. "He's not very stable right now, but stay with him, try to talk to him, try to reassure him, and don't let him near any weapons. He might be our best bet to find out what happened here. Our mission is to find this researcher, but if we can't, then we should try to figure out what happened."

Luca opened his mouth to protest further, but Bleiz denied him the opportunity, stern lines appearing on his face. "That's an order, Luca. I'll return within six hours. If I don't, assume I'm dead or captured and bring this man to Commerel. The viscount will know what to do."

Without giving Luca a chance to speak, Bleiz disappeared through the dense foliage toward the castle.

***

Bleiz carefully crept through the forest, wary of enemies. Upon emerging from the woods, he peeked through a ruined section of the castle wall and knew he was safe from ambush. There were no living beings left in the castle—or anywhere nearby for that matter.

Peering through what remained of the wall, Bleiz could see the chilling damage. Within the once twenty-foot-high walls, nothing now remained of the majestic inner keep but a large, black-green crater. Large fragments of rock that had once belonged to the keep were dotted all around the landscape, likely propelled by whatever had created the crater. The pieces were all badly charred as though a fire had ripped through them. But no normal fire could burn stone. Large sections of the wall had fallen down, or been broken through. Those sections still standing had been blackened by enormous scorch marks.

The gate itself seemed to be relatively unscathed, but the gatehouse and surrounding wall were now broken and crumbling along the perimeter of the crater. He felt a strange aura in the air. A tingling sensation crawled up his spine. It was as though the very air of the place had been perverted by what had happened here. But what *had* happened? The center of the crater was either the keep itself or just below it. Nothing remained but chunks of rubble.

Feeling distinctly unsettled by the atmosphere of the place, Bleiz elected to follow the wall along the inside rather than walk directly through the crater, stumbling as he navigated around pieces of charred, broken stone. He passed behind a piece of rubble near the gate and was startled to see what could only be human remains, though they were far too charred and blackened to glean anything from them. Strange pieces of what could have been steel were embedded around the edge of the crater, though they too were so malformed and discolored that Bleiz couldn't be sure of their identity. The air itself was perverted with a strange metallic taste.

The very center of the crater, dozens of feet down, was uniquely untouched and empty, as though that singular circular span, less than a man in size, had been protected from the devastation that had shattered the world around it. The site was suddenly making Bleiz feel sick. He was a veteran of many campaigns and was no stranger to death, but something about this place just didn't sit right with him. The castle wasn't lying in ruins, spread out over the courtyard and forests. Much of it was simply gone, blinked out of existence by some unknown force. It was an unnatural death.

Concluding his survey and noting the lateness of the hour, Bleiz started to make his way back to Luca and the stranger. While he had no idea who was responsible for the attack, the state of the former castle left one fact clear. Extremely powerful magic had been at work in this place.

Bleiz arrived back in the grove with time to spare. He was pleased to see Luca having a casual conversation with the man. While the shock of what he had seen must have been great, time with Luca seemed to have helped him.

Seeing Bleiz, Luca beckoned him over, then helped the shellshocked man to stand.

"What did you find out?" Luca asked, looking at his captain. "Were there any other survivors?" Luca realized the insensitivity of that question when he felt the weakened man's hand tighten on his shoulder and bowed his head in apology.

Nevertheless, it was a question that needed answering, and Bleiz did so in the way he knew was best to break bad news. Bluntly.

"I'm so sorry. I found none alive," Bleiz said before adding, "And honestly, I don't think anyone else *could* have survived. The castle is completely destroyed. Whatever destroyed the castle destroyed everything around it too. There's a large crater where the keep used to be, and all the remaining walls are badly charred. There may have been some who could have fled into town, but no one in the keep survived."

The man, having recovered more of his faculties now, had seemed to have restored a part of his sanity, and nodded slowly, gravely. Then he replied softly, "No one could have fled. The men who came were … very thorough."

"Who were these men?" Luca asked.

"I … I don't know," the stranger said, betraying his weariness and fragile psyche. "They were clad all in black. I was stabbed … then I … I fell off the wall."

"You should be dead twice then, and you're all the more fortunate because of it," Luca chimed in optimistically.

"No!" shouted the man, his guilt and grief permeating his words. "This is my fault. I should be dead with them! My friends, my family, everyone! Why should I, of all people, have survived?!" His voice rose continuously until he was shouting. Then his voice cracked, and he started sobbing quietly, leaning into Luca, who, unsure of what to do, awkwardly held the survivor to his shoulder.

Bleiz knelt next to him, grabbed his shoulder, and pulled him forward to face him.

"Listen, lad. You have had something truly terrible happen to you. And I know that right now you want to scream and shout and curse the gods and the earth. That's normal. But it's no way to live. Help us find out what happened, what's going on here, and maybe we can find the party responsible. This act will greatly upset the king, and he'll be keen to assist you however he can in seeking vengeance." Bleiz spoke now not patiently, but firmly. "Cry your tears, curse your gods, and rest for now. We'll bring you with us. You can tell us more tomorrow. But for now, rest."

"I *am* the responsible party! This is all my fault! I was the one at the gate! I could have stopped this! They're dead because of me. Because I was too weak!" The words came out in a half-choke and half-scream.

"And you got stabbed in the chest for it. And I suspect that whatever that crystal is, it's the only reason you're still alive," Bleiz replied. "This was not the act of one man." He sighed and dropped his hand. "It's late now. We will all rest and go into town tomorrow to learn more. You can tell us more when you feel ready."

The man gave up then and stopped struggling. He collapsed next to the ferns and lay there, quietly sobbing.

Bleiz grimaced, moving away from the two to stand at the edge of the grove. He motioned Luca over to him, placing an arm over his shoulder as they turned their backs to the man in quiet conference.

"This young man is clearly very damaged, but as it stands, he's the only who can tell us what happened. We might find out more from the townspeople tomorrow. But we should exercise caution regardless. I think he's harmless, but the people who did this to him could still be about." Bleiz said.

Luca stood in thought before giving voice to his concerns. "What if he's telling the truth? What if he *is* responsible for this? We have no idea what that crystal in his chest is for. It's clearly magical. What if that's what destroyed the castle and killed all of those people?"

"The crystal is discomforting, but it's not proof of wrongdoing. It looks like it was placed in him without his consent. And the scarring looks like he was badly injured before it was put in his chest." Glancing over at the sobbing wreck beside the ferns, Bleiz remarked, "His grief is real, but I suspect his guilt is imagined. If he was guarding the gate, he would have been among the first to fall. But whatever force was at play here was well beyond the abilities of this man. I suspect he may be the greatest victim of all."

"Do we know his name?" Luca realized suddenly.

"I thought you might have gotten it out of him?" Bleiz replied, to which Luca shook his head. "Well, we'd best leave him be. We can find out tomorrow. His life has been completely destroyed in the past couple days. He may yet go mad, though I hope not."

"I'll watch him tonight," Luca offered. "We didn't manage to speak about anything useful, but I feel like I should keep an eye on him for now."

Bleiz consented then retired, citing the long day.

Luca stood watch over the broken soul for the remainder of the evening, watching silently as his sobs became quieter and quieter until they subsided entirely. It was long into the night before the man succumbed to sleep, and Luca was looking forward to doing the same. However, even when he lay down and allowed Bleiz to relieve him, his mind churned. He thought of the man, of the castle as Bleiz had described it, and of the feeling of unrest that had plagued him for the last two days. So, it was approaching dawn when Luca finally slept, though he did so with the feeling that the day had been an omen for times to come.

Chapter 2

Whispered Murmurs

The mighty oak trees cast their shadows over the small clearing. The sunlight laid a steady beating down on the new leaves that were not yet in full bloom but still provided protection from the rays, distorting the passing of time until the sun approached its peak. Finding the flaws in the upper foliage, light shone through to illuminate the forest floor and accomplished its objective of waking the slumbering inhabitants of the clearing.

It was Luca who was first awakened by the light. After almost two days of little rest and great exertion, during which he had traveled almost three dozen leagues by night and day to reach the small clearing, he had succumbed to his fatigue. Although he had been subject to the same military training as his peers, he would have to undergo more to become a fully fledged Knight of the Wilds. As such, his body was unused to such exertion, having only recently left his family's manor, and this anomaly was protested by his body. Shifting from his half-reclined position in the curve of the large oak tree where he had lain, he glanced around the clearing.

It was approaching midday, based on the angle of the light penetrating the shady clearing. This would not make Bleiz happy. The older captain had become gruff and rigid as he had aged and would not take kindly to oversleeping, especially since he had obviously unwittingly fallen asleep on watch.

With his mind cleared of drowsiness, Luca gazed across the clearing at his companion. Bleiz lay on his side on the forest floor, having found his rest on a bed of moss. His snoring confirmed that his state of rest was ongoing. Although he would fall asleep standing up before he admitted it, Bleiz needed more rest than Luca did. The grizzled captain's spryness had given way to experience, which in turn had made him a wise and capable teacher. Although he was a Knight of the Wings by training, he no longer possessed the physical endurance needed for frontline duties but refused, unlike most older Knights, to involve himself in the politics of administration. Bleiz was a deeply impatient man when it came to politics and did whatever he could to avoid it, even going so far as to transfer to the Knights of the Wilds as, by his own admission, he would, "rather sleep in the mud of a swamp than preach the Obligation to aristocrats in palaces."

The Obligation was the foundational work of the Knights of Renderive and had been reportedly written by the legendary hero, Asta, founder of the Holy Knights, himself. The book was of similar importance to the Knights as the Founder Script, the central religious text of the Holy Church of Renderive, and described the ongoing responsibilities and obligations of every Knight sworn to defend the country. The full title read something along the lines of, *The Obligation of Every Knight Sworn to Serve the Holy Kingdom of Renderive, The King, and Sentential*, but every Knight who had to study it referred to it as simply, *"The Obligation."*

Luca looked back at the survivor they had found yesterday and saw him sleeping on the same knoll of ferns they had found him on. Going over to wake him, Luca could tell that his sleep had been far less fitful than his own. The man held the fine green cloak that covered him tight to his neck, covering his upper body entirely and obscuring the strange crystal that glowed in his chest. His face twitched frequently as though he was constantly trying to avert his gaze but couldn't. As he drew nearer, Luca could hear the man muttering feverishly under his breath, "No ... no ... I didn't mean to ... I ... I didn't want this. No ... I'm sorry, I'm so sorry ..."

Pitying the young man who appeared no older than Luca himself, he strode over and gently shook the stranger to wake him from his nightmares. It did not take great effort as the man started from his reverie immediately. Sitting up, he looked around quickly, breathing deeply, still clearly on edge.

Seeing Luca's youthful cheerful face staring at him, the man relaxed and regained his composure. Luca sat down next to him. "How are you feeling?" Luca asked in his typical chirpy fashion.

The young man sighed, rubbing his hands in his eyes, and he shook his head as if to clear away from his vison whatever demons had tormented him throughout the night. Looking up through the gap in the trees toward the sky, he replied, "Better, I think. I'm sorry for my outbursts yesterday. I just woke up and ... and panicked. I can barely remember anything. Just the gate. The men in black. And being carried here. Then the explosion. They're gone, aren't they? They're all gone?"

Luca's face darkened in response, realizing that the man had been slowly processing what had happened to him and wasn't completely aware of what was going on. In a somber and respectful tone, Luca replied. "I didn't go to the castle myself. Bleiz did, and he didn't want to talk much about it," Luca said before hesitantly adding, "Maybe some of the residents managed to flee into the village, but from what Bleiz said, well, he didn't have much hope for survivors."

The man accepted this with a grim darkening of his features. He glanced around the forest, perhaps searching for something to focus on. With nothing of interest available, he turned his focus back to Luca.

"From what I remember, it was a massacre. They would have killed everyone. My friends. My family ..." His voice trailed off for a moment, and he lost his voice again.

"They didn't kill everyone," Luca objected optimistically. "You're still here, though now that you're talking sense again, we need to know more about what happened. Then we can help you, and maybe you can help us. I'm Luca, by the way. What's your name?"

The man looked at him warily for a moment, appearing unsure of himself, before again asking, "Are we sure that no one else survived?" He was guarded in his query as if hoping that, if he asked again, the answer may change.

"I'm sorry, I don't know. But between what you and Bleiz have said, I think it's just you," Luca replied, still awaiting a response to his own question.

The stranger paused for a moment, a thoughtful look on his face and his brow furrowed. Then he replied cautiously, "My name is Calunoth. I was one of three men keeping watch in the gatehouse and a member of the Glathaous Castle Guard. I assume the man sleeping over there is Bleiz, yes?" He gestured to the slumbering body on the other side of the clearing. "We should wake him. We need to talk."

Bleiz was as grumpy as Luca expected when he was awoken to find midday past and rather unfairly took it out on the young noble.

"We're on a mission from the king himself! We need to be traveling from the break of dawn every single day. Why the blazes did you not wake me up? We've lost hours of traveling time!" he grumbled, rubbing his temples with his thumbs, trying to shift the fog of sleep from his mind.

Upon being reminded that they were still virtually on schedule as they had run through the night previously, Bleiz eased his grumbling somewhat, but he continued to groan and grimace as he rose, body creaking, from his overwrought slumber, complaining about how resting for too long reduced his capacity to move properly. Despite being well muscled for his age, the years had taken their toll on him, and Bleiz often had to stretch his back muscles out every morning to alleviate their soreness.

Once Bleiz had fully regained his mobility, he introduced himself to Calunoth formally and set about eating his breakfast, advising the other two to do the same while they spoke. Calunoth had no provisions or supplies and hadn't eaten in over two days, yet he was not as ravenously hungry as would have been expected. Keeping the cloak covering his bare torso in place, he gratefully accepted small pieces of bread and salted meat from the Knights and refused the offer of more.

After nibbling on the bread for a moment, Calunoth addressed the two. "I have only fleeting memories of what happened at the castle, and even fewer, strangely, of last night. But it is clear you saved me from being abandoned to the elements, and for that, I truly thank you." He spoke with the soft-spoken eloquence that bespoke a well-raised individual. "I expect you have many questions, but first I'd like to hear from you two. You have done enough to stop me from fleeing, but I would like to know your business in Glathaous before I say more. The reasons for my distrust will become clear soon enough."

Bleiz regarded him skeptically; Calunoth was far more coherent than the man they had found yesterday and seemed deeply distrustful given the aid they had given him thus far. Then he remembered the horrific scene he had seen at the castle, and he relented.

"We'll tell you our mission. As it stands, it may be that you're the only one who can help us," Bleiz said. "We've been sent by King Greshaun to meet a researcher from Akadaemia. She was to go to Glathaous Castle to act as a courier for something important, though we don't know what. She was supposed to have arrived at the castle to pick up the package on Spring Dawning Day. We traveled from Commerel, and before that Deirive. We hastened our pace when we saw the smoke rising from the direction of the castle. We found you by chance while scouting, and now we must find the researcher." Then Bleiz added, "Based on the scene at the castle, I think we need to find out if she still lives, and if she was even at the castle. And if we can't find her, we should at least try to determine what she was supposed to retrieve and find it if we can."

Calunoth listened to Bleiz intently then sat back pondering, clearly deciding whether or not to trust the two. Seeing his hesitancy, Luca knelt next to Calunoth and said, "I understand if you don't want to trust us, but we are of the Holy Knights of Renderive. We are obligated to protect the people of Renderive. And if you are concerned for your safety, we will defend you from attack." Luca, being fresh from his initial tutelage, remembered his oath to the Obligation well.

It must have been Luca's sincerity and seriousness that resolved Calunoth's reservations, for he at last spoke freely. "If you had wanted to capture or kill me, you would have done so already," Calunoth mused. "And to be honest, I really just want to have to someone to speak to about this. Holy Knights seem perfect for the situation …" Calunoth fiddled with the budding vegetation on the forest floor, twisting a piece of small, dark-green ivy. "All right," he resolved. "What do you want to know?"

Bleiz took up the questioning first, sitting down cross-legged across from Calunoth. "I went to see the castle, and it looked like a scene from one of the elder tales. An enormous crater spanned the entire perimeter of the castle, and it was sunk deep into the earth. Bodies were few and far between, and those I saw were so badly burned they were unrecognizable. Even the stones were deeply charred. I thought at first a meteorite had struck as the site resembled something I once saw to the north of the Llewyn Hills, but there was no unnatural rock debris here. And the likelihood of a meteorite falling on the castle is impossibly low. However, there were bits of mangled metal and steel lying around, so it looked to me like a battle had been ended by something terrible. The earth itself seemed dead. It was completely inhospitable."

Bleiz seemed about to describe more when he saw Calunoth's jaw clench and realized that the description had been, naturally, unsettling. So rather than continue, Bleiz launched into his questions. "What happened there? We know there was an attack. Do you know who it was? Did you know of any recent guests that may have been our researcher?"

"What happened at the castle …" Calunoth began haltingly, his voice faltering at first but growing stronger and more determined as he continued. "We were betrayed. Most of the guard was at the Spring Dawning Feast, and I was one of the few soldiers left to stand watch. Black-clad, hooded assailants approached us from behind, and there was a traitor in their midst. We fought valiantly, and almost won, but the last surviving attacker must have gotten to the gate because I heard it open as I fell off the wall."

"You have no right to be sitting here and talking about this my friend," Luca interrupted with a smile.

"I should be dead," Calunoth acknowledged. "But I'm not. I was barely conscious for the rest of this, so you'll have to forgive me for the lack of details. I was carried inside by one of the castle's mages. I couldn't move, and I could hear battle all around me. I heard … screaming." Calunoth swallowed, and the two Knights did not pressure him to go on; instead, they waited for him to continue at his own pace. After a moment to regain his composure, Calunoth did so. "I was taken somewhere underground, away from the battle. This part is especially fuzzy. I remember lights, and lying on a table, but nothing beyond that. Then I was moving through a tunnel, I think, and we were being followed."

"We?" interrupted Bleiz. "We found you alone. Were you accompanied by someone else?"

"Yes. I believe it was Archmage Aaron. He saved me and left me out here, then he went back into the tunnel. I think he was going to try to save more people. The last thing I remember was feeling the ground shaking. There was a great bang like when you pour too much oil on a fire. Then I heard something collapsing. I think Aaron destroyed the tunnel to prevent anyone from coming after me. Then … then there was another explosion, a much bigger one. From the castle. I could see it through that gap in the trees," he said, motioning upward. "It lit up the entire sky. I think it must have come from the laboratory, though I don't know what could have caused it. Possibly one of Lord Glathaous's inventions. Whatever caused it, there's no way anything could have survived it. The next thing I know, I'm waking up out here with this thing in my chest."

"We should look for this tunnel!" Luca said urgently, rising to his feet. "We may find more survivors in there."

Calunoth stiffened at his words, then shook his head. "We can try, but I can't take hope. Aaron was highly skilled. If he wanted the tunnel blocked, it would have been blocked."

As Calunoth spoke, Bleiz rose and started pacing the length of the clearing near the fern bed, tapping the ground with his feet and listening intently to each footstep. He noted the typical crunch of leaves and the shifting of dirt—until he heard something. The others heard it too. It sounded like someone knocking on hollow wood, only muffled. Reaching down and poking around in the vegetation, he discovered a thin edge. Easing the fingers of both hands' underneath, Bleiz pulled upward, revealing the passageway Calunoth had spoken of. It was deep, but after looking inside, Bleiz knew descending would be pointless. The tunnel was caved in almost to the entrance. It would take days and dozens of men to shift the rock. There was nothing to be done there.

"He's right, Luca. nothing else is making it out of there." Bleiz shook his head, closing the passage. "Good idea though, this," he murmured to himself thoughtfully. "We should get one of these in the palace." Turning back to Calunoth, he repeated his questions.

Calunoth sighed and rubbed his face before continuing. "I don't know exactly who attacked, but I have an idea. I don't know about your researcher. The only guest I'm aware of was the Sihleon minister, Lenocius. He was the one who organized the attack. It was his men clad in black." His tone darkened, and rage seeped into his voice as neared the end of his tale.

"How can you be sure?" Bleiz asked, turning sharply toward the young guard. "The Sihleons have never been aggressive. And attacking like that, under cover of night and without warning, slaughtering innocents? It's a violation of every rule of warfare. Were you even given the opportunity to surrender?"

Calunoth shook his head and said, "They came at us when we were weakest. They slaughtered without discrimination. Lenocius should have stayed for the feast, but he must have left early because he knew what was going to happen and—" Calunoth could not find his voice for a moment.

"And?" prompted Luca, his eyebrows raised.

"All I know is Lenocius spent most of the morning speaking to the traitor, the man who betrayed his people and opened the gates. That man ... that man was Alistair Glathaous," Calunoth concluded, his voice quivering on the last word.

"Isaac Glathaous' youngest son!?" Bleiz cursed vehemently. "What in blazes was he thinking? Did he not realize he was committing treason of the foulest nature? And what about the Sihleons? What do they get out of all this?"

"My guess is they wanted the magical technology from the laboratory, but I don't think they got it. It was probably all destroyed in the explosion," Calunoth replied.

Luca, who by nature was more troubled than Bleiz by the offensive acts of man, offered a more nuanced perspective. "I find it hard to believe the Sihleons would do something like this. Every Sihleon I've ever met has been so uptight and religiously virtuous they wouldn't be able to give you the time of day without chanting the praises of their god. I'd expect this from the Legrangians, but not from them."

Bleiz had remained standing and had continued to pace thoughtfully. Suddenly, he said, "Luca's right. It doesn't make sense for the Sihleons to attack us so suddenly like this, and without cause. Do you know of a reason they might do so, one we aren't aware of? And is it possible this Lenocius character was working alone?" He asked of Calunoth.

"The black-clad men definitely worked for Lenocius, but I suppose it's possible he was working with someone else, someone outside the castle," Calunoth replied. "But again, the only reason I can see for the Sihleons to attack would be to gain Lord Glathaous' technology. And to achieve that, they would have needed to determine its location. Only a select few in the kingdom knew about the technology our mages were creating; even fewer had access to it. I didn't think even Alistair knew. He was studious, but he never cared much for his father's experiments. I guess he paid more attention than anyone thought. I can't imagine the mages or the lord himself would have turned traitor."

"So we need to find Alistair then, to put all the pieces together," Luca pointed out.

"Alistair's dead. I stabbed him and threw him over the wall myself," Calunoth replied shortly, trying to rise though his knees were shaking with his anger. That same anger tainted his next words. "But that's not enough. His death was just the start. It's Lenocius I need to kill now. I have ... much to repay him for."

"Easy now, lad," Bleiz warned, moving to help Calunoth up. "I know you must want to hunt him down right now, but we should investigate more first. We should ask the townspeople if they've seen anything. And we need to find that researcher as well. I don't know anything about magic or Ynia technology, so I can't say what that stone in your chest is for. But she might know."

"We should get going now then," Luca remarked cheerfully, rising. "We should reach the town quickly enough, but gathering information could take time. And we might actually get to sleep under a roof tonight!"

Acknowledging the wisdom of Luca's words, Calunoth tied the green cloak ties firmly around his neck, securing it and concealing the crystal orb in his chest. With Luca supporting the weakened Calunoth, the new convoy returned to the road.

Bleiz led the way, with Calunoth, wrapped in his green cloak and still supported by Luca, following immediately behind. Calunoth was still so weak from his ordeal that he could hardly keep up with the Knights. He was certainly in no condition to fight should the need arise. He was surprised he could move at all, and he couldn't help but wonder if the crystal in his chest had something to do with it. The crystal had allowed him to recover from a fatal injury after all. What more was it capable of? Given the well-known genius of Isaac Glathaous, it wouldn't have surprised Calunoth if the crystal *could* revive the dead.

Because Calunoth had mentioned he had lost his sword when he had fallen, and was thus traveling without armor or weapons, Luca had lent him a short hunting dagger with a hilt carved in the shape of a wolf's head that the trainee Knight kept in his belt. Recognizing the value of the piece, Calunoth had thanked him and promised to return it as soon as possible.

As they traveled, Calunoth was forced to fend off questions about the crystal in his chest from an incessant Luca. Although not magically inclined himself, Luca took a keen interest in the field as he had been inundated with stories when he was young about great battles and exciting quests, many of which had been decided by the effective use of magic. He was finally dissuaded from his questions when Calunoth started coughing violently and asked to be relieved of the need to speak. Bleiz, listening to the conversation behind him, had the distinct impression Calunoth had been faking the cough, but he didn't blame him. Luca's curious nature was a great strength, but as his teacher, Bleiz knew it could become rapidly irritating if left unchecked.

Luca therefore took to talking at, rather than to, his fellow companions. He continued as they reached the crest of a hill until Bleiz issued a sharp hush. He stopped and held up his hand. The light from the sun rising behind them rendered the three men as silhouettes to prospective observers below.

"Hush, boy," he said sharply, gesturing to the side of the road. "Get in the trees, now!"

Luca obediently ceased speaking immediately and pulled Calunoth into the trees, with Bleiz following closely behind.

"What is it?" Luca whispered. "We should almost be at the town."

"That's just it," Bleiz replied, wincing as an errant branch scratched his forehead. "Calunoth, can you see the entrance to town? Who are those men standing guard?"

Calunoth extracted himself slightly to get a better view. The hill they had been climbing up sloped sharply down, obscuring the town from the south until the crest of the hill. Bleiz, leading, had seen the small town come into view and had pulled them aside upon inspecting the guards. They were neither Knights, nor militia, nor errant townsmen. The two men standing at the town gates were clad from the neck down in long black shirts beneath blackened leather armor. It was a familiar sight to Calunoth.

"They're part of the group who attacked the castle!" Calunoth exclaimed in a loud whisper. "Or at least they're wearing the same clothing! I'm sure of it!" Calunoth's eyes took on a devilish glint. "If we sneak along the sides, we can take them from opposite sides before they know we're there!" He had begun to move as he spoke before Bleiz put a hand on his shoulder and pulled him back.

"Not happening, not unless we have to," he said firmly. "Our mission right now is to acquire information, not storm the town. I know it's hard, but you must practice restraint for now. I can see some of the townsfolk from here. Don't go making their lives harder."

Calunoth struggled for a moment but finally relaxed and accepted the logic of the elder Knight.

"We'd better take the long way around and enter from the main road on the other side," Luca remarked, wincing as he felt the nettles around his ankle scratch against him. "Those guards look bored, and any traffic from the castle is going to be suspicious."

Agreeing with Luca's assessment, the three retreated back into the dense foliage of the forest, moving as swiftly as possible as they forged their own path along the edge of the trees. The forest encircled the town of Glathaous on all sides and was only breached by the roads leading to and from the castle. There were many stories of adventurers venturing into the forest only to become lost and disoriented. Such was the vastness of the treescape that one could easily lose themselves among the wooden trunks and never emerge back into civilization. As such, the three men kept within sight of the treeline throughout their trek around the town. Where the treeline was the least compact, the trio could see the wooden walls of Glathaous in the distance, obscuring the view of the town itself. After forging through the foliage for what felt like days, the three men emerged from the trees on the northern side of the town and swiftly joined the road heading into Glathaous.

As they neared the town on the northern road, they found the southern entrance guarded more strongly. With six black-clad men clustered around the entrance, it was clear they were watching for someone or something. A cart of goods was, as was usual, slowly making its way up the road in front of the trio. As they neared the gates, one of the black-clad men stopped it and began questioning the driver. As he was speaking, two of the other men started to search the cart.

"What do we do now?" Luca asked Bleiz, still supporting the weakened Calunoth. "We have to get in. The next nearest town is Crideir, and we don't have the supplies for that journey. Even if we did, we still need to find out what happened here and try to locate our researcher."

"We'll just have to talk our way in. It'll be easier than trying to force it," Bleiz said. "We'd best go now while half of them are distracted by that cart. Calunoth, lean on Luca as if you can't walk without him. It shouldn't be hard given the state you're in. Luca, give me your pack and let me do the talking."

Bleiz strode to the front and led the trio to the gates. When they reached the gates, one of the idle black-clad men confronted them.

"Halt!" he cried, holding his hand out in front of him. "What business do you have in Glathaous?"

"We hail from Caern Porth, sir. Here to join my mother's house for the Spring Dawning Feast," Bleiz responded, emphasizing the lilt in his speech characteristic of the Hillmen of Renderive.

"You're about three days too late, sir," replied the black-clad man. "And this area is not currently stable. I would advise you to return to your home." The man enunciated the words oddly, as though he was trying to hide an accent, but he did so well enough that the accent beneath was unrecognizable.

"We were delayed by poor weather on our way here," Bleiz replied smoothly. "And as you can see, one of my sons is not well and should not spend the night in the cold." He gestured at Calunoth, who now leaned heavily on Luca. "And with all due respect, sir, who are you to deny us passage? This is the first time we've seen these gates guarded in all our many visits here. What causes this?" Bleiz may have been a rough man in appearance and personality, but his experience had taught him that the right words to the right people could accomplish a great deal.

"There has been a major incident at Glathaous Castle. The lord's son, Alistair, is in charge now. He's hired our group to guard the town as he awaits word from the capital," the man replied. Bleiz maintained an innocent visage at this news; however, Calunoth was less capable, and he let out an exclamation that he quickly managed to turn into a violent cough. The reaction was fortunate, as it added weight to Bleiz's lie, despite the poor timing.

The guard examined the three, covered in leaves and mud from many days of travel, Calunoth wracked with coughing. They carried weapons, but with only two capable fighters, and only the big one holding his brother appearing capable of causing real trouble, the guard appeared to rationalize letting them into town. After thinking for a moment, he said, "We've been ordered to interfere with the townspeople as little as possible. As long as you do the same, you can enter. We will, however, have to search your belongings first."

"And why is that?" Bleiz countered with the same Hillmen lilt in his voice. "If you have been commanded to collect a toll, sir, we would rather pay you of our own free will."

"There is no toll," replied the guard. "But we have been ordered to search for something. A small white crystal orb, not dissimilar to a pearl. Possibly glowing. It is the Ynia object that caused the incident. Are you familiar with it?" Bleiz shook his head while Luca gazed at the ground to avoid giving anything away. "Regardless, I cannot grant you entry unless I've searched your packs. Please." The man's skin was unusually pale, but he did not appear to be a studious figure. Rather, he had the well-cut physique and short haircut associated with many in the military.

Bleiz, recognizing that the only peaceful way through this was to cooperate, handed over the two packs. As he did so, Luca repositioned Calunoth to ensure that the green cloak fully covered his chest and that the soft white light was not visible through it. The guard took the packs and searched through them thoroughly with the assistance of one of his comrades. Not finding anything of note, and with the other guards suddenly preoccupied with the pearl collection they had discovered in the cart, he waved them through. Bleiz thanked him politely and the three walked in unmolested. They stayed silent as they walked into the small town, Luca supporting Calunoth for the sake of their bluff until they were out of sight of the guards.

Once out of sight, Calunoth eased off Luca and stood freely. Bleiz looked at him sharply and murmured, "We'll discuss this later, not in plain sight. And cover your face. It's best if you aren't recognized." He motioned with his head toward the multitude of black-clad mercenaries dotted around the town. Calunoth obliged and pulled the hood of the cloak over his head, keeping his face obscured in shadow.

Glathaous was not a large town, but it was relatively wealthy for its size. Being Renderive's main supplier of lumber and woodwork, the town was filled with fine architecture made from the local wood and intricately decorated by talented woodworkers from all over the country. Many of the majestic houses were layered in sequential rows beyond the main street containing the local market. The town itself was surrounded by a large wooden wall erected by the town's own artisans. Usually, the town was bright, vibrant, and full of life with craftsmen, tradesmen, and their families actively engaging with their fellow townspeople.

However, there was no hint of that activity today. The mood was as dark as the encroaching storm clouds. The market was closed. Few people walked the streets. The ones who did moved quickly, shooting nervous looks at the strange mercenaries and the three companions who were also strangers to the townsfolk. They flitted from their house to their destination and did not stop to converse. The only businesses that appeared open were those deemed essential: the blacksmith, the inn, and the town hall. The town hall itself stood in the center of the town, heavily guarded by over two dozen more mercenaries. An aura of panic and despair permeated the air. It was far removed from the norm.

Noticing the approaching storm clouds, the three made for the tavern, The Ax and Stable, which, although relatively full, bore an air of distinct depression. The trio was regarded with suspicion by the patrons.

Thankfully however, only locals were present. A single soul sat as far into the shadows as possible in one corner, sipping wine under a light-gray cloak, their face obscured. The innkeeper stood scowling behind the bar, appearing to be in an even fouler mood than usual as he surveyed the three unwelcome additions to his tavern.

Bleiz, ever the negotiator, approached the innkeeper, Owen, to request room and board, and he looked like he well may refuse. He harbored a dislike of outsiders, and right now, even fellow Renderiveans were outsiders to him. However, after a brief and terse exchange with Bleiz, he accepted coins from Bleiz and handed him a key, scowling. Bleiz beckoned for his companions to follow him up the stairs at the back of the inn to their assigned room where they could finally speak without fear of being overheard.

"That con artist!" Bleiz complained as he shut the door behind him. "Eight sovereigns for one room and three meals for the night. Eight! Honestly, I had half a mind to sleep outside at that price." Removing his pack, he swung it down onto one of the four cots that lay against each wall of the small room. A small fireplace sat unlit but prepared in the far corner. Luca shed his pack and went to spark the fire, swearing quietly as he cut his hand on the grate before finally setting the fire alight, adding a hint of warmth and light to the room.

With Luca claiming the cot across from the door, Calunoth sat on the cot by the fireplace, unable to fully process what had happened. Luckily, Bleiz was on hand to guide the conversation.

"So, Alistair Glathaous is still alive. He's ordered the group that attacked the castle—whoever they are, or part of them at least—to pose as mercenaries to eventually take over the town. And they're all looking for the crystal that's stuck in your chest, Calunoth," Bleiz summed up expertly. "Well, this is quickly getting out of hand. Anyone have anything else to add?"

Calunoth stared at the floorboards as he addressed Bleiz. "There is no way Alistair could have survived. It's just not possible," he said slowly.

"There's no way that *you* could have survived," Luca interjected, "and yet here you are. The Sihleons are quite capable with Ynium technology. If they moved him out of the keep in time, they could have saved him, just as you were saved. Surely not all of Alistair's men died attacking the keep. They must have held some back."

"And now they're looking for this crystal that's stuck in my chest. Whatever this bloody thing is," Calunoth muttered. Then he looked up and spoke clearly, despite his weakness. "All right, here's the plan. I go to the town hall and tell them I have the crystal, but I can only give it to Alistair. They'll let me in, and I can kill the bastard before anyone stops me. You two don't have to stick around, but that's what I'll do."

Luca and Bleiz exchanged a concerned glance, and Bleiz countered with logic. "That's a great plan if you want to get killed. Who knows if you'll even survive if they take that thing out of your chest? Even if you do, it's unlikely they'll let you off easily for killing their boss, or trying to," Bleiz said. "We have to be rational now. It's obvious the technology this group is looking for is that crystal in your chest. They were willing to take on a castle to get it, so it must be valuable. Our priority now should be to stop them from getting it."

"Well then, how do we kill Alistair?" Calunoth replied tersely.

Bleiz chose his words carefully. Regardless of how weak he was, the captain had no doubt that Calunoth would try to fight all two dozen guards outside the hall and more to get to his opponent. Bleiz had to convince him to wait somehow.

"For now, we don't," Bleiz replied. At Calunoth's narrowed eyes, he hastily added, "Alistair is impossibly well protected right now. You might be able to get to him, but you'll certainly die in the process. And he's not the only one responsible. You mentioned the Sihleon minister, Lenocius? If he's also guilty, and we take this matter to the king, he may allow you the right to execute Lenocius *and* Alistair for their crimes. You can get your revenge and keep your life, but for now you have to wait."

Calunoth inhaled deeply, then exhaled. He had to concede to Bleiz. He was right. Throwing his life away while still one soul remained accountable for the Glathaous Massacre would be an offense to the dead.

"Could the king even try this Lenocius guy if he's a Sihleon?" Luca asked.

"Our country, our laws," Bleiz stated expertly. "Although he'd have to be in the king's custody for that rule to matter."

"If we're not going after Alistair yet, what are we going to do?" Calunoth asked.

"You and Luca go down to the inn, keep a table. Luca, try to get some information from the locals. See if anyone's seen that researcher. We may not have a description, but the locals will know about any new faces showing up recently. And keep an eye out for anything that looks out of place. Calunoth, you'd better not talk to anyone. We're vastly outnumbered, and if they find out you have that crystal, we'll be in trouble." Bleiz rose. "I'll go into town and look around. I'll be back in a few hours, hopefully before the storm hits. Stay out of trouble."

***

Calunoth sat alone at a pine table with a burning mug of bitter, soothing tea clasped between his hands. He was forced to keep his hood up and his face down, avoiding the curious and occasionally hostile stares of the other patrons in the tavern. He and Luca had both eaten their fill while Luca had regaled him with tales of his heroic elder brother, Felix, who had led the final charge against the Legrangian Empire during the Sieth Incursion. It was obvious Luca held his brother in high regard.

After they had sated their hunger, Luca had vanished into the steadily growing population of the tavern to engage with the locals. It was something Calunoth felt he should have done, but he was far less amicable than Luca, whose easy smile seemed to convey trust wherever he went. So, Calunoth was left alone with his thoughts while Luca scoured the public for information.

Luca mingled well, speaking to most, and although he was a stranger, his laughing nature had soon inundated him with the other patrons who seemed desperate for some good humor. The scent of roasting vegetables wafted through the common area, perking the interest of the patrons, many of whom stood close, whispering in hushed murmurs. Throughout his journey around the comfortable room, Luca had struck up many conversations, ranging from the fate of Glathaous Castle, to the appearance of the mercenary groups, to the whereabouts of the wayward researcher. Luca easily glided between the oiled wooden tables, using his charming good looks to tease information from the women in the room. Whether by purpose or happenstance, he was unable to get close enough to speak to the hooded figure in the shadowed corner, who appeared interested in his antics.

Luca returned to the table just before the storm hit, and Bleiz returned, soaked to the bone and carrying a parcel, shortly afterwards. He pulled aside a serving girl and ordered for himself before falling heavily into a chair next to Luca.

"What happened to you?" Luca asked Bleiz, gesturing to the small puddle of water now pooling around his seat.

"These bloody forest storms is what happened. It started raining over by the blacksmiths on the other side of town while it was still bone dry here. I don't understand how the weather works in this area," Bleiz replied, shaking his head. "Anyway, I didn't get much information, but I did get some. Luca?"

"I got a lot, so I can go first if you want," Luca offered, to which Bleiz nodded his assent. "From what the townspeople say, everyone went to the castle on the night of the explosion, but there was nothing to be done. No one came out of the castle, and the townspeople are scared. Really scared, and leaderless. Apparently, all the town's officials were at the castle that night. The mercenaries showed up in force the next morning and said they had been employed by Alistair Glathaous to manage the town while they waited for help from the capital. No one seems to know if these people had anything to do with what happened at the castle, so the mercenaries probably all arrived afterward. They've holed up in the town hall and are issuing orders from there."

"Wait!" Calunoth interrupted. "Has anyone actually seen Alistair? In person?"

"Well ... maybe, maybe not. Turns out he had never come into town before, and he kept to himself at the castle, so no one really knows what he looks like. They've just been taking orders through his surrogate, one of the mercenaries they call Adam. Everyone's been told to look for that white crystal though, and there's a sizable reward for anyone who finds it."

"How much?" Bleiz questioned, gratefully accepting a sip of Calunoth's tea while awaiting his own.

"Enough for me to consider handing the two of you over," Luca joked, clearly still in his information-gathering mood. "Well, maybe not that much. All I know is the crystal is some valuable experiment from the castle. I haven't heard anything else. I tried asking about our researcher, but with the town in the state that it's in, no one's noticed anything."

"Well, I got lucky then," Bleiz remarked. "I overheard a couple of the mercenaries saying that someone from Akadaemia had arrived in town yesterday and was asking some unfortunate questions. I tried to follow them, but it was too suspicious, so I quit. Akadaemia is on the other side of the country, so it's unlikely that it would be anyone other than our researcher. I heard the same rumors about the crystal orb that you did, I just didn't catch a price. Also …" He lowered his voice and leaned in closer. "I've heard rumors of war are growing. Apparently, huge lumber orders are coming in from the south. There's nothing official yet, but it sounds like Duke Byrant in the south is spending big on resources. What about you, Calunoth? Have you learned anything sitting here?"

Calunoth's eyes narrowed for a moment as Luca and Bleiz faced him. He could have sworn that the hooded figure in the corner had been trying to eavesdrop on their conversation, for as soon as he looked over Bleiz's shoulder at him, the figure quickly averted his head. "Nothing else, I'm afraid," he responded, keeping an eye on the figure.

"Well, at least we know the researcher is here. And we need to keep you hidden, Calunoth. We'll spend the night here and search for the researcher tomorrow. If we don't find her by then, we'll jump the wall and make our way to Deirive with you ourselves. We don't know for sure who this mysterious group is, what their affiliation with Alistair is, or where they came from. And the three of us are probably the only ones who know of their connection to the castle, so we have to get to the king and get the Knights involved in this affair. Greshaun might even send a Guardian to deal with this." Bleiz's stomach grumbled loudly, "But that's for tomorrow. Now I must eat. I'm starving."

The atmosphere in the tavern grew more and more raucous as the night grew on. Absent of anything else to take their minds from their fears, many of the patrons turned to drinking. As the fire was stoked higher and the ale was poured faster, the noise reached a fever pitch. It was clearly discomforting to some. The hooded figure in the corner rose and made for the stairs. He was not as tall as Calunoth had thought and walked with an awkward grace that belied his mysterious nature. One of the men drinking by the bar, a burly lumberjack taller even than Luca, who had been complaining to his colleagues about the number of outsiders currently in the tavern and clearly emboldened by the spirit, decided to intervene. Stepping in the path of the figure, he stopped him in his tracks.

"Where ya think *yer* goin'?" he asked, swaying where he stood. With one hand clutching his drink, he used his free hand to push the figure, knocking him over easily. The figure fell to the floor, and the hood fell back to reveal a long mane of light golden hair framing the pale, alabaster skin of a young woman. The woman, appearing frightened of the man, attempted to regain her feet but was unable to with the giant standing over her. "There'sh no room for you here!" The man reached down to grab her with the apparent intent of throwing her out, ignoring her protests that she had paid for her room.

Before he could lay his hands on the woman, the giant felt a firm hand on his shoulder. Luca, seeing the commotion and unable to stand idly by and let the man assault the woman further, had risen from the table to attempt to defuse the situation.

"Good sir," Luca said politely. "This woman has done nothing to harm you. Let her go."

"You're an oushider too!" the man yelled. "Why don't you get a room together in the foresht?" The man let go of the woman to grab Luca's arm and tried to pull him closer, simultaneously raising his glass to smash it into Luca's head. However, the man was unstable and unused to fighting anyone the same size as him. Rather than resist, Luca leaned into the pull and tackled the man to floor. The resulting brawl drew the attention of the entire bar as the two colossal men scrambled with each other on the floor. Fearing the arrival of the mercenaries, Bleiz and Calunoth leapt in to disentangle Luca from the mess. Evidently fearing the same outcome, two of the man's more sober friends dragged him back at the same time.

Bleiz dragged Luca up the stairs to their room. Unfortunately in the confusion, Luca's flailing left hand knocked Calunoth back, and as he fell, his cloak parted and exposed the crystal's light for a flashing moment before he gathered his cloak around him again. Fortunately, everyone in the tavern was too focused on the fight to notice him. As they left to a chorus of jeers, Calunoth looked among the crowd for the golden-haired girl. However, she appeared to have scarpered the moment Luca had distracted the giant.

Once back in the room, Bleiz scolded Luca for getting involved. "What did I say? Don't cause trouble! Don't get noticed! We're damn lucky those mercenaries didn't come, or there'd hell to pay."

"I couldn't just stand by and let that brute accost a woman like that. What's the point of being a Knight if you can't protect the defenseless?" Luca argued in response.

The content of the resulting argument was foreign to Calunoth as Luca and Bleiz argued over the purpose of the Obligation. Hoping to distract them from their fight, Calunoth interceded to bid them both good night. It only partially worked, for although they both began to retire, they continued arguing as they did so.

Finally, the bickering was replaced by Bleiz's heavy snoring. Outside, the storm raged, and Calunoth's dreams were once more tainted with the sound of the gate opening.

Chapter 3

Flight!

The storm that beset the small town of Glathaous that night was fierce and unrelenting. Normally shielded from such storms by the surrounding forests, the eye of the storm fixed its gaze directly upon the town, its eaves battering the forests while the town was subjected to its ire. The wind howled against the sturdy buildings as rain lashed against the windows, rattling them, and disturbing the sleep of many of the town's inhabitants. Rain crashed down like judgment from the heavens, turning the earthy ground into a slick mud that ensnared those who dared traverse it.

Calunoth was among those who found his sleep disturbed. The sound of the storm and the banging of an open gate against its post filled his ears as he lay awake in his cot. However, while others were kept awake by the screaming winds and claps of thunder, his sleep would have been fragmented without the forces of nature as his rest was tormented by the forces of his mind.

Dreams of black-clad soldiers with wicked grins and shining steel standing on the wall and laughing whirled through his mind. So too did the smell of smoke as fire lit up the world around him, the face of Alistair Glathaous as he fell over the wall, and the demonic smile of the man named Lenocius. But above all, there was that sound. That sound that tormented him more than any other: the grinding of the gates as they swung open to admit that deadly force.

Such were the state of his dreams that there was to be little rest for him. In truth, he preferred the pain of waking and walking and of acknowledging his failures, his weaknesses. In the lucid world, he could keep his mind focused. He could look forward to a time when those lost to the massacre would have their justice. But in his dreams, there was no control, no mercy. Just the same cackling laughter, the same pain, the same guilt, and those same green eyes that glared into his own as they fell away.

Calunoth, unable to resume his rest, glanced around the room, noting that his two companions slept soundly and deeply. They were not haunted by such thoughts, with Bleiz in particular seeming completely oblivious even to the storm. Luca, for his part, shifted more than was natural but did not awaken. *I'm lucky* they *found me and not the mercenaries,* thought Calunoth, pondering the forces of the world that had put them in that clearing. *I probably wouldn't have made it anywhere without their help, and they seem honorable. More so than me. And Sentential knows I need help right now.*

Then Calunoth heard something. A noise. A timid knocking on wood. The noise was almost imperceptible over the raging storm and the crashing of the gate outside, but it was not a natural sound. The knocking came again, more urgently this time. It was coming from their door!

Putting on the shirt that Bleiz had brought him from the blacksmiths and ensuring the light from the strange crystal in his chest was fully obscured, Calunoth moved cautiously to the door. He briefly considered waking his companions but decided against it. If this person was hostile, they wouldn't have knocked. And although a visitor was unusual at this late hour, it was likely just an errant worker or misguided reveler. It would be best if he acted naturally, as any suspicious activity could draw the attention of the mercenaries.

The knocking increased in volume and urgency. Aware that the sound could wake the others, Calunoth hastily opened the door. Expecting an innkeeper or servant, he was immensely surprised to see the hooded woman from earlier standing at his door. He opened his mouth to speak, but she put a finger to her lips, hushing him, as she nervously pushed him back into the room, closing the door behind her.

"Excuse me, but who are you?" Calunoth demanded, more surprised than concerned by the appearance of the young woman. Now inside the room, the young woman removed her hood and let the firelight illuminate her features. Now that he could see her clearly, Calunoth noted that this woman looked slightly different than his initial impression. She was extremely pale, with shadows under her eyes that spoke of many sleepless nights. Her golden hair had been tied back, and she had a mousy visage, with wide, furtive eyes and a narrow jawline.

"There's no time!" The woman spoke with the distinctive lilt of the Highlanders of the Galgre Range. "I saw the core in your chest, and so did the innkeeper. He's alerted the guards, and they're on their way here now. They can't get it. We have to get out of here, now!"

Calunoth stared at her blankly, unsure of how to react to this strange woman bursting into their room in the middle of the night. Seeing his dumbfounded reaction, the woman let out an exasperated sigh. "You're in danger! I know those men. They want the core you carried from the Glathaous laboratory. They've scoured the whole town looking for it. Get your things. I'll explain more later!"

Calunoth finally recovered his senses and asked, "Who are you? What are you talking about? What core? This crystal?"

The woman pushed him aside and strode to Luca's cot. Grabbing his shoulders, she roughly shook him awake, explaining as she did so. "My name's Lauren, and I'm from Akadaemia. I was sent here to collect the core. Get the other one up! I'll explain more when we're safe!" The woman's voice was quivering with nervousness despite the urgency it held.

She's the researcher Bleiz and Luca were supposed to escort! Calunoth realized, the pieces quickly falling into place. *And she knows the mercenaries are lying!* Heeding her instructions, he jumped across the room to Bleiz, shaking him roughly to pull him from his sleep. They had to move quickly. Luca rolled out of his cot with a dull thud, swearing, clearly startled to see the woman standing over him.

Bleiz had a more reserved reaction. Waking rapidly in response to the shaking, he instinctively rolled sideways from his cot, away from Calunoth, his hand wrapped around the hilt of his sword in moments. Seeing Calunoth standing urgently over him and the strange woman in the room, he opened his mouth to ask questions, but Calunoth cut him off.

"There's no time!" he said quickly. "The mercenaries are on their way. We need to leave now!" Calunoth grabbed his own cloak and the pack Bleiz had brought for him from town. They were ready in moments. After having woken Luca, Lauren stood anxiously by the open doorway, her eyes darting between the room where the men were readying themselves and the long empty hallway of the inn. Upon seeing the men ready to depart, she beckoned them to follow her.

"How far away are these mercenaries?" Bleiz whispered as they followed Lauren down the hallway. Lauren opened her mouth to speak, but she was interrupted by a loud bang as the heavy wooden front door opened and the pounding of armored boots stomped on the ground floor. That noise was enough to answer Bleiz's question. "Stop!" he called ahead, abandoning the need for secrecy. "They'll be here in seconds, and we can't fight our way past them all. We have to find another way out."

"We're on the third floor!" Luca replied, drawing his weapon. "We don't have a choice!"

"Put your sword away before you hurt yourself!" Bleiz barked, the old captain assuming his role. Addressing Lauren, he asked, "Is there a servant's stairwell or balcony we could use?"

Lauren shook her head. "I don't know. I've only been here for a day!" The panic was clearly setting in. The pounding footsteps were now on the stairwell, growing steadily closer. They were out of time.

Looking around the hallway, Calunoth forced himself to think. There were no balconies in any of the rooms that he knew of. And the windows in the rooms were tiny by design. Luca would never fit through them. Looking down the hallway, he saw the tavern's trademark stained-glass artwork railed off at the end of the hallway. It was the only large window in the place. It would have to do.

"Follow me!" Calunoth yelled, mustering his courage. The distance from where they stood to the stained glass was less than fifty strides. Gathering his strength, Calunoth held his cloak in front of this shoulder and sprinted explosively down the hallway. He covered the distance in seconds, his boots pounding loudly against the strong lumber of the floor. Conserving his momentum, he let out a strangled yell as he leapt over the railing, crashing heavily through the stained-glass window and into the empty space below. He swept his cloak away from his face, sending shards of broken glass flying with it. He had only a moment to analyze the situation before he felt himself falling freely through the air, the heavy storm winds buffeting him as he fell. Landing heavily onto the ground, Calunoth sank an inch into the mud before rolling forward and recovering safely to his feet.

Behind him, he heard Bleiz land in a similar fashion but did not hear Luca. Turning around, he could see Luca still standing at the opening, arguing with Lauren. As the sound of yelling grew audible even from outside, Luca took matters into his own hands. Grabbing Lauren as gently as he could under the circumstances, he threw her over his shoulder, and jumped down into the mud. Unlike Calunoth and Bleiz, Luca landed far more heavily and was unable to roll forward with Lauren over his shoulder. There was a distinct crack as the force of the landing went straight through him, and Luca let out a short exclamation of pain. Putting Lauren down, Luca rose slowly, his face contorted in a grimace.

"Luca!" Bleiz yelled, running to the young Knight's side. "Are you all right?" Luca gingerly stepped on his left foot, testing his weight. His grimace deepened as he put more weight on his foot.

"It's not good, but I'll make it," he replied through gritted teeth. "We need to go. Now!"

Through the opening above them, the group could see a swarm of black-clad mercenaries milling in the hallway. They had thought they had their prey trapped and now had to reorganize for the chase. The group didn't have much time. They ran toward the northern gate, the mercenaries in hot pursuit.

The groups' progress was aided by the heavy winds and violent rain of the storm overhead. It deepened the darkness of the night and significantly reduced their pursuers' visibility. The quartet, as they were now, splashed through the mud and the rapidly forming puddles; however, their progress was too slow. Luca was unable to keep up as they ran, and he let out a gasp of pain with every other footstep as his injured leg came down into the mud. At this rate, they would be caught within the hour.

Realizing this, Calunoth pressed them into the overhang of a nearby shop, its windows shuttered to protect them from the storm's winds.

"We're not going to make it at this pace. We're outnumbered and don't know this area," Bleiz stated, breathing heavily. "We won't even make it to the gate, never mind out of town." Luca had fallen over as they had come to a stop and now sat in the slimy mud under the shop window. His breathing was more labored than anyone else's.

"You won't make it with me," Luca said, panting, his voice containing none of its usual lightness. "Just leave me. I'll run and distract them. I should be able to draw at least a couple off you before they capture me."

"Dammit, boy, stop trying to play the hero. I'm not about to leave you here for them," Bleiz replied firmly, kneeling next to his charge. "We need to think of something else, and quickly. Ideas? Anyone?"

Calunoth wiped some of the torrential rain away from his eyes, then used his hand to cover them as he thought. Then an idea came to him.

"Follow me!" Calunoth said. "If we can get to the stables, we can ride the horses out of here. It's nearby. I think we can make it."

"We'll have to steal the horses, but needs must when the reaper calls." Bleiz recited the old adage regretfully. "Luca, come on. We'll carry you if we have to, but we have to move." Luca refused his offer but accepted a hand to his feet. He was made of far sterner stuff than most nobles and would not allow himself to become a burden.

The stables in town were smaller than those in the castle, but they still possessed enough choice for the group. Shattering the lock with the hilt of his new dagger, Calunoth swung open the stable door. In short order, they found two horses clearly bred for work but who looked strong and fit.

They had managed to lose their pursuers in the storm temporarily, but it was only a matter of time before they were found. Both entrances to town would be blocked off by now. They quickly saddled the horses with supplies from the stable and mounted them without pause. Bleiz rode with Luca while Calunoth was saddled with Lauren. With the experienced Bleiz holding onto the injured Luca, Calunoth led his horse through the gates of the stables, then galloped into the driving rain.

The town itself was becoming awash with activity. Even as the rain continued to pour, the efforts of the black-clad men to find them had awoken the town. Having lost their prey, the entire group of mercenaries was now out in force, banging on doors, demanding access to anywhere the fugitives could conceivably hide.

With the full force roaming the streets, Calunoth could now see the magnitude of the group. There were far too many of them to have hidden in town before the attack on the castle. They must have arrived after the attack. The destruction of the castle had clearly not been a part of their plans. The town itself was ill-equipped to accommodate such a large host, and no attacker with the forethought to attack the castle would have condemned it to destruction with such a host on the way.

Calunoth and his group had attracted the attention of the mercenaries by then. As the sole group galloping through the streets, they were hardly inconspicuous, and they soon had an array of men in pursuit. Steering his horse through the streets of the town, Calunoth soon led the group to within sight of the northern gate. The gate had been left open and abandoned as the storm battered the small town, but now it stood heavily guarded. As predicted, a large troupe of men barred the way, all with weapons drawn and hoods up. They had been expecting them. The gate itself seemed lodged open, stuck in the thick mud that had accumulated around the base of the doors.

Fortunately for the group, the mercenaries had not counted on the horses, and Calunoth and Bleiz adopted the same approach to the gate that had enabled their escape from the inn. Bleiz led the charge this time around, digging his heels into his horse and loosening his grip on the reins. The horse galloped toward the gate at full tilt, with Calunoth's horse close behind. The black-clad men were no cowards, but they all knew better than to stand in the way of speeding horses. To avoid being trampled, the men dove out of the way at the last second as Bleiz and Calunoth cleared a path right through the gate. A few of the men tried to hack at the horses' legs with their blades as they righted themselves, but by the time they had swung their blades, their targets were long past. The group passed through the gates at full speed, the wind of the storm now pushing at their backs and whistling over their heads. The rapid clacking of horse hooves on the road mingled with the clap of thunder as they fled the town and disappeared into the night.

***

The group spent the rest of the night fleeing on horseback. Unfortunately, not long after, they were forced to slow their pace to avoid exhausting their horses, even though they seemed energized at their newfound freedom.

The storm followed them for several leagues before finally relenting in its pursuit and dissipating to reveal the sun rising over the horizon, no longer shielded from the earth by the thunderclouds. With the sun high overhead as they reached the end of the forest road, the group beheld the great expanse of the plains.

Calunoth, for his part, was awestruck. Having spent virtually his entire life within the confines of the castle, all of his knowledge of the outside world came from other people or from books. He had heard tales of the great expanses of the Central Steppe of Renderive before, but seeing it with his own eyes took his breath away.

The land was flat for hundreds upon hundreds of miles all around, granting a clear view, from his elevated position, of the plains. He took in the vastness of the land as it began to slope up into the foothills of the Llewyn Hills to the east, the small town clustered halfway there just visible. But it was only with the view to the southeast that the true scope of the plains was revealed. In the far-off distance, a tiny walled city was visible from the hill, just a speck in the distance, with the faintest shadows of the even more distant mountains appearing behind.

The sight impressed Calunoth but had the opposite effect on Luca, who was less than excited to view the plains he and Bleiz had spent almost two weeks crossing only a few days ago. Although similarly impressed at first, he had quickly grown weary of the same sight day after day, only changing with the curvature of the land. It didn't help that his injury was now causing his ankle to swell up alarmingly, to the point where he had been forced to remove his boot to ease the discomfort. Sighting the town up ahead, he breathed a sigh of relief.

"Let's head there. It's only a few hours away, and we should be able to lose them in the town if they're still following us." He spoke in a voice that belied his discomfort. As he had been seated behind Bleiz, he had been able to rest far more than the captain, even falling asleep at one point. This was a feat similarly attained by their unlikely savior, Lauren, who as their pace had dropped, had fallen forward onto Calunoth's shoulder and still slept there. Calunoth had concluded the stress of the situation was unnatural for the young woman and had let her rest.

Bleiz was in a significantly less chipper mood, having had his rest disturbed and then forced to spend the night fleeing on horseback while fully soaked through with rain. "We'll have to head to the town, but we can't stay there long," he said, gesturing back at the plains. "Look at these fields. We'll be visible to them a hundred leagues away. We can rest in Crideir for the night as the horses won't go much further. But we'll have to leave early in the morning."

Crideir was the name of the small prairie town that served as an intersection between Commerel, Caern Vaughn, and Caern Porth. As such, there was always a healthy flow of travelers and tradesmen passing through and several available accommodations. It was the perfect place to recover and regroup—for a short while at least.

The group arrived at the town just as dusk began to settle, and the warm day's air seeped away across the prairies to be replaced by the chilly winds from the hills. This place had been designed as a throughway town with wide paved roads dotted with merchants selling their wares and the occasional bootblack peddling their services. The road itself was quieter than usual as most of the conventional travelers had arrived earlier in the day, and most of the populace had begun to retire for the evening.

Lauren awoke shortly before they arrived. Calunoth had many questions for her, but he elected to wait until they stopped as it was only fair for Bleiz and Luca to hear as well. Lauren seemed to understand that and instead kept up a more casual exchange. She credited him for his quick thinking earlier at the inn. The conversation was pleasant, but though Lauren came across as highly intelligent, he also couldn't help noticing how young she was. To his knowledge, anyone who worked at Akadaemia was typically over thirty, and Lauren appeared only a little older than Calunoth.

When Calunoth raised this point to her over his shoulder, she merely shrugged and replied, "Most of the professors are old and bearded, but they take on capable students of all ages if they think the students can handle the work." There was a hint of pride in her voice as she spoke, and Calunoth took her at her word.

The four companions soon pulled off the main road and onto the side streets in search of a low-profile inn to rest themselves and their horses. Their search proved fruitful, and they soon found themselves at a small inn called The White Horse quietly tucked away on the northern side of town. After almost a full day and night in the saddle, Bleiz and Calunoth dismounted gingerly, with Bleiz in particularly bad spirits. Despite his mood, he successfully procured a room from the round-faced, friendly innkeeper while the rest of the group tended to the horses. Once the necessary affairs were in order and dusk began to creep into night, the group finally retired to their room to convene a discussion.

Calunoth, as exhausted as he was, had to help Luca up the stairs, and upon reaching their room, unceremoniously dumped him on the nearest cot. Bleiz went to examine Luca's injury, though he did so with a mug of strong liquor he'd brought up from the inn's bar. After taking a long sip, Bleiz collected himself and knelt down by the bed next to Luca.

"It's definitely broken," Bleiz remarked, inspecting the swelling that now encompassed the entirety of Luca's ankle. "That was a hard impact, and having to ride through the day didn't help it. We'll bind it, but you're going to be useless for a couple weeks, unless we can find a medic in town."

Lauren cleared her throat to attract their attention before speaking. "If you're comfortable with it, I have some knowledge of medical Ynia techniques that could help reduce the swelling and the pain. I don't think I can repair it entirely, but I can probably cut the recovery time in half, maybe more," she offered before adding, "This is my fault anyway. I was scared to jump, and those men were right behind us. If I had jumped like I was supposed to, he wouldn't have hurt himself."

"Trust me, girl, the boy has an unnatural tendency to try to be the hero. This whole affair is just going to go straight to his head," Bleiz said wryly. It was then Calunoth remembered Bleiz and Luca didn't even know Lauren's name, such had been the panic leaving Glathaous.

Luca grinned. "Come on, Bleiz, someone's gotta be the hero!" Turning to Lauren, he said, "If you can help, feel free. If not, no worries. It's a Knight's job to help those in need."

"You'll be in need of more than a blasted healer if you don't smarten up!" Bleiz scolded. The combination of fatigue, stress, and concern for Luca had frayed his nerves to the point where he was in danger of losing his usual control.

Lauren began to work on Luca, so Bleiz, aware that working the complex Ynium formulas required the utmost focus and concentration, instead turned to Calunoth to ask his questions. "Right, we've fled with you from a group of armed assailants who are after that thing in your chest. I get that. Who's the woman, and how do you know her?"

"I met her about three seconds before you did," Calunoth replied, partially distracted by Lauren's process as she weaved formulae into the air. "She told me a little more on the way here. Her name is Lauren, and she's a researcher from Akadaemia, the same person you were sent to escort. She's supposed to be transporting this crystal somewhere, and she seems to know who those men chasing us are. More than that, you'll have to ask her."

Bleiz accepted Calunoth's report with a weary nod and reverted to sipping his liquor as Lauren worked on Luca. She had taken a small book from her pack and was reciting words from it as she held her left hand over Luca's injury, leaving the right hand to weave formulae. As Lauren worked her craft, the innkeeper brought up the food and drink Bleiz had requested, and he took it with a mumble of thanks. The captain's gray eyes matched the weariness of his movements.

Calunoth had a basic understanding of how Ynia worked. It wasn't magic of the sort that could be found in tales of dragons and faeries but instead constituted one of the primary fields of technological research in the world, though it was frequently called magic by the common folk, and the term had become synonymous with Ynium mechanisms. From what Calunoth knew, Ynia was natural energy manipulated in different manners, conjured primarily through the use of formulae weaved into the air by the spellcaster. Although typically advanced magic had to be cast using strictly defined formulae and words that allowed the spellcasters' will to shape the energy, those who were proficient enough could wield basic or even advanced magic with only a word. However, this was a level only obtained by mages with the skill of an archmage or higher. Anyone in theory could learn; however, the study was rigorous, and apparently dangerous, and many individuals gave up before casting even a single spell.

Eventually, Lauren released the magic and fell back with a heavy sigh. The fireplace in the corner of the room flickered softly in the silence as the young researcher sank onto Luca's cot. The use of magic extracted a heavy toll on the body. However, her treatment seemed effective. The swelling around Luca's ankle had entirely disappeared, and he no longer appeared to be in any pain. Eyeing the injury warily, Luca resumed his feet and gingerly tested it. He was able to stand unsupported.

"Wow, that's really something," he remarked. "It feels slightly weaker than before it was broken, but I could run on it now if I had to. Thank you, my lady." He bowed to Lauren, whose cheeks flushed a light pink. "But now I sense my companions and I must question you in detail, so I suggest you get comfortable."

"Of course," Lauren replied, easing further down into the bed Luca had just deserted. "My name is Lauren Abraham, and I'm a researcher from the University of Renderivean Akadaemia. I assume you're all guards from Glathaous Castle?" she asked, looking around at them.

Calunoth replied first. "I am, but these two are Knights of Renderive. This is Bleiz, Captain of the Wilds, and Luca, his student. They found me in the forest after I had been carried out of Glathaous Castle during the massacre." His voice grew bitter as he recalled it.

"So where is everyone else? What about Lord Isaac Glathaous? Or Archmage Aaron Gelon?" Lauren asked before realizing Calunoth's last words. "Massacre? What massacre? What happened there?" Bleiz looked at her in surprise.

"We were rather hoping you knew. Or at least in part," said Bleiz. "We'll tell you our account, and then you can tell us yours." Bleiz then proceeded to recount the story of the Glathaous Massacre as he had heard it from Calunoth. Upon hearing the news of the black-clad men attacking without mercy, Lauren grew despondent. By the time Bleiz had finished the story, Lauren appeared visibly upset.

"Lord Glathaous was a visionary in his field, and to know he died like that is very discomforting. You have my condolences, Calunoth. I'd heard he was a great lord as well as an academic," she said before launching into her own story. "I suppose it's my turn now. I was dispatched from Akadaemia by my supervisor, Professor Newt Callagher, on a special mission from the king himself. He told me that the Glathaous laboratory had concocted the magical breakthrough of the century, and he wanted me to bring it back to him. I was to be accompanied by two Knights on my return trip to help guard the results of the experiment. Originally, I was to reach Glathaous Castle on Spring Dawning Day, but I was slowed by poor weather on the plains and had to spend an extra day in Commerel, so I arrived a day late. The townspeople were rushing up to the castle by then, terrified, and finding it destroyed. It was heartbreaking. No one knew what had happened. I didn't understand fully either at first. The crater made sense, but the number of casualties and the timing didn't. Why would they conduct dangerous experiments when there were so many people in the castle, and where were the guards?"

Lauren sighed and rubbed her eyes. "Everyone returned to town when we saw that army of supposed mercenaries coming from the north. They claimed they'd been sent by Alistair Glathaous to govern the town until the king's men arrived, but everyone could tell they were a hostile force. Many were ethnically Legrangian, and it didn't make sense for them to have arrived so quickly. People were expecting Knights not mercenaries. On top of it all, they're too organized to be mercenaries, and no one's even seen Alistair. I think they might just be using the name." She paused and took a sip from the steaming cup the innkeeper had brought up for her.

"Do you think he's alive?" Calunoth asked directly, his green eyes narrowing.

"I don't know. I didn't see him, nor did I meet anyone else who had seen him. Apparently, he was the only one who had survived the incident, but they wouldn't let me see him. I thought something was amiss when I heard that. Lord Glathaous wouldn't have been careless with his experiments like that. I went to the town hall to meet with Alistair, but he was wounded in the incident and they said he needed time to recover."

"It makes sense for him to have survived, though I don't know how he did," Bleiz remarked. "As the one who opened the gates, he would have been able to get away before the battle started in earnest, even if he was wounded."

"Do you doubt me?" Calunoth asked bitterly, upset at the direction this conversation was heading.

"I don't doubt your skill, only your memory," Bleiz replied tactically, taking another swig. "You were horrendously wounded yourself at the time, so it's possible your aim was not as true as you thought. Regardless, Lauren, please continue. You say you know what caused that crater. I thought perhaps a meteorite."

"To call down a meteorite from beyond the skies would be madness," Lauren replied. "I don't think even the Grand Council could do it. No, that crater was created by a magical explosion. I thought it was an accident, but based on your story, it may well have been deliberate. Lord Glathaous had been experimenting with the ancient Selevirnian technology called Pralia. We have very few records left from that era, but we know the Selevirnians were far more technologically advanced than we are. They came from beyond the Faar Mountains and colonized most of Northern Creidyl. We still don't know what caused the Selevirn Union to fall two and a half thousand years ago, but we have been able to recover some of their old technology from archaeological digs in The Wastes. Pralia technology amplifies Natural Ynia in an incredibly efficient manner, but we don't really understand how. If this technology could be mastered, we'd be able to utilize magic on a scale hitherto unheard of. It would make Renderive the dominant country on the continent." Her eyes lit up as she spoke, imagining the potential this new technology could have in the world.

"And that crystal in Calunoth's chest? That's this 'praylie' technology you're talking about?" Bleiz questioned, woefully out of his depth with this new magic. "Does all that old magic have the same power Cal's does? He should be dead, but that thing seems to have saved him."

"May I see it?" Lauren asked, turning to Calunoth. Calunoth was keen for answers and quickly removed his cloak and undershirt to expose the crystal, which now glowed with warmth and light. Lauren approached him and delicately touched the surface of the crystal, of which only a partial, rounded portion was raised from Calunoth's chest. The crystal was almost as big as Lauren's hand and glowed even brighter as she put her fingers on its surface. Seemingly transfixed by it, she was jolted out of her reverie by Calunoth's voice.

"Can you take it out? If it's so important, I shouldn't hold onto it. Could you take it?" he asked.

Lauren examined the crystal with pursed lips and then shook her head. "I cannot remove it. And even if I could, I wouldn't. If this is a Pralia Core, it is the most advanced piece of technology our nation has ever created. Its properties are not fully known, but from the regular reports we received from Lord Glathaous …" Her voice trailed off as she disappeared into her thoughts, her eyes reflecting the glow of the core. Briefly returning from her reverie, she asked Calunoth, "You were seriously wounded when this core was implanted into your chest, weren't you?"

"Yes. But if it's an energy amplifier, then wouldn't that just mean it was used to amplify a medical spell? To the point where it could heal even mortal injuries?" Calunoth asked her.

Lauren looked at the core again, her eyes shrouded, then cast her gaze to the open window allowing the cool night air to flow into the room from the attached alleyway. After a long while, she spoke. "This core was designed to act as a generator for the laboratory, a power source, so to speak, that could power all sorts of magical technology. It seems to create huge amounts of energy out of virtually nothing. By implanting it in you, your body must have been able to take the energy of the core and use it to heal yourself. I can only guess at the finer details. Even my understanding is vague. Only the human body can use Natural Ynia to cast spells, so this core should act only as a repository in theory. This technology is ancient in nature, but new to our civilization. We'd have to take it to Akadaemia to find out more. But I hope that's enough of an explanation to satisfy you." She rose and added, "Other nations desperately want this technology, and as long as you have it, you'll be hunted for it."

"That explains a lot, but you haven't explained the crater yet," Bleiz interjected. "You said a deliberate explosion? Is that core in Calunoth's chest going to do the same thing?"

Calunoth's heart skipped a beat at the thought.

"No, it's stable. I think," Lauren responded. "If continually fed a huge amount of energy, it could theoretically explode, but I don't know where such a source could even be found. The explosion was most likely caused by Lord Glathaous trying to prevent those so-called mercenaries from getting the perfected core. There would have been a lot of equipment around that wasn't as stable. The crater was most likely the result of Lord Glathaous destroying all of the other equipment simultaneously."

"What about those soldiers pursuing us?" Luca asked. "Do you know anything about them?"

Lauren shook her head. "No, they're working for someone, but I have no idea who. They could be Sihleons, but they all appeared to be either Renderivean or Legrangian to me. The Sihleons have very distinctive accents, and their skin is a shade darker. Also, they rarely engage with the outside world, so to see so many of them in one place would be odd indeed." She turned back to Calunoth and said, "You can put your shirt back on. It's probably a good idea to keep it as hidden as possible."

Calunoth obliged the young researcher, slipping his shirt back over his head.

"Well," Bleiz said with a whistle. "This is a much bigger deal than I thought I was getting myself into. We should head north tomorrow. Those men pursuing us will have to rest as well, and with luck, they'll waste a good deal of time searching Crideir. We could get to Caern Porth within a few days on the horses."

"Why not head to Deirive? It's where we were supposed to go anyway," Luca asked.

"Caern Porth is safer and closer. There's a Knight garrison there, and we shouldn't be traveling around carrying something this important. We can get an armed escort there and then return to the capital," Bleiz replied, yawning loudly.

Calunoth noticed that the lines in the captain's face seemed deeper than they had when he had met him in the grove.

"My apologies," Bleiz said. "These past two days have been taxing on me. I'm not as fit as I was ten years ago. We'll have to move early in the morning, and I'd better get some sleep. You had all better sleep as well. You never know when your next chance at a bed will be.

"Getting old, Captain?" Luca chirped from his position on his cot.

"Wait twenty years and you'll see where that attitude gets you," Bleiz retorted, clambering onto his own cot. "Don't stay up too late." The grizzled old captain said no more and instead drifted summarily off to his rest.

Calunoth attempted to the do the same, but sleep eluded him still. Luca and Lauren stayed awake talking as both had slept well on the way to Crideir. Their conversation was gentle and quiet, but his thoughts had turned to other matters. He lay on his cot and attempted to sleep, but his mind raced with the knowledge of what he had learned. The Pralia Core in his chest was now the subject of a national manhunt. And it was what Lenocius was after. Now, at long last, Calunoth had a reason to smile. He had the reason for the Glathaous Massacre implanted in his chest. If Lenocius wanted it, he would have to come and get it.

After many hours of lying awake with thoughts of redemption for his failure running through his mind, Calunoth finally slipped into sleep, going back once more to the company of the cackling black-clad men, the fires, and the gate.

Chapter 4

An Ill-Traveled Path

The small town of Crideir was bustling even more than usual as the companions set out to leave their comfortable abode. Well fed and well rested, the mood had improved markedly from the previous evening, although Bleiz still grumbled about his sores as he mounted his chestnut horse. Luca volunteered to take the reins from the older captain, an offer that was not refused. Although fit for his age, Bleiz had many years of weariness in his bones and subsequently was not as quick to recover from exertion as his younger charges.

Having ridden through the night and day previously, the group had been grateful for the opportunity to rest more substantially. Even Luca and Lauren had eventually taken advantage of this opportunity to sleep well into the morning while Bleiz, the consummate soldier, had chosen to eat a hot breakfast early and then venture into the markets to replenish their supplies. Calunoth, for whom sleep was becoming increasingly elusive, had joined him, woefully aware of the fact that he had no money to his name, having not kept his purse on his person while on guard duty at the castle. Therefore, Calunoth found himself beholden to the captain for supplies and materials.

Because Calunoth had lost his sword in the massacre, he had since been carrying only the small dagger he had borrowed from Luca to defend himself. While the dagger would be useful in close combat, it was no substitute for a proper weapon. But swords were not cheap, so Calunoth spent much of the morning admiring the weaponry for purchase, lamenting their high price but saying nothing. Bleiz had already done so much for him, and he could not in good conscious ask him to purchase a blade when he still had some means to defend himself.

However, as they walked back through the market with their packs restocked with provisions, Bleiz noted Calunoth eyeing the weapons stalls wistfully, and when Calunoth stopped to admire a particularly fine longsword, the captain took charge.

"I see you have an eye for the finer weapons," Bleiz remarked casually as Calunoth handled a sword with an ornate hilt inlaid with gold and a thin, sharp blade. "But a fine weapon isn't a good one. The blade on that one is so thin, it'll snap in half if you hit anything harder than a piece of cloth. You need something more practical." He reached into the stall and extracted a standard-issue army longsword. With a plain metal cross guard and a dulled, tempered blade, the weapon appeared completely unremarkable.

Calunoth carefully handed the ornate weapon back to the vendor and said, shaking his head, "I would love something better to fight with, but I haven't the coin for even a cheap blade. I'll just have to make do with the dagger until I can find some money or a new weapon."

"Nonsense!" snorted the captain. "We've been able to run so far, but now that you have your strength back, we must be prepared to fight our way out of situations that demand it!" He turned to the vendor and negotiated a price. Fortunately, the blade in question appeared dull and did little more than take up space in the merchant's inventory, so Bleiz was able to acquire it for a lower price than Calunoth would have anticipated. With negotiations concluded, the old captain handed the blade and its scabbard to Calunoth, who accepted it hesitantly.

"I appreciate it, Bleiz, but I have no way to pay you back. You've covered the costs of everything so far, and I have nothing to contribute," Calunoth replied, frustrated by his lack of usefulness.

"If we have to fight those men, and you end up taking one out before it can hamstring me, I'll consider us even," Bleiz replied. "Besides, I can go back to the quartermaster of the Knights at Caern Porth, and they'll give me the money back. We can receive compensation for emergency purchases made in the field, and arming an unarmed companion certainly meets that threshold. If I'd bought that ornament you'd picked up, they would have had some questions, but a reliable piece of steel they won't question."

Calunoth accepted his reasoning gratefully and remarked, "I can imagine some Knights try to abuse that opportunity," as he examined his new blade.

"A lot try, but not many succeed," Bleiz replied. "I heard tell once of a Knight who tried to claim a bottle of single-malt Galgre whiskey as a necessary expense for guarding the harbor during a rainstorm."

"Did he succeed?" Calunoth asked.

"He actually did the first time!" Bleiz replied laughing. "But after he tried the second time, he was told to just buy a thicker gambeson."

The two men grew somber and furtive as they returned to the inn, frequently casting their gaze into the shadows for any sign the mercenaries had caught up to them. They thought they had avoided detection until Calunoth caught sight of the swishing of black fabric at the far side of the market. Pulling Bleiz into a side alley, the two men waited anxiously as the black-clad men passed them by.

The two men were whispering quietly as they moved past their shrouded prey, but all Calunoth could hear was, "Crideir," and "Pralia," but nothing beyond that. With a grim exchange of glances, Calunoth and Bleiz hurried back to the inn to collect their companions and disappear from the town.

***

The group hastily mounted their steeds and swiftly trotted to the town's northernmost gate. The road to Caern Porth was well maintained and busy, but most traffic was moving south and began to thin and become less regular the further the group journeyed north.

Caern Porth was the northernmost city of Renderive and the location of the main border fortress that served as the first line of defense against invasion from the Legrangian Empire. Although lost for several months to the Legrangian Forces in the Sieth Incursion twelve years ago, the city had been retaken in the last push by Felix Draca, Luca's eldest brother, in which the Legrangian forces were expelled from Renderive and the most recent peace had been established. As a deterrent to Legrangian aggression, the city and fortress were always heavily fortified and manned by a large contingent of the Holy Knights of Renderive.

The Holy Knights derived their name from the Holy Church of Renderive, from which their order originally sprang. Although the Church in Renderive did not hold the same absolute political power as the Church of the One did in neighboring Sihleo, it still retained its position as a moral and cultural force of Renderive.

Renderive itself was once part of the Legrangian Empire, with the oldest records of the continent dating back over three thousand years. At one point a united state, a deep divide had begun to grow around twenty-three hundred years ago between the deeply religious Renderivean Province and the increasingly secular Legrangian Empire. The divide eventually deepened until the First Schism War broke out, in which Renderive united under the hero, Asta, disciple of Sentential, and cast the Legrangians out of the province, thereby establishing Renderivean independence. Since that time, the Legrangian Empire had been a constant aggressor, continually seeking to reclaim the land lost. Although the last Legrangian attack over the Sieth River had been significant, the offensive had not reached the height of the Fourth Schism War, presided over by the current King Greshaun forty years previously.

The Legrangian disdain for the Renderiveans was deep and inbred. After disposing entirely of the Legrangian Church five hundred years ago, the emperor had established himself as the sole provider of reason and morale for the Legrangian Empire. As a result, the empire had expanded its technological abilities and kept its people industrious, if not free. Now the Legrangian Empire was the single greatest threat posed to the country of Renderive. And it was a threat that was taken seriously.

The terrain north of Crideir changed beyond the vast, flat expanse of the Central Steppe and began to rise slowly in elevation as the Llewyn Hills neared. Although the road did not slope as substantially as the hills to the east did, the change in elevation was welcomed by both Luca and Bleiz, who still remembered the dull days trekking across the Central Steppe. The day passed without incident until late afternoon when the group started to cross over one of the largest hills yet, and the vantage point rendered a clear vision of the path they had just tread.

"Look! Behind us!" Lauren called from her perch behind Calunoth on the bay horse. Given her position, she had been assigned to watch the road behind them for their pursuers as Bleiz scanned the road ahead.

Turning his horse, Calunoth could barely see the diminishing outline of Crideir in the distance, many miles down. What he could see clearly now that they had the high ground was a large group of mercenaries following their trail. They were all mounted on horseback and moving more quickly than the group was.

"Damn. They must have picked up our trail. I knew we waited in that town too long," Bleiz cursed. Turning to the others, he said, "We'll increase our speed. There are still a few hours of light left, and they're moving faster than us. If we can keep away until nightfall, we might be able to lose them in the dark." Switching places with Luca, he grasped the reins and spurred the horses into a gallop once more. Following suit, Calunoth and Lauren kept pace close behind as they attempted to distance themselves from their pursuers.

The hours passed and the road remained strangely quiet while they fled their pursuers. Bleiz was clearly discomforted, and his discomfort was aggravated when the group crossed over the crest of the hill and sighted a small troop of soldiers heading down the road on foot toward them. The men wore mismatched equipment and bore no insignia that connected them to any banner. Bleiz examined them from afar. They were too poorly equipped to be mercenaries but moved with the intent of men marching to battle. The incline of the hill was such that the men were visible to the companions before the reverse was true. As a Knight's captain, Bleiz technically had the authority to order any armed combatant of Renderivean descent as he saw reasonably fit. Regardless, Bleiz was taking no chances with the suspicious men and ordered his companions to hide in the ditch to avoid drawing attention to themselves.

"Hail, men of Renderive!" Bleiz called as the men approached him. Dismounting, he approached them with the confidence of an experienced veteran. "Which way do you head?" he asked.

The men were all dressed in differing attire, but they were all armed and appeared at closer inspection to be at least somewhat competent with a blade, however poorly equipped they may be. At the older Knight's approach, the men looked alarmingly at each other before their leader, a short man with a crop of dirty blond hair and a matching beard, stepped forward to address him.

"We are men headed to war and would rather know your name first, traveler," the man said gruffly, eyeing Bleiz warily.

Bleiz was visibly startled by the manner of this reply but acquiesced nonetheless. "My name is Bleiz Terin, Captain of the Wilds, Fourteenth Division of the Holy Knights of Renderive."

"Captain Terin, we are currently heading south to join our brethren. We have also been told to watch for a small group of travelers. Have you perchance come across a young man with a white crystal attached to his chest?" the man asked.

Bleiz's instinctive reaction nearly betrayed his mind. His gray eyes widening and beard twitching, he had to suppress an urge to immediately reach for his sword. Sensing tension, the men all put their hands to their weapons. Forcing himself to stay calm, Bleiz attempted to speak to the man. "I have come across many travelers over the past two weeks, sir, but none who would match that description. And I believe I would notice such an unusual trait." Bleiz continued evenly, "What business would you have with this man?"

"We have been ordered to search for this man and his companions. He has something very important to Duke Byrant, whose army we are to meet in Southern Renderive. We were also advised that a pair of Knights had aided and abetted these travelers and that they were headed in this direction," the leader replied. When Bleiz grew tense, he continued. "If you have anything you would like to tell us, Captain Terin, now would be the best time for you to do it." The man drew his weapon, and his charges followed suit.

"Are you sure about this, sir?" A young but scraggly man asked. "He's a proper Knight, and we're looking for a group of people. This might be a mistake."

"You should listen to your—" Bleiz began in a warning fashion, but he was cut off by a bellowing battle cry from the side of the road. In a flurry, Luca had jumped out of the ditch and started sprinting toward the group with his weapon drawn. When all the men had drawn their weapons, he had panicked and assumed the worst, rushing forward to assist the veteran Knight. Calunoth leapt out of the ditch, sword drawn, and followed suit.

With all hope for a diplomatic resolution disappearing before a charging Luca, Bleiz drew his sword and struck out at the leader before he could recover from his surprise at seeing the younger Knight charge at him. However, the leader was experienced himself and reacted quickly to raise his sword to parry Bleiz's attack. With a lighting quick riposte, the leader responded in kind and counterattacked. Sparks flew as Bleiz and the leader dueled ferociously. Bleiz, as a Knight, had far more skill than his opponent, but the leader was soon joined by one of his companions. Now in a two-to-one battle, Bleiz had his hands full as he dodged, ducked, and parried against both of his opponents simultaneously.

Luca's charge had taken the group of men by surprise, and he was upon them before they could raise their weapons. Luca dispatched an ax-wielding soldier with a neat flick of his wrist that defied his size before being confronted by the remaining three soldiers. Although a capable and powerful Knight, fighting off three men at once was a challenge for any warrior. Fortunately, the men were disorganized and coordinated with each other sloppily, with never more than two of them striking at the same time. One of the men managed to loop around Luca and went to deliver a fatal blow while the big man was distracted fending off two blades at once only to find the edge of his blade banging against the flexible, tempered steel of Calunoth's new sword as he arrived on the scene.

Luca's initial attack had improved their odds, but they were still outnumbered. The three fought the five remaining capably, exchanging small nicks for major cuts. But the battle was turning against them; these men were able fighters, and their coordination improved as they fell into the rhythm of battle. After several moments trading blows, the leader managed to push Bleiz back, causing him to backpedal and trip over a small rock in the road several feet away. As his companion moved forward to finish Bleiz off, the leader looked at the two other men attacking his party. Recognizing the one they needed, he called out to his men.

"Take the black-haired one! Lenocius wants him alive!" the leader called, pleased to see the fight turning in his favor.

However, he was celebrating far too soon. Bleiz swept the advancing man's leg out from beneath him, giving himself time to regain his feet and continue his defense. Growling, the man rose and strode forward to put an end to the pesky Knight when he heard a guttural scream behind him.

Calunoth and Luca had been fighting evenly with the three men, but the orders of their leader had reached them as clearly as it had reached his men. The order flicked a switch in Calunoth. His breathing suddenly became fast and ragged. His eyes lit up with a demonic glow. Nights of sleeplessness, the specter of his nightmares, and the remembrance of his near death awoke something in Calunoth. Something that had been lurking beneath the surface since the night of the massacre. Something that had been triggered by the name of the man he held responsible for the massacre. Lenocius.

Emitting a ravaging roar, the white-hot rage that had been burning in Calunoth's chest and mind burst forward to make itself known. These men were responsible for the massacre. Whether they had been there or not didn't matter. They worked for the man who did. They were men who could be held accountable, the first in a long line. Anger and resentment poured from Calunoth as his rage took over. This was his first opportunity to fight them, to make them pay. And fight them he would. He would take on anyone associated with the black-clad men who had destroyed his world.

And he didn't hold back. Free of his cautious sensibilities, he attacked recklessly, relentlessly, his jet-black hair following his motions as he swept into a rage. Swinging his blade with wild abandon, unaffected by pain or fear, he attacked with the ferocity of a demon, and the men knew instantly they wouldn't get away. Luca jumped out of the way of Calunoth's sword, the blade that had just saved his life almost taking it only moments later, leaving Calunoth alone to face the three men.

Rushing wildly forward, Calunoth jumped through a gap in the men and swung his sword powerfully as he spun backward, decapitating the central man. Without stopping, he leapt to the left, parrying an oncoming blade as he did so, and ran his sword through that man's stomach. It took him but a moment to extract the blade, but that allowed the last man to jump forward and cut a large diagonal slash across Calunoth's back. However, the blade did not bite deeply as Calunoth's momentum had carried him away from the blow and into the body of the second man. Pushing the second man off his blade, Calunoth swung wildly again at the man who had just slashed him, completely oblivious to the pain of the shallow cut across his back. Calunoth's blade bit much deeper. It sliced into the last man from shoulder to hip, almost cutting him half and causing him to fall back instantly as the blade sliced through several of his internal organs. He was dead in seconds.

With rage still clouding his mind and the red mist still shrouding his vision, Calunoth ran toward the remaining two men, including the leader. Unsure of how to react with the tide of the battle turning so suddenly against him, the leader raised his sword to block Calunoth's oncoming swing. Calunoth brought the blade down with such force a crack appeared at the edge of the leader's blade, and shockwaves reverberated down his arm, numbing his fingers and loosening his grip on the blade. Calunoth disarmed the man in short order and ran him through, leaving only one man still engaging with Bleiz.

Seeing the blood-crazed Calunoth rushing toward him, the man jumped away from Bleiz and dropped his weapon, his greasy brown hair falling into his terror-stricken brown eyes.

"I surrender!" he screamed, hoping to avoid the same fate as his colleagues as he lifted his hands to cover his face.

The man might well have. Calunoth didn't hear the cries of surrender, and he wouldn't have cared if he did. These men were evil. They worked for Lenocius. Killing them would hurt Lenocius. So they had to die. But Bleiz stepped in the way, blocking the killing blow with his own blade.

"Calunoth! That's enough!" he shouted at the young man. But Calunoth wasn't listening. He was possessed entirely by his rage, and parried Bleiz's blow, moving to shove him out of the way. The man who had surrendered was cowering now, tears streaming down his face as he begged for his life.

His pleas may have gone unheeded had Luca not rushed in from behind to tackle Calunoth to the ground. Calunoth's blade went flying out of his hand as Luca's crushing weight fell on top of him. He struggled wildly, consumed by anger, but for all his rage, he could not shift Luca's great weight off. As Bleiz retrieved his fallen sword, Calunoth slowly calmed, feeling the rush of adrenaline leave his body and the red mist start to rise out of his vision. He became aware that he was breathing heavily and that his back was giving off a dull ache. Then he noticed Luca was speaking to him.

"Calm down, Cal! Gods! You almost attacked Bleiz! Get a grip man!" Luca shouted at him as he lay face down on the road. Calunoth's mind slowed from its racing pace, and his breathing normalized.

"I'm all right now, Luca," he muttered. "Let me up."

Luca eyed Calunoth carefully, ensuring that his faculties had indeed been restored, before rising and helping him to his feet. Calunoth accepted his hand gratefully and took stock of the situation as he stood.

The road was littered with bodies. The man that Luca had killed had fallen off the side of the road and now lay in the ditch face down. The men Calunoth had killed dotted the road, the extent of their gruesome injuries on full display. Blood was spattered all over the road, and the dirt had been unsettled by their footwork as they had dueled. Bleiz had bound the arms and legs of the man who had surrendered and now stood speaking to him.

"You're still alive because you surrendered. Your continued health is dependent on you answering my questions quickly and fully. Understand?" Bleiz spoke roughly with an edge to his voice. At the man's nod, Bleiz asked, "Who gave you your orders? Who are you working for?"

The man was young, barely older than Calunoth and Luca, and was clearly shaken at seeing Calunoth tear through his companions. Tears streamed down his face, and he spoke with a tremor in his voice.

"We're just commoners! From a village near Caern Porth. Vince, our boss, was contacted by Reil. He promised there would be a better place for us in the new Renderive once the king was dead! He swore we wouldn't have to work the fields so hard with him in charge!"

Bleiz interrupted the terrified young man with a roar. "Once the king is dead?! Are you admitting you were going to attempt to kill the king, boy?!"

"No, sir!" squeaked the boy. "We were just going to fight in the war is all. Duke Byrant is gathering men to remove Greshaun from the throne. Reil's one of his top men, and he promised us a better life if we fought for Byrant. That's where we were going."

"Gods!" Luca cursed. "Byrant's going to start a civil war? What is he thinking?"

"Well, now we know why there's been so much activity in the south now," Bleiz responded. "But he had to have been keeping this quiet for a long time. If he's mustering men now, then that means his attack must be imminent." Turning back to the boy, he asked, "And who told you of us? How do you know the man called Lenocius?"

"I don't know!" the boy said. "Vince met with a bunch of the other captains. He came back saying Byrant's top ally needs this crystal. Some Sihleon minister. We only heard yesterday from one of Byrant's men it might be coming this way. He gave us your descriptions. The bounty on you is enormous! We could live comfortably for the rest of our lives with that money! But I don't know who Lenocius is, honest!"

Bleiz seemed about to ask more of the boy before Lauren, who had come out from the ditch once the fighting had ended, interjected. "Wait, did you say there are other people coming this way? Where are they? What about the Knights at Caern Porth?" she asked.

"There's a whole pile of us marching tomorrow. We left early because Vince wanted to get a head start on the hunt for the crystal," the boy replied, information now flowing freely. "The Knights are still at Caern Porth as far as I know, but the rest of our guys are on their way here."

"Damn!" Bleiz cursed. "That means that the road ahead will be blocked. We can't go forward, or we'll run into Byrant's men, and we can't go back because we'll run into those mercenary bastards! We're trapped!"

"We should get off of the road," Calunoth said, having regained his senses entirely. "We're losing time either way. And from what's left of this battle, it'll be easy for either group to figure out we were here."

Bleiz acknowledged him grimly. With the hilt of his sword, he bashed the trussed-up young man in the temple, rendering him unconscious and causing him to fall onto the ground. Then he handed Calunoth's sword back to him. "We'll speak about your actions later," he warned. The captain turned and addressed the others. "But for now, we need to run. Leave the horses. They'll only slow us down in the wild. Luca, can you run?"

Luca was wiping the blood off his sword as he responded with an affirmative nod. "Lauren did a great job. The ankle aches a little, but I'll be fine," he said.

The group rushed to unload the horses with an air of disappointment. The horses had been good to them and had saved them a great deal of labor, but they would only get in the way in the wilds. They were built for the plains and pastures, not the rugged countryside surrounding the Llewyn Hills. Once they had removed all of their possessions, Luca sent the horses packing down the road with a heavy slap on each rump. The horses gave out a great neighing and galloped off down the path.

The group hurried off the road and found shelter in a small rocky alcove beneath a hill while they discussed their next move. Bleiz drew a map out of his pack, and the rest of the quartet clustered around to examine it in the rapidly failing sunlight.

"Right. Caern Porth is no longer an option," Bleiz said examining the map. "We'd never be able to sneak past those men if there are as many as the boy said there were. We can't go back to Crideir either with that other group chasing us. But at least now we know to be careful of who we trust. If Byrant wants that crystal, we need to get it to the king as soon as possible."

"We can't go west," Lauren said pointing at the map. "The hills level out into the plains, then into the Terrestia Forest. We might be able to lose both groups in the forest, but we'd never find our way out ourselves."

"So then we go east. Caern Vaughn is our only option," Calunoth surmised. "We'll have to pass through these swamps though. What does this skull mean?" He pointed to the markings to the east.

Bleiz and Luca looked darkly at each other before Luca answered. "That's the Caerwyn Bogs. It's a cursed swamp. We can't go there. No one who does ever ventures out. I've heard plenty of stories from the other Knights. Stories of men who lose their way and run in circles for days only to be preyed upon by the bog ghouls. We should avoid it at all costs."

Lauren chimed in then. "There's no such thing as curses. But I have heard from some of my professors that there's powerful magic at work in the area. It would probably be best to avoid it if we can."

"Where else do you suggest we go then?" Calunoth demanded. "We can't just wait here to be caught and slaughtered."

Bleiz continued to quietly study the map, playing his fingers over it and murmuring to himself. After several moments of contemplation, he spoke.

"This has become a much graver matter. We must reach Caern Vaughn. The lord there is one of the most devoted allies of the king. He can be trusted, if anyone can. The king must be informed about this coup as soon as possible. If we go north or south, we will most certainly be caught." His fingers rested on the map for a moment, then he drew a line to the bogs. "We have no choice. We will be safe from our pursuers in the bogs. No one will follow us in there. Whatever magic or demon lies there, we will simply have to face it." Rolling up the map, he stowed it in his pack, ignoring Luca's protestations.

"We're out of time. We must press on. Come. The Caerwyn Bogs await."

Chapter 5

An Unlikely Meeting

    It was a clear night with no clouds covering the moon nor obscuring the stars. Beams of moonlight journeyed down from beyond the sky to reveal the way through the rocky terrain that constituted the lower hills. The moonlight made quick work of the shadows of beasts and other unknown forces that usually prowl the night, yet the light granted by the moon was of no comfort to the group as they slowly traversed the rocks. Although their way was clear, the night granted no blanket or cloud to shroud the eyes of those who hounded them. If they were to continue deeper into the hills, they would be at the mercy of their pursuers by dawn. The only way to evade capture now was to tread the ground that no man would dare tread, and so they marched with the haunted expression of the hunted.
    The group marched on through the night, but the grim reality they were facing was now becoming clear. Bleiz, as the unofficial leader of the group, felt it the most. He had seen many winters and many battles and had developed a hardened view of the world. However, the young charges he was leading had suffered greatly, and now he must lead them through even more and hope they could cope.
    Lauren, for example, was coping as well as could be expected, but she was only a researcher. She couldn't fight, and she didn't belong here. As an intellectual, she should be writing formulae in labs not trekking through the mud. And while she was willful, she lacked the stamina of the men, and that could become a serious impediment soon. It was the young guard, Calunoth, who concerned Bleiz the most though. In the span of seven days, he had seen his home destroyed, all his friends slaughtered, been driven out of his hometown, and now it seemed like he was the target of a regional manhunt not just by some mysterious group of mercenaries, but also by the entire army of the nation's third most powerful noble.
    Bleiz cast his gaze to Calunoth warily and saw the black-haired young man trotting along appropriately. He hadn't slept well in days. And that rage that had taken hold of him had been frightening to behold. Bleiz had seen a man rage like that only once before. That man had flung himself into battle and slain over three dozen men single-handedly before succumbing to innumerable wounds. It was a rage

that was well-placed, Bleiz did not doubt. If he was in the same position, he would likely have reacted the same way. But that rage was dangerous. It made Calunoth a liability. If he had the chance to kill Lenocius or Alistair, he might take it, even if it guaranteed their deaths.

Aware of Bleiz watching him, Calunoth shrugged his shoulders, wondering what Bleiz was looking at. Deciding the sooner they had this conversation the better, Bleiz edged closer to Calunoth without reducing his gait.

"How are you feeling, Cal?" Bleiz asked. "We didn't even take the time to staunch that wound. Are you managing?"

"I'm fine, thanks for asking," Calunoth replied between breaths. They were all beginning to pant as the pace wore on their lungs. He knew what Bleiz was going to talk about, so he pre-empted the captain. "I'm sorry for my actions back there. I wasn't trying to hurt you. I don't know what came over me."

"What came over you was pain and anger, a blood rage. I've seen it before, though maybe not to that extreme. If we'd put an entire army in front of you, I think you would have cut them all to pieces. No, that's not the problem," Bleiz began. "The problem is how you controlled it—or didn't. I'm not going to try to understand what you're going through, but I know you just want to tear down the world to get to the people responsible for your loss. That anger can be good, it can motivate you, and I think you'll need that motivation to get to them. But we need you to control it better. As it stands, if you went off like that uncontrolled again, you might get the rest of us killed. We want to help you, but we have to know that we can trust you to listen, obey orders, and most importantly, control your rage. Am I being clear?"

Calunoth had been quiet throughout the lecture, and when it was over, he replied with a nod and an apology. Bleiz returned to the front of the group and was replaced by Luca, who was maintaining his trademark positive attitude.

"Don't worry too much if the old man lectures you," Luca said smiling. "He does that to everyone. I'm expecting Lauren will be hearing from him soon about something. He's just trying his best to be in charge."

"He's a captain, isn't he?" Calunoth asked in response. "Isn't being in charge part of his job?"

Luca gave out a short snicker that he managed to turn into a cough. "Well, yeah, but he hates being in charge. He only does it because his sense of duty is harder than a rock. If someone else could lead, he'd much prefer that. He's happy to advise, but he's never enjoyed leading." Luca stopped talking as the moonlight began to grow dim and a putrid smell began to fill the air. His eyes narrowed and he said, "We're nearly there."

The four companions reached the edges of the bog at the onset of dawn, and the tenuous nature of their flight became apparent. On the hills behind them, not an hour's ride away, the black-clad men appeared at the crest of the hill and could easily see the group at the edge of the bogs. These men too would have to abandon their horses soon to manage the terrain, but they seemed driven to push their steeds further than the companions had. The group's only choice was to keep moving, so move they did, refusing to look back until the hard rocky ground of the low hills eased into a soft, marshy quagmire and the air was permeated with the thick stench of peat and sulfur. After several miles of slogging over the spongy ground, Bleiz grimly announced they had reached the Caerwyn Bogs.

For the first few miles, Calunoth wasn't sure what his companions had been so apprehensive about. The place stank, to be sure, and the watery mud was difficult to forge through. But there was no hint of the magical interference of the place, nor any sign of ghouls or spirits. However, as they continued their trek into the interior, he began to change his mind. The light from the morning sun faded as twisted trees began to obscure the sky. The trees grew thicker as they walked until no sunbeams at all breached the upper foliage, and the bogs molded into an eerie twilight abyss. Mist rose from the dark pools of water to obscure the surrounding areas, causing Lauren to grab onto Luca or risk losing him in the encroaching fog. Unconsciously, the group began to walk closer together. There was something distinctly unnatural about the place.

As Calunoth looked around at the shadows that shifted effortlessly through the bog, he swore he could hear whispering beyond the surrounding trees. After several more minutes of carefully listening to the sounds around him, he realized why he found their environment so unnerving. The bog was entirely silent but for the sounds of their movement and the whispering of the winds through the trees. No frogs croaked; no fish swam. The bog was devoid of any natural sounds of life. And above all, he had a feeling that he struggled to dismiss, the feeling they were being watched.

Lauren was now teetering on the edge of collapse, and Luca was practically carrying her as they moved through the swamp. Bleiz turned to look at them at one point, seemingly about to ask if they wanted to make camp, but he was quickly dissuaded of that notion. No one wanted to stay in this eerie place for any longer than required.

The group trudged along for hours without speaking for fear of disturbing whatever unnatural force watched over the bog. It was not until they saw a light up ahead that they broke their silence. Weapon drawn, Bleiz cut through the undergrowth to create a path to the light. A single campfire burned brightly in a small clearing with firm ground. This was no ordinary campfire, however. It burned with an eerie green glow that betrayed it as a source of magic, for no ordinary fire would burn green. A tent and various worldly possessions lay scattered around the clearing.

"What th—" Bleiz began from the front of the group, but he was interrupted by a flashing shadow. Instantly, the shadow had disarmed him and rendered him unconscious. Luca and Calunoth scrambled for their weapons. In their haste, Luca was forced to drop Lauren, but they weren't quick enough. Calunoth felt his sword leave his hand, and then there was nothing but blackness.

***

When Calunoth awoke, he was surrounded by a nearly absolute darkness. The eerie light that had snuck through the dark and twisted trees earlier had vanished, only to be replaced by a pitch-black layer of nothingness. It would have been impossible to see anything at all but for the light of a strange campfire. The green light of the fire cast flickering shadows and bursts of light onto the ground as it battled eternally against the blackness, fighting to protect the small clearing from the encroaching darkness. The clearing itself was a sanctum. The ground was firm, unlike the sinking sludge of the surrounding areas, and the trees formed a tight circle around it, leaving enough space to move comfortably but not so much as to render a frightened mind discomforted by thoughts of what might be hidden within. In such places, the mind could create phantasms more terrifying than any the earth could create, but the clearing was of such a size that there was no unlit space from which such a phantasm might appear. It was an expertly chosen spot.

All this Calunoth could see from where he sat with his back pressed against the cold bark of a twisted tree. His hands were bound tightly behind him, though with what he could not say. Looking around, he saw all his companions in similar positions dotted around the clearing. Luca had been tied to a particularly large tree to accommodate his girth, and he currently sat there unconscious, head down, his muddy blond hair hiding his face. Lauren and Bleiz were tied up between Luca and Calunoth. All were still unconscious.

Looking around the clearing, Calunoth replayed the attack. It had come so quickly, so efficiently, that they'd been unable to react in time. Whatever had attacked them was not a foe they could defeat easily, if at all. All Calunoth could remember was a shadowy blur, a flash of steel, and then the sensation of falling. At least they all appeared to be alive, which was more than they had a right to expect. Calunoth thought briefly about what it would have been like to die here, so suddenly, in this dank and disparate mire. His life had been in danger continuously since the Glathaous Massacre, as he now referred to the event in his mind, but the thought of being suddenly struck down by some strange spirit and left to do nought but feed the micro denizens of the bog sent chills down his spine. That was no way to die, and with him would die the truth of the Glathaous Massacre. So too would justice for the perpetrator.

A rustling beyond the fire drew his attention. They were not the sole inhabitants of this clearing. A shadowed figure sat back from the magical fire on the other side of the clearing. They blended in so completely with the background that Calunoth would not have noticed them had they not moved. The figure rose and strode toward the prisoners. Calunoth quickly dropped his head back down, feigning unconsciousness. His bonds were strong but not unbreakable. If he could untie the knot, he could slip away when the figure was distracted then rescue his friends. For that plan to work, the figure had to believe they were in no danger of losing their prisoners, and there was no more secure captive than one who wasn't conscious.

His ruse failed embarrassingly. The figure continued to approach, and Calunoth soon heard them speak.

"You can drop the act," a deep voice said, sounding amused. "You're not going anywhere. Those bindings are magically sealed and imbued with energy from the swamp. They can't be broken or undone by anyone but me. Feigning sleep won't do anything for you."

Calunoth, his heart pounding, ignored the voice, hoping to convince his captor he was mistaken. The voice continued, noting Calunoth's inaction with a small snort.

"All right, have it your way." The voice was laced with the musical lilt of the Renderivean Hillmen. "I don't like repeating myself anyway. I'll sort you all out once everyone's awoken." The voice spoke with a confidence unlike any Calunoth had heard before. It was not the confidence of a boisterous guard after too much ale, nor was it with the haughty arrogance that many of the researchers at the castle possessed. It was almost factual. The voice was in complete control of the situation, and it was so obvious that it seemed foolish to doubt it. Unable to justify his continued feint, Calunoth looked up and saw the source of the voice.

The figure was no monster, nor was he a spiritual creature of the swamp. It was just a man. He was tall and powerfully built, with long brown hair that draped partially over his left eye. His eyes were a piercing green and hid beneath a perpetually furrowed brow. He may once have been dressed in fine leather armor, but the original color was impossible to distinguish beneath what seemed like layers upon layers of thickly caked mud. This stranger had clearly been in the bog for some time and was obviously quite capable. He appeared completely at ease in the dark and cursed swamp and was unintimidated by the blackness beyond the trees. The group was completely at his mercy.

Calunoth attempted to speak to him, but the man ignored him, turning instead to the fire. It seemed he was committed to waiting for the rest of them to awaken before engaging with them. He instead began formulating some concoction in a pot above the magical fire, occasionally throwing in ingredients and stirring it. Calunoth had no idea what it was, but the smell of the swamp could not blot out the potent aroma of crushed herbs and roots given off by the mixture. Perhaps the man was some sort of druid? Calunoth had heard stories of the druids of the hills, who combined magic and herbalism to create concoctions that could heal the spirit and the mind but also allowed them to see into the future. He had always doubted their fortune-telling abilities as he discounted entirely the notion that chemically induced visions could do anything but addle the mind. But how could a druid be so strong as to single-handedly incapacitate two Knights, a former guard, and a novice mage in moments? Calunoth would have to wait for answers and hope the man had no intention of adding any of them to the simmering brew.

Luca was the next to wake, and he was far less compliant than Calunoth. He opened his eyes, saw their beleaguered situation, and reacted distinctly hot-headedly. After furiously trying to escape his bindings, he began to shout at the man now nestled comfortably by the fire.

"Who are you?! Why don't you come over here and face us? Untie us! Or are you afraid of what we'll do?!" Luca shouted, his voice echoing through the trees. This shouting seemed to irritate, rather than concern, the man. He walked to within six feet of the big Knight, who was continuing to shout, and focused his gaze on him with narrowed eyes.

"Silence!" he barked, waving a hand at Luca. Calunoth did not expect such a response to have any effect on the outraged Luca but was staggered when his booming voice went silent. Luca had not stopped shouting, his mouth still moved, but no sound came out! The man had used magic to silence him. Fearing he may permanently muzzle Luca, Calunoth called out to the man.

"Stop! Get away from him!" he called, only to see the man turn his piercing green eyes in his direction. The man repeated the same command and motion as with Luca, and Calunoth braced himself, preparing to be stuck with the same spell that had silenced Luca. But nothing happened. Calunoth felt the Pralia Core in his chest warm with a gentle glow that failed to show through his clothing. And that was all. Calunoth noticed nothing else amiss, so seeing Luca continuing to protest unsuccessfully, Calunoth spoke again. "What did you do to him?" he called out to the man who had turned his back.

The man whipped around with alarming speed and stared at Calunoth in surprise. The stranger repeated the motion and bid him to silence, but Calunoth repeated his question. His brow deeply furrowed, the man walked over and knelt beside him.

"Oh, now what sort of spirit are you? Magical resistance is a rare trait, but magical immunity I've never even heard of." He seemed to be speaking to himself rather than to Calunoth, and he surveyed Calunoth carefully, now much more wary of him. His musings were interrupted by a groan as Bleiz and Lauren began to stir. Luca's shouts had disturbed their rest enough to rouse them from their slumber, and Bleiz was quick to adapt to the situation. Feeling his hands bound and himself attached to the tree, his first reaction was to negotiate rather than struggle.

"You're human!" he said seeing the man leaning over Calunoth. "This is just a misunderstanding, sir. We mean you no harm!" The man, still interested in Calunoth, glanced over to meet the gray eyes of the captain, who had reacted rather differently than his companions. Finally catching a glimpse of the man's face unobscured, Bleiz let out an exclamation. "Valthor?! Valthor Tarragon? Is that you? What are you doing in this place?" The man Bleiz had called Valthor was now fully on guard, and his hand crept to his waist where a standard military-issue sword adorned his belt.

"What manner of spirit are you? How do you know my name?" Valthor queried, his hand now fully grasping his sword. That his magic had failed on Calunoth and he had been recognized in this desolate place was clearly discomforting to him, and he was ready to dispatch them immediately if the need arose.

"We are no spirits!" Bleiz replied. "We were traveling through the bog when we were attacked. Presumably by you. We mean you no harm. Even if we could hurt you." The last sentence was added as an afterthought as he remembered they were bound and unarmed.

"No men ever venture through this bog. There is ancient magic here that turns the bog alive. It is madness for normal travelers to attempt to pass through. And one of you is immune to magic. Those are properties of spirits not men. So, I repeat my question. How do you know my name?" Valthor asked.

"We fought together for King Greshaun in the Sieth Incursion! You led the Fourth Division; I led the Second. We pushed the Legrangians back over the river and drove them back to Regigaard." There was a note in Bleiz's voice that deeply disturbed both Calunoth and Luca, a note that they had not imagined the experienced and grizzled captain would emote. He was afraid. "We were forced in here by our pursuers. We had no other recourse, but we must get to Caern Vaughn. You must believe me!"

Valthor contemplated him for a moment, then asked another more specific question. "Spirits can often read the minds of the people they imitate. Let me ask you something only a Knight of Renderive would know." He paused to think for a moment, then asked Bleiz, "What are the seven principles in common that underly the Obligation specific to the orders of the Wilds, the Wings, and the Waves?"

Calunoth looked on at the interaction, praying that this was a question that Bleiz could answer well. To his despair however, Bleiz's lined face took on a blank and indignant look immediately upon hearing the question.

"What? That question doesn't even make sense! There's no— What?" Bleiz responded. Calunoth could see Lauren cringe at Bleiz's reaction, and he empathized with her. They were surely in trouble now. However, Valthor's face took on a much less severe countenance, and he relaxed.

"Huh, so you aren't a spirit," Valthor said. "Who are you then? It seems we've met before, but I'm afraid my memory fails me." At Bleiz's confused expression, he explained his actions. "When the spirits of this bog find a body, they take on its form, thus killing the host. They can then read and remember the memories of the dead, and it can be very difficult to distinguish them from the real thing. If you had taken time to think about your answer, I would have to assume you were scanning the body's memories for the answer. But of course, it was a trick question—literally unanswerable—which you realized immediately. But I must ask again. Who are you? And what force would drive sane men into this place?"

Bleiz was relieved at Valthor's explanation. He accepted it with a nod and answered, now calmer, though a cold sweat still dripped down his face.

"My name is Captain Bleiz Terin, serving in the Fourteenth Division of the Knights of the Wilds. These are my companions," he said, gesturing. "Luca, son of Conan Draca, Lauren Abraham of Akadaemia, and Calunoth Leiron of the Glathaous Castle Guard. We were forced into the bogs by two separate groups. Although we're not familiar with the identity of one, the other are men from the north, coming to fight for Duke Byrant. They all seek something we carry." Hearing Calunoth exclaim at his last revelation, Bleiz directed his next comment to him. "Valthor is one of the Six Guardians of Renderive and one of the most loyal servants of the king. He's on our side. If we can't trust him, we can't trust anyone."

Valthor digested the information and nodded. "Now I remember you! Your forces held the bank while we got our men across. You didn't have that beard then. It ages you about a hundred years. But weren't you a Commander of the Wings? What did you do to get demoted like that?"

"I was not demoted by force, sir," Bleiz replied. "I chose this position in the Wilds to avoid the politics of the higher commands. I am less well compensated but much happier for it."

"I don't blame you. If I had to live in the Bastion with Calethor for more than a week, I'd chuck myself off the tower," Valthor replied, now abandoning all semblance of formality. "Well, I buy your story. Give me a minute, I'll untie you." Valthor then proceeded to do just that, muttering a word to break the magical reinforcement of the restraints before cutting their hands free. He spent considerably longer on Calunoth's bindings casting additional spells as he did, clearly perplexed by how they did not affect Calunoth. Each time the Guardian muttered a word, Calunoth felt the warm glow in his chest again and strangely began to feel stronger.

After everyone was untied, Valthor beckoned them over to his strange campfire. He was just about to sit down when Luca tapped him on the shoulder and motioned at his mouth, still unable to speak. Remembering that he had not reversed his spell, Valthor hastily apologized and made another motion with his hand, this time barking, "Speak!" Luca's voice was restored.

With the five now all gathered around the glowing green fire, which emitted a heat that felt warmer than it naturally should be, Valthor addressed them again.

"I apologize for the mix up. I hope you can understand my reservations. I've seen far more spirits than men in this place, and it seemed beyond foolish for any human to come here," he said, settling down on a firm patch of earth.

"You're here though," Lauren pointed out. "What are you doing in this place?"

"He's one of the six Guardians!" Luca exclaimed excitedly, completely abandoning his reservations. "He's no ordinary man! He's one of the strongest human beings in Renderive, more! In the world even! This is nothing for someone like him!"

Calunoth had read about the Guardians in one of the books back at the castle library. The Six Guardians of Renderive were a group of six of the most powerful warriors in the country. Hand selected by the king, each was a pre-eminent leader, fighter, and tactician. They answered to the king directly, and, though they were not formally part of the Knights or had any official noble lineage, their authority in Renderive was surpassed only by the king. Most had a history in the Knights, but some had served as mages, researchers, or as retainers to the royal family. Some were expert instructors. But they were all extremely dangerous. Valthor Tarragon even more so. He had made history by being inducted into the Guardians at the age of nineteen because of his incredible achievements in the Sieth Incursion. Rumors abounded that his strength was derived from experiments performed on him in the laboratories beneath Akadaemia, but regardless of the source of his strength, he had distinguished himself in his service to the king and was now considered one of the king's closest and most trusted advisors.

"I don't think that answers the young lady's question," Valthor said, peering over the fire at Luca. "I'm here on a mission from the king. These bogs have been a source of trouble for many travelers over the years, but they were so out of the way that it wasn't really a problem. But a little over two months ago, we received some disturbing news. We've always known there was some sort of powerful magic at work in the bogs. A team of researchers from Akadaemia came in by their own accord to investigate, not dissuaded by reports of spirits. These were people of science after all!" He added the last sentence almost mockingly. "But of course they didn't come out when they were supposed to, so the king sent a battalion of Knights in to find them. They vanished too. That's when he decided to send me. I'm to investigate the cause of the disappearances and resolve it if possible."

"Spirits have never been proven to exist," Lauren interjected pointedly, clearly offended by Valthor's jab. "There is no proof of any supernatural force that can be observed outside of old wives' tales. They were right to investigate."

"Oh, I'm not debating the researchers' character, only their intelligence," Valthor replied amicably. "But both science and steel failed here. The king considered sending in some of the Willow Knights to see if their faith would help, but then he elected to just send me. He wants this matter resolved, and quickly. Rumors of an entire battalion going missing without cause are bad for morale, especially given the reports we've heard about Byrant in the south."

Calunoth sidled up to Luca and asked quietly, "Who are the Willow Knights?" not wanting to appear uneducated before the impressive Guardian.

"They're the military arm of the clergy. They operate within the Knights," Luca replied. "They answer to the archpriest instead of the field marshal like the rest of us."

"If the researchers came in two months ago, how long have you been here?" Calunoth asked Valthor, trying to do the math in his head.

"Almost a month," Valthor replied. "And I'm almost done. I was planning on resolving the issue tomorrow. I wouldn't mind some help, if you're willing."

Valthor had the right as a Guardian to order any one of them however he saw fit. This was a right he rarely exercised, however, as he understood that the best work came from people who wanted to help rather than those who were pressed into it. Bleiz responded with this knowledge in mind.

"We are always keen to assist a Guardian, sire," he began. "However, our mission has become so important, I fear we cannot spare the time. Even a day. We believe civil war lies on the horizon, and we must inform the king as soon as possible." With that statement, he recounted their experience since fleeing from Glathaous and concluded with his interrogation of the young boy on the road.

Valthor listened intently, without interruption, while Bleiz recited the story. When he spoke of escaping through the stained glass of The Ax and Stable, the Guardian let out a quiet snicker but otherwise remained silent. When Bleiz finished, Valthor gazed into the green fire, his eyes veiled, contemplating the captain's account. After a few moments, he turned to Calunoth.

"I've visited Glathaous Castle on many occasions over the past ten years. Isaac Glathaous was a great friend to me, and to Renderive. I'm sorry you had to experience what you did, but now I need to hear your part of the story." His voice was gentle and reassuring, and Calunoth felt as comfortable as he could be retelling the night of the massacre and how he ended up with the Pralia Core in his chest.

When he was finished, Valthor reverted to gazing into the fire. He remained quiet for several minutes until Bleiz cleared his throat and startled him out of his reverie. Looking back at the group, he spoke again. "I understand your concern, but this talk of civil war long predates you. We've heard rumblings out of Byrantia for months now, and the king is prepared. Warning him of the immediate outbreak will not change preparations altogether. I am, however, much more interested in this other group. The black-clad mercenaries. I cannot identify them with any group in Renderive, yet they seem driven to pursue our technology. Technology now stuck in Calunoth." He paused for a moment to think before continuing. "I will travel with you for now. We will head to Caern Vaughn. Berwyn is the lord there and the last person I saw outside of this accursed swamp. I will have him mobilize his forces to send south. I would like to guard this technology in your chest personally though, Cal." He pinned his gaze on Calunoth. "Anyone willing to go those lengths for this technology is a threat, and I am obligated to see you safely to the capital. However, I must conclude my business here first."

Bleiz looked surprised but pleased by his offer. Traveling with a Guardian was as close to safe as could be guaranteed. It would be good for the group to travel in Valthor's company for a while. He was apprehensive about Valthor's plans for the bog though. Any problem that compelled the king to send his best man was a serious problem indeed, a point he raised to Valthor, who was not dissuaded.

"We should be all right," he responded. "I have a plan that should have worked with just me. With three fighters, it will make my job much easier. But this is a conversation for the morning. The night grows long, and I should rest at least a little before tomorrow. You have given me much to consider, and we can discuss it at greater length tomorrow." Bidding them goodnight, Valthor laid back on the ground where had sat and spoke no more.

Bleiz offered to take the first watch while his companions rested, feeling as safe as they could be in the eerie mire of the swamp. Luca and Lauren fell asleep quickly, their fatigue overcoming them. Calunoth stayed awake for several hours staring up at the dimly lit undergrowth of the surrounding trees, aware of the growing warmth spreading from his core, until he too surrendered to his rest, the dark spirits that haunted the bog abandoning their contest for the attention of his mind and yielding to the darker spirits of his mind that plagued his sleep.

Chapter 6

Secrets of the Core

    Calunoth was awoken to the metallic ringing of swords clanging. Alarmed, he rolled over and off the fuzzy bed of moss that he had lain on for the last few hours and pulled his sword from its sheath. He was on his feet in moments only to be greeted by a quizzical look from Bleiz, who sat on a nearby stump polishing his sword. Relaxing, Calunoth turned to the source of the noise on the other side of the clearing where Luca and Valthor were sparring, a starry-eyed Lauren in attendance.

    Luca was the larger of the men in girth, but they were matched in height, and it was clear from the first few exchanges that he was hopelessly outclassed. Valthor had two primary weapons: a short sword carried at his belt and a strange double-bladed staff slung across his back. A weapon of his own design, the staff's blades were forged of steel and inlaid with magical formulae that provided strength and flexibility to the blades. They were mounted to a hardened ebony staff further laced with magical properties. It was a frightening and imposing weapon to face, but it was not the one that Luca faced now. He instead had to contend with the simple short sword Valthor carried as his off-hand weapon. The blade had no special properties and was merely a standard-issue commander's blade.

    Luca should have held the advantage, pitching the length of his long sword against Valthor's short sword in the wide-open space, but he found himself constantly on the defensive. Valthor moved so fast, Calunoth could barely see the blade as it whipped through the air. The heavy clang and Luca's sluggish reactions to each blow told Calunoth Valthor was not just quick but strong too. Even if they had met him fully armed, he could still have easily beaten them all.

    Not wanting to disturb them, Calunoth instead went to sit next to Bleiz, who motioned for him to bring his sword. Sitting down next to him, he watched the older man's callused hands gently rub polishing oil on the blade and carefully wipe it down with a clean white cloth. Bleiz stored the clear liquid in a small vial and used it sparingly. The stench was pungent even from a distance.

    "There are many things that the Knights try to drill into your head when you're in training," Bleiz remarked as Calunoth watched him in silence. "The political and religious stuff is part of it of course, but equipment maintenance is the most important. I've been waiting for an opportunity to do this for days. Keeping the metal clean prevents it from rusting. And I'd rather go into a battle armless than with a rusty blade." The elder Knight seemed remarkably relaxed and oblivious to the dark nature of his surroundings. Some light had returned with the rising of the sun, so the bog wasn't completely blanketed in darkness, but somehow the return to the eerie gray mist and the twilight atmosphere was more unsettling to Calunoth than the darkness.

Yet Bleiz was completely relaxed. His trust in Valthor's ability to defend the group was absolute. Combined with the calming effect of polishing his weaponry, Calunoth could see many of the stress lines that had marred his face were much shallower than they had been on previous nights. Not yet forty, Bleiz's well-kept beard was tinged with silver-gray hairs, and his face was drawn with lines of hard work. Calunoth began to realize then what toll the burden of command had put on Bleiz, and he felt worse for it. The elder Knight was essentially in his retirement, yet by finding him in that grove, Calunoth had forced him back into a position of leadership.

A pang of guilt struck Calunoth. Before they had met Valthor, Bleiz had been protecting Luca, and when the time came, he had worked hard to protect Calunoth and Lauren as well. So it was good to see him without the weight of his charges resting as heavily on his shoulders.

"Do you need to use my polishing kit, Cal?" Bleiz inquired. Calunoth drew his sword from his scabbard and showed it to him. Bleiz nodded and carefully put the small vial of oil on the ground. "I noticed when we bought it that it was duller than it should have been. It doesn't completely ruin it, but it certainly makes it less useful than it could be. There are a couple notches in the blade that can be sharpened out. You know how to sharpen a sword, I trust?"

"Uhh, yes," Calunoth replied hesitantly, thinking back to his previous studies. Sensing his hesitation, Bleiz said nothing more, instead electing to look at him skeptically. Unable to refute the gaze, Calunoth relented. "The armory always took care of weapon maintenance. If we needed something, we just went to them. We were never far enough away from the castle to have to do it ourselves."

"Well then, it seems I must teach you. We'll see if we can do this before Luca gives up. He's a stubborn one, but I can't imagine he'll last too long against Valthor. I just hope he doesn't tire himself out. It sounds like we've got a big job ahead of us today," Bleiz said, smiling. Carefully putting away his own sword, Bleiz took Calunoth's sword and demonstrated in exquisite detail the specifics of sword maintenance.

The lecture continued until Luca finally gave up, and his sword was cast spiraling into the dirt, sinking almost halfway into the marshy ground. Luca collapsed next to it, breathing heavily, his forehead glistening with sweat from the exertion of the bout. Valthor sheathed his blade and helped him to his feet before walking over to Bleiz and Calunoth.

"That was a good bit of exercise!" he said, sounding rejuvenated. Compared to Luca, who staggered over to the pair, Valthor was not even breathing heavily. "It's been weeks since I had anyone to practice with. Anyway, we had best get going. Our destination is in the center of the bog, and I'd like to return to the camp before nightfall. Trying to navigate this place in the dark is a pain."

The group quickly gathered up their belongings and followed Valthor through the bog. Calunoth found himself at the front of the group with Valthor, who wished to speak to him at length. The Guardian's powerfully built frame contrasted sharply with Calunoth's slight build, and despite being of almost equal height, Calunoth felt out of place next to Valthor.

"So, you've had a Pralia Core stuck into your chest, have you? What's that like?" Valthor asked, seemingly unperturbed by the strange nature of his questioning.

"It's okay, though I've been feeling it getting warmer the further we move into the swamp. I feel like it's reacting to something," Calunoth replied before cursing as he made a misstep into a waterlogged divot.

Valthor pondered for a moment before answering. "I'm familiar with the technology, at least in theory. Isaac had been working on this project for a long time, and he was always keen to share with me. That was one of his faults, Sentential rest his soul. He always wanted to talk about his experiments and rarely had someone new to share his excitement with. The stuff he was working on went over the king's head, but I understood mos—" Valthor stopped mid-sentence with a half-choked cry and fell to one knee clutching his chest. Startled, the group converged around him attempting to help, but he waved them away with his other hand. With his teeth gritted and his fine features contorted, he reached for a large flask he kept at his waist, snapped open the cap, and drank deeply from it. Coughing, he fell back onto his backside on the ground and slowly removed his hand from his chest, his face pale.

"Are you all right?" Calunoth cried out, kneeling beside him. Valthor held up a single finger, implicitly asking for a moment. After a minute of panting and regaining his strength, he resumed his feet, seemingly unaffected by the incident. Closing the flask, he returned it to the holster at his waist. Calunoth smelled the same pungent aroma that had emanated from the pot Valthor had kept over the fire. It was clearly some kind of medicine. Valthor then removed a second flask from his belt and drank a small portion of its contents before addressing the group.

"My apologies. I should have mentioned that can happen," Valthor finally said. "Don't worry, I'll be fine."

"Sire, what was that? I've seen older men than you by far succumb to their health in a similar fashion. Are you healthy?" Bleiz asked, representing everyone's concerns.

"I'm as healthy as I can be," responded Valthor curtly. "You may have heard that I was subjected to magical experiments when I was younger? The results made me far stronger than anyone else, but they came with some nasty side effects. My body metabolizes and operates at twice the rate of a normal person. Unfortunately, that places a great deal of strain on my heart. I have a medicine that helps alleviate the symptoms, but these fits can come on randomly. I apologize again for startling you. I don't usually get them more than a couple times a month."

The group continued to regard his ashen face with concern, but he dismissed them. Turning his attention back to Calunoth, he resumed their conversation, ignoring the concerned gazes of the other companions as they resumed following him in silence.

"What was I saying? Oh yes, Isaac's experiments. Well, I journeyed frequently to his lab, always in secret of course—the less attention that laboratory received from prying eyes the better—and he was always keen to discuss his work. Would you like to know more, or are you happier not knowing about the core in your chest?" Valthor silently waited for Calunoth's reply.

"I didn't ask for any of this, but this is what's come my way," Calunoth replied. "It might be easier not knowing, but if I don't learn,

I'll end up just being a tool for others. At least if I know, I might have some control over decisions regarding my fate."

"Better to jump before you're pushed in essence? Wise words," Valthor said. "Very well, I'll tell you what I know, but first I should speak to your friends about our task. I'm surprised they've come along this far without asking actually." Turning, while continuing to walk backward, Valthor addressed the group.

"Right. I've figured out that the source of the magic in the bog comes from some sort of arcane Ynia stone beneath the waters at the center of the bog. I don't know exactly what this stone is, and I haven't been able to get to it because it's guarded by a great swamp beast. I'm not even sure what else to call the creature. It's some sort of magical construct, though I don't know where it came from. It probably gets its strength and form from the stone. Our goal is to kill the beast and retrieve the stone. Any questions?" Valthor announced his plan in short order, quickly and to the point.

"I have one," Lauren said raising her hand. "How do we kill the beast if it's magical? Don't we have to destroy the stone first if it's the source of the beast's power?"

Valthor laughed in reply, although no one else understood what was funny. "It's simple," he replied. "We chop it to pieces, then grab the stone. My job is to suppress the stone's magic with my own while the three of you do the chopping and the grabbing. Lauren, you stay back and drag the bodies out of the water if it kills any of us." The cheerful manner in which he reported his plan did little to bolster confidence. Dismissing the air of uncertainty from the group, Valthor turned back to Calunoth and asked, "How much do you know about Ynia?"

"Not much," Calunoth admitted. "I could barely understand anything Lauren was explaining earlier. I've read about it briefly, but I never really understood the theory."

"All right, blank slate, much easier to work with," Valthor replied cheerfully. "I'll keep it basic for now, but if you want to discuss it in detail later, we can. So, Ynia is the energy that permeates the world. Manipulating that Ynia was called magic in olden times, and that name stuck. Magic is not magic in the way you hear of in fairy tales. Magic is, in its simplest form, the unnatural manipulation of Ynia, or energy. Ynia exists all around us, mostly in the form of Natural Ynia, the energy you get from fire, wind, water, earth, and the like. There are other forms of energy, Life Ynia, which is what keeps all of us alive, and Immaterial Ynia, which is just floating around and mingling with other forms of energy."

"What's the difference between Natural and Life Ynia then, sire?" Bleiz asked, moving closer behind them as Luca fell back to chat amicably with an uncharacteristically quiet Lauren. The captain's graying beard had seen some of its natural brown color restored artificially by the numerous flecks of mud that now matted it.

"Life Ynia is far more complex than Natural Ynia and is used to sustain life rather than natural processes, hence the name," the Guardian answered before helping himself to another gulp from his flask. "There are other forms of Ynia, but Natural Ynia is the big one. Using Natural Ynia, a spellcaster can create magic by drawing in and channeling Ynia through the caster's body, then manipulating, using formulae or sheer focus, that energy into a different, more specific function. For example, I created that fire back in camp by drawing natural energy from the earth and converting it into a source of heat, from which I was able to create the fire. And those bonds I used on you and your friends were inlaid with Natural Ynia. I essentially funneled energy from the earth into a form that bound the fibers of the rope together and made them unbreakable. Well, you could have broken them in theory, but you would have had to exhaust all the Natural Ynia in this area for that to occur, which seems pretty unlikely to me."

Calunoth replied slowly, his brow furrowed as he tried to process the information. "I think so, but how did you steal Luca's voice from him?"

"Oh, that. I'm not entirely sure of the mechanics, but it uses the same principle. I drew energy from the earth, funneled it through my body, and bent it to my will. There are two main ways to conduct Ynia. One is through the *Slliared*, or force of will, in the Hillmen tongue. This involves you focusing your mind to achieve what you want the Ynia to achieve. The command is used to convert the focus into action."

"That sounds like it could be dangerous," Bleiz observed. "It wouldn't be hard to get distracted and miscast a spell. That's enough for me to avoid using it."

"Well quite. That's why the second method exists," Valthor conceded. "The second is through the use of formulae, which involves weaving symbols in the air and using chants to focus the mind. Most mages, or manipulators of Ynia, need to use formulae. It's not guaranteed to be safe, but it's safer than the alternative. I can get by using the first method on basic things, but even I have to use formulae for advanced magic."

"Is there a limit on what can be done with magic? And why doesn't everyone try to learn magic if it's so useful? I understand the first method may be difficult, but the second method seems doable for anyone with the formulae," Calunoth replied, pausing as Valthor used his sword to cut through a particularly intrusive hanging vine ahead of them.

Valthor held his tongue for a moment as he considered the best way to phrase his answer. "There are limits," he responded after a moment. "The first is that you cannot use magic to accomplish the impossible. Ynia is a source of fuel to do something, but if something cannot be done, then no amount of fuel will ever make it happen. I could not, for example, move a mountain with a single spell, at least, not one that could ever be maintained."

Valthor paused to glance at Calunoth. "The second reason I hope will answer both questions. You're not naturally supposed to mix Life Ynia and Natural Ynia because your body acts as a conduit for the energy. The spellcaster themself is the link between the natural energy and the act. However, the interaction between Life and Natural Ynia damages the body badly. In small amounts, Natural Ynia has no adverse effects, but in larger quantities, with more natural energy flowing through your body, the reaction is greater. The greatest limiting factor for magic is the spellcasters body. Once a caster begins a spell, they must complete it. If they're torn from the source or the target of the energy, then the Natural Ynia will continue to circulate through their body until they can release it. Normally, that results in the spellcaster's death, though of course it depends on the magnitude of the spell being cast. Starting a campfire is no great problem. Sending a fireball into an enemy camp? Might be an issue. While those who are more intellectually inclined aren't intimidated by the challenge, the process is foreign and intimidating to people who can get by just by swinging a sword."

Valthor snorted. "Besides, if every novice thought they could cast with ease, they'd end up setting the countryside on fire, so nonprofessional use of Ynia is discouraged. Does that all make sense?"

"I think I get it," Calunoth responded, scratching his face. "So, if you were to begin a spell, and it was interrupted and you couldn't complete that spell, then the Natural Ynia would destroy your body?"

"Exactly. You're a quick study," Valthor said approvingly. "Half my classmates at Akadaemia spent a week with their heads in their textbooks trying to figure that out. But then, it would take most of them a few days to work out a simple maths problem, so I suppose that's no great praise."

"What would happen if you ran out of Natural Ynia to channel, sire? Would that also end the spell?" Bleiz asked the Guardian.

"No, the principle holds. You still have to finish the spell. So when that happens, the Life Ynia that flows in your body and keeps you alive is utilized to complete the spell, but if that happens, you're probably as good as dead already," Valthor answered. "You only have a finite amount of Life Ynia in your body. When it's depleted, you die. Life Ynia has a higher potential, as a source of energy, but as there is a relatively small amount in your body, trying to use it as an energy source would deplete it rapidly. You'd likely be able to complete the spell you're casting, but you would die immediately afterward. It'll work, but it won't get you very far."

"So then, this stone that's causing the problems in the bogs is a source of energy? Or a conduit like a human?" Calunoth asked, ducking as he passed under a twisted black branch.

"The latter, I think," Valthor replied. "I believe it's been centralizing Natural Ynia from the earth into the living creatures in the swamps. In theory, it should have killed them, but for some reason, it's just distorted them. Then the spirits and other beings come for an easy source of Natural Ynia. Throw in a bit of fog and the imagination of children and you have a cursed swamp, ready for sale. Hold on." He stopped, putting an arm in front of Calunoth. "We'll have to resume this conversation later. We're nearly there."

The group emerged from the brush and mossy trees into a large lagoon. The water looked shallow, two feet deep at most, but it was pitch black and appeared devoid of life. Bleiz and Luca moved into the clearing while Lauren stayed as far away as she could. She had tied her long blond hair back, but like the rest of her companions, she was still covered in mud. At the water's edge, Calunoth and Valthor awaited the men, Calunoth now actively distracted by the Pralia Core in his chest. It had been growing warmer and warmer as they had approached the lagoon, and now it was so hot that it was almost burning his chest. Casting his gaze across the water, he saw a strange creature lying in wait for them.

The creature seemed to be composed of the bog itself. Standing over eight feet high with a gown of moss and vegetation concealing a body seemingly compacted with mud, wood, and water, the creature had the appearance of a large deer standing on its hind legs. The creature had thick tree trunks as arms and legs to match, though its legs were mostly covered by the strange vegetation it wore. Calunoth's observation was interrupted by Lauren's gasp of horror.

"What the hell is that?" she whispered urgently to Valthor.

"That, lady and gentlemen, is the guardian of the stone. Ugly brute, isn't it?" he replied with a cheekily raised eyebrow.

"It looks like something out of a story to frighten children!" Bleiz exclaimed. "How are we supposed to fight that thing?"

"I'm not. You are," Valthor replied jokingly but quickly became serious seeing the glowering gaze of the captain. "I haven't fought the guardian before, but it's main advantages are that it's big and bulky. I can't imagine it's very fast. The stone is the problem. Maybe Lauren can feel it, but since the rest of you don't use Ynia consciously, you can't tell, but the stone we need is hidden under the water just past the guardian, and it's giving the guardian energy. Remove the stone, and the guardian should fall."

"How will we find it?" Calunoth asked. "This water is pitch black. I don't like the idea of getting in it as it is."

"The stone is emitting a sort of barrier that will become visible when I go to suppress it. You just have to keep the guardian busy until I can overcome the barrier. Once I do, it will disappear, and you'll just have to keep an eye on where the stone falls. There's no current, so it shouldn't be difficult," Valthor replied. "Any other questions?"

"How long do we need to keep that thing busy for?" Luca asked, his hand resting uncomfortably on the hilt of his sword.

Valthor hesitated before replying. "I think, five minutes at most. I'm going to have to focus on the stone though, so you can't let it get near me, or there'll be trouble. Right, is everyone ready?"

The three men nodded their assent and drew their weapons. At Valthor's signal, they leapt into the water. Calunoth jumped in after Luca. The water came up past the guard's knees, limiting his movement, and the muddy lagoon bed slowed him even more. But he kept pushing toward the creature. Behind him, he heard Valthor begin to chant strange words, and looking behind him, he saw the Guardian weaving symbols in the air. His face was contorted in focus, both eyes closed under the partial fringe that obscured his left eye. He had already started his battle. Now it was time for Calunoth to begin his.

A shimmering light appeared in the water to the swamp guardian's right, and the construct turned its attention to the three warriors charging at it through the mud. The crystal stone became visible then as the black water immediately surrounding it turned as clear as day. Calunoth's chest grew even hotter the closer he got to the stone, now becoming painful.

Unfortunately, he had little time to ponder the issue. The creature moved swiftly, far more swiftly than they had been expecting, and bore down upon them in seconds. With a bark from Luca, the three men split, with Luca jumping to the creature's right, Calunoth to the left, and Bleiz jumping back just in time as the two tree-trunk arms slammed down on the water where Bleiz had just been standing. The creature moved faster than they'd anticipated, swinging its left arm at Luca, who wisely chose to duck rather than attempt to parry the blow. The creature's arm swung over his head, missing him by inches but allowing Luca the time he needed to counterattack. Swinging his sword with both hands and all of his strength behind him, Luca crashed his sword deep into the construct's leg, penetrating halfway. Given that a blow like that could have cut a man in half, Luca was unprepared for his blade to stop, but halfway through the stump, it became lodged in the creature's leg. Unable to extract it before the next blow came, Luca was forced to abandon his weapon and had to dive to the side as the creature swung at him again.

Calunoth had kept his run and darted behind the creature, coming closest to the crystal stone behind it. Casting a fleeting glance behind him, he saw the crystal glowing with a bright yellow light and felt the heat being emitted from the strange stone coming in such volume that it was causing the surrounding water to boil and evaporate. Turning his attention back to the creature, Calunoth hacked at its back twice, thrice, before he was knocked to the side by the creature's flailing arm as it sailed past Luca and continued into him. The blow knocked the wind out of him, but he recovered quickly and charged back in.

Bleiz, after jumping back to avoid the first attack, had now rushed forward to strike at the creature's face. Although it did not seem to have eyes, the captain's quick jabs seemed to irritate it, and it took a step back, swinging at Bleiz with its arm and leaving the right flank exposed for Calunoth to continue hacking at. Their efforts were successful in keeping the beast occupied, but it appeared to be immune to pain and resistant to damage. The creature's speed seemed unaffected by the sword lodged deep in its left leg, and as Calunoth watched in horror, the large slash marks he had made in the beast healed and closed. The beast was regenerating itself! About to look at Valthor for guidance before remembering that he could not assist them in this fight, Calunoth instead jumped in front of the beast to fight alongside Bleiz. The water around the crystal stone seemed to boil even more rapidly as the stone's battle with Valthor continued.

Then the shimmering light stopped, and the water ceased boiling. Calunoth looked over at the shoreline, hoping to see Valthor walking toward them, but instead he felt icy spikes of fear begin to prickle into his skin. Valthor was hunched over on the shore, clutching his chest, Lauren by his side. He had suffered one of his fits during the battle! Cursing, Calunoth coordinated with Bleiz to prick at the creature from both sides, antagonizing rather than hurting it as they were slowly driven back toward the bank. Luca stood back, effectively useless with his only weapon now lodged in the limb of the raging beast. The two were slowly but surely being beaten, and it was only a matter of time before one of them slipped and allowed the beast to deliver a fatal blow.

Suddenly, the shimmering light returned behind the creature. On the bank, Valthor, now perched on one knee and sweating profusely, had reengaged with the crystal. However, it was obvious to Calunoth that they didn't have long. Valthor was struggling. They had to end this as quickly as possible. And he had a plan.

"Luca, catch!" Calunoth yelled, throwing his own sword over to him, leaving himself unarmed. Luca caught the sword handily and splashed heavily to the fore to pair with Bleiz. Seeing him move toward his own position, Calunoth ducked and jumped under the creature's swinging arm, propelling himself toward its left leg. Missing the creature's attack by a hair, Calunoth grasped both hands around Luca's embedded sword, and, with all his strength and forward momentum, finished the blow that Luca had started, shearing through the thick wooden trunk and separating it into two. The creature gave a mighty bellow and fell heavily onto its uneven stump. In a rage, the beast renewed its assault on Bleiz and Luca, unable now to turn and deal with Calunoth. Calunoth saw his chance.

He sprinted through the water toward the crystal as fast as he could, sending enormous splashes of water behind him as he thrashed through the lagoon. His core was now on fire, burning his chest with a searing heat as he neared the crystal. But he would not be stopped. He plunged his hand down and reached to grab it. But the barrier prevented him from reaching the crystal, and for a moment, Calunoth was filled with an incredible surge of energy. All of the fatigue accumulated in his body over the past week was wiped away, and he could feel the scar on his back begin to seal. For the briefest moment, he was connected to the bog and every creature in it. He could feel fear, real fear, embodied by the swamp guardian who now thrashed around in a frenzy, catching Bleiz and sending him flying across the swamp. But there was nothing it could do. The crystal stone seemed to falter at Calunoth's touch, and that was the only opportunity Valthor needed. Calunoth felt the barrier crumble as Valthor's magic tore through it, shattering it and allowing Calunoth to reach into the water for the stone.

As he touched it, the crystal burned his hand as its energy flailed, trying to save itself. But it was too late. Ignoring the searing heat, Calunoth wrapped his hand around the stone and went to tear it from the water. But he never had the chance.

As his hand closed around the crystal, an even greater surge of energy flowed through him from his core to the crystal, and suddenly heat and light burst forth from the crystal, forcing Calunoth to yank his hand away and watch in awe as cracks began to spiderweb through the stone. The stone gave out one more burst of light and heat, then the light died, and the stone crumbled into pieces in the water, completely destroyed.

The creature, about to execute the now solo Luca, stopped in its tracks and then slowly began to disintegrate as the source that had powered it for generations failed. The swamp guardian fell apart into the individual natural components that formed it, leaving roots and tree trunks floating lazily on the water. On the bank, Valthor collapsed, unconscious. Calunoth and Luca ran to help Bleiz out of the water where he had fallen. He was severely winded but otherwise unhurt. Luca and Calunoth likewise had escaped with only minor injuries, Luca with a cut on his arm and Calunoth with burn marks on the palm of his hand. Valthor had no physical injuries, but he was clearly exhausted.

    Returning to the bank, Calunoth helped Luca carry the comatose Valthor back to their camp, aware as they left that the mist had begun to lift and they could at last hear frogs croaking in the water.

Chapter 7

Fresh Air

Calunoth found the changed atmosphere of the bog startling as he helped carry the unconscious Valthor through the undergrowth. The fog that had beckoned shadows from beyond the grave and spirits from other worlds into its midst had now dissipated from the bog floor, laying bare the fervent greenery of the mossy trees for all the world to see. The sunlight still struggled to filter through the trees, but it no longer appeared as an unwelcome stranger at the door but as a gentle well-wisher granting an optimistic air to the bog. Without the menacing shadows and fog that had so obfuscated their path on the way into the bog, the place was relaxed, tranquil, and would have been almost pleasant had it not been for the lingering stench of peat and sulfur.

Lauren was the only one of their group not caked in yet more water and mud. Valthor had fallen partially into the water when he had collapsed and again when Luca had slipped as he had tried to gain a foothold in the mud. As a result, the companions blended in well with the green and brown of the bog as they returned to their camp.

Luca swore as he regained his footing, shifting the comatose Valthor back onto his right shoulder. "I don't get it," he whined. "Valthor is supposed to be one of the most powerful warriors in Renderive. Why is he the only one out of commission after a fight like that?"

Calunoth was curious about that too. His only understanding of magic came from the brief explanation Valthor had given earlier, but given the aura of strength Valthor emitted, he had not expected him to prove so flimsy in a fight. He couldn't offer an explanation, but Lauren dropped back from the front to provide one.

"Combat with magic is very different from combat with weapons," she said. "I don't even understand it very well, but from where I was standing, it looked like he was trying to suppress the energy of that Ynia stone. In other words, he was basically trying to suppress all of the Natural Ynia coming out of the bog. When you add in that strange fit he had halfway through, it's no surprise that he's exhausted. That kind of effort would have killed most people."

"Do you know what that Ynia stone was, Lauren?" Calunoth asked. "I can't explain what happened, but it shattered as soon as I touched it. I picked up a couple shards, but I can't tell what they are."

Calunoth gave the shards to Lauren, who examined them closely as she walked. Her eyebrows furrowed. Once it had been removed from the water, the stone had adopted a strange amber color and ceased to emit heat. The surface had once been flawless but was now riddled with cracks. The shards were surprisingly flexible but sturdy, solid, and opaque. Lauren examined it for a moment before passing it back to Calunoth, shaking her head.

"I'm sorry, I have no idea what it is. I've studied stones with stored Natural Ynia before, but never ones that have conducted it. I'm afraid I'm not much use to any of you." Lauren said the last sentence with a note of resentment in her voice. Luca, catching on to that note, spoke before Calunoth could.

"Nonsense! If it hadn't been for you, we'd have been chopped to pieces while we slept. You saved our lives!" Luca responded, reverting to his usual cheerful self. Lauren bit her lip and made to respond. She had clearly been holding these feelings in for a while.

"And since then, I've just been baggage slowing everyone down. I can't fight, and I don't even know anything about this strange technology we're dealing with. This is supposed to be my specialty, and I don't even know that!" Lauren's voice quivered. "And I just had to spend the last hour watching all of you get pummeled without being able to do anything to help! I'm one of the best students Akadaemia has to offer, and I'm useless out here!"

Both Luca and Calunoth were taken aback. They had enjoyed Lauren's company but had never expected her to feel so strongly about standing back from the action. Luca tried to respond first with his knightly reasoning. "But a lady shouldn't have to fight with the men. Let us do the fighting and the getting injured so you can stay safe."

Calunoth swore he could physically feel the indignation flowing out of Lauren as she responded. "Oh, so because I'm a woman, I can't fight like a man? Despite being at the top of my class since I was twelve and being far smarter than most men?" Lauren replied caustically.

"Brains have nothing to do with it." The weary voice came from Valthor, who had begun to stir between Luca and Calunoth. Opening his eyes, he looked up at her blearily. "Women simply aren't as strong as men physically. They're not expected to fight because no amount of skill can make up for that physical disadvantage. If you were really smart, you wouldn't want to fight at all." Valthor closed his eyes as he spoke and grimaced with pain. He motioned for the two young men to put him down, so they set him down on a nearby tree stump. "If you really want to fight, you're going to have to come up with a different strategy than glaring at me," he finished, noting Lauren's glare as he sat.

"That beast you just fought was much bigger than all of you and you still prevailed!" Lauren objected.

"And we were damn lucky not to be killed in the process," Bleiz interrupted, coming over to them. "How are you feeling, sire? Are you well enough to continue?" he asked as Valthor combed his fingers through his hair.

"I'll live," Valthor replied, dropping his hands. He looked like he hadn't slept in weeks. "That did not go the way it was supposed to. We should've turned back after my first fit. They can be triggered by extreme stress, but I didn't anticipate this mission would cause that kind of stress. If I'd have taken it on by myself, I doubt I would have made it. What happened to that monster? Did you kill it?" He looked around at the group.

"The beast fell apart once Calunoth destroyed the stone," Bleiz responded. "You collapsed at about the same time. I wasn't entirely sure what happened myself."

"You had just broken the long jump national record, Captain," Luca interjected, trying to diffuse some of the tension that had arisen between Valthor and Lauren. "Twenty feet you must have jumped avoiding that thing's arms!" His comments had their desired effect as Bleiz gave out a hearty laugh and Lauren was forced to smile, though she tried to suppress it.

Valthor himself was so tired he could only nod in response to Bleiz's report. Then he shook his head clear of the fog surrounding his vision and slowly rose to his feet. His legs buckled as he rose from the stump, and he had to be caught by Calunoth, who helped him back up.

"Thank you." He nodded at Calunoth. "Let's get back to camp. We're nearly there, and it's a far better place to rest than here. We can talk later." Calunoth went to put his arm around Valthor to support him back to the camp, but Valthor rebuked his offer. With barely enough strength to walk, sheer pride alone kept him on his feet, but that was enough.

Once they reached the camp, Valthor made his way back to his place by the fire and collapsed. Bleiz watched over him for a few moments before turning and announcing that he was merely sleeping and should recover without further intervention. With the news that they would have to remain in the camp for a while longer, Luca and Bleiz attempted to remove some of the mud from their clothing.

Calunoth tried to do the same using the hunting knife he had borrowed from Luca to shear large curdles of mud from his belt. He had no armor, having had his guard's armor shorn off on the night of the massacre, and consequently had far fewer items to clean. Seeing him less preoccupied than his other companions, Lauren came to speak with him.

"Hey, Calunoth?" she asked. "Can we talk for a moment?" Calunoth was surprised by her hesitant tone and motioned for her to sit down next to him on the fallen tree. Sitting down gracefully, she started speaking in her Galgre accent.

"You're not as old-fashioned as the Knights over there. You might understand. I'm tired of having to sit back and do nothing as you all get hurt. Bleiz could have had his chest caved in with that attack, and Luca … well, he could have gotten badly hurt as well, and there wouldn't have been anything I could do about it." Her gaze trailed over to the young Knight, who appeared to have given up trying to scrub his armor and was now attempting to beat off the mud with the hilt of his sword. "I've never felt useless before. And I hate it. So …" her voice trailed off, but then she found her resolve and spoke with confidence. "Will you teach me how to fight?"

Her request surprised Calunoth greatly. He had the least experience and the least training of all the men in the clearing. He could keep up with Luca for a while, but he would eventually be bested by the trained Knight's skill. Valthor would beat him within seconds. And there was the unfortunate truth to contend with as well, which Calunoth knew he had to speak diplomatically about.

"I'm flattered, but the others are much more capable fighters than I, and besides, Valthor's got a point. You belong in a lab where you're at your best. The Knights belong in the field where they're at their best, and," he hesitated before adding, "there's that physical difference between men and women. It doesn't matter how smart you are, it's going to be extremely difficult for any woman to make up that difference, regardless of her skill."

"The priestesses of the Church of the One are women warriors!" Lauren objected. "If they can do it, why can't I?"

"Yes, but they fight with their clerical magic behind them. And they're trained from birth. It's not something you can just pick up," Calunoth responded.

"Try me," Lauren said, daring him with her eyes.

Seeing this was not a fight he was going to win, Calunoth stared back into her determined eyes and felt compelled to help her. Lauren had saved their lives once, and he had grown to appreciate her as he spent more time traveling with her. Although he had only been traveling with the group for a short while, he felt a connection to them brought about by their flight through danger together. He had lost everyone he had cared about in the massacre, and that pain was still fresh. But in this group, he had found new people he considered friends. People he wanted to help. And he hoped they felt the same way about him.

Thinking back to how he'd had to watch all his loved ones die and been unable to help them even as he was being carried, dying, through the castle, he could empathize with Lauren. Looking into her bright eyes, he couldn't help but relent. Besides, even if she couldn't fight on the front lines, it made sense for her to at least learn to defend herself against assailants.

"All right," he relented. "I can teach you the basics, but you can't leap into a fight right away. The guards trained for three years before they were allowed to fight. I'll teach you what I know on the condition that you'll only jump in if it's absolutely necessary. Regardless of your gender, novices with a sword can do a lot of damage, to yourself and everyone else." Calunoth felt his decision validated as Lauren's face lit up with excitement. Initially very timid, she was beginning to emerge from her shell as she spent more time with the group. Running over to the comatose Valthor, she detached his short sword from his belt and ran back to Calunoth. The Guardian didn't flinch. He was so exhausted he could have been mistaken for dead had it not been for the gentle rising of his chest. Even so, grabbing his sword had been a bold—and risky—move.

"Right, I'm ready! How should I swing this?" She held the short sword with two hands and brandished it at Calunoth.

"Okay! First things first!" Calunoth said, laughing for the first time in weeks. "To start, no real weapons when you first begin training. Second, I'm pretty sure it's a felony to steal a weapon from a Guardian, so put that back and use this instead." Calunoth held out a long, supple tree branch he had snapped from a fallen tree. It had no leaves and was relatively consistent in diameter along the length of the branch. He had procured the two best branches he could find, ones similar in form and function to the wooden training swords that had dotted the chests of the training room back at Glathaous Castle. Lauren flushed and hastily returned the sword to the unconscious Guardian. He had not stirred the entire time and would be none the wiser when he woke up.

Returning to Calunoth, Lauren took up a place opposite him and held the stick firmly in her hand. Calunoth took a moment to observe her form, moving around her, as Oscar, the captain of the Glathaous guards, had done for him on so many occasions.

"Back straight, chin down, spread your feet a little more. You need a solid base to revert back to," Calunoth said, adjusting her stance as he spoke. "Positioning is the most important thing to remember when fighting. You should have a default position that you always return to after making any attack. It allows you to also act defensively. Your mind should always be thinking about protecting yourself first. My teacher always used to say, 'You've got lots of enemies but only one you, so prioritize.'"

Calunoth continued to instruct Lauren to the best of his knowledge for the remainder of the afternoon. She was a quick study and an attentive student. She adapted quickly to the theory but struggled with the practice of swordplay. After several hours of instruction, they were both weary, and Valthor had begun to stir, so they concluded their practice with the promise that they would continue in the nights as they traveled. Returning to the campfire to rejoin the marginally cleaner Luca and Bleiz, they sat and prepared a meal from their supplies.

Valthor finally awoke to the smell of the overcooked meat that Bleiz was cooking. Bleiz cursed the unnatural heat of the fire and quickly removed the pan from the flames. Valthor snapped to attention instantly, all traces of drowsiness eradicated from his piercing eyes. He was sharp and bright once more, and he called Bleiz over from the fallen tree on which he sat.

"Bleiz, what did you all do while I was asleep? And what time is it?" Valthor asked, glancing up, unable to see though the thick overgrowth.

"Very little, sire," the captain replied. "We simply cleaned our equipment and rested our limbs while you slept. It's hard to tell the time right now, but I suspect it's close to sundown."

Valthor accepted his report and began to pace around the clearing, stretching as he did so. From the other side of the clearing, he beckoned to Calunoth, who darted over.

Drawing his sword as Calunoth approached, Valthor readied it. "Let's spar for a spell while Bleiz overcooks the rest of the food." Then he added an explanation. "You did well against that swamp beast, but I'm keen to understand the abilities of my traveling companions, and I need to know how well you can defend yourself against human threats."

Although he was tired from the day's exertions, Calunoth could not refuse the Guardian his request. Drawing his own sword, he held it in his hand and waited for Valthor to make the first move.

Valthor obliged him, leaping forward in a blur of motion to stab rapidly into his left shoulder. Calunoth didn't even have time to think. He reacted instinctively, diverting the penetrating thrust past him and blocking the immediate follow-up blow. The force of Valthor's sword sent shockwaves down his arm, vibrating the small muscles of his right hand as they absorbed the force of the impact. Valthor continued his offensive, striking hard, fast, and seemingly at random. But even as Calunoth was defending at the edge of his wits, he was aware Valthor was going easy on him.

Recognizing that Valthor was trying to gauge his ability, Calunoth knew he had to attack eventually, so after a feinted backpedal, he ducked under Valthor's sweeping sword and moved to jab the Guardian's knee. Valthor moved so quickly he was almost imperceptible. Sparks showered the ground as the Guardian ran the length of his sword down Calunoth's, deflecting his blow easily.

The sparring continued for several more minutes until Calunoth's body finally gave in to fatigue, and Valthor's strike sent his blade spinning from his hands, embedding itself in the boggy ground and knocking Calunoth on his backside.

Valthor eyed him curiously for a moment, then moved to help him up.

"You said you were a guard at Glathaous? You fight well for a guard. Better than Luca, to be frank. He's too heavy with his attacks. It gives him less time to recover."

"I was taught by a former Knight of the Wings," Calunoth replied, catching his breath.

"Then he did his duty well," Valthor remarked, "Come, eat and rest. We will have to travel quite the distance tomorrow. We should reach Caern Vaugh as fast as possible. We've wasted too much time recovering here. The world continues outside of this bog. At least this place is a bit less frightening now with that stone gone."

Remembering the stone, Calunoth reached into his pocket and removed the shards of the stone from the lagoon. He handed them to Valthor, who observed them carefully.

"Do you know what it was?" Calunoth asked. "I asked Lauren earlier, but she had no idea."

Valthor was silent for a moment as he contemplated the shards. Then he said, "I think so, but I'm not sure. I'll spend the night studying them. I've already slept more today than I usually do in a week, so I'll have energy to spare. We can speak of it, and other matters, tomorrow. Our conversation this morning was rather unfortunately curtailed, and I owe you a proper explanation."

The group ate their dinner, trading cheerful stories around the green campfire. With the crystal gone, life had begun to return to the bog, and it no longer seemed frightening or cursed. The warmth of the fire, the protection of the company, and the knowledge that they were no longer being actively pursued led to an evening of fine company and rest for the group such as they had not yet enjoyed together. Even at Crideir, they had needed to keep looking over their shoulders, but in this place, for the moment, they were safe, comfortable, and among friends. And as Calunoth retired to his rest, he couldn't help but appreciate that simple comfort after weeks of turmoil. But for Calunoth as always, even the tranquility of his surroundings could not prevent him from falling back into the dark world of his mind. The sound of the gate remained foremost in his mind even as he repeatedly watched Alistair Glathaous fall off of the wall.

***

The group left early the next morning, with Valthor keen to be off. He had waited for them all night, staying awake as he conducted small experiments on the crystal shards Calunoth had given him. The success of his meddling was unknown to the group as he had removed the shards from the fire and stored them in his pocket. Valthor extinguished the green campfire with a word and set off through the bogs, leading the way for the group.

It took an additional three days of travel before the group finally emerged from the Caerwyn Bogs. The muddy nature of the ground made it difficult to move quickly, and they covered in three days a distance that would have normally taken a single day. Nevertheless, the group was thrilled to emerge from the shadowy boughs of the trees into the warm spring sunlight and smell the fresh air blowing down from the hills. The wind carried the scent of fresh dew from the rain-swept hills, lending the air a chill dampness that was piercing but welcome after the dead air of the bog. Valthor was particularly excited to be rid of the bogs. Having spent the last month within, he had emerged onto the rocky steps of the Llewyn Hills and promptly knelt down to kiss the ground.

He had been an excellent traveling companion, Calunoth noted with amusement as the Guardian of Renderive was brought to his knees at the sight of firm ground. Once fully recovered from his ordeal, he had led them surely and safely through the bog, all the while keeping them entertained with light-hearted stories and jests. Upon being reminded that the specter of civil war loomed over them, he merely shrugged it off. Although obviously reliable, it soon became clear that Valthor took very little seriously. He was always quick to laugh, and he grew on everyone, even Lauren, who grudgingly admitted that his company was better than none.

When he rarely did broach serious topics, he did so with a calm and composed demeanor. Only twice in three days had he done so. The first had been when Bleiz asked after the quality of his health, which led to him explaining his actions in the swamp.

"Well, I thought going in that it was a lodestone," he had said. "A piece of meteorite ore that pulls energy from its surroundings as it falls and eventually sits concentrating all the energy around it: the Natural Ynia from the sky, the stars, and the like combining to become a concentrated mass in the bog creating a breeding ground for magical interactions."

Noticing the men were completely lost by the Guardian's explanation, Lauren translated. "Basically, it's a magnet for Natural Ynia. Too much energy was concentrated in the bog, and it provided a magical source for the spirits and other strange creatures of the bog to operate in. But it wasn't a lodestone. A piece that small shouldn't have been able to attract that much energy."

"Exactly. I couldn't see the size, but all of the other evidence led me to believe it was just a lodestone. In which case, I would have just had to block the flow of Ynia flowing toward it, disrupting the barrier and allowing Calunoth to remove it from the earth. The energy would no longer be attracted to it and would instead dissipate upward, following the path of least resistance," Valthor reasoned, gesturing as he explained. "But when I engaged with the Ynia around the crystal, it was clear immediately the stone was something else entirely. This crystal wasn't drawing energy toward it. It was—how do I say this?—magnifying the Natural Ynia in the earth. Cutting that off from its source meant suppressing all the Natural Ynia in the bog for long enough for someone to remove the stone from its source of energy. Calunoth had great timing because I wasn't able to disrupt the flow for more than a few seconds."

"How did you actually suppress it, Valthor?" Luca asked, the big man coming up behind the Guardian. "I learned a bit about it from my tutor, and I know you have to get your own energy from somewhere as well." It was clear over the last several days that Luca was trying to impress the Guardian however he could, for he rarely flaunted his privileged upbringing otherwise.

"That was the worst part," Valthor replied, a slightly remorseful tone to his voice. "I started with the wrong formulae, which didn't help, but I had to draw the Natural Ynia from the same source as the crystal I was trying to suppress. It was like moving water from the bottom of a waterfall back to the top to stop the current. It worked, but I would advise against trying it yourselves. The amount of energy that went through me could have lit up a small city, I swear, hence my heart issue flaring up again. As for the crystal itself, I can't say for certain what it is. But whatever it is, it's ancient. At least two thousand years old, based on its energy signature. I can't tell you much more than that. None of my experiments showed me anything useful."

"Valthor, when I got close to the crystal, it felt like the orb in my chest was on fire. It got hotter the closer I got to the crystal, then the crystal exploded when I grabbed it," Calunoth said. "Is there a connection between the two?"

Valthor hesitated before responding, then finally said, "I can tell you what I know about that orb, that core in your chest, but it's personal to you, and a national secret. We can speak privately if you wish for this business to remain between us only."

"My companions have fought to protect it and me," Calunoth responded plainly. "They have as much right to this knowledge as I do."

"Good," Valthor replied. "I was going to tell them anyway since they're involved now, but the faith you show in your companions speaks to your intentions. Very well, I'll tell you what I know." He paused to enjoy the expression on Calunoth's face before growing serious and raising his voice so the others could hear him. Lauren had trailed back from the pack slightly as they walked and appeared to have trouble keeping up with the Guardian's relentless pace.

"I believe that the orb in your chest is a Pralia Core. Designed from ancient Selevirnian technology, the Pralia Core is designed to seamlessly conduct Natural Ynia, amplifying it in the process." Valthor had only begun speaking when Lauren hurried to the front of the pack to interrupt him, her intellectual curiosity overriding her physical exhaustion.

"But I thought that conducting Natural Ynia can only be done by humans. If you could do it through an object, you could generate literally an unlimited amount of energy for spellcasting. That would revolutionize the world as we know it!" she exclaimed.

"Exactly," Valthor said. "And the Selevirnians managed to do it somehow. The specifics we don't know, but what we do know is that since the Marveuz Excavation eight years ago, every nation on the continent has been racing to replicate it. Transferring energy through an object may not seem hard, but it's fraught with difficulties and consequences. Can you name some, Ms. Abraham?" Valthor was enjoying his role playing the teacher.

"Well, any object that conducts Natural Ynia has no ability to control it. It will just keep storing the energy until it's at capacity, and when it becomes overloaded, it will explode, releasing the energy outward," Lauren recited, her intelligence evident. "Also, the Ynia capacity of most objects is extremely low. Some of the newest Ynium technology can store a lot, but those have to be specially designed to do it."

"Huh. Maybe those morons up at Akadaemia are teaching you some useful items after all," Valthor replied. "In other words, it can't be done, but with these Pralia Cores, any amount of energy can be channeled through them, bypassing the need for the body to act as the conduit. This would enable massive stores of energy to pass through them as they don't possess the Life Ynia that limits humans. If put to military purposes, anyone using these cores could conquer the continent with ease. We need them for our own protection, as do the other nations."

"So, I have a priceless piece of technology that could conquer the continent embedded in my chest?" Calunoth asked incredulously.

"Maybe,"' Valthor replied without breaking his stride. "The Glathaous laboratory was one of three major labs developing Pralia Cores and the only one that has produced any kind of workable result. Akadaemia and the Royal Galgrenon weren't getting anywhere. I don't know if this design is a half-finished product or if it does something else entirely different from what it was designed to do. That was the issue with Isaac. He'd set out to discover something and get distracted with something else that he found more interesting along the way. I know that he poked and prodded me all of the time, but I don't know if what he finally created is a functioning Pralia Core or not. It will be up for the researchers at Deirive to decide that. I'm afraid I know no more about the cores. As to why the stone exploded, it's possible it was exposed to too much energy from Cal's core, but I'd only be speculating."

Valthor knew no more of the subject so instead turned to speaking of the wonders of their destination, the ancient city of Caern Vaughn. As a native of the Hills, Valthor knew a great deal of the history of the Llewyn Hills and entertained the group until they reached the capital of the Hills, relieved to at last return to civilization.

Chapter 8

Caern Vaughn

Caern Vaugh was the oldest city on the continent of Creidyl. Originally founded by the native Hillmen before the settling and founding of the Legrangian Empire, the town was clustered around Cynid Yfir, the great hill, which towered above the surrounding countryside and served as the home of Vaughn Keep. With the neighboring town spread out beneath it, the keep's tower stood vigil over the hills and the plains, granting a clear vision of the surroundings for miles around. The old town had been erected inside the ancient stonewalls surrounding the base of the hill, but newer settlements continued to spring up just outside.

Under the guidance of the Berwyn family for generations, Caern Vaugh served as the cultural and political capital of the ethnic Hillmen. As the first known inhabitants of the continent, the Hillmen had welcomed the new Legrangian settlers with open arms, then had chosen to fight alongside the separatist Renderiveans in the First Schism War. The first King Relstert had rewarded them with the Llewyn Hills and the friendship of Renderive until time immemorial. As time passed, the Hillmen eventually acceded formally to Renderivean rule. As a result, though they maintained much of their own culture, they enjoyed the benefits of living under the security and prosperity of a united nation.

The group of unlikely friends, unofficially led by Valthor, now hurried through the town and soon found themselves at the sealed oaken doors of Vaughn Keep. Two guards stood outside holding spears, waiting to interrogate anyone wishing to pass through the gates. Upon seeing Valthor, they immediately called for the gate to be opened and bowed deeply as he passed.

"You're something of a celebrity around these parts, sire," Bleiz remarked, noting the reverence they paid to the mud-splattered Guardian.

"I've told them to stop doing that. It draws too much attention," Valthor replied offhandedly. He turned in a circle without breaking his stride. "Now, where's Parker? Ah, here he comes."

The interior courtyard was large and spacious with well-maintained gardens. Ivy clung to the interior of the walls and crept its way up to the battlements. The central courtyard gave way to the Great Hall and was connected by a grand set of staircases that an elderly man draped in green-and-gold robes now shuffled down. Valthor greeted him warmly and went to meet him. Following suit, the group greeted the man, who was elated to see them.

"So very long you've been gone, Master Valthor!" the man named Parker exclaimed in a squeaky voice. "Lord Berwyn had given you up for dead. We all had!"

"I swear, if he's arranged my funeral again, I'll never forgive him," Valthor replied jokingly. Turning to the group, he introduced the man. "This is Parker, caretaker of Vaughn Keep, and for all intents and purposes, part of the stonework here. He's been serving Lord Berwyn since before any of us were born." Valthor looked past Parker. "Where is the old bastard? We have a lot we need to discuss."

"Forgive me, Master Valthor," Parker squeaked again. "Lord Berwyn has gone off on a hunting trip and will not return until tomorrow. We can, of course, have the guest rooms set up for you and your companions until he returns." He then beckoned to a passing servant to lead the bedraggled companions into the keep.

Once inside, Calunoth couldn't help but be impressed by the interior. The keep was well carpeted throughout, with a broad array of tapestries hanging from the walls, leaving little of the cold stone beneath exposed. The carpet was warm and well fitting, with intricate patterns inlaid within. The tapestries depicted Llewyn history from the founding of Caern Vaughn to the heroics of the current Lord Berwyn during the Fourth Schism War. The ceiling was high and modeled with masterfully crafted archways that granted the ceiling a majestic appearance.

The central hall was arrayed with a series of long oaken tables that also adhered to the beauty of the hall, the oak well lacquered with oils to produce a smooth sheen depicting the grain of the wood. Most impressive of all though were the meticulously crafted stained-glass windows that dotted the upper echelons of the entrance hall. Patterns of roses and Knights melded with bards and poets practicing their craft. The setting sun sent beams of light through the glass that pervaded the color of the light, bathing the interior in a rosy glow.

At Calunoth's agape jaw, Valthor let out a chuckle. "Impressive, isn't it? My people have always been expert artisans. Our skills in crafting and architecture are matched only by our ability to weave words and songs," he boasted. "I know we're all hungry and filthy, but permit me to arrange a short detour from the dining hall." Turning to the servant, Brynn, he spoke in the strange Llewyn language to her.

The girl nodded and replied in the same language. Luca coughed awkwardly and spoke to Valthor. "Valthor, can you speak the common tongue when we're together? I don't like not knowing what's being said." Calunoth privately agreed, but he would never have given voice to his concern for risk of offending the Guardian. Fortunately, Luca had no such reservations, perhaps in part due to his noble upbringing. The language Valthor had spoken was alien to Calunoth, sounding both lyrical and guttural at the same time.

"You stand on Llewyn land, you should expect to hear the Llewyn tongue, Luca." Valthor replied caustically, "But for your sake, I shall maintain Common while you're guests in these halls."

Luca flushed a bright red and mumbled a quiet gratitude, retaining his silence from that point onward as Brynn led them through the central grand doors at the furthest end of the hall. The Guardian walked beside her, enjoying a fluent conversation with the serving girl in their native tongue. Brynn was initially flustered and nervous speaking to the Guardian, but his easygoing manner soon alleviated her nervous disposition.

The two led the group into a large rectangular room that rose up to a dais at the far end. Atop the dais stood a mighty throne of stone. The throne itself was as much a work of art as the hall in which it stood, with obsidian layers carved in the shape of ivy wrapped around the stonework, giving a smooth, polished appearance to the otherwise ordinary granite. But it was the sight behind the throne that truly captured the eyes and hearts of the group.

Virtually the entire back wall behind the throne was composed of the same stained glass that comprised the smaller windows of the entrance hall. But the scale of craftsmanship of the designs was of an entirely different stratum. This glass depicted the aftermath of a battle, a single man kneeling and raising a sapphire sword to the heavens and a bearded figure enveloped in clouds reaching down to lay his hand upon the sapphire sword. The kaleidoscopic image was brought into full glory by the sun setting behind the glass, casting the entire room in a surreal, almost religious light.

"By Sentential, I've never seen a sight like it," Bleiz whispered, the image stealing the words of the others. "I've heard about the *Gwydr*

Sylfaenydd before, but it's clear what I heard did no justice to the truth."

Valthor, satisfied by their reaction, turned to the group and explained the significance of the sight. "Gwydr Sylfaenydd, or I guess the common translation would be, The Foundation Glass, or Founder Glass, depicts the victory of the first Lord Teyrnon over the warring clans of this land, the unification of our people, and the founding of Caern Vaughn. It was constructed millennia ago now, but it remains our people's most prized accomplishment. Anyone seeking to meet with the Lord of the Hills must do so in awe of what we can accomplish."

Calunoth found his words next after Bleiz and felt compelled to question Valthor about the masterpiece. "Who is that figure in the clouds, Valthor? And what is that sword in the image?"

"The figure in the clouds is our original god, Llwerenye. However, in our religious literature, he fell out of favor with our people after the destruction of much of our lands during the Schism Wars. Instead, people turned to your god, Sentential, and adopted the Holy Church of Renderive. The sword in question is the Holy Weapon, Ynelia. One of the five known Holy Weapons, it remains the only one unaccounted for."

"I've heard of the Five Holy Weapons!" Luca exclaimed excitedly, breaking his silence. "They're legendary weapons forged exclusively by the greatest swordsmiths of the age. Legend says the forging of the weapon required the smiths to sacrifice their lives to forge their very essence into the blade by pushing the limits of magic and their own mastery. These weapons have only ever been wielded by heroes in the stories."

"The only Holy Weapon in Renderivean hands is the Relsarter, wielded by Asta himself in the First Schism War," Valthor acknowledged. "And that's currently locked up in the Commandant's Bastion. The Legrangians have two others, the Sihleons have one, but the Ynelia remains lost. But I think that's enough history for today. Let us eat and rest. I daresay, we may not have the opportunity to enjoy such luxuries for a while after this. And we should not impose on Miss Brynn's hospitality indefinitely."

The serving girl blushed and said she was happy to help however she could. Calunoth couldn't help but notice how well Valthor treated the servants. As a Guardian, his rank was surpassed only by the king, and he could have ordered the girl to act as his footstool had he the inclination. Yet Valthor treated the servants the same way he treated everyone else.

I suppose, reasoned Calunoth internally, *if everyone is below him, he doesn't have to account for the differences in rank and stature like the rest of us do. He has no need to distinguish between servants and dukes. They're all the same to him.*

Brynn then led the group back to the dining hall where the cooks brought out hot lamb and fine spirit. After weeks on rations with only the occasional hot meal, the food offered was a feast, and they enjoyed it immensely. Forbidding depressing topics as business for tomorrow, Valthor and Bleiz led a merry evening of drinking and storytelling, with the experienced men keen to regale their younger companions of tales from their own youth. Calunoth, Luca, and Lauren listened cheerfully, the warmth of the food and the castle allowing them to forget their troubles for a short while at least.

Several hours later, the group was escorted to their rooms and given the opportunity to bathe before retiring for the evening. Everyone had been given their own room, and Calunoth was grateful to finally have an opportunity to relax in comfort he had not enjoyed since the massacre. In this place, they were well taken care of, comfortable, and, most importantly, safe. As a result, Calunoth's fatigue finally caught up with him as weeks of sleepless nights and heavy exertion took their toll on his body. Such was his exhaustion that when he concluded scrubbing all the mud and dirt from his body, he fell to his bed and slept immediately. However, even in his exhausted state, the demons that tormented his rest found energy aplenty to prickle his mind with sinister laughter and flickering flames, even as the gate ground open once more in his mind.

***

Calunoth woke late the next morning. The sun of the previous day had given way to a gentle rain shower that pattered lightly against the dark stone of the castle. The dull, dreary morning rain gave a rather different perspective to the world around him. Climbing out of his bed reinvigorated, Calunoth went out onto the balcony. The guest rooms had been built into the westernmost tower and provided a beautiful visage of the hills from their high vantage point. The stonework that made up the balcony floor was riveted with ridges, allowing water to flow through them and down the sides of the balcony. The Llewyn Hills themselves were famous for their rainy season. The rich and fertile ground was frequently the subject of the darks clouds that rolled over the mountains from the Selevirn Ocean.

After taking the time to let the rain wash away the last bit of drowsiness from his limbs, Calunoth went back into the room to dress. He had removed his dirty clothing and slept without it, his only accessory the Pralia Core implanted in his chest. The core glowed with a warm white light. Calunoth had not had much time to examine it, nor to consider the conditions that had brought him to this point. They had been so consumed with fleeing their pursuers that he had had little time to consider the madness of the situation. Though he had resolved to banish memories of the Glathaous Massacre from his mind however he could, his actions and failures on that day were not easily struck off. The grating of the gates was a sound that was beginning to blur the line between his dreams and his waking hours. Although it was the source of the motivation that drove him to even bother carrying on with life, the pain of it was fresh—and crippling. If he did not cast off the shadows in his mind, they would overcome his sensibilities, and the victims of the Glathaous Massacre would be left wanting for true justice.

Casting the dark thoughts to the side, Calunoth searched for his clothing, only to find it had been replaced with a set of entirely new garments. The garments were simple but clean and appeared freshly woven. Donning the plain white shirt and earth-brown trousers, he found that his boots and weapons had been restored to their natural appearance. The days trekking through the bog must have made the chore significant for the servants, and Calunoth made a mental note to extend his gratitude to them later. Leaving his room, he went in search of his companions.

Quickly finding Luca admiring the view from the top of the tower, Calunoth joined the blond giant as he gazed out at the sprawling city below. They had only been traveling together for a short time, but already Calunoth held an appreciation for the young Draca noble. He had not had any friends his own age at the castle, and Luca, with his easygoing nature and quick smile, proved to be a fast friend.

"Morning, Cal," Luca said cheerfully. His bright blue eyes reflected the refreshing effect a safe night's rest had had on them both. "Quite a view, isn't it?" He gestured at the ancient city and the surrounding hillscape. While the stone tower of the keep loomed over the town, its majesty was diminished by the height of the surrounding hills. A low mist shrouded the base of the hills even as the rain fell gently from the heavens. In the distance, Calunoth thought he could see a herd of sheep being corralled down one of the slopes of the distant hills, but the distance proved the better of his eyesight, and he could only detect a ripple of white against the otherwise staunch hillside.

"It's certainly better than miles of the Terrestia Forest," Calunoth agreed going to stand next to him. "I just wish we were here under better circumstances."

"Really?" Luca replied, glancing over at him. "It's adventures like these that make me glad I enlisted with the Knights. I spent my entire childhood listening to my brothers' exploits in the Sieth Incursion. The stories they would tell! I can go back to them and tell them my own stories now. Maybe I could even find a bard to make a song out of it! Wouldn't that be something, Cal?"

Calunoth regarded the young Knight skeptically. "This isn't like any adventure I've ever wanted. I was perfectly happy back at the castle. Why do you care so much about what your brothers think anyway?"

Luca regarded the former guard in surprise before answering. "Well, my father is Conan Draca, one of the heroes who fought alongside the king and Lord Berwyn in the Fourth Schism War. When the Sieth Incursion came twelve years ago, my eldest brother, Felix, led the charge over the river. He was a year younger than I am now when his commander was slain, yet he rallied the men and fought back to win against the Legrangians in what seemed a hopeless battle. Being a hero runs in my family. I guess I want to live up to that, and joining the Knights seemed like the best way to do it. I know if I work hard and comport myself with honor, I can become a greater hero than any of them!" Luca's bright eyes shone with passion and optimism.

Calunoth tried to avoid raising his eyebrows. Luca was a capable warrior and a promising Knight, but Calunoth had the impression that the young Knight had spent too much time reading epic tales. There were few heroes in the real world, and it didn't seem like something that could simply be pursued. Rather than risk offending Luca, Calunoth just smiled and agreed with the young Knight before suggesting they should wake the others before the morning grew too late.

The two were pleased to find Lauren awake, and she joined them knocking on Bleiz's door. The older captain emerged fully alert. He had been awake for hours, he reported, but had taken the time to enjoy the morning view. As a group, they journeyed down the stairs and were intercepted on the way by the servant, Carys, who informed them Berwyn and Valthor were awaiting them in the throne room. Thanking her, the group made their way to the base of the tower.

They had all taken the opportunity to bathe and refresh themselves. Their clothing had been discarded and replaced, and the Knights had had their armor cleaned and treated. Bleiz lamented the treatment was not to his standards, but he did so quietly, aware of the amount of dirt that had been caked on the hardened leather armor.

As they entered the throne room, the group was greeted by Valthor and a large, jovial man Calunoth assumed was Lord Berwyn. The large man had a flowing white beard and was himself muddied, though he wore the finest clothing, with a lambswool gambeson finely interlaid with dyes depicting the rams head that served as the crest of his house keeping him warm in the chill of the rainy season. Valthor had discarded his previous leather armor entirely and now stood in the hall arrayed in a new, beautifully tooled set of hardened leather armor emblazoned with the Berwyn crest. He had clearly determined his previous apparel was beyond saving and instead elected to don a new outfit entirely.

"Greetings, friends!" Berwyn exclaimed in a booming voice, his double chin bobbing up and down as he spoke. "I hear you helped Valthor sort out that mess in the bogs? You have my thanks. I've been hearing complaints about them for years but never had the ability to deal with it until Valthor came along. That's one less problem to deal with."

"And you have our thanks for the generosity of your hall, Lord Berwyn," Bleiz responded formally with the sentiment felt by all. Having washed his hair and beard clean of the mud that had stained it, Bleiz stood regally in his freshly scrubbed armor.

"Think nothing of it!" Berwyn boomed. "If I can't tend to my guests, I do not deserve these halls at all. Now, to business. Valthor has told me of your adventures thus far. Which one of you goes by the name Calunoth?"

Calunoth stepped forward and bowed to the large man. "I am, sir."

Berwyn waved his hand and said, "You can dismiss the formalities lad. You're not in Deirive. Call me Berwyn, for 'tis my name. Valthor told me of the Glathaous Massacre. I am pained to hear of it. It smacks of a plot most foul. Were it up to me, I would rouse my men and go hunting for the fiends responsible with you myself, but I'm afraid more pressing matters are at hand. I am informed that you are in possession of the technology these attackers are trying to procure?" Calunoth nodded his assent. "Then they have made themselves an enemy without any reward. I cannot speak much of this technology. Isaac was always an eccentric fellow. But if the king has sent for it, then the king should have it. There are dark days ahead for Renderive, I fear."

Valthor continued explaining. "We've spent the morning in council, and I'm afraid I haven't got much good news for you. Many reliable sources coming out of Byrantia say Gerard Byrant is moving to depose the king and is amassing an army to do so. He is moving secretly to avoid attracting the attention of the Knights until he's ready, but we estimate he'll make his move before the month is out."

"Why does Duke Byrant wish to depose the king?" Bleiz asked. "He is among the most powerful men in Renderive, but the king surely commands more support?" He stroked his beard in thought.

"Among the hills and the eastern coast, that's certainly true," Berwyn replied. "But Byrant rules much of the land to the south around Byrantia, and the people there do not think nearly so highly of the king."

"Why is that?" Luca asked. "King Greshaun led us to victory in the last Schism War and has protected our borders from invaders time and again. The granaries are full, the treasuries are flowing. In fact, life in Renderive has never been better!"

"There are always people born in comfort who demand more," Berwyn answered. "Byrant has become an icon of sorts to them and has recently made a menace of himself at court by proclaiming the need to give more wealth to the people. Of course, he has no interest in giving up his own wealth, so instead he's been attacking the other nobles. He's a believer, but also a hypocrite, and there are many who are the former who lack the capacity of being the latter, merchants, large farmers, and the like. So, he's begun to develop a movement, the type of movement many are willing to fight for."

"Many of his ideas would help so many people though!" Lauren interrupted, stepping forward. "There's a limit to what the wealthy can spend on luxury, so what's so bad about giving some of it to someone to buy food for their family?"

"The politics is not the problem at the moment," Valthor said, ignoring Lauren's criticisms, "The problem is that it has begun to spread, and there is now enough dissent among the southern plains to create a serious problem for the king. Byrant can easily claim the area south past Commerel and the Galgre region. His ideas are far more popular in those regions, and there are enough individuals disquieted with the king that they would likely take his side. Revleir, however, is relatively affluent due to their trade with Chelia, and neither one of those places are likely to side with him."

"The bigger problem," Berwyn added, "is that a civil war, while disastrous to the country, will make us vulnerable to an attack from the Legrangians or the Sihleons."

"A common tactic," Bleiz observed. "Wait for two enemies to destroy each other then march in at full strength and defeat them both. But surely the king has the support to defeat Byrant?"

"Ordinarily, yes," Valthor continued, "But there's another player at work here: the player that you have had the unfortunate advantage of meeting. These black-clad mercenaries."

"Are they working for Byrant then? Who are they?" Luca asked, glancing back and forth between Berwyn and Valthor.

"This is where Berwyn's spies have been useful," Valthor answered. "We don't have a lot of information regarding this group yet, but we do know they're working for the Sihleon minister, Lenocius, whom we know thanks to Cal, is the orchestrator of the Glathaous Massacre. Lenocius himself is working with Byrant, and we suspect Byrant wants to use the Pralia Cores to turn the war in his favor. Whether he can harness that technology quickly enough is another matter. And what Lenocius gets out of this is still unclear."

"However, our spies have informed us the Sihleons and the Legrangians are both working on their own Pralia Cores. So, it's possible Lenocius is just using Byrant to get the technology for Sihleo," Berwyn contended.

"So, if we go to Byrant, we find Lenocius?" Calunoth interrupted, his eyes blazing at the name.

"In theory, yes," Valthor replied, crossing his arms. "But it seems like there's going to be a civil war standing between you and Lenocius.

If Lenocius is, as we believe he is, working with or for Byrant, we can't just walk up to the gates of Byrantia and ask for him."

"What about the Sihleons themselves? Is this Lenocius acting alone, or are these mercenaries from Sihleo as well perhaps?" Bleiz asked. He was far more knowledgeable of the geopolitics of the region than the younger members of the group.

"We don't believe Lenocius is acting alone, but we don't think the Sihleons are otherwise involved. They've never been interested in attacking Renderive, and as it stands, they have their own internal struggles to deal with at the moment. There is a growing divide between the Church of the One and the Politik. Neither wants a war with the outside world right now," Berwyn said.

"And this is where those mercenaries who took over Glathaous came in," Valthor continued. "I received regular reports at Caern Vaughn from the king that accumulated while I was in the bog. Now that I've had a chance to review them, I've learned that Cress, another Guardian, has discovered traces of these mercenaries all over the country. She managed to capture one and interrogate him. Apparently, these mercenaries are part of a larger group called 'PRIMAL.' There have been reports of them cropping up in Sihleo and Legrangia as well." Valthor paused and glanced warily at Calunoth. "Lenocius came up in the interrogation. It seems he's the leader of this group in Renderive. Although how this ties into his duties as a Sihleon minister is currently unknown. Unfortunately, they seem to be professionals, and Cress wasn't able to get much more reliable information out of him."

"If we've had his name and his association with this PRIMAL group confirmed by a Guardian, couldn't the king formally request some answers from the Sihleon government?" Bleiz asked, looking pointedly at Berwyn.

"The king has sent messengers to Sihleo, but they've thus far been rebuked," Berwyn replied, stroking his beard. "We're not on good or bad terms with them, but if they don't want to talk, or if Lenocius is acting on his own, there's not much more we can do. Of course, it's only been two weeks, so there is perhaps time for answers to return."

"So, what do we do now?" Luca asked as most of the conversation had gone over his head.

"We get Calunoth to Deirive and let the king decide what to do from there," Valthor replied. "He could want Cal either on the front lines or locked away in a tower in Akadaemia. Regardless of what he decides, Deirive should be our destination."

Turning to Valthor and then back at the group, Berwyn added, "Indeed, but the road to Deirive is long and could be dangerous. You have only just arrived out of danger yourself," Berwyn interjected. "Valthor has agreed to escort you, but you should rest here for a couple more days. You are as safe as you can be within these walls, and besides, I have asked Valthor to deal with a matter that will likely take a couple days. I will send a message ahead to Deirive to inform the king of your arrival here and imminent journey to Deirive. We can deliver Valthor's new information about Glathaous to the king as well."

Valthor nodded. "Berwyn has asked me to investigate a matter regarding a strange magical field in a small village to the east of here. It's disrupting Ynia casting and making life difficult for the shepherds and farmers. I'll leave tomorrow morning. It shouldn't take long to deal with, but in the meantime, you can stay here." He went to stand before Bleiz and Lauren and added, "Captain Bleiz of the Knights of the Wild and Lauren Abraham of Akadaemia, under my authority as a Guardian of Renderive, I hereby dismiss you of your mission to escort the Pralia Core back to Akadaemia. You may go wherever you choose now. I will assume responsibility for Calunoth's safety."

Luca made to speak, but Bleiz cut him off expertly. "Sire, with all due respect, if we are to go wherever we choose, we would like to continue escorting Calunoth. This matter seems rife with strange intentions, and we would like to do our part to ensure the security of Renderive."

Valthor looked at him, amused, before turning to Luca and Lauren for their thoughts. Luca responded as expected. "I'm not about to ditch Cal. We're committed now." Lauren agreed with their assessment.

Valthor did not seem remotely surprised. "Very well. I suppose ten eyes are better than four." He glanced back at Berwyn as he continued, "But no more. We need to move quickly and quietly. If I wanted an army, I'd get one." He put his arms behind his back, turned, and went back to Berwyn's side. "I'll be leaving early tomorrow. You can all rest here until I return."

With that, Valthor dismissed the group, and they exited the throne room, leaving the Guardian and the lord to continue their discussion of matters far above their group's varied stations.

Chapter 9

An Unseen Force

The companions were practicing in the training yard when Valthor came for them the following morning. Lauren had been learning quickly from Calunoth, and, seeing the sense in Lauren being able to defend herself, Luca and Bleiz had accommodated her in their drills.

The sparring sessions also gave Calunoth an opportunity to acclimatize to his new armor. Having spent the last few weeks armored only by the wool of his shirt, he and Luca had visited the castle's armory and had received, at Berwyn's command, special attention from the quartermasters employed therein. Calunoth had been fully outfitted in a tanned leather armor similar to Valthor's gear, though notably less expensive. He was also finally able to return Luca's dagger as not only had his sword been sharpened on a grindstone by the castle's armorers, he had obtained a replacement dagger. The armorers had raised a few eyebrows when they had returned to the armory with Lauren in tow shortly after they'd concluded their business. Her presence drew a few quizzical looks from the men stationed in the armory, but she was given similar treatment.

With most armor being too heavy and ill suited to her body shape, Lauren had instead adopted light scouting armor, similarly made of leather but lighter and thinner than Calunoth's. She wouldn't have as much protection, but her movement would be unimpaired, and the protection offered was better than nothing. She had also been outfitted with a short sword. Though not muscular by nature, having spent most of her life in the library rather than the training yard, the hard traveling and training was slowly increasing the strength of her limbs, and she bore the exertion without complaint. While still far weaker than her male compatriots, she was at least well equipped.

Bleiz had been particularly impressed by their rejuvenated appearances. When they arrived in the yard after being outfitted, he was waiting for them and whistled at the new armor Calunoth and Lauren had received.

"Lord Berwyn is certainly generous," he said. "These materials must have cost a fortune."

"Just hope he hasn't got a bill waiting for us when we leave!" Luca said, laughing. "Come on, old man, let's see what you've got!"

They had been practicing for over an hour when they were disrupted by Valthor's appearance in the courtyard. Ceasing their sparring, the group turned their attention to the Guardian, who did not appear to be in the mood to mince words. He looked pale and drawn. *He must have conducted a lot of Ynia using the circle*, Lauren thought. She knew he had been using one of the Ynia-powered transport circles to send a message to the king. A relatively new invention from the industrial city of Galgrenon, the new technology allowed messages to be transmitted between circles in moments rather than taking days to deliver by foot. However, these devices could only move small items currently, primarily a special type of light parchment, and even those took a large amount of Ynia to transport. There were only five such devices in the country—Caern Vaughn, Galgrenon, Asta's Gate, Caern Porth, and Deirive—so their use was not widespread and typically only reserved for important messages between high-ranking officials.

"I've heard more reports from Clynwyl, the village Berwyn asked me to investigate." Valthor announced wearily. "I suspect a similar force to the one we found in the bogs could be at play. I'd like Calunoth to come with me." He conveyed it as a request, but the tone of his voice made it clear that he considered it an order. "The rest of you can come if you like."

Calunoth did not question the Guardian. Although he would have preferred to have taken the opportunity to rest, he owed his life to Valthor, and likely his continued security. Whatever Valthor wanted ought to be obliged in Calunoth's mind. The remainder of the group reached the same conclusion and communicated as much. Valthor accepted their decisions with a nod and turned on his heel to disappear into the castle.

***

The group made quick work of their preparations, and within an hour, were following the Guardian out of the gates of Caern Vaughn.

Refreshingly, the group could travel this time without fear of pursuit or unnatural danger—for now. The road to the village was clean and well kept as it wound through the hills. Their progress was slowed only by the fatigue of consistently navigating up steep inclines and trying not to fall on the way down. Valthor had told them to try to balance their pace, making up for lost time going uphill by racing downhill. Unfortunately, the rigorous nature of this exercise soon overcame their abilities, clearly evidenced when Calunoth tripped running down a particularly steep incline and rolled the remaining sixty feet down the grassy hill, landing in a heap at the bottom. The resulting dizziness had almost caused him to walk off a nearby ledge, and it was decided after that that the group would just go at the pace they could manage.

Having started the journey late in the day, night began to fall after six hours of journeying, but Valthor ordered the group to push on. It was not until the darkness was so all-encompassing that the road ahead was invisible that the Guardian finally pulled them aside and led them into a comfortable cave built into the side of the hill.

"This is the perfect spot to make camp," Bleiz remarked, "Do you know this area well then, sire?"

Valthor replied after barking a short magical command to spark a glowing green fire. "I grew up not far from here. The village we're going to, Clynwyl, is one of our rival villages. We used to compete with them in the Hill Games many years ago."

"When did the games stop?" Luca asked curiously.

"They didn't," Valthor said. "I just haven't partaken in them since becoming a Guardian. My responsibility is to all Renderiveans equally. I can't be seen favoring one over the other."

The night passed quickly for those who rested. Bleiz and Luca took on the responsibility of the night watch.

"These hills are not particularly dangerous at this time of year. Especially not with me here. You'd be better off sleeping," Valthor said to the grizzled captain, who had taken up a position at the mouth of the cave.

"While that may be true, sire, it is a Knight's obligation to stay aware of potential threats, even in apparently threatless areas," Bleiz replied, peering out from his position beyond the edges of the campfire that illuminated the surroundings, never taking his gaze away from the darkness. "Luca will watch with me. He's a good Knight candidate, despite his noble lineage. I fear he will have to stand watch in far darker times ahead, and it's best to chisel the mind and body for it while he's still young."

"He's quite different from his elder brother, I have to say. Felix was one of my classmates back at Akadaemia before the Sieth Incursion," Valthor noted, glancing over at the young Knight, who was currently readjusting the straps of his leather armor. "Luca hasn't yet been tested by the world like Felix had at this age. Still, they share a strength unique to the Draca line, even if he hasn't discovered it yet."

Bleiz gave a small smile at the Guardian's words. "Aye, he's a good lad. I'll have to knock him into proper shape before I retire though. He has spirit aplenty, but a bit more discipline would do him good. Even if my generation is running out of time, I have to make sure I leave the Knights better than I found them."

"I'm sure you will," Valthor replied, before calling out for the young Knight. "Luca! You have the distinct privilege of standing watch with your captain tonight. I'll relieve you halfway through." With those words, the Guardian retired to achieve the few hours of sleep he usually did.

***

After a blessedly uneventful night, Valthor hastened the group off at first light.

They arrived in the village of Clynwyl before noon and were promptly welcomed by the local village elder, a strange druid with wrinkled eyebrows and skin so hardened it looked akin to smoked leather. The man carried a staff with what appeared to be a large goat horn built into the end. Valthor began conversing with the man fluently in Llewyn. Once the conversation ended, the elder turned and started to head out east of the village. Motioning for the companions to follow him, Valthor walked alongside the elder, continuing the conversation as he did so.

After another hour of walking, hindered by the slow-moving elder, the group came to a field. The field was grassy and fenced off but devoid of livestock. Calunoth had begun to feel the Pralia Core in his chest slowly warm as they had walked, though the difference was so slight he hardly noticed it. Upon reaching the field, the elder bade them farewell and returned to the village. Once he was out of earshot, Valthor resumed speaking in Common.

"What an idiot," he said, clearly annoyed. "It's a twenty-minute walk here. He could have just pointed us in the right direction."

"What did he tell you?" Lauren asked. "I've been feeling something strange as we got closer and closer, but the place seems completely unremarkable."

"He basically told me they needed an elder druid, not a Guardian. This village has never liked me," Valthor grumbled, an annoyed look on his face. "But he also said the sheep populating this field were growing sickly and dying early. The druids have felt a strange presence here too, and the herbs aren't growing as they should. He spouted a bunch of nonsense about the wrath of the spirits too, but I managed to tune most of that out," Valthor said caustically. Kneeling, he quietly worked a formula and formed a small campfire on the road. The green fire appeared once more but appeared much smaller and duller than the one from the previous night. Then, continuing, Valthor said, "Berwyn's reports were right though. There is something interfering with the energy transferrals in this area. It's not terrible in this spot, but it could be worse further in."

Without another word, Valthor jogged toward the field. Vaulting the wooden fence, he tried to replicate his magical fire in the center of the field. The fire still appeared but was even duller and weaker than the one in the road and disappeared within a few minutes without Valthor's command.

As the group followed Valthor into the center of the field, the core in Calunoth's chest continued to burn hotter until it became uncomfortable as he reached the center.

Noting his discomfort, Valthor rose from his contemplations and addressed him. "You good, Cal?" he asked.

"It's nothing," Calunoth replied. "It's just that this core is warming up a bit more than usual. It'll probably pass. I'll be fine."

Rising from the remains of the fire, Valthor approached Calunoth and put his hand over the core. Feeling the heat through the leather armor, he withdrew his hand and instead put it to his forehead, thinking. After a moment he spoke. "This core has been increasing in temperature the further we got into the field, correct?" Calunoth nodded his assent, so the Guardian continued. "Then it looks like bringing you here was the right choice after all. Lead the way. Whichever direction increases the heat, go that way. We'll be right behind you."

Startled at suddenly being given the order to lead, Calunoth walked in a wide circle around the field. Feeling the largest spike in warmth on the north side, he slowly began to walk in that direction, altering his course slightly when he felt the core's heat begin to wane. He climbed over the fence on the northern side of the field, and the group followed Calunoth through the hills, now exchanging the green pastures for the rocky steppes that covered a great deal of the eastern hills leading to the foothills.

The warmth in Calunoth's chest was growing steadily warmer as he abandoned the path and began clambering over rocks, deviating far from the beaten path. The core continued to warm until he slipped down a narrow gully and suddenly found himself face to face with a boulder, his chest growing warmer than ever.

"There's something near here," Calunoth called to his companions as they followed him down the gully.

Valthor came first and examined the boulder that had arrested Calunoth's momentum. His eyes narrowed, and he declared, "This is no ordinary boulder."

"What do you mean, sire?" Bleiz asked as he followed him down, Luca and Lauren following closely behind.

"I mean it shouldn't be here. The moss is exposed on the top of the boulder, which can only have happened if it's rolled away from somewhere. There are no grooves or unusual patterns anywhere that would suggest it had fallen, so someone has moved it from somewhere. We'll have to move it and see what it's covering."

Calunoth grabbed the boulder with Valthor and pushed. The boulder didn't budge. Bleiz and Luca added their strength to the cause, and the boulder shifted slightly. Finally, Lauren put her slight weight to the boulder, and the five slowly pushed it aside, tipping it onto a downward slope and letting it roll down, almost flattening Bleiz in the process.

"Well, well, well, what do we have here?" Valthor muttered to himself. The boulder had been hiding a small entrance to a dark tunnel that curved downward toward the center of the earth. "Does anyone want to volunteer to go first?"

Seeing no takers for his offer, Valthor tried to summon a green flame in his hand to light their way. The flame blazed once, brilliantly, then vanished without a trace. "No magic here I guess, but then ..." Valthor muttered, his words fading away as he clambered down into the tunnel. Calunoth followed him down, Luca and Lauren followed, and Bleiz took up the rear.

The darkness did not last long. Not long after they began stumbling through the dark, the cave slowly became illuminated by bioluminescent moss dotted all around the tunnel. It began glowing in small blue patches at first but slowly grew in size and magnitude until it covered the entirety of the tunnel, making the darkness disappear as though the tunnel was bathed in full daylight. There were signs of human activity littered in the tunnel: a piece of flint dropped on the floor, directions engraved into the wall, and patches of moss that had clearly been burned away.

The group traveled warily through the underground tunnels silently, their weapons drawn. The glow of the moss lent an eerie vibe to the place, and it seemed as though the tunnels went ever deeper, leading them into the core of the earth itself. The air began to grow thick and dense as they moved further away from the entrance. Valthor had examined the moss and declared it harmless, but the group shared a growing sense of dread as they descended further into the eerie glow.

Finally, the tunnel split and forked into two separate paths, one leading up and one leading down. Both ways were clearly illuminated by the moss, and both appeared to have been recently traveled.

"Which way should we go?" Calunoth whispered, the echoes absorbed by the moss on the walls.

"Either one of these paths could be the way, and I'd like to limit our time in this place if possible. Which way does the core react more strongly to?" Valthor replied.

Calunoth shifted to the front of the column and paused to observe the changing temperatures of his chest. Hesitating a moment, he decided and pointed toward the path leading up.

"That way is stronger. Whatever is causing the interference should be up ahead," Calunoth reported.

Valthor attempted again to light the magical green fire. This time, nothing happened at all. The Guardian's eyes narrowed, and he turned to Calunoth.

"How are you feeling, Calunoth? Stronger or weaker than normal?" the Guardian asked.

"Um, well now that you mention it, I'm actually feeling pretty good. Better than I was when I woke up honestly," Calunoth replied, unaware of the strength in his limbs until the Guardian had raised the issue.

"Huh, interesting. Do you notice anything off about this place, Lauren?" Valthor's voice echoed softly as he called back to the trailing researcher.

"There's some kind of Ynia imbalance here," Lauren replied, jogging up to the Guardian. "It's hard for the others to notice since they don't use Ynia, but it almost feels like the Natural Ynia's being pulled away to somewhere else. Further down the tunnel. What do you think is happening?"

"I have a theory, but that's all right now. I'd like to confirm it first. But there is something sinister about this whole place. We shouldn't leave any of it unchecked. Let's split up." He turned to the others. "Cal, Bleiz, and Luca, take the descending path. I can sense the Ynia flow about as well as that core in your chest now, Cal, so you can lead the others. Because two of us can follow the energy, this will be faster. If you come across something nasty, scream and I'll come for you. If not, follow the path to the end and then turn back up the main passage. It's only one way so we'll have to run into each other. Lauren, you're with me."

Calunoth grimaced at the thought of being separated from the powerful Guardian, but he understood the rationale. Whatever was here was not natural and required their full attention. Besides, he did not wish to spend any more time here than required either. Nodding his assent, Calunoth steeled his nerves and followed the path down into the earth, Luca and Bleiz following closely behind.

Once they were gone, Valthor traveled up the other path with Lauren hurrying behind. Feeling the icy tension in the air, Lauren mustered the courage to speak to Valthor.

"You don't like me, do you, Valthor?" she said, giving voice to the misgivings that had been developing since she had met the Guardian in the bogs.

Valthor seemed completely unbothered by her question, answering bluntly, "I don't dislike you. I'm just indifferent to you."

Bristling slightly at the callous nature of his words, Lauren replied curtly, "And why is that? Is it because I'm a woman?"

Valthor continued walking without missing a beat. "No, I know plenty of capable women, the Viscount of Commerel being the best example. But no, it's that Akadaemia types aren't generally to my liking. You're all so ...out of touch."

"What do you mean? Didn't you go to Akadaemia as well? You studied history if I recall correctly," Lauren retorted, almost offended.

"Yes, I went to Akadaemia, and it was a waste of time," Valthor responded. "The history professors didn't understand the material they were teaching. They were just teaching it the way they interpreted it rather than how it actually happened. Don't even get me started on the economics and governorship professors. They wouldn't know the real world if it hit them in the head. They're so caught up in their own smug theories that only work on paper that they never take the time to see the real world. Then that gets passed on to their students. They're all convinced they're right about everything because they've been taught to think that way."

Lauren was startled by his rationale. Having studied at Akadaemia for years, she too had been taught to believe scientific theories that mocked the supernatural beliefs of the common folk. There was a scientific explanation for everything. People who attributed things to spiritual or supernatural forces did so because they couldn't understand how the world really worked. The idea Valthor floated ran squarely against that belief. Taking a moment to compose herself, she responded haughtily. "Maybe that's because it's the right way to think. Technological advancement that improves lives comes from us. We can find new ideas because we have the knowledge to examine old ideas." She tried to articulate her point as clearly and succinctly as possible.

"But how do you know?" Valthor replied caustically. "If you're only ever taught one version of something, how can you know it's the right one? The current state of Akadaemia is such that the professors teach only one version of the ideas that they believe in but none of the other possibilities. And how are you supposed to know that you're right if you don't consider contradictory theories? Hence, you're taught to listen and obey rather than to think, which was the original point of the school. And then we get people like you as a result."

Lauren was about to issue a harsh reproach but was curtailed by an urgent motion from Valthor. "But enough of this. Be quiet. I see light ahead."

***

Calunoth, Luca, and Bleiz continued walking deep down into the earth. The tunnel seemed to grow lighter the further down they went as though the moss embraced the challenge of lighting the darkness the further they dared traverse. The passageway was wide enough for two people to walk side by side, so Luca and Calunoth took point, and

Bleiz kept an eye on the rear. Sensing the tense mood, Luca attempted to lighten the mood by jokingly suggesting that they could eat the moss to glow in the dark themselves, but he was quickly hushed. Calunoth and Bleiz were not in the mood for jokes.

They did not have to travel for long before they came to a door in a metal grid that blocked the way down the tunnel. The grid was made of forged steel and would have required special equipment or magic to cut through if it hadn't been unlocked. The trio passed through the grate unimpeded with the same thought: was the grate designed to keep people in or out?

Slowly, the tunnel morphed into a larger and larger space, culminating in a large hallway that all three men could comfortably stand abreast in. A pungent smell permeated the air, causing Calunoth to wrinkle his nose as he entered the room. The luminous moss that had previously dotted the caverns had begun to fade but still illuminated the space just enough for Calunoth to see a sconce on the wall. The rest of the room was obscured in darkness. Calunoth pointed at the sconce on the wall, and Bleiz nodded and drew flint from his pack. He sent sparks flying from it into the oil, igniting it and illuminating the room. Looking around, the three companions felt their hearts skip several beats as they realized where they were.

They were standing in a prison.

The walls had been carved out, and grids of the same thick, forged steel as the entrance separated the alcoves from the center of the room. There were at least eight cells, and the room ended in a pit of blackness at the far end. Moving slowly, warily, the group moved toward the end of the room, examining the cells as they went.

"I don't know who or what was kept in here," Bleiz muttered, cursing, "But they're not here now. These cells are empty, and thankfully, there's no bodies in them either."

Calunoth reached the pit at the end of the room first and had to choke back his scream. Hanging above the pit was a single cage, dangling from the ceiling of the cave by a cast-iron chain. The cage was the only inhabited cell in the prison, and it was inhabited by a single decaying body, a body unnatural in its decomposition. Its skin was pulled tight around the bones, and the teeth and hair had fallen out. Clothing hung around its skeleton, far outstripping the size of its wearer. The skin appeared paper thin, and the corpse, which could have been male or female, had died with an expression of agony plastered across its face.

"Gods!" Bleiz exclaimed, moving forward to join Calunoth at the edge of the pit. Luca brought along a short piece of wood that had been lying on the ground and used it to carry some of the flame Bleiz had struck to life on the other side of the room. Grimacing at the sight, Luca lowered the torch to two sconces that jutted out from the wall. With them lit, the entirety of the pit was clearly illuminated, and the trio as a one gave out at rattled breath of horror.

Recovering first, Luca gave voice to what they were all thinking. "Well, now we know why the cells are empty."

The bottom of the pit was filled with human bones.

Chapter 10

An Ancient Darkness

    The light that glowed ahead of Lauren and Valthor was of a different composition than the light of the cave. While the bioluminescent moss glowed with a soft bluish hue, the light creeping around the corner of the passage was a powerful red that fluctuated in a rhythm as they approached it. Holding his hand up to halt Lauren's advance, Valthor crept forward to the corner by himself and held his back flat against the wall, careful to avoid any deliberate movement that could give away his location.

    Lauren's heart pounded in her chest. They were still several miles beneath the earth at this point, and escape was not a realistic option given the narrow nature of the tunnel. If anyone, or anything, came around the corner, she would have to fight it. Preparing herself, Lauren carefully drew the short sword she had retrieved from Caern Vaughn and held it in her trembling hands.

    Though she had been a quick learner training with Calunoth, she still lacked the resolve to wield her gifted sword in real combat. Also, with Valthor up front, she would probably just get in the way. At the very least, she hoped that she didn't hit Valthor.

    Valthor, for his part, was unconcerned with her presence. Typically accustomed to completing missions alone, he had elected to ignore her existence and instead focused on what he saw around the corner. The passage was one way. Unless someone from the outside entered the tunnel, the only people who could come up behind them were their own companions, so the rear was well covered.

    Peeking around the corner, the Guardian paused a moment to listen, then hearing and seeing nothing, carefully snuck out from behind the wall, watching for any unexpected movement.

    He heard nothing. He saw no one. With his short sword still firmly grasped in his sword hand and motioning for Lauren to follow him with his other, Valthor slowly stepped out of the tunnel and into a large cavern. Following his lead, Lauren entered the cavern behind him.

    The cavern itself was a source of bewilderment to Lauren. While the tunnel that led to it held the natural appearance of hewn rock that had been dug through, the cavern had the grace and structure of some of the most structurally sound buildings in Renderive. Large carved stone pillars at the corners of the room provided support for the roof of the cave, which alone retained the natural surface of the surrounding cavern. The exposed walls were comprised of heavy sandstone bricks precisely laid, giving the impression they had just walked into an ordinary castle hall. However, the walls were not bare. Instead, the entirety of the wall to their right was obscured by a complex mesh of machinery. Large steel instruments were connected to each other with strange metal tubes that glowed with the odd red light that had oozed into the tunnel. High bookshelves stood empty all around the room, and a couple of wooden desks dotted the space haphazardly.

However, the main source of the bright red light came from the center of the room. The tubes leading from the surrounding machinery converged into a strange pedestal, on which rested a small metal platform. And on it, thick sheets of an unknown, silver metal supported a vise. Red light shone brilliantly from within the vise, but whatever the clamp had been holding was unclear as it now stood empty and unfilled. The surrounding machinery gave off a dull hum as it appeared to remain operational.

"There's no one here. This place looks abandoned," Valthor reported back to Lauren, sheathing his weapon. Pointing to a large gate on the far side of the cave. "There's a proper entrance on the other side of the cave. I don't know where it leads, but it doesn't matter. It's caved in, so we won't be able to go that way." The gate held the same architectural detailing as the rest of the cavern, with ornate patterns carved into the gateposts and the solid, unyielding stability of the other pillars evident even from a distance. The tunnel past the gate was much larger than the one they'd just traversed, but the collapsed rock beyond made it impossible to determine more.

"What is this place?" Lauren asked, feeling strangely unsettled at the sound of the machinery. She recognized some of it as Ynium conversion technology, but the design was far more intricate than anything she had seen in her studies. Parts of it looked like some of the Ynium research labs at Akadaemia, except these pipes were made of argent. Argent was the best conductor of energy ever discovered but certainly did not come cheap.

What happened to the other entrance? she wondered. To Valthor, she said, "This place looks like it was only recently abandoned.

Whoever was here left behind a lot of equipment and notes. Maybe they didn't have time to collect them before they had to escape?"

"No, that cave-in wasn't natural. Someone caused it. The architecture of these tunnels is magnificent. It wouldn't have collapsed by itself. Besides, the tunnel we came through looked like an emergency exit. The miners would have carved it out as soon as they got here, so they would have source for air and a way to get out if the cavern collapsed. Combining the cave-in with the boulder where we came in, this place was meant to be abandoned and never discovered again," Valthor replied as he continued examining the space. He walked over to the pedestal at the center of the room. "This device appears to be the source of all the interference, though I can't tell what it is. Whatever had been held by this clamp has been removed."

Lauren began to file through the papers that lay strewn over a workbench to the right of the room, searching for information about the technology and the lab while Valthor mused about how to destroy the device causing the disturbance. As she did so, she thought she could detect the dull hum of the machines steadily growing louder even as she immersed herself in the notes.

***

"What kind of place is this?" Bleiz demanded, staring down into the pit of bones. "Who keeps prisoners this far underground? And for what purpose?"

Calunoth had turned away from the pit, his stomach churning. The smell of the dead lingered in the air, causing him to gag inwardly as he scanned the room, now brightly lit by the torches Luca had set ablaze.

The prison was small, with eight tightly confined cells inset into the wall. The glistening rock walls were bare and reflected the flickering torchlight back into the room. The room was completely devoid of furniture or feature, barring the cells and a small table that now came into view opposite the pit. A single chair was tucked in behind the table, and a neat stack of papers sat off to the side. Whoever had been here before hadn't been gone long.

Approaching the table, Calunoth picked up the papers and began shifting through them. "You two, come here. I've found something," he said, calling Bleiz and Luca away from the pit. Grateful for the opportunity to look away from the sinister collection of bones, they approached the desk. Joining Calunoth in sifting through the papers, Bleiz focused on one in particular labeled, "COPY," squinting to read it clearly in the limited light of the torches. Once he could see the scribbled black lines, he recited their contents to his companions.

"'The results are good so far,'" Bleiz read out loud. "'But we need more prisoners to sustain the experiment. Try to bring us some that last more than half a day next time.' It's signed, 'L.'" He looked up at them. "What kind of experiments were they doing? Human experiments? Those have been outlawed for over a hundred years!"

"If this is the result, then I can see why," Calunoth replied grimly. "Here's another one. 'Some of the prisoners have been showing declining conditions since their turn. Should we try to keep them healthy or just get more?' Signed, 'Kl.' The response reads, 'Do both. We'll watch both groups to determine differences.' Signed, 'L' again."

"What kind of experiment drains the very life out of its participants?" Bleiz wondered, shaking his head darkly. "This is evil of the foulest kind. We must put a stop to it. There must be dozens of people in that pit, maybe more. How did Berwyn let that many people disappear under his nose like that?"

At that point, Luca interrupted their conversation to do what they all felt like doing and was promptly sick in the corner. Wiping his mouth with his sleeve, he cursed. "Let's go find Valthor and Lauren. There's nothing else here, and I don't want to stay in this place any longer."

Bleiz and Calunoth agreed. Calunoth took the notes, folded them away into his pocket, then helped Luca up from his knees and guided them out of the room. He couldn't help but feel a sense of dread as he did so. He had thought he had seen the maddest of the world when he had faced the guardian of the Caerwyn Bogs. But it was becoming clear that there was something sinister afoot in the world. Contemplating these thoughts, he led the group back to the bifurcation point and followed the trail of Valthor and Lauren. All throughout, his core continued to smolder.

***

Lauren rifled through her own set of papers with a deeply furrowed brow. The light of the central apparatus was such that the cavern was lit up as though in full daylight, giving off the uneasy impression of being outside despite being surrounded by solid walls.

Lauren read quickly. While she was no great warrior, her experience as a researcher and student allowed her to read through the complex notes with ease. The notes in question were filled with complex formulae and observations. Though many of these she recognized as cornerstones of Ynium technology theory, many were beyond her understanding. The structure of the notes was such that it was like trying to read a fire-damaged textbook. Although whole, the gaps in her knowledge as the notes detailed increasingly convoluted equations required her to infer much of what was intended to be understood from the indecipherable passages. Among her greatest troubles was the fact that many equations contained symbols she had never even seen before mixed in with the common symbols used by researchers across the continent. These same symbols, she noticed, were consistent with symbols inlaid into the machinery that dominated much of the laboratory.

Her contemplations were interrupted and her heart leapt at a loud banging behind her. Almost dropping the papers, she whipped around ready for a confrontation only to see Valthor bashing the vise with the hilt of his sword.

Seeing her whirl around with an astonished expression on her face, Valthor stopped to offer an explanation. "This thing is the cause of the interference, but it's so powerful down here that none of my magic will work. It just disappears as soon as I cast it. So, since I can't use magic to destroy this thing, I've gotta try something a bit more old-fashioned," he said before noticing the notes in her hand. "What have you got there?"

Lauren went over to him, keen to explain what she had found. "I think they were making something here. See this?" she pointed out a section of the paper covered in complex symbols. "This is a creation formulae combined with the Kefla Equation to create what looks like a transduction system." Lauren was excited at the opportunity to show off her knowledge, but her effort was lost on the Guardian, who took the notes from her hand to examine them himself.

"Yes, but half of these symbols are wrong. This formula is supposed to detail energy transferal, but it looks like they were trying to turn it into an energy conversion formula," Valthor remarked, flipping through the pages, scanning them as he did so. Reaching the last page, his eyes narrowed, and he pointed out a table on the back cover. "Look at this. It's a translation guide for these symbols, or part of one at least. It seems like not all of this work is their own."

"They're the same symbols inscribed on these devices!" Lauren exclaimed, delighted that Valthor had missed this observation. She pointed to the complex machinery against the wall. Valthor went over to one, holding the notes up and comparing them to the symbols on the machine. After several moments of examining them, his eyes widened, and he let a soft gasp. "What is it?" Lauren asked. "What do you see?"

Valthor cleared his throat and looked around the cave before returning to the conversation and answering. "This is not Renderivean technology, nor is it the work of druids, mages, spirits, or any other force on the continent. This is ancient Selevirnian technology. *Functioning* Selevirnian technology, similar to what was pulled out of the Marveuz Excavation site. This technology predates the nation under which it lies, and yet it still works, or has been restored to work at least."

"Gods ..." whispered Lauren, "But then who did this? What were they making? Could there still be Selevirnians living?"

Valthor shook his head. "We don't know much about the Selevirn Union. We know they came from beyond the Faar Mountains and were the first to colonize Creidyl. We also know that they were far more advanced than we are now, and the technology we found proved that. But none could have survived. The records from the time of their fall are virtually nonexistent. All we have are old folk tales passed down about the gods filling the skies with ash and scarring the earth with their fire. We have no idea what actually happened to them." Valthor's explanation was interrupted by the sudden pounding of footsteps from the direction of the tunnel. Drawing his sword instinctively, Valthor took up a position just outside of the entrance, ready to surprise any unexpected visitors.

His vigil was unnecessary however as Calunoth slowly emerged from the shadows, relaxing as he saw Lauren standing near the center of the room. Bleiz and Luca followed after him, and the group was reunited once more.

Calunoth spoke quickly in a panicked voice, and it was clear that the entire group was deeply disturbed by their findings. Valthor listened carefully without reaction.

"We found a prison down the other tunnel," Calunoth reported. "There was no one in there though. But we found a huge pit filled with human bones. We also found these orders." He withdrew the papers from his pocket and showed them to the Guardian. "We don't know what they were doing, but they were conducting some form of experiment on humans. They kept the prisoners for that purpose."

"And now we know where they were experimented on," Bleiz added grimly, staring at the equipment. "Whatever magic this is, we need to find whoever is responsible for it. What have you two found out?"

Bleiz's question was halted by Valthor, who approached Calunoth curiously. "Cal, you look distinctly uncomfortable. Is it your core?"

Calunoth shifted as he spoke. "It's getting really warm now. It's almost burning. It's been getting worse the closer I get to these machines."

"These machines appear to be drawing in all of the Natural Ynia from the surroundings, although for what purpose we don't yet know," Valthor replied, holding his hand close to the core. "It's possible that being so close to a concentrated source of Ynia is causing your core to work overtime amplifying it. Just bear with it for now. We'll try to be quick. It shouldn't cause you any permanent problems."

Lauren reported their findings, describing how the lab was using ancient Selevirnian technology to make something, though they didn't know what yet. "The notes are very complex. I'll need a lot more time to decipher them fully," she said.

"Well, this place is abandoned and will stay that way, so why don't you do that, Lauren?" Valthor ordered. "We've got time, and we need to figure out who's behind this if possible. I can and try help you later, but I'm more useful searching for more information right now."

Lauren nodded and took up residence at one of the workbenches, head down studiously over the notes.

The newly arrived trio were far less happy with this arrangement. They wanted to leave as soon as possible, but Valthor dismissed their fears. Whatever was responsible was gone from this place and likely wouldn't return.

So, while Lauren poured over the notes, the remaining members of the group combed the laboratory for more information. They found a medley of items and apparatuses that provided no clue as to the identity of the experimenters, and they were slowed by Bleiz constantly asking whether an item he had found held any value. Because of a deep distrust of Ynia and virtually no understanding of its function, Bleiz was unable to distinguish between a magical object and a normal one, which was irritating to Valthor in particular. As the most knowledgeable among them, he was called on to identify the unearthed items. However, after having to tell Bleiz that a silver candlestick was not a magical object, he established a rule that unless an item was glowing, they shouldn't bother him with it.

It was Luca who found the first useful piece of information. Standing on a chair, he had reached up to pull a box down from the top of one of the high bookcases lining the walls. Most of the shelves had been cleaned out and everything else of value taken, but this box had blended so well into the shadows created by the red light that whoever had scoured the rest of the laboratory of features must have missed it. Bringing the box down, Luca opened it to reveal even more stacks of papers. Calling the companions over, the group dove into the box, trying to find some explanation about what happened here.

Calunoth found the telling paper first. Apparently a draft, the paper had several corrections for grammar and honorific language. After reading through it himself and choking down an exclamation, Calunoth read out the letter, also labeled, "COPY," to his companions.

"'Dear Rightful King Byrant, I am pleased to inform you that you may rely on PRIMAL's ability to supply you with Pralia technology for the upcoming conflict and support you in other required covert activities. Our members have been working hard at all our bases to ensure you will have the military technology required to successfully defend Byrantia against any force Greshaun can muster. We will be delivering the technology to you from our Llewyn base shortly and hope this will serve as a strong indication of our continued investment in both our interests.' It's signed 'L,' just like the letters in the other room."

Valthor gave a great sigh and fell back into the chair he had been leaning on, putting down the document he had been scanning.

"Well, that's made the job harder," Valthor muttered to himself.

Luca appeared bewildered by Valthor's and Calunoth's reactions. "Wait, I don't get it. PRIMAL? That group from Valthor's reports? What technology are they talking about?"

Valthor ignored him and instead looked blearily down at the paper he had been reading. The hum of the machinery grew steadily louder in the background. "If Byrant has access to military-grade Pralia technology, this war will not end well for us." Turning back to Calunoth, the Guardian gestured at the sheaf of paper he'd been reading.

"Cal, you're going to want to hear this. It's a report from Glathaous," Valthor said before reciting from the page. "'L, Efforts by PRIMAL operatives to seize Pralia technology rumored to be at Glathaous Castle were unsuccessful. Glathaous Castle destroyed. Casualties unknown. Assumed command of the town under AG's name. Reports emerged of a small group of survivors, potentially including Archmage Aaron, likely in possession of Glathaous Core. AG's cooperation overseeing operations in Glathaous ensured to continue. Pursuit of group in progress. Will report again when more details known.' Signed, AR. Well, now we know."

Bleiz's mind was reeling. "So this group, PRIMAL? They're responsible for the Glathaous Massacre?" Bleiz demanded.

"It would appear so. It seems this PRIMAL group is working for or with Byrant to provide him with Pralia technology. They're the ones who attacked Glathaous Castle, and it can be assumed from the letter that 'AG' is Alistair Glathaous. Everything matches up except for this part about the archmage having the core," Valthor replied.

"I was wearing Aaron's cloak when Bleiz and Luca found me. It was distinctive enough that some of the townspeople could have thought it was him, and I kept my face hidden the whole time we were there," Calunoth replied "But if they were coming after this Pralia Core in my chest, what were they trying to make in here?"

"I might be able to answer that," Lauren interjected, walking over to them from her perch. "The equipment here was unearthed deep underground. They didn't make it themselves. But they were able to use it to create a Pralia Core. They use the letters 'PC' in here, but that must be what it stands for. But apparently they weren't successful. They weren't able to make a true core but something close. They probably wanted to use the Glathaous Core to perfect their own."

"But if the core they made here wasn't complete, then what did they make? And what did they send to Byrant?" Bleiz asked. Lauren could only shake her head.

"I don't know. I'm still trying to figure it out. This isn't a manual, more like a spare notebook for thoughts. This PRIMAL group was pretty thorough cleaning the place out."

"I think we've found all we need to," Calunoth said bitterly. "Let's get out of here. My chest is on fire as it is."

Valthor stopped him as he turned to leave. "Hold on. We need to destroy this equipment first. This Pralia technology is disrupting all of the Ynia in the area. We can't just leave it."

"It's gotten pretty loud too, hasn't it?" Luca noted. "It was buzzing a lot more quietly when we got here." He looked at Lauren, hoping for an explanation. "And why would they just abandon it if it's so rare?"

"It hasn't been abandoned long," Valthor remarked. "Maybe a couple of days. There isn't even any dust on the equipment. I suppose we could try cutting the tubes off, though I'm not sure if that would work. This metal is made of stern stuff. It's going to take a lot of hammering to break it."

"Sire, is it a good idea to break it? I saw the result of a Pralia explosion at Glathaous Castle. If we get caught in a similar explosion, we'd likely take half of the hill with us," Bleiz pointed out, remembering the crater that had decimated the castle courtyard.

"Based on the sound it's making, it might do that anyway," Luca joked. Lauren did not find his joke amusing as she had reached the end of the notebook and had begun reciting the last lines in her head.

> *Once the product has been created, the unstable energy flow will likely build up, and without an output for the energy, accumulate in the machinery. We have the ability now to recreate this machinery, and we need Byrant for the plan to work. Once we remove the core, we will deliver it to Byrant and remove ourselves from this lab. It will not be safe when the energy builds to a critical level.*

Raising her head, she became aware that the quiet hum of the machinery had gradually grown into a mechanical roar. Realizing what was about to happen, she screamed at the companions.

"RUN!" Lauren screamed, and, holding the notes close to her chest, bolted toward the tunnel.

The companions looked at each other for a moment, perplexed and startled by the young researcher's exclamation. Then, as one, they all burst into a sprint, realizing the ramifications of her warning.

They followed Lauren back out of the passage, letting her lead the way. The moss that had been glowing brightly had begun to dim and obscured their vision. Lauren knew what was going to happen to the equipment in the lab, and they had to be as far away as possible when it did. Reaching the intersection where they had split up, Lauren shouted, "Follow me!" and dashed down the tunnel toward the prison.

With panic setting in for most of the companions, and with the whir of the machinery now audible even from their position, they followed her down into the prison. The noise grew louder and louder as they raced down to the gruesome cells, Lauren in front, Valthor in the rear. They ran through the small prison, and Lauren, unfamiliar with the room, ran straight up to the pit, skidding to an abrupt stop on the edge, and was greeted with the sinister site of the bones. Calunoth, Bleiz, and Luca all knew what was coming and stopped her at the edge. Luca grabbed Lauren so her momentum wouldn't carry her into the pit. Valthor had no such awareness, however. Still sprinting fast, he was unprepared for the sudden stop that the foursome made at the edge of the pit and couldn't slow down in time to stop. Instead, he crashed into them from behind, sending all five of them tumbling into the pit of bones. It was well he did as a blinding light suddenly filled the chamber, illuminating the air above them as they fell into the pit, followed by a noise that shook the caverns and reverberated down the tunnel.

With nothing to stop them, the companions plummeted to join the bones in their grim celebration of death.

Chapter 11

Over Hill and Dale

The reverberations continued to echo around the room after the initial flare. The light that had exploded into the prison would have illuminated a continent, but it faded quickly. The five companions stayed low, huddled together in the grim graveyard of human remains, silently awaiting the echoing of the blast to die down. They were uninjured, though only by chance, as Calunoth had landed facedown in the pit and had been fortunate to escape having his eye gouged out by a protruding rib as the other companions piled on top of him and Lauren and rolled onto the brittle bones that provided a deeply disturbing cushion to soften the landing from their ten-foot descent into the pit. Many of the bones shattered on impact. The shockwave had extinguished the sconces on the wall, plunging them into darkness after the blast of light.

After several tense minutes, the reverberations stopped, and Calunoth was acutely aware that the fire that had been roaring in his chest had disappeared entirely. He could feel his other companions nearby, but in the pitch blackness of the cavern, he could not see them. The silence was finally broken by Valthor exclaiming, "Light!" At that word from the Guardian, the cavern lit up with a greenish glow that appeared to have no source or direction and illuminated the companions as they lay sprawled among the bones below the hanging cage. Lauren let out a scream at the sight, while Valthor maintained his composure.

"Well, that could have gone better," Valthor remarked casually. Although his voice held its usual confidence, Calunoth could see by the green glow that Valthor's expression defied that confidence. He was as shaken as the rest of them.

"What the hell was that?" Bleiz demanded, extricating himself from the bones that, when standing, came up past his shins.

"Let's get out of this pit first. No offense to present company, but I'd rather not stay in here," Valthor replied, nodding at the remains.

Luca became the foundation of the group's escape from the pit. As tall and strong as he was, he boosted the Guardian up high enough for him to climb out. From there, the two worked in tandem to rescue the rest of the companions. Luca came up last, with Valthor using the long staff-sword on his back to reach the young Knight and pull him up.

Once they had regained the floor, they could see the effect the blast had had on the cavern thanks to Valthor's green light. The walls appeared to still be sound, without significant threat of collapse, but small cracks had begun to appear on the floor and ceiling. The rocks themselves appeared to be singed, and the air had a strange metallic taste to it. What had once been the prison door had been blasted away and now lay in several pieces scattered across the prison floor.

"That very well could have been us," Valthor remarked, observing the smoldering pieces of metal. He turned to Lauren. "Thank you, Lauren. I daresay you just saved our lives." Lauren looked shocked at the approval.

The others agreed. Then Luca asked, "Do you know what that was? What just happened Lauren?" he asked turning to the blond researcher.

"I think so …" Lauren began hesitantly. "There was a set of formulae at the end of the book that detailed what would happen to the machinery once the product was removed. If it had been replaced, or had the machinery been properly turned off, then that wouldn't have happened. I think the energy that had been used to power the experiment was trapped and growing. Without the core, it had nowhere to go and built up until the machinery couldn't handle it anymore. When the limiters were breached, the energy had to go somewhere, and it was released all at once, leading to that explosion."

"Why wouldn't PRIMAL have turned it off though?" Calunoth asked. "That machinery must have been priceless. Why would they just leave it like that if they knew what was going to happen?"

"Probably because they wanted the place destroyed," Valthor answered. "You saw the cave-in? They had what they wanted. And those machines are embedded into the wall, so they couldn't have been moved. Better for them to be destroyed and hide their tracks."

"I don't think it's as complex as that," Lauren answered. "They left quickly, but still left behind important documents? I think they removed the core prematurely and couldn't figure out how to switch off the machine. They knew what was going to happen, and they couldn't stop it without replacing the core, so they had to abandon the place to get the core out."

"The second explanation seems more likely," Calunoth said. "It doesn't sound like they managed to even make a proper Pralia Core. I don't think they fully understand what they're doing with this technology. We should go back up there and see if there's anything left."

The group acceded to that wisdom, and Valthor led the way back up to the former laboratory, the green light he had summoned seeming to follow him as he walked. Traveling back up through the tunnels, the effects of the explosion were clear on the surrounding walls. The luminous moss had been completely incinerated, and the walls were now smooth and clear, albeit blackened. As they approached the entrance to the laboratory, the effects were even more dramatic. Sections of the wall had not just been blackened but had even begun to melt, with strange trails of liquid seeping down the rock until they cooled and hardened after the explosion, leaving unique patterns decorating the walls.

The laboratory had been obliterated. Large chunks of steel from the machinery lay smoking and scattered around the room. The tables, the shelves, the workbenches, all had been erased as though they had never existed. The only structure left in the room was the pedestal containing the vise that had held the experimental core, and it had not escaped unscathed. The vise itself had shattered into pieces and now lay scattered on the other side of the cavern. The pedestal had begun to melt on the side facing the bulk of the machinery, while the other side bore the impressions of the blackened ash that had painted the prison door.

There was nothing to be salvaged.

"Let's return to Caern Vaughn," Valthor said warily eyeing the scene. "There's nothing here anymore, and the source of the disturbance is gone. Also, I've got a feeling that we shouldn't linger here. Something feels … off in the air. Let's go." The group, as a whole rattled by the destroyed laboratory, agreed heartily, and they began to make their way back to the entrance.

The further they walked, the more they realized just how extensive the explosion had been. Marked by the disappearance of the luminous moss from the walls, the explosion had blasted far into the tunnel, further than they would have been able to run had they made for the entrance.

"Good thinking, Lauren." Luca complimented the researcher as he viewed the steadily decreasing marks on the walls of the tunnel. "I would have just run straight on and gotten caught in this. How did you know to go down instead of out?"

Lauren blushed at the praise from the young Knight as she answered. "To be honest, I was thinking about the blast radius and figured it would be better to have layers of stone between us and it rather than distance. I can't believe it came out this far though. There must have been an exorbitant amount of Ynia accumulating in those machines."

The luminous moss began to line the walls again as they moved closer to the exit. After spending most of the day wandering the tunnels, the exchange of fresh air for the strange metallic air that had permeated the cavern was welcome. Exiting the cavern, the harsh light pierced their eyes, temporarily blinding them as they adjusted to the light of the surface.

The sun was beginning to dip down below the horizon as the group returned to Clynwyl, with Valthor able to report back to the elder druid that the issue of the disrupted magical field had been resolved. After spending the night in the village, with individual families gratefully giving up their beds for their guests, the group returned to the road and made their way back to Caern Vaughn.

***

The road back to Caern Vaughn the next morning was uneventful, so the group discussed the events in the cavern. Lauren spent a great deal of the journey reading from the notes she'd found as she walked, and after several hours of study, enlightened the rest of the group.

"It seems the machinery in that cave was discovered several months ago, but it was unusable. PRIMAL spent a great deal of time restoring it. Their goal was to create a Pralia Core that could amplify energy without risk to a spellcaster, but their experiments kept failing. In the end, their final product could conduct energy but did so in an unstable manner, and it couldn't reliably maintain the flow. It seems that they were able to create a workable core in the end, but it has limitations that it's not supposed to," Lauren reported. "I think it would work as a Pralia Core, but it wouldn't be as efficient, or as stable, as it should be to be used safely."

"So, there's a group of PRIMAL operatives running around with a magical oil drum in their pocket? Great." Valthor responded to the report with his typical cavalier attitude. "Byrant's a capable military leader, and if he gets his hands on even a semi-functional Pralia Core, it's going to be bad news for us."

"It seems they were focused on using it defensively more than offensively, based on the formulas they were attempting with it," Lauren continued, ignoring the Guardian. "They were using barrier and blocking formulae mostly. The notes say they tried to use it with offensive formulae, but the results were too unstable to be used in the enclosed space they had. They may be taking it somewhere else to develop those offensive capabilities though."

"And they tried to take the Pralia Core they knew was in Glathaous Castle when their experiments kept failing," Bleiz noted. "But how would they know that Lord Glathaous was conducting that research?"

"Byrant probably found out," Valthor replied. "He has access to higher security classifications, so he likely knew about the research. We don't know enough about this PRIMAL group though. Where did they come from? What are they doing with Byrant?"

"We may yet find out, especially if Byrant tries to take over the kingdom," Bleiz replied.

With that observation, the group fell silent and remained that way until they found themselves back at the gates of Caern Vaughn, few hours of sunlight left in the sky.

They were greeted exuberantly by the enormous Lord Berwyn, who bade them to come inside to rest and eat. He had just been about to engage in his own dinner and invited the group to join him. Over dinner, the group regaled their experiences in the caverns.

When Valthor raised the point of the Selevirnian architecture, Berwyn interrupted in his booming fashion. "We've known those tunnels exist for decades now, but they're mostly inaccessible. They're dotted all around under the hills. I'm surprised that there was anything down there. In theory, they should connect to the underground network that extends into the Faar Mountains built back in the Glory Age, but so much of it has caved in that we've never bothered to investigate down there. Even with the recent reports, I would have expected the source to be some radical druid sect operating in the open, not a secret society operating underground." Berwyn spoke with the enthusiasm that betrayed his love of history.

Valthor nodded at the heavily bearded lord and continued his report. When he was finished, Berwyn leaned back in his chair at the head of the table and stroked his bushy mustache, lost in thought. Finally, he said, "Thank you for your assistance in this matter, Valthor. It seems I've sent you on quite the set of adventures over the past months. You have my gratitude."

Valthor responded that it was his pleasure to help, and Berwyn continued, shaking his head. "I must say, all this talk of these mercenary types—this PRIMAL group, you called it?—it eats at my nerves. I've noticed that there's been something foul in the air. I can't tell what it is, but I can sense it in my soul. I fear Byrant may be up to far more than just a simple uprising. If he's working with these characters, then that can only mean trouble. Still, young master Calunoth, you must be pleased." He directed his attention toward Calunoth. "You now have a name for your enemy and some information about their leader. Signed 'L,' you said those notes were? You have figured out who that is, I presume?"

Calunoth nodded, "It's almost certainly Lenocius, though I don't know how he's connected to Byrant. It confirms what we heard from Valthor's reports, that Lenocius is PRIMAL's leader."

"It also seems," Bleiz interjected, "that Alistair Glathaous is part of this PRIMAL group as well. That speaks of the depth to which this PRIMAL rot may go. We should be careful. If someone like the son of Isaac Glathaous can be corrupted by these people, then we must be careful who we trust."

"Indeed, and I fear now the rot may have settled in elsewhere," Berwyn said. "I've had reports from the Galgre Range that the Highlanders are militating. They've always been a proud and independent folk. If they see a shot with Byrant, they could take it."

"If Byrant can effectively utilize the Pralia technology we discovered in combat and gains the support of the Highlanders and the rest of Southern Renderive, then he may very well be able to overthrow the king," Valthor replied worriedly. "We know who most of the factors will align with if we cannot defuse the situation. I trust the king can count on the support of the Hillmen, Berwyn?"

Berwyn nodded his head with certainty. "So long as the Hillmen blood flows through these hills, the king will have my support. You know of my history with Aiden. I would sooner cut off my own head than betray him. My support is unconditional," he said emphatically.

"But I do have concerns about your own colleagues, Valthor. If it comes to blows, will the Guardians all stand by the king? Having even one defect would seriously bolster the legitimacy of Byrant's challenge."

"I can only speak for myself unfortunately," Valthor replied. "You know that the Guardians typically operate independently. At our investitures, we swear to protect the people and nation of Renderive. If Byrant can convince any of the Guardians he's acting in the best interests of Renderive, then they may choose to defect. He can't convince me of that though. His ideas are utopian. Unattainable, with a lot of bodies on the ground before he can figure out that they're unattainable."

"How do you know that?" Lauren interrupted the Guardian indignantly. "Have you ever taken the time to read any of his works? Or listen to any of his speeches?"

"I've read enough to know the man's mind is not rooted in reality. These types of revolutionaries are all the same. They think they're the hero when really they're the villain in disguise," Valthor answered bluntly, casting a disparaging glance at the fiery young researcher.

"And the Knights are primarily concentrated in the north and the capital," Bleiz added, clearing his throat to ease the tension. "They will side with the king, barring a few southern defectors. So, most of the army will be arrayed against Byrant. Who else do we have?"

"Well, with us," Berwyn said, "the ten thousand or so Knights that garrison the capital and the Bastion, and many of the men-at-arms in the north and the capital, you'll have easily twenty thousand. The Chelians will stay neutral or side with the king if this war is not protracted. They may not have an opportunity to mobilize from the isles though if this is a quick war. The only unknown here is Commerel."

"Commerel is the heart of the Renderivean economy," Valthor said. "Viscount Latoya will not want a war. It's bad for business, and any civil war will be heavily contested around Commerel. She'll likely support whoever she believes can end the war fastest."

"While that's true, she's also familiar with Byrant's ideals," Berwyn posited. "She won't want to support someone whose ideals would destroy the wealth that her city has accrued. If the fight were between two traditionalists, she may not have a preference, but with that radical in the mix, she might favor the king."

"Well, it's something I can speak with her about myself," Valthor said. "I intend to take Cal through Commerel on my way to the capital. If we take the wild route, we won't reach the capital for weeks, and we need to get there as soon as we can."

Calunoth started at the mention of his name. He had been trying to pay attention to the conversation to avoid appearing rude, but the complex talk of politics and alliances went largely over his head. The younger members of the group were all somewhat apathetic about the politics of the nation. Calunoth was preoccupied with finding Lenocius and taking his revenge, and thoughts of this nature had distracted him from the conversation for the most part. Hearing Valthor mention his name, he refocused on the conversation. "So we'll head to Commerel, then to Deirive? When do we go searching for Lenocius?" Calunoth asked.

"If it comes to war, I don't know. We have to keep watch for Alistair now as well. We still don't know for certain if he survived the massacre or if PRIMAL is just using his name. I won't lie and guarantee you'll be able to hunt and kill them yourself, but I will do all in my power to ensure you have that opportunity," Valthor replied. "Our first priority should be getting you to the king, and he can decide what to do from there."

"I'll do whatever it takes to get to Lenocius. You know that." Calunoth's eyes blazed with the dark fire within that threatened to engulf his soul. Anger at the prospect that he may not be able to actively pursue the minister nearly boiled over.

"Greshaun could lock you in a room in the capital. He could also send you to the front lines. I don't know. But you're now a piece in a much bigger puzzle. The country comes first, and you need to remember that." Valthor scolded the young guard.

His cheeks burning, Calunoth muttered an apology, and the conversation moved on to other aspects of war, from supply line discussions to territorially advantageous battlegrounds. The talk was spirited between Bleiz, Valthor, and Berwyn, but the youngest three grew drowsy from the cinnamon wine and roasted meats. After sufficient time had passed to avoid offending their host, the three made their excuses and retired. While the young companions rested and prepared for the next day, the elder men stayed up conversing well into the night and did not retire until the sun had long since disappeared below the horizon.

***

The group left early the next morning. Rising early as usual, Valthor had banged on their doors in the dawning hour, jolting them from their slumber. He always seemed to be in a hurry to go places. The younger members of the group had taken no issue with this, having spent much of the night resting. Even Calunoth had managed to achieve more sleep than usual, though it remained a tormented sleep that was starting to eat at his senses. Bleiz had not been as easy to budge. Now that he was no longer sleeping in the wilds, he was much less alert to his surroundings and had grumbled a great deal as he had fallen out of bed. This grumbling had continued throughout much of breakfast, during which Valthor had outlined their plans. Now that he'd had time to digest what he had learned in the caverns and his conversations with Berwyn, he was clearly in a hyperactive state as he moved to plan their next move.

The group planned to travel on the main road from Caern Vaughn to Commerel, in the heart of Renderive. Valthor wished to meet with the Viscount of Commerel. From there, they would journey east to Deirive, passing through the Knight's central stronghold at the Commandant's Bastion. The journey would take over two weeks on foot. Berwyn had offered them horses, but Valthor had refused without giving cause, much to Bleiz's chagrin, who had tried to protest but gotten nowhere. And so, with their supplies replenished by the good Lord Berwyn, they thanked him for his hospitality and set out from the ancient carved gates of Caern Vaugh south through the Llewyn Hills.

The journey away from Caern Vaughn was superior to the journey to it. Absent of the mud of the swamp and the threat of pursuit from PRIMAL, it was not difficult to improve on that journey, but the natural beauty of the Llewyn Hills gave the companions new life as they made their way southward. The hills were awash with the signs of spring fading into summer. Frequent rainfall provided nourishment to the lush plant life that decorated the hills, causing an explosion of fervent green to paint the ground. The rising hills sloped gently upward, granting the travelers an unparalleled view of valleys and dales filled with a cool gentle mist that slowly dissipated upward as the days wore on.

The scenery was breathtaking for the group members who had not traveled this route before. Valthor had trod this road many times, as had Bleiz in one of his earlier campaigns. For all the evil circumstances that surrounded his journey, Calunoth couldn't help but feel grateful that he now had the opportunity to see the beauty of the natural world, and he could sense his companions felt the same.

Calunoth and Luca spoke freely, Luca's cavalier nature wearing away at Calunoth's brooding demeanor. Emboldened by the natural beauty of their surroundings, Calunoth grew less somber as they walked, though his increasingly dwindling sleep was starting to wear on his mind, and he had to shake his head often to clear the fog from his vision.

Valthor walked silently at the head of the group, appearing completely preoccupied with his own thoughts. Lauren, too, was strangely silent, and with his other companions engaged, Bleiz fell back to speak with the young woman.

"Beautiful scenery here, isn't it?" Bleiz remarked. "The Llewyn Hills are more breathtaking than Shellthrone Lake or the Faargaard Oasis in my mind. Granted, I've only seen the latter in paintings." Lauren only nodded silently. After many years as a captain and leader of men, Bleiz had developed a keen sense for detecting disquiet in his ranks. Usually, it was the result of cowardice, nervousness, or trepidation, but sometimes there were deeper issues to address. And issues with one soldier must be dealt with before they spread to other soldiers. Pressing her on her silence, Bleiz asked, "What's wrong? You've been unusually quiet since we left Caern Vaughn. Are you worried about something? We're more than capable of defending you against any threat that may come our way."

Lauren turned her head to look at the grizzled elder captain, her bright green eyes studying him. He had tidied up his graying beard and mustache while at Caern Vaughn and had rested well enough to fill his clear gray eyes with wisdom and patience. Looking into those eyes and taking in his rugged, earnest face, she felt reassured. She felt like Luca and Calunoth lacked the maturity to fully understand, and Valthor clearly had no respect for her, but in Bleiz, she thought she might find a kindred soul.

"It's nothing. I was just thinking about Duke Byrant and what he stands for," she replied.

"Ah, of course," Bleiz nodded. "You're a Highlander, so if it comes to war, you're concerned about your people's welfare if they side with him."

"Not quite," Lauren said. "It's just that I've read a great deal about Duke Byrant and his ideals. He's very popular at Akadaemia, and I can't help but wonder if he has a point. He wants to help people less fortunate at the expense of the more fortunate. What's wrong with that? Surely the wealthy should feel compelled to help the poor? And if the local nobility or governors help that to happen, then why should the king oppose it? It's easy for him to say to them that they can work for themselves and earn their way when he's sitting on a gilded throne. I guess I just, well, I understand why people would follow him."

Bleiz, forever the negotiator, answered the young woman with a carefully constructed reply. "Well, yes, but there's a reason the world works the way it does. Could it be better? Absolutely. Could be worse? Yes, much worse. And if the world works right now, do you want to risk that world for only a chance of a better one? What if it ends up worse? It's taken thousands of years for us to get here. Are Byrant's ideals the next step? Maybe. But maybe not. And the consequences of being wrong in this case are far worse than the benefits of being right. The king has an obligation to protect his people from both external and internal forces. After centuries of his family's rule, we have security, strength, and for many, prosperity. Even the poor among us can easily put food on the table. It wasn't that many years ago that even a noble family could go hungry."

Lauren chose not to listen to the captain's response intently, instead immediately replying, "But why should anybody go hungry while the noblemen feast? How much of the food that is thrown out of Lord Berwyn's kitchen could go to someone who needs it? There is such disparity between those in the city and those in the villages. I don't see how any idea that fixes that can be so bad. Every victory comes at a cost after all."

"And the victories that we have attained so far came at a very high cost. They should not be discounted so easily. And with the threat of civil war looming, the cost of Byrant's victory would be much too high," Bleiz responded, suddenly aware of the age difference between him and the young woman. He had seen far too much bloodshed in his life to risk more for an uncertain reward. This idea was lost on Lauren, who pursed her lips and turned away.

Bleiz sighed and decided not to pursue the matter further. The young researcher was incredibly smart and passionate, and he was sure that this was a fight he could not win with words. He was no scholar; he was merely a soldier. And although he felt that experience would diminish the young woman's misguided passions eventually, he could offer nothing but his own experience to the discussion. So, he instead relied upon retelling his favorite story, where in his younger days he had misplaced his commanders' helmet in an ill-advised sojourn at the local tavern, which brought tears of mirth streaming down the young woman's face.

With Lauren now pulled out of her reverie by the skilled Bleiz, the journey proceeded more smoothly, and within a week, the group emerged from the Llewyn Hills and descended onto the Central Steppe. The sprawling city of Commerel lay now less than two days away, and they would likely not spend more than one more night in the wilds. This was a source of some disappointment to Lauren, as while camping in the wilderness, she and Calunoth had made significant progress in her training. She had mastered the theory of footwork and parrying and had made strong inroads into the practical application of that theory. On one night, Bleiz had even taken her aside and gone through, in exquisitely painful detail, how to properly maintain her sword and equipment. The short sword she had been given at the Caern Vaughn armory was composed primarily of aluminum and was far lighter than the steel weapons carried by her companions. While that made it light enough for her to wield, it also made it much less durable, which was a point beaten into her head by a fastidious Bleiz.

After another two days of traveling with the looming sight of Commerel's walls coming steadily closer, the group finally reached the outer regions. The group had felt entirely safe on this journey, and the tendrils of war had not yet pervaded the minds of other travelers that they had passed on the road. However, as they neared the gates of Commerel, the merchants and travelers leaving the city appeared to be increasingly furtive. This was not lost on Valthor, and he stealthily accosted one such individual three miles out of the city. He spoke with the man in a quiet undertone and slipped him a coin as a gesture of his appreciation before sending him on his way.

"There's something amiss in the city," the Guardian reported. "According to that man, many of the guards have grown harsh and appear to be searching for someone. My guess is either me or Calunoth based on the reports I heard."

"Did PRIMAL take over Commerel too then?" Bleiz demanded.

"Glathaous was much smaller than Commerel, and they were taken unawares. Also, Commerel is the center of the nation. I can't imagine Commerel falling that easily, and if there had been a fight, we would have long since heard of it. No, something else is going on, but we'll have to get inside to find out," Valthor replied.

"We could go around," Luca suggested. "We have enough supplies to make it to the Bastion, even if we don't go into Commerel."

"No, I must speak with the viscount," Valthor replied. "We must go in, but we should exercise caution. Calunoth, keep your hood up. Lauren, take Ddedfryd. It probably stands out the most. Just hold it like a walking stick." He removed the sheathed, bladed staff from his back and handed it to her. "Bleiz, you do the talking. If the guards ask us for our names, make something up." He dropped his own hood over his head and fell behind to walk with Lauren.

The gates of Commerel were among the most impressive in the country. Barring a traveler's way in tandem with the thirty-foot walls that guarded the prosperous trade city, they were replicated in a foursome along each wall of the city. Guarded religiously by toll collectors and inspectors with the help of the city guards, no goods traveled in or out of Commerel without proper inspection and payment.

Bleiz led the way, striding confidently toward the guards—whose steel plate-mail was peppered with dust that obscured the balanced scales that were Commerel's insignia—standing watch under the arches of the thirty-foot gate. They appeared to be close to the end of their shift, and they were annoyed people were still entering the city.

"Halt! What goods do you and your companions bring to Commerel, Sir Knight?" The guard was heavily mustached but had a coarse voice that spoke to the length of the day and his apparent weariness.

"No goods for trading, sir. We are merely passing through and wish to rest the evening in your fine city," Bleiz responded smartly, his authority ringing in his deep voice.

"Where do you hail from, Sir Knight? We usually receive reports of Knights passing through the city. And you appear to be accompanied by members not of the knighthood. This typically requires registration with Commerel authorities. I must insist you leave your names and intended place of residence for the evening." The guard's bushy mustache quivered as he spoke. Behind the guard, Calunoth saw a small group of the guard's colleagues conferencing in hushed whispers, casting curious glances at his group. It was an unusual group to be traveling together to be sure, but surely not one that would require further investigation.

Bleiz leaned in close to the guard to whisper in his ear. "My friend, we travel in secrecy under the authority of the field marshal with some important representatives from Sihleo." He gestured at his hooded companions before pressing some coins from his purse into the guard's hands. "Suitable compensation is in order for individuals who assist with the safe and secret delivery of said representatives. I trust we have an understanding?" He finished with a confident smile that years of command afforded him.

The guard weighed the coins discreetly in his hands before nodding. "Aye, the roads be dangerous these days. I daresay a couple quiet individuals won't do any harm." The guard then moved out of their way and beckoned for Bleiz to lead his companions unimpeded into the city.

Calunoth marveled at the captain's negotiating skills as he followed him through the gates. The group appeared to pass through the gates without incident when Valthor suddenly seized and fell on one knee to the ground, clutching his chest. It was startling enough to draw the attention of the surrounding guards, but Luca, acting quickly, hoisted the Guardian to his feet even as he pushed through his fit and waved off the encroaching guards. Once they were clear of the gates, Valthor pulled Luca with him into the first side alley so he could drink his potions and rest for a few minutes as he recovered from his fit. Once he had regained his strength, he wiped his mouth clean of the foul-smelling concoction, and they headed into the city to find suitable lodgings for the evening.

Chapter 12

The Inn of the Flying Raptor

 The city of Commerel was one of the youngest cities in Renderive. Originally a small hunting village in the plains, its ideal location as a crossroads between the capital and the north resulted in a large influx of travel through the small village. Inns and taverns had sprung up to accommodate travelers, followed soon after by merchant shops and a local militia. The commercialization of the city brought great wealth to its inhabitants, and soon thousands of people had begun to flock to the city to find their fortune. The city had developed to accommodate the flow of goods and money, and as a result, was now the wealthiest city in Renderive and served as a financial capital for the nation.

 There had, at one point, been an attempt to designate Commerel as the capital of the entire country, removing the designation from Deirive, but these attempts had been thwarted by the relative vulnerability of Commerel compared to Deirive. Although Commerel was well defended with its own militia, imposing walls, and the best defensive technology money could buy, it was still an easier target than the ancient capital, which had the natural defenses of the sea and mountains and the impregnable fortress of the Commandant's Bastion to defend it.

 So, Commerel had been relegated away from royal responsibilities and instead took on the heart of the Renderivean economy as its charge. The central market crossed several streets and proved a repository for goods from across the continent. Commerel Castle lay to the north of the market, surrounded by the residential regions that housed the upper classes and the wealthy merchants of the city. The castle itself rivaled the Royal Palace in Deirive, with three towering peaks of smooth stone carved painstakingly into the sky. The castle was the abode of Viscount Latoya, who had ruled over Commerel for the last thirty years. A popular ruler, she had reduced the rate of tolls and taxes in the city and allowed business to flow unimpeded by excessive governance. As money flowed into the city, she received a small portion in the taxes that accumulated and allowed the expansion of the city, such that there were now settlements blossoming outside the eastern wall of the city. The result of her governorship was a city that flowed with food, wine, commerce, and laughter.

However, it seemed to Calunoth that the times were not so kind to Commerel as they had previously been. Most people walked with their heads down, keen to avoid attention. The market stalls were as busy as always, but the merchants who cried out to their potential customers appeared to do so with less fervor than one might expect. The air seemed taut and tense, with many people continuously looking over their shoulders and huddling together and talking in hushed whispers.

"Let's go," Valthor said with a grimace, still clearly in some discomfort. "I know of an inn where we can stay the night. The tavern keeper is well known by travelers. I think it's as good a place as any to rest." He guided them through the sprawling maze of Commerel's cobblestone streets. The streets were clean and well maintained on the main roads, but many side roads and alleyways were in far worse condition. The city seemed hopelessly confusing to navigate to Calunoth, who had never before stepped into a city of this size, and he walked close to Bleiz, concerned that if he were separated from the group, he would not be able to find them again.

Valthor himself seemed lost on occasion, having to pause to examine the street signs, once even stopping a passerby to ask for directions. Fortunately, he had been here often enough to be able to navigate the complex mess of streets without insurmountable difficulty, and they shortly found themselves standing outside a large and loud inn several streets removed from the central market. The inn was several stories high and was emblazoned with a large sign above the door that read, "The Inn of the Flying Raptor."

Valthor opened the door for his companions, ushering them in quickly. The sun was fading, and although the cool spring air was beginning to give way to the warm summer glow in the twilight, the streets carried an atmosphere of uncertainty that begged none to take their time retreating inside. The inn itself was busy, but not so busy that it was crowded. The tables were recently adorned with workers, businesspeople, and their clients who were now beginning to retire back to their homes to prepare for the next day's work. The room itself was well lit, with lanterns brightening every table and hanging from every wall. The place appeared well worn but in good condition otherwise.

Calunoth's observations were interrupted by the explosive entry of the jovial innkeeper. Jumping out from behind the bar, he approached them with a great smile that seemed to light up the room more than any of the lanterns that adorned the walls.

"Good evening, friends! I don't believe I've seen ya around these parts before. The name's Dahaffy. I'm the proud owner of this establishment. How can I help ya today?" Dahaffy cheerfully asked, the toil of the evening thus far evidenced by a glistening brow below short, coal-dark hair.

Valthor, who had been the last to enter the inn, pushed his way to the front, speaking on behalf of the group who seemed slightly put off by the man's jovial exposition.

"Dahaffy, it's me," Valthor said in an undertone. "But I'm hear on quiet business. I don't want anyone knowing we're here, all right?"

"Mum's the word, Mr. Kernle!" Dahaffy said winking with a smile, taking the instruction in stride. "What do you and your friends need in Commerel?"

"For now, just food and rest," Valthor answered, "Do you have any rooms left? Preferably ones close together."

"Indeed I do my friend! Just follow me!" Reaching behind the bar, Dahaffy pulled out a set of keys and guided them up a staircase on the near side of the inn only a few feet away from the door. The wooden staircase creaked as they moved, but their footsteps were muffled by a long rug that ran the length of the stairs. Dahaffy brought them up several flights and came to a stop on the top floor. He opened a door on the fourth landing and beckoned them inside. The group filed in slowly, with Dahaffy following them in.

"Make yourselves at home!" he exclaimed. "This room and the one across the hall are yours. I'll have some food sent up for you. Will you need anything else while you're in town, Mr. Kernle?"

"Maybe information, Dahaffy, but for now, I think we'd best rest. Thank you," Valthor replied, seeming to be more at ease now that they were off the street.

"Sounds good to me. I'll send some food up for you. See ya tomorrow!" Dahaffy replied, and in a flash, he disappeared back down the stairs.

"What an unusual fellow," Bleiz remarked, surveying the large, well-appointed room.

"He seemed very ... cheerful." Lauren noted, adding to Bleiz's thought as she sat at a small wooden table near a crackling fireplace. The room was of the same sturdy brick construction as most of

Commerel, and the fire warmed the stones and kept the chill breeze of the night at bay. Aside from the table, three comfortable beds garnished each wall save for the wall taken up by the fireplace, creating a space that was crowded but not cramped for the companions to converse.

"He takes some getting used to, but once you do, you'll find no finer man this side of the Sieth," Valthor replied. "I usually stay at this inn when I come to Commerel, when I'm not stuck in the castle that is. I know he's trustworthy, which I think is what we'll need based on what we've seen so far."

"What's our plan of action, sire? Should we head to the castle now?" Bleiz asked.

Valthor took several minutes to think before answering. "No. Not today. And maybe not tomorrow either. Something's not right here, but we need to find out what. It's possible PRIMAL has gotten to the viscount, in which case, going to the castle would mean walking into the enemy camp."

"In that case, we'd best rest. We could be in for some trouble here, and we'll handle it better if we've slept. We can make a plan tomorrow," Bleiz decided.

Everyone agreed. They had been traveling for almost two weeks, and opportunities to sleep well outdoors were few and far between. Combined with the relentless pace that Valthor had driven them at, they all wished for sleep. Calunoth and Valthor elected to take the opposite room, leaving the Knights and Lauren to their rest.

Calunoth went expediently to his rest while Valthor was too restless for sleep and instead spent the entire evening with his eyes on the door. It was fortuitous to their companions that the pair had chosen the other room to themselves as, although fatigued, neither rested. Calunoth attempted to drift off into the sweet release of sleep, but he was constantly pulled back to the world of the waking by shadowy figures with green eyes and mocking laughter that tormented his mind. He shifted and grimaced as he drifted in and out of consciousness, drawing Valthor's attention but not his interest. This was not a battle the Guardian could fight for the young guard. So, Calunoth was left to relive his nightmares as he fell from the Glathaous gates again and again until at last he forsook sleep and lay in his cot, counting the seconds until he took his turn at the watch.

***

The companions regrouped the next morning in the room that Bleiz, Lauren, and Luca had shared. Valthor himself had hardly slept, only being relieved by Calunoth from his watch in the early hours of the morning so the Guardian could sleep for a couple hours. He was on edge but did not seem to be adversely affected by his lack of sleep. Citing the magical enhancements of his body, he reminded them he could usually get by on one or two hours of sleep a night.

With everyone in attendance, Valthor laid out his plan for the day. "We should ask around and see why some of the guards are acting strangely. We also need to find out if Viscount Latoya has been seen recently." Valthor's serious tone was a marked departure from his usual casual disposition. The Guardian's brow was furrowed, and his narrowed eyes darted around the room. Regardless, his voice still carried the factual confidence that made his presence so reassuring to his companions. The Guardian seemed stressed, but was hiding it well. "Commerel is a big city, so we'll need to split up to gather what information we can. Is anyone familiar with Commerel?" Bleiz and Lauren raised their hands. "Good, then you can travel in pairs, and I'll go alone. Bleiz, you and Cal go together. Lauren and Luca together," Valthor said, pointing at each team in turn. "Bleiz go to the shopping district. It's just to the east of the central market. Luca, you and Lauren go to the market. It's big enough that you two shouldn't overlap, but you'll still be close enough to help each other if need be." Here he paused and looked each person in the eye. "If anything goes wrong and you have to flee the city, there's a landmark called the Lonely Tree about fifteen miles southwest of here. If you don't return to the inn before night falls, I'll assume you've fled there, and I'll come and get you. Any questions?"

"Do we really need a plan to flee the city?" Luca asked, eyebrows raised. "I don't see how simple information gathering could go so wrong that we'd need a plan like that."

"Experience, lad," Bleiz explained to his charge. "Hope for the best, plan for the worst. You'd be amazed at how quickly missions can go wrong. In fact," he said with a low chuckle, "did you forget how far from our original mission we are right now?"

"We're still on track, roughly," Luca protested with a sheepish smile before acceding to the wisdom of his superiors.

The group did not dissent further, and they left with the rising of the morning sun to search the streets for information.

Calunoth and Bleiz found themselves in the shopping district within the hour. The shopping district differed from the market in that the wealthiest merchants congregated in the shopping district. While the marketplace was chock full of vendors selling their wares from sturdy wooden stalls, many of the more successful merchants had accrued enough wealth to establish true shops and could simultaneously enjoy a roof over their heads and a steady stream of wealthy clientele. As a result, the shopping district was among the wealthiest areas in the city and was home to many stores selling goods ranging from cooking utensils and pastries to ornate vases and weapons.

Calunoth had been impressed by the smorgasbord of goods available in Crideir, but the markets of Commerel were a different story entirely. It seemed that all of the goods and gold of the world flowed through the streets of this city. The people of Commerel walked the streets finely dressed in silken garments and plumed hats that became the comely nature of the entrepreneurs. Calunoth felt distinctly out of place. Although the armor he had received in Caern Vaugh was finely wrought, he felt like he did not belong among these people. Passing an apparel store, his eyes were drawn to a long coat that seemed to be made entirely of smooth leather patterned after snakeskin. It would have fit him well, but the price of the garment was exorbitant, more than any guard would have received in a year, so he turned his gaze away.

Bleiz was less self-conscious. Dressed in his distinctive Holy Knights armor, he stood out as much as Calunoth, but because the Knights were highly respected in Commerel, he did not receive the same looks of disdain Calunoth felt directed his way. Additionally, the way he held his back straight and his shoulders square seemed to invite respect while Calunoth walked slightly slouched besides him, making him look shorter despite the two being about the same height.

"You said that you know your way around Commerel, Bleiz?" Calunoth asked. "How is that? Have you lived here before?"

"No, nothing like that," Bleiz replied. "I was born in Caern Porth and moved to Deirive after being initiated into the Knights. I've never lived anywhere else. But I have had to travel through Commerel on many occasions, usually when traveling to Caern Porth. I don't know every street, but I know enough to find my way around. What of yourself? Did you ever see the world outside the castle?"

"No," Calunoth said, shaking his head. "I never really had the chance to leave the castle. I could see the town, but not much beyond that. The forests stretched out around the castle for miles. It might have been boring at times, but it was what I had." Changing the subject, he motioned to the people milling around them. "I see the people here like the Knights. Is that why you became one?"

Bleiz let out a short laugh. "Did I become a Knight so people would like me? Well, as a young lad, I had hoped that more young ladies would find me more attractive, but that wasn't the main reason. No, my father was a Knight who perished in the Third Schism War. Following in his footsteps and protecting my home just seemed like the right thing to do."

"I'm sorry, I didn't intend to bring up bad memories," Calunoth apologized, but Bleiz waved his apology away.

"Think nothing of it. Time heals all wounds. It was a raw loss at the time. I was only five, but it was a long time ago. I hope you'll be able to find a similar peace," the captain said, his voice growing somber. "I won't say I understand what you went through because I can't, but I can tell you were affected by what happened. You've recovered more quickly than what I might have expected on the surface, but you still have demons haunting you, don't you?"

Calunoth swallowed. "I'll kill Lenocius. Alistair too, if he still lives. And then we'll see what the demons do. But let's speak of other matters. Where should we start looking?"

Bleiz let the young man divert the conversation. Every man dealt with grief differently, and Calunoth's was more offensive than most. Instead, the captain addressed his question. "We should talk to some of the wealthy merchants, suppliers to the castle in particular. If there is something going on behind the scenes, they'll know. They'll have connections all over the city, so that should significantly reduce the required legwork."

The pair then toured the streets of the shopping district, frequenting every shop along the way. The shopkeepers were friendly and genial, but none were forthcoming with information. Most just elected to smile and ignore their questions. The pair spent most of the day going from shop to shop being constantly frustrated by cheerful smiles that told them nothing. They were beginning to grow desperate until they happened upon a small grocer.

The shop itself was deserted but for an elderly woman transferring carrots from a box into a stand. Approaching who must have been the shopkeeper with the weary frustration of a man whose patience was wearing dangerously thin, Bleiz greeted the old woman.

"Excuse me, good madam. How are you this day?" he asked politely.

"Terrible!" replied the elderly woman bluntly. "Hardly a customer all day and barely a word from the castle in weeks. I'll die before I retire, but by Sentential, Sir Knight, I've had happier days."

Calunoth was amused by the brusque tone the woman took. She had clearly been running this shop for decades and was long past the point of caring about perceptions. Bleiz too appreciated the candor and continued with his line of questioning.

"What news of the castle? I've been speaking to your fellow shopkeepers all day, and no one is willing to tell me anything," Bleiz said.

"I'll tell you news of the castle, I will!" The elderly lady began to rant. "Fifteen years I was the sole supplier of food to the castle I was. Then three weeks ago, some obnoxious guard comes in and tells me to lower my prices or they won't buy from me. Fifteen years! All this malarkey happened as soon as Latoya fell ill. If she doesn't recover, the whole city will fall apart!"

"Forgive me, but what's this about Viscount Latoya being ill? I've not heard anything about that in the city," Bleiz interrupted.

"Those guards came down and told us not to worry about it. She hasn't been seen in weeks, but none of the shopkeepers are asking questions. The guards came and told us we should just continue on, business as usual, while some Reil character takes charge while the viscount's indisposed. Also said if we told anyone, they couldn't guarantee the security of our shops." The old woman shook her head. "I remember when the guards of this city used to stand for something. When they used to be decent."

Calunoth and Bleiz were startled by the woman's revelations. Calunoth followed up on Bleiz's questioning and asked, "Will you be safe telling us this?"

The old woman snorted. "What are they going to do? Burn my shop down? I've been serving the people of Commerel and the castle for nigh on four decades. They wouldn't dare touch me. And if they do, oh well. I haven't got many years left in me anyway."

Calunoth couldn't help but be impressed by the strength of the elderly woman. Bleiz thanked her for her words and nudged Calunoth to buy some of the apples on display by the door. They were expensive but delicious, and the elderly woman clearly appreciated their business. The pair continued to check in the remaining shops, but could find nothing further, so they decided to return to the inn.

***

Many streets away, Luca and Lauren were being knocked around the market, quite literally. The Commerel Plaza Market was renowned around the world as a hub for budding merchants and peddlers. Hundreds of people seemed to be thronged around the plaza conversing with each other, haggling with the merchants, and being bewitched by peddlers who shouted promises of miracle cures. The market was so busy that Lauren ended up having to hold on to Luca's muscular arm as the pair waded their way through the cacophony of noise and people.

"At least if we have to run, we can lose them in here!" Luca shouted to Lauren, who had to lean close to his face to hear him. Lauren nodded, but frustrated with the noise, began to pull the big man out of the plaza and onto one of the side streets. Although the central plaza contained many of the stalls, the market didn't end there. Rather, it stretched out in an ever-expanding circle into the surrounding streets. Those streets, unlike the central area, were much less crowded, and for the pair's purposes, would be better to canvas. Finally stopping in front of a merchant selling shoes, they took the opportunity to catch their breath.

"Why on earth would anyone ever go into that mess willingly?" Luca demanded, breathing more heavily than a Knight should have been.

Lauren answered as she dodged out of the way of a bulky mercenary. "Lots of people are looking for the best deal they can find, and when money's involved, people get crazy."

"I can't imagine something like this back home," Luca said shaking his head.

"Where is home for you?" Lauren asked, "I heard your last name was Draca, but I'm assuming you're not related to Conan Draca."

"Actually, he's my father. I'm his fourth son," Luca replied casually, his eye catching a helm with a large peacock feather sprouting from the top on display.

"Wait, so you're a noble?!" Lauren said, appearing surprised. "But how? You're so *un*-noble!" Seeing Luca's hurt expression, she hastily clarified. "I mean, you're kind and giving and don't seem obsessed with collecting money from people."

"What kind of nobles have you been meeting?" Luca asked. "Some are bad apples, yeah, but Greshaun's honor system keeps most of them honest enough."

Lauren flushed. "Well, I haven't actually met any nobles. I've just read about them. I read that Greshaun's honor system just lets the king control the court completely, monopolizing his power."

Luca stared at her blankly for a moment. "Monopolizing meaning …" His voice trailed off, waiting for clarification.

Lauren was caught off guard. She wasn't used to having to explain the words she used, even though many were perhaps more academic than what others may have chosen. "It means centralizing, like, he has all of the power in his court and no one else has any."

"Oh," Luca said, understanding her point now. "Well, not really. I was never a great study of politics—my brothers all did that—but the way it was explained to me is that any Renderivean noble acting in a manner neglectful or abusive of their people can be removed at the king's discretion. But he can also be overruled by a unanimous vote of the Renderivean Council. That's never happened before though. Greshaun knows what he's doing. He once removed the Lord of Coleir for repeatedly jailing dissenters without trial. It's a hard system to abuse though, given that the king can't elect the council."

"I see," Lauren said. "I didn't know the council could do that. Well, I guess I'm just surprised you're a noble."

"I'm just a Knight," Luca said, looking around. "I don't want to be a noble. Come on. Let's ask around to see if anyone knows anything."

The pair began separately questioning a series of vendors, many of whom were forthcoming. After confirming their information with several other merchants, Lauren and Luca stepped into the shade of an alleyway to discuss their findings.

"All the whisperings I've heard point to the same thing. There are forces amassing in the south, in the region around Byrantia. And lots of supplies are going that way, with just as much money coming the other way. I had one merchant tell me he's never seen such a demand for bolts in his lifetime," Luca reported.

Lauren nodded and said, "I've been hearing the same thing, but none of these merchants seem to know anything about Commerel itself. Most of them traveled from other places and are only here for a short while."

The pair continued to comb the market and its customers, but between the noise, the crowds, and the transient nature of their surroundings, they were unable to derive any more knowledge from the market, and as twilight began to encroach, they cut their losses and returned to the inn.

***

The companions reconvened at the Inn of the Flying Raptor late in the afternoon. Luca and Lauren arrived first and seated themselves in a corner of the tavern. They were joined by Bleiz and Calunoth less than an hour later but were forced to wait well into the evening before Valthor finally emerged in the doorway of the inn, hooded and cloaked.

"Sire, you had us worried for a while there. We were about to leave the city to meet you," Bleiz remarked as Valthor plopped himself down on the table bench. Motioning to one of the serving girls, he ordered a drink of strong liquor, never letting his hood fall from his face. When the drink arrived, he downed it in one shot and ordered a second.

"Rough day, Valthor?" Luca questioned jokingly, to which Valthor glowered at him before responding.

"I don't know what good news you've heard to put you in a joking mood, but it's sure as hell gotta be better than what I've found out." The Guardian spoke quietly.

"We didn't hear anything about Commerel," Lauren said for Luca. "But we did hear forces are amassing in the south, with lots of supplies headed that way. It seems like Byrant is getting serious with his preparations."

Valthor nodded before turning his gaze to Bleiz, who answered the gaze with a report. "We've discovered that the Viscount of Commerel is ill and has been for several weeks. She hasn't been seen for over a month. They're trying to keep that quiet though. We could only get one person to talk to us about it," Bleiz said.

"Well, we know for sure now that Byrant's ready for a war," Valthor began. "The motive we had already, but if he's bringing supplies and men at a noticeable rate, he must be close to ready."

Calunoth nodded in agreement. "Those men we fought on the road to Caern Porth were traveling in secret. If Byrant's not hiding his men's movement anymore, he must be confident that he's past diplomacy—or secrecy."

"Oh, the bastard's well past diplomacy," Valthor replied. "He's skipped chivalry and gone straight to subterfuge. What you've learned about the viscount fits with my findings as well. I went to the lower districts where most of the servants live, and they were terrified out of their minds. I had to reveal my identity to get one to trust me. Willful woman, she was."

"What did you learn, sire?" Bleiz asked the Guardian.

"I've learned that we're in real trouble," Valthor replied. "You've heard reports of the guards acting strangely? Byrant got into the head of some bureaucrat named Reil. This Reil has taken over the guards and seized control of the castle. From what I can tell, they were assisted by some of Byrant's men and a few others, although the details weren't great. All of the servants have been threatened with death for them and their families if they tell anyone of this matter. But the word is out among the poorer folk, and it's spread up to some of the wealthy as well. That's why everyone here is so on edge."

"Sentential's light!" Bleiz cursed under his breath. "Then does the viscount still live, or is the city completely under Reil's control?"

"I would imagine she still lives," Valthor mused. "She is exceptionally capable. Commerel is not an easy city to run. She's likely managing the economic upkeep of the city from behind bars. Without her knowledge, Reil would crash this place within months. As it stands, it seems like he's making a mess of it even with her help."

"So what do we do? Should we try to rescue her?" Luca asked.

"What we do," Valthor said, "is leave Commerel at dawn and go to the Bastion. I'll bring back a squadron of Knights to arrest Reil and hope that Byrant hasn't launched his attack yet. If Commerel belongs to Byrant, this war will not go well for us. If just the five of us try something, we'll get cut to pieces trying to get inside the castle."

"And what of the rest of us then?" Bleiz asked, stroking his beard. "I will happily help you in this endeavor, if it is your command."

Valthor shook his head. "No, there are plenty of Knights who can help me with this job. It will require my direct intervention unless another Guardian is at the Bastion right now. And given the amount of treachery abounding right now, you're the only one I can trust to get Cal to the king. I'll write a letter for you to give to the king later. It should hel—"

Valthor' instructions were interrupted by a crash as the front door suddenly slammed open, and a battalion of guards filed into the inn. The men moved quickly to identify the patrons, and in short order, they were upon the companions.

"Here! He's here!" one of the guards called, pointing at Valthor. Swearing, Valthor rose to his feet and pulled his double-bladed staff from his back. Luca, Calunoth, and Bleiz jumped up, also drawing their weapons.

"Valthor Tarragon!" A guard captain stepped out from the crowd, reading from a writ. "You are under arrest on charges of sedition, trespass, and use of a fake identity in violation of the laws of Commerel and Lord Steward Reil. Come with us, and we will ensure no harm comes to you."

"Grr, they must have recognized me at the gate," Valthor growled. Then he raised his voice and threw all his authority into it. "As a Guardian of Renderive, I have authority over all of you! Desist and drop your weapons, or I cannot be held accountable for what may happen to you!"

Calunoth thought this was an optimistic attempt at negotiation considering the number of guards who had piled into the tavern outnumbered them at least three to one.

"We have orders to arrest you regardless of your status, and Lord Steward Reil has authorized us, in the name of Viscount Latoya, to bring you in. Drop your weapon!" the captain of the guard barked back at him. Calunoth realized that the man had a hint of fear in his voice. In fact, all the guards, despite their overwhelming advantage, looked terribly nervous facing down the Guardian.

Valthor was not phased. "Last chance to leave with your lives," he said calmly.

"So be it. Arrest him!" the captain barked. The guards surged forward, weapons drawn.

Calunoth and Luca found themselves back-to-back against the four that had snuck up behind them. Bleiz had his hands full protecting Lauren, who had stayed seated seemingly petrified by the occurrence, from three men who had edged forward beside him. At first glance, Valthor seemed impossibly overwhelmed with at least ten men including the captain charging at him.

They didn't stand a chance.

Valthor became a blur of speed and sound as he crashed headlong into the oncoming crowd, using his dual-bladed weapon for both attack and defense. In moments, he had slain three men with his blade and sent another crashing to floor, magical fire searing through his clothes.

Calunoth did not have time to observe more as he had his own soldiers to fight. He and Luca had not been fighting together long, but they had already created a bond that allowed them to flow well together as they ducked and wove through the men. They fought as one unit against four individuals, rather than two individuals on four. Fortunately for them, the guards they were fighting were inexperienced and clumsy, one even managing to cut his ally with a misplaced spear thrust. As it was, Luca and Calunoth easily dispatched the men. Bleiz had felled one but was pinned against the table while Lauren held her sword helplessly in her hand. In a brave move, Bleiz lunged forward, aiming to split the two men and break through the semicircle they had trapped him in. But as he lunged forward, he slipped on a spirit that had spilled on the floor, and his strike went wild, chopping off the hand of one of the men rather than his head and causing Bleiz to land heavily on the floor, his uninjured opponent poised to deliver the fatal blow.

But the blow never came. Instead, Lauren's hardened aluminum sword protruded through a hole in the man's armor, causing his weapon to fall from lifeless hands and the man's body to follow soon afterward. Pulling her sword back, the young researcher fell back onto her chair, tears emerging in her wild eyes.

Valthor, meanwhile, had made quick work of his opponents, his blows landing swiftly and harshly. He parried and attacked in the same motion and moved with such a practiced grace that the guards attacking him seemed unable to keep up. With ten bodies dotted around him, Valthor turned deftly and finished off Bleiz's injured opponent, who had sunk to his knees clutching his stump of a hand.

Valthor collapsed to one knee, panting heavily. Taking on ten opponents in a confined space was a challenge even for a Guardian.

Looking around at the disturbing image of the bodies strewn all around the tavern, Valthor cursed. He needed time to think. But it wasn't incoming. What was incoming was the heavy footfall of guards on the cobblestone streets outside. There would be dozens more guards here soon. And they didn't have the strength to fight off dozens of men at once.

Fortunately, he didn't have to think because he was grabbed roughly by the arm and dragged to the back of the tavern by the innkeeper, Dahaffy.

"Go! Take your friends out the back door! We'll cover for you. Save the viscount," he whispered in his cheerful, uplifting voice. Bleiz grabbed Lauren roughly by the arm and dragged her out, overcoming her shocked state. Valthor and Luca followed him out the back door, which led into a dark, covered alleyway. Calunoth turned to thank Dahaffy as he left, but the innkeeper waved him away with a cheerful smile and a, "See ya tomorrow!" before slamming the door in Calunoth's face.

"Come on," Luca said, panting. "We've got to get out of here." He went to turn and run but had to stop before almost impaling himself on a silver sliver of metal jutting out of the darkness. On the other end of the sword was a figure dressed entirely in black, a hood over his features. The shadowy figure grabbed Luca and wrapped an arm around his neck, a blade soon following.

Chapter 13

Resistance

Luca froze where he stood, holding his hands in the air. The hooded figure commanded him to drop his weapon, a request with which Luca complied. Calunoth cursed inwardly. They outnumbered and almost certainly outmatched the man, but they couldn't get close enough to act before the man could kill Luca, drawing the blade across the throat of the big man. Valthor had caught his breath and slowly moved forward with his hands up, away from his weapon. He was acutely aware of the growing noise behind him as the inn filled with soldiers. There was no time to waste with this man.

"Unhand our companion, sir," Valthor demanded softly, the politeness in his voice creating a threat volume could not match. "If you want money, we can arrange that, but we haven't got time. If you couldn't hear, half the city's guards are about thirty feet behind us. I'm sure they wouldn't mind arresting you as well. So let us conduct our business quickly."

The hooded figure cast his eyes furtively over the Guardian's shoulder, looking at the door Bleiz had barred behind them. The noise of the guards was clear and at a fever pitch through the open windows of the inn. Then, the man spied the distinctive weapon known as Ddedfryd slung across Valthor's back. A deep voice emanated from under the hood.

"Are you the Guardian Valthor?" the man asked without shifting his blade from Luca's throat.

"I am, and you should be aware of the consequences of your actions because of that," Valthor replied.

"Who do you serve? Who do you call the King of Renderive?" the hooded figure demanded, steadfast in his actions despite currently threatening one of the most dangerous men on the continent.

Valthor's eyes narrowed as he studied the figure, close to losing his patience and making a move. He couldn't reach Luca in time if he moved, nor could he risk hitting the Knight accidentally with a magical attack, but if he could use magic to destroy the lantern that lit the shadowy alleyway behind the figure, he could distract him long enough to move in.

"I serve the nation of Renderive under the command of His Majesty, King Aiden Greshaun the Second," Valthor replied, slowly bringing his right leg back, preparing to spring at the man.

But the attack proved unneeded. The figure growled, "Good enough," and removed his sword from Luca's throat. Luca staggered forward, landing on his knees but swiftly rising to face his captor. The figure sheathed the sword and spoke softly.

"Follow me. We need to get away from the guards. We have a place to hide. If they find us, there'll be hell to pay," he said. Turning, he broke into a jog down the alleyway, leaving the companions slightly baffled in his wake.

Valthor was likewise surprised, but he could now hear the guards battering on the door behind them. This shady character had not had the air of a common cutthroat, and without a thorough knowledge of the winding back alleys of Commerel, the group was as liable to walk directly into the guard station as they were to find a suitable hiding place. Motioning to his companions to follow him, the Guardian matched the jog of the hooded figure, who moved with a distinct lack of grace. Whoever he was, he was not used to sneaking around, that much was clear. The companions followed Valthor, Bleiz practically dragging Lauren behind them.

The group followed the hooded figure through a complex mess of narrow streets and curving alleyways. Many of the alleyways were dimly lit. Some weren't lit at all. The neat cobblestone only decorated the main roads while many of the back alleys were composed simply of packed dirt. They raced through the streets of Commerel, only crossing the main road twice, and once, Calunoth thought, cutting through someone's rear garden, though it was too dark to tell properly.

Finally, after they were well and truly lost, the man stopped in front of a closed paper shop close to where Calunoth thought the shopping district was. The shop itself was small and simple, unlike the shops Calunoth had visited earlier in the day. A small glass window that allowed light in but wasn't designed to catch the interest of customers, a single wooden door, and a sign labeling the place as, "Farrow's Paper and Print" was all the group could see in the darkness.

The guards now blanketed the city, disturbing the rest of every citizen and shopkeeper in their pursuit. On several occasions, the group had darted close behind a set of guards as they ducked from street to street but had thus far evaded notice. The hooded figure did not appear interested in taking liberties with their luck and looked around carefully to ensure they had not been followed before knocking on the door.

A gravelly voice floated through the door asking, "What time is it?"

"Time to hide," the hooded figure responded in his deep voice.

The exchange must have constituted some sort of password because the door swung open, and the hooded figure hustled them into the shop, stress lacing his voice. Whoever the man was, he was clearly fit as he was relatively unwinded despite having just run across half of the city. As the group filed into the shop, which lay blanketed in darkness, a voice emerged from the other side of the door.

"Galen! You've brought half an army with you!" The gravelly voice came from a stout, bearded man standing behind the door. Calunoth could only detect the vague outlines of the man from the little light that trickled in from the streetlamps.

"And I've got the other half looking for us," the hooded figure named Galen replied caustically. "Have the guards come by looking yet?"

"Not yet, but it won't be long. It sounds like they've woken up half the city at this point," the owner of the gravelly voice replied. "Get on downstairs. Best if I'm alone when they come by."

"Thanks, Farrow," Galen said, heading toward the back of the shop. He moved by instinct rather than by light, and Calunoth could hear the steady slide of a rug being moved, followed by the sound of a hatch opening. It was only then that light filtered into the shop, emitted from lanterns inside a hole in the floor. With the light providing a brief flash of the interior of the shop, Calunoth saw that the walls were lined with sheaves of paper neatly bundled together with string. The smell of ink pervaded around the shop. But that was all he was able to notice in the short time that he had, for he was yanked down into the open cellar.

He followed Bleiz down a short ladder that led them into a brightly lit basement. Galen came last, closing the cellar door and bolting it shut. Now locked in the basement and safe from the guards at least, the group could turn their attention to the potential new threat they had encountered.

The basement was larger than expected, somehow larger than the shop above. The room was unfurnished but for a single table, on which lay a jumble of documents ranging from maps to mathematical tables.

Lanterns on all four walls hungrily consumed their oil as they lit the room as though the sun was akin to them. The walls were made of solid stone, providing the foundation for the brickwork of the shop and causing the cellar to feel cramped and stuffy despite its size. Nine men were clustered around the walls, and various pieces of weaponry and armor were strewn about the floor.

All of the men, many of whom who had been sleeping, jumped to their feet when the cellar door opened, only to relax when they saw Galen, who had now removed his hood to reveal a young, albeit grim, face. He appeared to be only slightly older than Calunoth yet seemed to bear the weight of the world on his shoulders. His walnut hair was cut short and accented the bags under his eyes that belied nights of unrest.

"Galen, you found them! And I'm glad to see you return." An older man stepped forward. Addressing the group, he said warmly, "Greetings, friends. My name is Edward Thomas, Deputy Captain of the Commerel Guard. I hope you will forgive the circumstances of our meeting." The man appeared genuinely relieved to see them, and although his manner made Calunoth feel at ease, Bleiz was not as convinced.

"We were almost killed by the Commerel Guards just now," he growled. "What is the meaning of this?"

Thomas raised his hands. "I am deeply sorry for the circumstances of your encounters. The men who attacked you are no guards of Commerel. Most are traitors, supplemented with men-at-arms from the south. I can promise you that we will cause you no harm while you're here."

"Captain Thomas," Galen said, saluting. "I found Guardian Valthor outside the Inn of the Flying Raptor, as reported. Many of the enemy guards were massing outside the inn when I arrived, so I snuck around the back to find them."

"You did well, Galen," the captain acknowledged. "The guards got into the inn though?"

Galen hesitated before Valthor interjected on his behalf. "Less than two dozen in the first wave. We managed them, but we would have been in far more trouble had we stayed. I can surmise enough about what's going on based on this meeting place. I assume you're all hiding from the guards as well?"

Thomas nodded and said, "We are the surviving members of the guard who managed to escape the attack on the castle. The third in command of the guards, a swine named Jarl, aligned with the Steward Reil to betray us. He mobilized about a quarter of the Commerel Guards in rebellion and seized control of the castle from under our noses. They were helped by a group of men dressed entirely in black who have since donned Commerel Guard uniforms and even now prowl the streets above our heads."

"PRIMAL," Calunoth growled. "Probably assisted by Byrant. But why did they replace the guards? Surely it would be easier to just take over the city, particularly if they have the manpower?"

"That's just it. There weren't enough of them to seize the city entirely," Thomas replied. "And a hostile takeover would have brought the ire of the merchants, and perhaps even brought the Knights marching in from the Bastion. This operation had to be done quietly, covertly, without anyone the wiser. As it stands, the official word from the castle is that Reil has assumed control of the city while the viscount is ill. The new guards have been busy threatening the most powerful merchants with license removals and other unsavory means. As a result, they successfully managed a coup without anyone being able to publicly prove it."

Valthor carefully considered the man as he gave his report, the Guardian's piercing gaze embodying his authority. Once Thomas had finished speaking, he made his thoughts known. "It lines up with what I've discovered. It could be worse, but not by much. Am I right in assuming that the rest of the original guard are either dead or incapacitated?"

"No, that many bodies in the streets would have been too difficult to hide. Some died in the attack, but most were made to surrender and locked in the prisons beneath the castle. I would have been among those killed had Galen not roused us and helped us escape," Thomas answered, indicating the young man who had found the group at the inn.

"So, you're in as much trouble here as we are. But how did they find us? Do you know what they want with us? It takes a lot of guts to try and arrest a Guardian," Valthor asked, leaning a shoulder against the wall.

Thomas scratched his head and said, "You were spotted by one of the guards at the gate. It's widely known that you suffer from fits. I hear they were watching for you, though I don't know what they want with you in particular. From the reports we've heard, the entire force of the castle is looking for a white crystal orb your group is rumored to possess.".

"Byrant and PRIMAL must be getting awfully confident to try something like this," Luca interjected, glancing at Valthor. "First, they take Glathaous and now Commerel. It sounds like we're going to have to be even more careful with who we trust going forward."

Bleiz crossed his arms and clarified Luca's observation. "They haven't taken Commerel officially, but with Reil in charge, it basically belongs to Byrant. We need the Knights from the Bastion to march on Commerel, which Valthor can order. The army could be here within two weeks."

"There may be nothing more we can do," Valthor acknowledged. "With this move, Byrant will likely move his army to defend Commerel, and it will become the central battlefield of the first stage of the war. If he can dig in here, this war will last a long time."

"Lord Valthor, if I may?" Thomas interrupted the men. "Many of my men are still trapped in the prisons. They may not survive long enough to wait for the Knights. And they certainly won't if it escalates into a larger conflict. We have a plan, and we want you to be part of it."

Valthor bit his lip, clearly conflicted about the right course of action, but indicated Thomas should continue regardless.

"We have almost three hundred men locked in the prisons below the castle. We've spent the last three weeks trying to find a way in without walking through the gates, and we've found one. It's not pretty, but it'll work. Once in the castle, we can release the prisoners and take back the castle." He spoke quickly and clearly. This was a plan that had been long in the making.

"Why didn't you send for help from the Knights?" Bleiz interrupted. "If we had a squadron to help, that would be doable, but with just us, we'll be heading to our deaths."

"With all due respect, Sir Knight," Galen replied for his captain, "We have seen our home suddenly taken from us from people we thought we could trust and our captain killed. We have a hard time trusting anyone right now."

"But you trust us?" Bleiz replied.

"If you've got a thousand men combing the city for you, we could guess that you were on our side," Galen said. Calunoth could not fault his logic. And he felt something deeper. An angry creature reared in the pit of his stomach at the young guard's words. They too had been betrayed and lost everything. He could empathize with how the men in the brightly lit cellar were feeling. They wanted to take their revenge and destroy the people responsible for their loss. It was not something he could deny.

"Valthor, however the plan may sound, we should help them," Calunoth asserted. "I won't leave them to fight this battle alone."

Valthor looked at him curiously for a moment before relenting. "Of course, I would not leave Commerel in the hands of some treacherous leech. But we need to be logical. Nothing will be gained by us throwing our lives away. Captain Thomas, I trust the plan you gave me is a summary? Give me the details. If we can reclaim Commerel without provoking Byrant's army, then it will mean many more lives will be saved. So, let's hear it."

Captain Thomas nodded and said, "Yes, sir, we've planned every step of it. We can gain access to the castle through the sewers. We've spent the last few weeks mapping them, and we found a way in last night. We intend to go in the morning. We'll split into four groups. One will release the prisoners, one will secure the armory, one will secure the viscount, and one will find Reil. If we can secure the armory, the prisoners can be armed, and we can retake the castle from the inside."

"Do you know if the viscount lives?" Valthor interrupted. "I'm guessing she does, but something more concrete would be useful." Here he started pacing, his key tell that he was thinking.

"She lives," said a man from behind Thomas who had thus far remained silent. He was a middle-aged, grizzled man with several scars scattered across his face. "We have contacts with the servants who still serve in the castle. The viscount has been locked in her quarters and is assisting Reil with the management of the city. The place would fall apart without her, and they both know it. She should still be safe."

"Carius speaks truthfully," Thomas confirmed. "Her quarters are in the Western Tower. Realistically, we need to secure her before Reil. If it goes badly, he may try to use her as a hostage."

"Will the prisoners be in a fit state to fight? Three weeks locked in a prison tends to knock the spirit out of a man. And even if they are, will they be enough? From the numbers I'm reading, we'll still be outnumbered three to one," Bleiz asked, probing the captain and holding out the sheet of figures he had picked up to peruse.

"They may be weak but far from useless. And with the fire of fury in their blood, they will fight fearlessly against this foe," Thomas replied. "As for being outnumbered, that's true, but we have a plan. One you and your friends have unwittingly assisted with. I know that you have not been in Commerel long, but have you had any interaction with the merchants? Or the townsfolk?"

"We've spoken with both merchants and some of the locals," Calunoth reported. "With the exception of that innkeeper, Dahaffy, they were all nervous and difficult to talk to."

Remembering the cheerful innkeeper, Lauren broke from her stupor to interject. "Will Dahaffy be okay? Will he get in trouble for helping us escape?"

"Dahaffy will be fine," Valthor replied, glancing at her, irritation in his eyes. This was not something he had time to worry about right now. "The man's a national treasure to people around these parts, and even the traitor guards know it. He's served most of them before. They won't hurt him else they'll have half the city of Commerel banging down the castle gate. They're not that stupid."

"Come to think of it, the last thing he said was, 'Save the viscount!' Does he know what's going on then?" Calunoth asked Thomas, who nodded in reply.

"Most people know what's going on, even if none can say it out loud. The new guard is trying to clamp down on the rumors as much as possible, but everyone sees through them. The population hasn't acted yet out of fear for their own lives," Thomas explained, "but we've spoken to many of them, and they're all willing to assist us. In fact, they've been supplying us while we've been stuck down here."

"And no one has said anything out loud yet for fear of their own life," Valthor mused. "The whole operation is extremely clever. Though it could never last indefinitely, but for a while, it's genius. Very well, what role do the people play in this operation?"

"Dahaffy, Enid, and a number of the other merchants have been working to stoke unrest. They're going to inflame that with an illegal rally tomorrow morning, and we have friends who are going to stoke it into a riot. We hope it will spread throughout the entire city," Thomas explained. "We expect it to keep most of the guards occupied in the city while we sneak into the castle and reclaim it."

Valthor went over to the table and contemplated the various aspects of the plan, milling silently through the papers that formed the blueprint of the plan. He stood in thought for several moments before concluding, "It's a good plan. And it just might work. With us here to boost the infiltration team, we have a real chance of pulling it off."

"So instead of leaving at dawn, we're storming the castle?" Luca asked cheerfully, though how he could still be cheerful, Calunoth could only guess.

"It seems that way. I swear, Cal, you're a problem magnet," Valthor said jokingly. "The plan is good, but we need to make some alterations, especially now that we're involved."

The Guardian sat at the table and started pouring over the plans in detail, assuming command of the operation. The planning went on long into the night, with the companions all keen to offer what help they could. As a result, the night went long for them, and they did not retire until past midnight, thoughts of the upcoming battle blazing in their minds.

Calunoth retired in the farthest corner where no light reached, absorbed in his own thoughts. It was a relief the lantern light did not reach him, leaving him in shadow. The shadows felt more comfortable than the light, and he fell into the sorry half-sleep that dogged him as he returned to the land of his demons beyond the physical plane of waking consciousness. Several times throughout the night Calunoth woke in a hypervigilant state, expecting to see the black-clad men of PRIMAL storming into the cellar, accompanied by the honey voice of their leader, Lenocius. But such a reprisal never came, and Calunoth was left to balance on the border of waking and sleeping.

Calunoth was not the only companion who found no rest that evening. Lauren too failed to find refuge in the free land of dreams and instead stayed awake, sitting forgotten in another corner. Tears streamed down her face as she silently wept behind hands that, once clean, now bore the blood of the dead guard.

Chapter 14

The Battle for Commerel

The air was thick with anticipation when Calunoth gave up the battle for sleep. The cellar they rested in was hot and stuffy, with the dead air inside only infrequently exchanged for the fresh air of the paper shop above when the cellar door was opened to allow for the guards to pass freely in and out. The shop owner himself, Farrow, Calunoth had learned, had been the one to find the guards rather than the other way around. Galen and Thomas had been the first to escape the castle and had collapsed, exhausted in the streets near the man's store. Rather than call the so-called authorities on them, Farrow had instead dragged them back to his shop and hidden them in the cellar, rehabilitating them as they recovered from their escape. After they had recovered, they had found other surviving members of the guards hidden around the city and had brought them back to the paper shop, which now essentially served as the base of operations for the Commerel resistance.

The guards themselves were tired after weeks of being hunted, but they were all possessed by the passion of anger that motivated them to reclaim their home, and Calunoth had no reservations about their efficacy in the coming attack as he watched them prepare.

The details of the plan had been hammered out by Valthor, Thomas, and Bleiz the night before and detailed to them in the morning. Valthor had written a missive bearing his official seal to be borne to the Holy Knights garrisoned at the Commandant's Bastion detailing their instructions should their attempt to retake the castle be unsuccessful. He had designated this task to the swiftest guard with the intention that, even if they fell, the Knights would prepare to march on Commerel immediately. The trio had then divvied up roles accordingly to the skill and knowledge of the remaining members. Calunoth had been grouped with his companions, Bleiz and Luca, with the young guard, Galen, serving as their guide. Their job was to sneak into the prison and release the prisoners. Valthor would travel alone and would be responsible for rescuing the viscount. It was decided he would be the best person for the job as the viscount already knew and trusted him. And trust was becoming increasingly hard to find in these times. Captain Thomas would take two of his men and attempt to arrest Reil. Carius would take the remaining four men and secure the armory.

Calunoth was glad to be working with Galen. The young man had impressed him in the short time he had known him. Although few good friendships begin with one of the parties holding the other at sword point, he had heard enough from and about Galen to appreciate his company. As Luca had remarked, it took stones to stand in the way of a Guardian. Besides, Galen knew the layout of the castle well and would be able to guide them quickly through the unfamiliar halls.

Valthor had excluded Lauren, and she had been mostly forgotten about in the excitement. The Guardian had made clear his lack of confidence in the young researcher's abilities, so she had spent most of the night alone, coming to terms with the fact that she had just ended another person's life. Calunoth had noticed but had no idea how to approach her. His failings had resulted in the deaths of everyone he had ever loved, and he had lost all respect for the sanctity of life as a result. After all, if he could be at fault for the deaths of his loved ones, why should he care about the life of some stranger who was trying to kill him? Lauren did not have such a cynical view of the matter, however, and would likely not respond well to it.

With Calunoth found wanting and Bleiz and Valthor engaged in their plans, the burden fell to Luca to revive her spirits. He had approached her and woken her before the others, and they had spoken in whispers for almost an hour before the others woke. Calunoth had no idea what Luca might have said, but his words seemed to have had the intended effect, for Lauren wiped her eyes and appeared to resolve herself.

It was then Galen told her she had not been included in the plans and was instead to assist in stoking the riot in the market. After a brief, tense moment, she strode up to the Guardian and let her feelings be known quite explosively. At Bleiz's nod of confirmation, Valthor relented and told her to join her companions on the prison-break team. With all the preparations finally made, Thomas led the companions and the guards out of the paper shop.

This day had been weeks in the planning. The merchant's guild had been informed that everything was ready and were even now setting up a stage in the marketplace from which to begin their protest. The shopkeepers had prepared themselves and their attendants to proclaim a wide loss of faith in the local government, all the while shuttering their windows to protect their property should the riots spread as they were intended to. Farrow had made himself useful, going out in the early morning and nailing pamphlets to incite the riots. The city of Commerel was about to be rocked by the rage of the people who refused to bow down to a false leader.

Once outside, the group had split into two groups—half led by Thomas and half led by Carius, the scar-faced guard who served as Thomas's second-in-command—who had then taken separate routes to the sewer drain nearest the western wall of the city, far away from the castle. After half an hour of discreet movement through the city, the groups arrived at the sewer drain that collected Commerel's run-off. Removing the loose grate, the teams jumped down into the dark, dingy, disgusting sewers of Commerel.

Calunoth was almost overwhelmed by the stench of sewage and excrement that flowed through the sewage system. Constructed only thirty years ago to modernize the city, the sewer system was made of brick and mortar, with the floors composed of smooth stone that had been carved to effectively channel the run-off into the vast caverns deep below the town. The caverns flowed with water that was believed to run eventually to the Southern Ocean and thus carried all the waste far away to a place that was no longer Commerel's problem. The tunnels were wider than Calunoth had expected, with enough space in the main tunnels to walk five abreast. Wide as it was, they still had to wade through the streaming wastewater, which no one appreciated.

The reunited group then traveled together for over two hours, being forced to follow the winding design of the sewers. Their effort was not helped by the uniformity of the sewers; every wall looked the same, causing the group to twice hit dead ends and forcing them to backtrack. Thomas repeatedly consulted his map as he guided them through the dank sewers. At least the group was well equipped with lanterns that clearly illuminated their way and made it easy to read the diagrams Thomas had sketched. Above their heads, Calunoth could clearly hear the rousing of Commerel through the grates as the merchants and commoners began to go about their day.

Finally, the group reached an intersection where they broke into teams. While the armory and prison were relatively close together, the Western Tower and central office, where the viscount and Reil were suspected to be respectively, were not. Valthor broke off first, seizing the map from Thomas and comparing it to his own, which he had drawn for himself last night, before handing the map back, saluting them, and disappearing down a side tunnel. Thomas broke off second, handing his map to Carius before climbing up a ladder to the central offices. Galen and Calunoth's group broke off third, with Galen leading them determinedly through a descending secondary tunnel, leaving Carius's group to make their way to the armory.

Calunoth's group traveled quickly, but the tunnel kept sloping downward, prompting Calunoth to ask Galen, "Are you sure we're going the right way? We shouldn't still be going down, should we?"

Galen shook his head and said, "The prisons are large and far underground. But all the drains in there are sealed tightly shut with Ynium locks, so we can't get directly into the prison. We'll have to cut through the kitchens, so we're about where I would expect. We're aiming to reach the sewer tunnel that runs beneath the kitchen's cellars. It should only be a few more minutes."

The young guard proved himself right, and the group soon found themselves below the correct drain in a narrow tunnel that required the tall Luca to duck to avoid hitting his head.

"This is the drain. It should eventually lead right into the storehouse behind the castle. From there, we can easily access the kitchen and then the prisons," Galen reported. "Everyone clear on the plan? We move quickly and quietly until the prisoners are out. Don't hurt the servants. If they startle and try to raise the alarm, you can knock them out, but try to be gentle. They won't be expecting us and might think we're intruders. Once we're in the prison, we take out the guards, get our guys out, and lead them to the armory. From there, we retake the castle. Any last-minute questions?" The companions shook their heads, and Galan took that as a sign to begin. With Luca's help, the two men raised the grate from the ground, breaking the thin metal bindings that held it. Luca climbed out first, then assisted Galen up, followed by the rest of the group.

Calunoth emerged last and could see they were in a large, dusty warehouse full of crates. The walls were wooden, unlike the stone that made up the inner walls of the castle. Thankfully, the storehouse was deserted. Moving stealthily, Galen led the group through the storeroom out into a side courtyard. Guards patrolled the large walls of the inner fortifications of Commerel, but they were always looking outward, not inward, so they failed to notice the companions as they moved furtively into the castle through an open wooden door.

The companions emerged just outside of a bustling kitchen as the servants were beginning to prepare breakfast for the castle's inhabitants. The room was large but densely packed and filled with the alluring aroma of bacon slowly smoking over a large central firepit.

"How do we get through here?" Bleiz demanded. "The place is packed!"

Galen assuaged the captain's fears. "See that door? The nearly invisible one right beside the kitchen? That's a hallway that runs parallel to the kitchen, used to reduce congestion. It could still be busy, but right now, most of the servants are working in the kitchen." Galen went to open the door, and they all slipped quietly through it, only to freeze at the sound of armored feet pounding nearby. Thinking quickly, Galen hustled them into an adjacent pantry covered by a long curtain.

The five managed to hide just in time as a pudgy castle guard emerged heavily from around the corner, failing to notice the swinging of the curtain. "Girl, what's the deal with breakfast? We're getting bloody fed up of waiting for you trouts!" he bellowed at one of the maids who had appeared before him.

"We're sorry, sir. It is not yet time for the hot food to be served. We'll bring it to you as soon as it's ready." The maid appeared slightly flustered, and Calunoth could hear Galen exude a rattling breath beside him.

"Well, don't send me away with nothing, girl, or I'll come back for you tonight! Get me something cold then and double the hot food," the pudgy guard roared at the maid.

"Yes, sir," the maid said, and Calunoth heard footsteps shuffling down the hallway.

"Shit," muttered Galen. "Try not to startle her."

The curtain was suddenly yanked back, and the maid stood in the entrance to the pantry. Upon seeing the strange, smelly amalgamation of armed intruders kneeling in the pantry, she made to let out a scream that began as a startled gasp before she let the scream die quietly in her throat.

"Galen!" she exclaimed in a whisper. "You're alive?"

"Yes, Trish, I'm alive, and I'd like to stay that way. Don't let them find us!" Galen whispered back furiously.

The maid named Trish gave a start as the pudgy guard boomed after her, demanding to know what was taking her so long.

"I'll be right there!" she called back and reached past the group for cheese and sliced ham. She paused for a moment, and a spark of electricity burst in her brown eyes as she looked at the young guard. "What do you need us to do?"

"Keep quiet and stay out of the way. The castle's about to become a battleground. Get the other servants and bar them in the kitchen. Don't come out until the noise ends," Galen whispered.

Trish nodded, and made to move away, her hands now full of ingredients. "Save the viscount, and …" she hesitated before finishing. "… please come back safely." The curtain swung shut and the maid was gone. She deftly dealt with the pudgy guard, who, after eating his fill of the cold meat, stomped away from the kitchen.

"Look at Mr. Popular here!" Luca whispered, nudging Galen. "Friend of yours?"

"This mission doesn't have to be without casualties," Galen responded, glaring at the young Knight, who brushed off the sarcastic response with a subdued chuckle.

With the hallway clear, the group made it through the hallway to the wide spiral stairs leading down to the prison without incident. Drawing their weapons, they moved swiftly, Galen and Calunoth leading. After descending several flights, they held the element of surprise over the guards at the entrance. They had been in the midst of a shift rotation when the group fell on them, with two of the four guards weary from a night of standing guard. The weary guards fell almost immediately, so surprised and tired they didn't even raise their weapons. Calunoth ran his blade through the midriff of one while Galen pressed his own blade through the throat of the other, knocking both guards back into their colleagues.

Luca and Bleiz pushed through Calunoth and Galen, swords raised, ready to engage their enemy. The two remaining guards, though fresh, were ill-equipped for the fight. Carrying long spears that served to block the entrance of the prison, their weapons were useless in the tightly confined stone corridors. They moved to point their spears at the oncoming Knights, but their movements were blocked as the butts of their spears rammed into the wall behind them, relegating the sharp blade of the spear high into the air and ineffective against the Knights, who dispatched the guards with ease. With the way into the prison now clear, Galen seized the key from one of the fallen guards and opened the door, prepared for more guards within. They were not disappointed.

Six guards were patrolling the interior of the large prison, mostly centered around two large cages in the center of the room. The cages covered most of the room and contained hundreds of men, many slumped weakly on the floor and against the bars of the cages. Seeing Galen, one of the men in the cage reached an arm out of the bars and pulled the closest guard hard into the cage, shattering his nose in the process, then finished the guard off with a fatal snap of the neck.

The remaining five guards were caught off guard by the unexpected demise of their colleague. The thick steel prison door had shielded them from the commotion outside, so they had not been prepared for the armed invaders. Galen ran to the guards, Luca and Calunoth close behind. The battle was short and deadly. Galen took out two men in a quick fit of rage while Luca and Calunoth handily dispatched the remaining three.

The battle had roused the men in the cells, and their commanders had to hush them as the companions did their work. Bleiz found the key for the cages, and in short order, the imprisoned guards were no longer imprisoned. Before all the guards had filed out, one particularly tall man fought his way through the crowd to the cage door. With brilliant orange hair streaked with white and a flowing mustache to match, he stood out from the other guards, and the men around him parted respectfully as he moved past them.

"Captain Frederick! Are you all right, sir?" Galen asked the tall man.

"Galen, you still live! You're a sight for sore eyes, I'll tell you that for free," Frederick answered in a crass Galgre accent. "Most of us are fine. They haven't been feeding us well, but that's done some of the men good. Wiped the fat out of their bellies it did. What's the plan?"

"Lieutenant Captain Thomas led us in. He's gone to find Reil. Carius is seizing the armory as we speak. Can everyone fight? Is anyone injured?" Galen replied, inspecting the prisoners as best he could.

"We're fine. The lads in the other cage are better. They got locked up with some visiting Sihleon healer. We'll drive these bastards out with our bare hands if need be. What of the viscount?" Frederick asked.

"She lives. Guardian Tarragon is going for her himself," Galen replied.

Frederick swore softly. "Well, Sentential himself is looking out for us today, lads! Let's go!" he called to the other men. "Time to take back our castle!"

Calunoth had taken the keys from Bleiz and opened the other large cage as Frederick and Galen conversed. Dozens upon dozens of emancipated guards trotted out, heeding their captain's words. They all appeared malnourished and gaunt, but with the promise of freedom, a new fire burned in their eyes, and they moved unimpeded.

There was an anomaly among the long line of dirty, tired men who filed out of the cages. At the end of the line was a young woman unlike any Calunoth had seen before. Long raven hair was tied behind her head in a practical manner that somehow enhanced her delicate features. She was coated in a thin layer of dirt, like the rest of the inhabitants of the cage, but underneath, her skin was a dark olive. She wore the remains of a flowing green robe, a diminished, dust-covered hue that fell far short of her piercing red-and-blue heterochromatic eyes. Taller than the average woman, she carried an air of majesty that belied her weeks spent in the cell.

She was, Calunoth noted, exceedingly beautiful.

Luca had the good sense to bow respectfully to the lady, and Calunoth followed somewhat belatedly. She did not seem impressed with their reaction and responded brusquely, "Where is the viscount? We must ensure her safety at once." She spoke coldly and quickly with a light Sihleon accent.

"My lady, Guardian Tarragon is securing her as we speak. The rest of the guard will now attempt retake the castle. Perhaps it would be safest for you to stay down he—" Luca was left stuttering as the woman swept past them toward Frederick. Calunoth noted a distinct aroma of juniper berries and pine in the air as the woman swept past them. The exotic woman and Frederick conversed quickly about the state of the guards as they hurried to the exit.

Left somewhat dumbfounded by the woman's haughty dismissal, Calunoth and Luca rejoined their companions at the head of the column as the guards filed swiftly out of the prison. Galen consulted with Frederick and the Sihleon as they led the guards in a jog through the hallways of the castle, no longer interested in keeping their presence unknown.

"How did they manage to get everyone to surrender like that, sir?" Galen asked his captain.

Frederick growled before answering. "An unhealthy combination of spiked drinks, unarmed guards, and threatening the viscount's life. Whoever these men are that Reil's teamed up with, they're professionals, unlike the low-life scum who joined with Jarl to take us out. Neither Riel nor Jarl could ever organize something like this alone. And I'd never seen those men before. Some other group, an outside force, is helping them."

The group sped toward the armory, from which Calunoth could hear the sounds of battle echoing. Carius and his men must have run into more trouble than they had.

Because Calunoth's friends were the only ones armed, they led the charge into the massive room that doubled as both Commerel's training room and armory for the Commerel Guard. Long mats lay out on the floor for sparring, and the walls were decorated by hundreds of the shields, swords, and spears that made up the Commerel Guard's default equipment. Calunoth could see two of Carius's men backed into a corner, furiously fighting back a contingent of a dozen false guards. It appeared that Carius himself hadn't made it. They wouldn't have had a chance had Calunoth's group failed to arrive when they did, but with Reil's men finding themselves now surrounded and cornered, they were forced to fight on two fronts.

Calunoth, Bleiz, and Luca jumped into the fray, striking at the men's backs and forcing them to split their attention. The freed guards behind them began unhinging swords from the walls and racks and moved in to overwhelm the false guards with sheer numbers. However, in the time it took to equip themselves, the trio found they had their hands full. Lauren trailed behind them, anxiously looking to prove her worth, her light aluminum sword held loosely in her trembling hands. She was soon overtaken by a flash of raven hair speeding past her as she loitered uncertainly at the edge of the battle, biting her lip.

Bleiz and Luca each skilfully delivered a swift death to two of their attackers and Calunoth dealt with one only to be forced back by a guard menacingly swinging a mace. Calunoth found himself being driven back by the false guard's aggressive swinging, tripping backward over a rut in the floor as he moved back to dodge an attack. The rut made him fall on his backside, the mace whistling through the space he had previously occupied. The impact of the fall jarred his hand and caused his sword to clatter to the floor. Calunoth felt a rush of fear course through his veins as his enemy stood over him with the blunt mace, ready to deliver the fatal strike.

But the strike never came. Calunoth heard a female voice behind him yell, "Caesure!" and the man arrested his blow, coming to a complete standstill mid-strike. Then the raven-haired woman sprung into view above Calunoth, swiftly slashing across the man's neck with a guard-issue sword. The man remained where he stood, not falling despite his death until the woman issued a second command, at which point he fell to the floor and did not move again.

The woman held out her hand to Calunoth, who sat stunned by her intervention before gratefully accepting the assistance. The remainder of the false guards had been rapidly overwhelmed as the freed guards had come storming through the room, rage guiding their blades, and the room was now filled with men raiding the armory.

"Thank you," Calunoth said to the woman as he rose to his feet, "Um, sorry, I don't think I got your name."

"Claere Heriong, Second Division of the Church of the One's Priestess Core. I understand you're one of our rescuers?" At Calunoth's nod, she added, "Then I thank you in return. We may speak later, but now we must find the viscount. This Reil fool is involved in matters far darker than a simple power grab." She made to move away but was distracted by Frederick's sudden bellowing. He had jumped up on a large chest at the back of the room.

"Arm yourselves well, lads, and show no fear! Now is our time to take our dignity back from Reil's dogs! We retake the courtyard, the castle, and then the city!" he roared in a rousing voice his men responded to with a cheer before rushing out. Calunoth and Claere found themselves joined by Luca, Bleiz, and Lauren as they were swept out of the room by the surging crowd of armed and angry guards. The group had little choice but to follow as the crowd rushed like a flood of rage through the halls of the castle, terrifying the groups of soldiers they encountered for the brief moments before their demise. The storm of men finally erupted out of the castle keep and into the open grassy courtyard within the castle's inner walls where they could spread out and revel in the sunlight that had been denied them for weeks.

By this point, the false defenders of the castle had been alerted to the prison break and had organized to face the escapees in the central courtyard. However, the pretenders found themselves deprived of manpower as a huge portion of the guards had been called into the city to suppress the protests that had erupted into riots spreading from the market to the upper quarters, spurred on by the people rising up to reclaim their city for their captured viscount. Divided, but not defeated, the false guards made their stand in the central courtyard, fresher than the emancipated prisoners but dwarfed by the passion and ferocity of their assault. The battle met with the battle cries of the guards, the cursing of the commanders, the clash of sword on shield, and the steadily rising outrage of the people wafting in from beyond the walls.

Calunoth and his friends emerged last into the chaos of the courtyard alongside the priestess, Claere. The air was filled with the metallic scent of blood, the screams of the dying, and the smoke that was now spreading over the city as the rioters began to burn Commerel. Each guard, false or true, was similarly equipped, making it impossible to determine who was fighting for whom. Or who was winning.

Frederick and Galen had disappeared into the fray as the guards fought to reclaim their castle from the intruders, leaving the group to fend for themselves as the battle raged around them. The sensations of battle seeped into Calunoth's mind and heart, causing a red mist to descend on his vision as he felt the rage he had felt before return. These men were traitors. And they deserved a traitor's death. Calunoth moved to charge in, sword brandished, only to be stopped by a hand on his shoulder. The hand was like cool water on the forehead of a feverish man, clearing his sight of the mist and bringing the world back from the brink into a sharp relief, if only momentarily. Looking over his shoulder, he saw the delicate features of Claere looking intently into his eyes.

"We need to find the viscount. We can only add to the chaos here, not alleviate it." She spoke in a cool, calming voice that bore the same trademark iciness she had exhibited earlier.

"She's right, Cal!" Bleiz shouted at him. "I'll stay here and help command the guards. The rest of you, go and find Valthor!"

Calunoth obeyed the older man's orders. Now that his mind was clear and he was away from the carnage, he knew that he would only make the situation worse. He couldn't tell the difference between the men they had freed and their opponents like they could. Luca seemed to hesitate but was pulled back by Lauren, which was enough to convince him to follow.

Breaking away from the edge of the battle, Claere led them through the now empty keep. The guards had poured into the courtyard in force. The fight for Commerel would be determined there rather than within the castle itself. Claere seemed to know the keep well and traveled swiftly, the remains of her robes swinging freely above her knees as she ran expertly, sword in hand. Lauren kept pace with the woman, despite being considerably less fit.

"Who is this woman, and why is she fitter than me?' Luca asked as he ran alongside Calunoth, panting heavily with the exertion of the sprint.

"Her name's Claere. She's a Sihleon priestess or something," Calunoth yelled back. "I don't know why, but she can wield magic and fight as well!"

"What is the Church teaching over in Sihleo?" Luca asked, a disbelieving grin plastered on his face.

Calunoth couldn't respond as he was forced to focus on pushing the air through his lungs to fuel their dash. He could have sworn he had read about the Order of Sihleon Priestesses at some point, but in the heat of the moment, he could not recall. Lauren, overhearing their conversation from ahead, could only recall the entry she had read in the Akadaemia library.

Sihleon priestesses were a special order of warriors who served the Church of the One. Raised from birth to carry out the orders of the Church, the order was exclusively female as dictated by The Word, the doctrine of the Church of the One, and were steadily infused with Natural Ynia from a young age. This infusion made them far stronger physically than most women and was combined with extensive training in magic and arms, so they were among the most potent fighting forces on Creidyl. Serving as the personal arm of the Speaker of the One, the head of the Church in the theocratic Sihleo and the earthly representative of the Sihleon deity known as the One, the priestess order delivered the judgment and wishes of the One in the physical plane. As much as she wanted to, Lauren had no time to speak to Claere as they rounded a corner and burst through the entrance to the throne room.

The throne room of Commerel was indicative of the wealth the viscount had brought to the city. The stone walls were decorated with exquisitely carved marble busts depicting previous Commerel viscounts. The throne stood on a raised dais and was likewise carved of fine marble. The back of the throne was engraved with the balanced coin-laden scales that embodied the mindset and vision of Commerel. At the foot of the throne lay Thomas, his sword shattered against the marble of the dais and his hand clutching his stomach. The two other guards from the cellar lay where they had fallen among the bodies of the four men they had slain in their last stand.

The group hurried over to Thomas, who was coughing up blood as Claere helped him to sit up.

"You're here ..." he whispered faintly. "Did the others make it?"

"They're raising hell for you in the courtyard as we speak," Luca answered, trying to comfort the man.

"What happened to you?" Calunoth asked, kneeling next to the man.

"We found Jarl and Reil. We fought ... Jarl escaped with Reil and another traitor. Jarl ... he's ... he's not normal." Thomas's breaths came in short wheezes interspersed with coughing fits that had him trying to wipe the red liquid from his mouth.

"And the viscount?" Claere asked as she exposed the deep gash in his stomach. Thomas opened his mouth only to begin a severe coughing fit. "Hold still!" Claere ordered, and she began to cast formulae in the air over the wound. Calunoth watched in amazement as the wound began to slowly close, only to stop just below the surface as Claere lost her balance and fell sideways.

Calunoth moved to catch her, at which point she grimaced. "After all that time in the cage, I haven't the strength to heal him fully right now and still go on, but now he has a chance."

Thomas opened his eyes and nodded weakly. "Thank you for the chance. Latoya's in the Western Tower. Valthor should be there by now." His voiced dripped with weariness, and he appeared to be on the verge of losing consciousness.

"Are any of you medics?" Claere asked the group.

Lauren said, "I'm not an expert, but I know the basics."

"Then you stay here with him. Make sure he doesn't pass out. We're going to the Western Tower," Claere ordered.

Lauren nodded resolutely. After being swept along during the entire invasion, she was glad to have a real purpose to which she could assist. Her determination to come along would be vindicated after all.

"Shouldn't we chase Reil and Jarl?" Calunoth asked the priestess, firmly aware he was not in charge.

"We can get them later. If your Guardian has failed, the viscount might be in danger. Let's go!" Claere replied before resuming her feet and jogging to the door.

Calunoth and Luca looked back at Lauren, now tending to Thomas's less severe injuries. She answered the question in their gaze firmly. "Go. I'll be fine." she told them before turning her attention back to the captain.

Luca and Calunoth nodded to each other and set out behind Claere, seeking the Western Tower even as the battle for Commerel raged in the courtyard outside, and the carrions perched on the castle parapets, eagerly awaiting their upcoming feast.

Chapter 15

Fate of the Traitors

The inner keep was almost deserted. Only the occasional beleaguered guard crossed their path as Calunoth, Luca, and Claere dashed through the stone corridors of the castle. The noise floating into the castle stayed steady, though in truth, it became louder the closer the rioting crowds came to the castle even as the trio moved further away from the courtyard. The trio made good progress despite the castle's large size thanks to Claere's familiarity with the castle's interior, which she used to guide them effortlessly toward the Western Tower.

They struck down the few hostile guards they encountered quickly and easily. No one was in the mood for a prolonged fight while the chaos outside threatened to interrupt their endeavors. Alert to the dangers around him, Calunoth's mind went to Valthor. The Guardian had been the first to break off from the infiltration team, and though he had the furthest distance to travel, Calunoth couldn't help but wonder at his continued absence. As capable as he was, one could not rule out the possibility that he had fallen or been captured, especially given the likely heavy security around the viscount. Calunoth dismissed those thoughts quickly; Valthor was the best of them. He would pull through this ordeal. Calunoth's musings were interrupted when Claere abruptly stopped at a large staircase that spiraled up toward the highest floors of the castle.

"Up here!" Claere urged them, slightly out of breath herself. "The viscount will likely be in her quarters at the top of the tower." With that, she started to climb the stairs with Calunoth and Luca in close pursuit. The stairs were not overly steep, but the speed at which they scaled them caused Calunoth's legs to protest at the strain and his lungs to burn. His companions were of a similar condition; as they moved higher and higher into the tower, their breathing became as heavy as his. But they all refused to stop, knowing that the chaos below them could soon be close behind, and time was of the essence.

Calunoth privately hoped the guards watching the viscount would have descended to assist their comrades in the courtyard as his legs were at risk of turning to jelly at the rate they were going, but he was disappointed as they reached the top of the staircase. The stone spiral staircase terminated finally in a long, carpeted hallway hundreds of feet above the ground. The hallway was adorned with oil paintings along both walls from the staircase to the door opposite. The sole inhabitant of the hallway was a single guard dressed in full armor, his hand resting on his steel sword hilt, his features obscured by an iron helmet. He was clearly a more experienced fighter than many of his peers based solely on the comfortable manner in which he leaned on the pommel of his sword, and he must have been selected to guard the viscount's quarters for that same reason.

Seeing the trio emerge from the stairs, the guard slid his blade from its sheath and stood ready to engage them. He had expected them to continue their pace, but the journey up the stairs had winded them, and all three were forced to lean against the wall at the top of the stairs, requiring time to recover. Realizing this, the guard shifted and advanced on Luca, who appeared to be the most threating assailant even as he leaned against the wall panting heavily.

Fortunately for Luca, the length of the hallway combined with the guard's hesitation combined to give him the time he needed to recover, simultaneously blocking the guard's strike as he drew his sword from his side. By attacking Luca first, the guard had surged past Claere, dismissing the young woman as a threat and was shortly, and fatally, corrected of that notion when the priestess slipped her own weapon through a gap in the guard's armor, wounding him and allowing Luca the opportunity to disarm and strike the man down.

Calunoth was grateful for the expertise of his fit companions as he would have been unable to defend himself had the guard come for him first. The rigorous training undergone by both the Knights and the priestess order afforded them far more endurance than what was required of a simple guard. Taking a moment to recover, the trio advanced to the end of the hallway where Claere tried to open the door. It was locked, but the commotion outside had commanded the attention of the room's inhabitants, and a muffled voice sounded from behind the door.

"Who's there? What's happening out there?" The voice sounded strong and slightly irate as though annoyed they had been disturbed by something as trivial as an uprising.

"Viscount Latoya! It's me, Claere! We've come to rescue you!" Claere shouted through the door. "Please let us in!"

"Claere?"

The group heard a shuffling followed by multiple locks clicking open. After a moment, the door swung open to reveal the Viscount of Commerel. She was a tall woman with the dark skin that betrayed her Chelian upbringing, mahogany hair, and a stern, arresting gaze. Like Valthor, she radiated confidence. "What's going on? I can see a battle in the courtyard below. Have the Knights arrived?"

"No madam, your own guards have escaped and are currently trying to reclaim the castle from the imposters. Have you been harmed in any way? Do you require healing?" the young priestess asked the imposing woman, who snorted in reply.

"These fools couldn't hurt me. The city would be bankrupt within a week if they did. Where's that scum, Reil? Has he been killed yet?"

"He's likely escaping as we speak, though we don't know where to, madam. His men and Jarl defeated our own forces," Luca answered.

"Well, what are you standing around for then?" the viscount demanded. "Get after him! Alive if possible. I've half a mind to execute him personally!" The viscount was clearly in no mood to wait. As a woman of fortitude, she was quick to order the trio into action.

"Madam, have you seen the Guardian Valthor Tarragon yet?" Calunoth asked, concerned about the Guardian's whereabouts.

The viscount shook her head in reply. "You're the first people I've seen in almost a month, though I saw him about three weeks before this whole affair started. He was headed to Caern Vaughn at the time. Is he here somewhere?"

"We'd better go after Reil, Cal," Luca interjected. "I don't know where Valthor is, but with the viscount safe, we should try to chase the traitor down."

Calunoth agreed, now very concerned about the Guardian but unable to act upon it. Claere resolved to stay with the viscount, citing her need for protection until the castle was restored to peace again. With Claere guarding the viscount, Bleiz marshaling the courtyard battle, Thomas on the edge of death, and Valthor missing in action, the responsibility of finding Reil now fell to Calunoth and Luca.

The pair thanked Claere for her assistance and ran back down the stairs. The way down was far easier than the way up, but the slope of the stairs accelerated Calunoth and Luca's speed to a dizzying pace to the point where they were unable to arrest their own momentum and began to fly at a speed beyond their control. The stairs were adorned with a long rug that provided the grip required to prevent them from slipping, but the angle of the stairs coupled with the burning sensation in his legs told Calunoth he would have to keep running into the hallway or risk his momentum carrying him face first down the remainder of the stairs.

Unfortunately, the stairs were not uninhabited, and as Calunoth rounded the second floor, he found himself facing, for a brief moment, a dark figure that strongly bore the unmistakable stench of sewage. The moment was brief as neither had been expecting the other, and Calunoth crashed heavily into the figure, slowing down just enough for Luca to barrel into his back and send all three of them tumbling down the stairs. There were only a few steps left, but Calunoth flew down most of them, his landing and Luca's cushioned by the figure they had crashed into, who recovered quickly, dislodging them both as he drew his sword and scrambled to his feet.

Neither Calunoth nor Luca were able to respond in kind as between their exertion on the stairs and the winding caused by their abrupt landing, they now lay in a heap, stunned and incapable of reacting to the situation.

The figure, instead of attacking, sheathed his sword as he observed the two young men groaning on the floor in front of him. "What do you two think you're doing? Where's the viscount? Where are the others?"

Calunoth shook his head to clear the stars flashing in his vision and looked at the man, recognizing his voice. "Valthor?" Calunoth questioned. He certainly sounded like the Guardian, but his clothing and face were obscured by a thick crust of what looked like mud. He was also dripping wet. But there was no mistaking the unusual weapon slung over his back or the Hillmen accent that lilted his voice. "You're alive!"

"Of course I'm sodding alive!" retorted Valthor angrily. "Answer the questions, man!" Whatever had delayed the Guardian had put him in an extremely foul mood.

Calunoth sat up and updated him, secretly relieved at this opportunity to rest for a moment. "The viscount's safe. She's with Claere, a Sihleon priestess we discovered in the prison. Bleiz is in the courtyard fighting. Galen too. Thomas was badly injured, but Lauren's with him now. We're going after Reil now ourselves. He and Jarl escaped from Thomas."

Valthor shook his head, flecks of grime and water dripping from his hair. "If Thomas isn't dead yet, I'll bloody do him in myself. His map sent me entirely the wrong way." It was at this point that Calunoth associated the stench of sewage with another smell and began to wonder if it was actually mud that the Guardian was covered in. "No matter, Reil's probably headed to the Eastern Tower. There's a postern gate near there I'm sure they'll try to get to. They'd be mad to try and get out the front. I saw the courtyard on the way over here. The place is a mess."

Refusing a hand from the Guardian, Calunoth and Luca rose to their feet, grateful for the momentary respite. With Valthor back in their midst, the trio began to move swiftly back through the castle, the noise growing ever louder as they moved nearer the courtyard. As they approached the central wing of the castle, Valthor called them to a stop.

"If we're all chasing them, they can just keep on running. I'll cut across outside to the exit of the postern gate. I might be able to cut them off," he announced. "You two, keep following these hallways. The castle's like a mirror. The east is designed to reflect the west, so it's all exactly the same." With those instructions, Valthor disappeared down another hallway, moving more swiftly alone than he could have with the fatigued Calunoth and Luca.

Calunoth and Luca followed the Guardian's instructions and resumed their swift jog through the hallways. After climbing another staircase to the second floor to avoid a couple skirmishes, they ran across the archway dominating the entrance hall. With a brief glance down, Calunoth saw the battle in the courtyard had spilled into the entrance hall, and it was no longer just guards involved in the fray. The protests that had erupted into riots to attract the attention of the false guards in the city had been far more destructive than what the plan had intended, and now the false guards who had gone out to suppress the people had been driven back into the castle. The rioters had followed them in, and now the courtyard, entrance hall, and the gates had descended into anarchy as the false guards desperately tried to fight off the true guards and rioters who had now began roaming unchecked through the castle halls.

Jogging next to him, Luca witnessed the carnage unfolding in the hall and saw a familiar face in the crowd. Valthor had cut through the entrance hall, intending to round the postern gate from the other side.

But he had not counted on the fight spreading to the entrance hall. He now found himself buffeted by the roiling tide of battle and significantly slowed as he weaved and ducked through the frenzied screaming mob of rioters, freed guards, and Reil's men. Seeing the Guardian in trouble, he called it to Calunoth's attention.

"There's nothing we can do, Luca! If we go down there, we'll just end up in the same mess!" Calunoth called back to him over the bellow of the mob below.

"Then it's just you and me left, Cal," Luca replied, grinning. "Let's give ourselves a good showing, shall we?"

Calunoth did not share the young Knight's cavalier attitude. His heart began to pound as he realized how the plan had fallen apart. Thomas had failed. Bleiz was somewhere in the courtyard. Valthor was now out of the picture. It would now be up to him and Luca to catch the people responsible for this coup. The fever pitch and noise of the mob played into his fears, and he began to hesitate and doubt himself. The image of the dying Captain Thomas floated into his mind. Thomas was the type of man to be dealing with this issue. Or Valthor, the Guardian of Renderive. Calunoth had no place in this battlefield of guards and traitors! But then another image flashed in his mind. An image that haunted his dreams and tore at his soul. The image of the laughing Lenocius and the face he had seen falling from the battlements of Glathaous Castle. This was just a different snake of the same species. And they would do no more to destroy the city of Commerel. Calunoth resolved himself. If he was to kill Lenocius, he would have to take up the mantle of justice again. This was just a practice run.

The pair moved quickly through the corridors, running past the throne room where Thomas had fought Reil and Jarl. The floor outside the door was marred with a trail of blood, drops of red staining the floor at regular intervals. There was a clear trail, so at least one escapee had been wounded. The pair followed the trail swiftly, and Calunoth was beginning to grow concerned that they had taken too long. With the Eastern Tower fast approaching, there was still no sign of the escaping Reil until the pair turned the corner to the last hallway before the spiral staircase. Limping through the hallway and bleeding heavily from a leg wound, a burly guard shielded a much smaller, chubbier man in green robes from their view. The two escaping men were almost at the end of the hallway and would soon head down the staircase to the first floor. If that happened, they'd be free to exit through the postern gate. It was highly unlikely that Valthor would be there to intercept them in time.

Knowing this, Luca sprinted down the hallway with his sword drawn, Calunoth close behind. He lunged around the guard, deftly moving past him and jumping in front of the stairs, blocking the escaping Reil. The guard, who must have been Jarl, still had his wits about him and knocked Calunoth to the side with a mailed fist as he attempted to emulate Luca's move. Calunoth clattered into the stone wall and was briefly stunned, giving Jarl the chance to move in on Luca. Seizing the opportunity, Reil began to run away from Luca, heading up the stairs to the tower and leaving Jarl to deal with the attackers. Luca went to chase the flabby aristocrat but found his way blocked by Jarl.

The leader of the treacherous guards was a strong man by all respects. Tall, powerfully built, and possessing an indomitable will to defeat his opponents, Jarl was a threat to even the most experienced opponent, despite his lack of technique. This became quickly apparent to Luca as he blocked Jarl's first attack and felt lightning crash down his arm with the force of the impact. Luca, of equal height to the false guard, shoved him back onto his wounded leg, and the two began their bout in earnest. Calunoth jumped in beside Luca, who was struggling to hold his own against the heavy man's blows. For a fleeting moment, Calunoth felt warmth emanating from the core in his chest, but he dismissed it as the result of the heat of battle.

Calunoth was forced to alter his fighting style against the strength of Jarl's blows. The man seemed to hit even harder than Valthor did, although Valthor had only been testing him when they had sparred. Calunoth shifted his left hand to support the flat of his blade, reinforcing it against the crushing weight of Jarl's broadsword before the giant turned to fend off Luca's strike. Focused exclusively on holding his own against this formidable opponent, Calunoth failed to notice the chip that had developed in his blade, the hardened edge pushed beyond its limit by the force of Jarl's attack.

Luca attacked Jarl, his blade clattering against the guard's own, but Jarl had no time to capitalize as Calunoth came in swinging to deliver a two-handed slash down on his head. Neither man was prepared for what happened next. The guard raised his blade above his head and Calunoth's blade met his in midair, shattering along the chipped edge and splitting Calunoth's sword in two, leaving him holding the hilt and half the blade. The other half spun over Jarl's with the impact, and as Jarl's sword rushed over Calunoth's head, the fragment of Calunoth's sword whipped across the guard's face, dispossessing him of his left eye.

Jarl screamed and fell back, cursing. "You bastards! Everything was perfect! How dare you do this to me?" Jarl was now bleeding even more heavily from his leg wound, and he knelt with one hand holding his ruined eye. Even wounded as he was, the rage inherent in the man's voice deterred both Calunoth and Luca from attacking momentarily. But the advantage was with them, and they had to seize it before it disappeared. Jarl swung blindly with his massive sword, trying to fend them off in a frenzied defense, but Luca's Knight's training proved impervious to the guard's attempts. Deftly sidestepping the guard's mad attack, Luca slashed at the man's uninjured thigh, severing the quadriceps and dropping him to the ground. He finished off the guard with a neat slash across his throat, causing the man to gurgle his last curses at them as he fell to the floor at the base of the stairs, dead. Calunoth and Luca both dropped to the floor. Calunoth's arm was still vibrating from the force that had shattered his blade. Luca was feeling similarly battered, having engaged Jarl longer.

"He was strong," Luca said, panting and kneeling on the floor. "Too strong. He was hitting as hard as Valthor does."

Calunoth rose, still clutching his vibrating arm, and examined the body. He noticed the core in his chest now, still emitting a warm glow. He could not see anything unnatural about the body. Jarl had been a strong man, evidenced by the rippling muscles exposed through the gashes in his armor, but he was no true giant. He shouldn't have been strong enough to snap Calunoth's sword in half. Jarl's sword too was nothing special. Locked in the guard's death grip, the broadsword was of the standard-issue tempered steel expected of a Commerel Guard. Calunoth had started to walk away thinking he would perhaps ask Valthor or Lauren to examine the body later when he noticed something. A strange glow from inside the man's bracer. Knowing Reil wasn't going anywhere now that he had trapped himself in the tower, Calunoth undid the laces on the bracer, removing Jarl's plate-mail glove in the process. With the guard's arm exposed, Calunoth saw a faint red light coming from within. Calunoth had at first thought it was from something stashed in the man's armor, but the glow was coming from within the guard's arm itself!

Joining him, Luca used his dagger to carve out a section of the man's arm. The cut was not deep and came out with little gore. Surgically, Luca pulled a small shard of crystal from his flesh, marveling at the glowing red light it emitted. Calunoth held out a hand, and Luca placed the crystal in it. But Calunoth did not have the chance to look at it. The moment it touched his hand, the crystal's light vanished, and the shard cracked and disintegrated in his palm. At the same time, the aching in his legs subsided, and the cut on his arm from the previous fight melted away, leaving his skin flawless. Calunoth did not notice the cessation of the dull ache from the cut, instead being too preoccupied with the dust that now adorned his hand.

"Is it the same thing that happened in the bog?" Luca asked. "The crystal there broke too. Was this what was making Jarl so strong?"

Calunoth nodded, slowly realizing the ramifications of this discovery. "This must be a Pralia Core, or part of one anyway. We knew PRIMAL was involved, we just didn't know how much."

"We'll have to talk to Valthor and the viscount when this is all over. They'll know what to do next," Luca said, refocusing his gaze on staircase. "For now, we should arrest Reil. He didn't look like much to be scared of, but we should be careful regardless. Do you have any other weapons?"

Calunoth looked down at the remains of his sword dismayed; he had not had the blade long, and already it was in pieces. "No," he replied, "but the edges of the sword are still sharp. I can still cause some damage if I need to."

Luca nodded and led the way up the stairs. They moved much more slowly now, knowing the steward was trapped, and took the time to investigate the rooms and hallways along the way, ensuring he couldn't slip past them. Calunoth was beginning to grow wary they might have missed something, that Reil had found a way to escape, but his concerns were alleviated as they reached the top of the tower. The steward had taken up hiding in his own room at the peak of the Eastern Tower. Mirroring the viscount's room in the Western Tower, it was luxuriously decorated with fine furs and an assortment of drinks and perfumes from across the continent. Life in Commerel had been good for Reil, but not for much longer.

Calunoth and Luca scanned the room and failed to find the chubby little man. Calunoth spotted the open balcony doors, and he motioned to Luca. The balcony was carved of gray stone, like many of the new additions to the castle, and encompassed almost as much space as the room from which it projected. The wind was billowing at their altitude, sweeping down from the Llewyn Hills to the north and setting the flags flying above the central spire of Commerel Castle. Reil stood at the edge of the balcony, his race run. He leaned on the railing, sweat dripping down his forehead.

"It's over Reil! There's nowhere left to run! Surrender now!" Luca called to the steward, who failed to respond for a moment and slumped over the railing before turning to address them.

"You're not the guards. Who are you two?" His voice was high-pitched with fear.

"Luca Draca of The Holy Knights of Renderive and Calunoth Leiron of the Glathaous Castle Guard. We have every authority to arrest you for your crimes against the Viscount of Commerel and your treason against His Majesty King Greshaun the Second," Luca replied, invoking his formal Knight's training for making an arrest.

"You're just a Knight, fighting for the greater good. And you're just a poor castle guard, well, not much of a castle if what I heard from Lenocius is right, but not well off by any means." Reil spread his arms and smiled a wan, toad-like smile. "You could, of course, arrest me right now, but why should you? If you protect me and see me out of here, I can make you wealthy—"

Calunoth cut off his offer as he jumped forward to lift the man by his collar.

"What do you know about Lenocius? Speak! I command you, you worm!" Calunoth roared. He hadn't realized he had moved forward to strike at the sad little man. The name, Lenocius, had triggered something inside him, the rage that had built up inside his heart and soul, consuming him.

Realizing bribery was not his best avenue of escape from this situation, Reil wiped his sweaty palms on his robes and attempted negotiation instead.

"If you want to know about Lenocius, I'd be happy to tell you," Reil replied wisely, his business acumen easing his anxiety. "He's the one Byrant sent. It was Lenocius' idea to replace all the guards and seize Commerel. He even brought those devices of his, those Pralia Cores, I think he called them. He put a shard in Jarl's arm to demonstrate the power Byrant wields. You know what's coming, don't you?" Calunoth glared into the man's eyes. Clearing his throat, Reil continued his pitch, "Byrant is going to run roughshod over Renderive. He'll be the next king, and when he is, he'll remember everyone who helped him along the way. This could be your opportunity!"

Calunoth prevented Reil from continuing by shaking him even harder and pulling him over the railing of the balcony. Calunoth was now the only force preventing the Lord Steward from dropping hundreds of feet to the courtyard below as he roared, "Where is Lenocius?! Tell me!"

"If you kill me, you won't learn anything!" Reil shouted, panicked that his negotiations had not gone to plan. "Put me down and help me escape, and I'll lead you to Lenocius. I won't fail Byrant, unlike that failure Alistair. Byrant can make us both richer than you could ever imagine!"

"Cal!" Luca yelled, coming up behind him and grabbing Reil. "Stop this! You won't learn anything like this." Looking into his friend's eyes as Calunoth stared down the Lord Steward, Luca was scared. He was no coward by any means, but the glaze that had taken over Calunoth's rage-filled eyes was unnatural, inhuman, and it chilled him to the bone.

Calunoth didn't hear Luca. He didn't care anyways. This man was a servant of Lenocius. He was the Alistair Glathaous of Commerel Castle. And he would get what he deserved.

With a strangled yell, Calunoth yanked the chubby man over back over the railing, leaving him sprawled on the balcony floor. Reil began to rise to his feet, to attempt to flee again, but Calunoth didn't give him the chance. Drawing the jagged remains of his sword from his sheath, he lunged upon the steward, with the broken sword hilt turned up toward the sky. In a swift, rampant motion, he brought the remains of the sword down on the flabby man once, twice, three times. Again. Again. Again. Again. Stabbing downward, Calunoth's mind was blank as he brought the blade down for the eighth time. He was not stabbing Reil. He was stabbing Alistair. The puppet of Lenocius who had destroyed Glathaous Castle. Again and again the broken blade came down. He couldn't see; he couldn't think. All he could feel was the white-hot anger and guilt that tore through his body, and he released it in a catharsis of rage. Again. He thought that he felt a strong set of hands pulling him back from the body, but he ignored and overpowered them. Again.

Then he felt another set of hands grab him around his chest, and together, they pulled him away from Reil. His wrist snapped as his weapon was knocked from his hand. Fighting back, he tried to push forward again, to beat Reil to death with his fists alone if need be. But for all of his rage, he couldn't overpower the hands that held him back, though it was a close contest.

Then a hard knock across his face brought him back. He was panting heavily, unsure of what was happening. Looking up, Valthor's dirty face came into focus. Wincing at the pain pervading from the left side of his face, he slowly rose to his feet. He saw Reil lying several feet away, so mangled he was almost unrecognizable.

"What did the viscount say?" Luca asked Cal, staring at him in disbelief. "Bring Reil in, 'Alive, if possible?' What was that? There's nothing left of the man!"

"I ... I don't know. I'm sorry, I just ... I just lost control. He's one of Lenocius' pawns. I couldn't control myself," Calunoth stammered in response, looking away from Luca's astonished face.

Valthor regarded him curiously, staring at him for a moment, appearing to be deep in thought, before shrugging off whatever he was thinking. "Well, what's done is done. We can't revive the dead, and if we could, we wouldn't waste it on this guy," Valthor announced, kicking the corpse with his foot. "We should return to the viscount. She's gone down to the throne room to control the riots. The battle was just clearing up as I got through it. Do you want to tell her the truth, or should we make something up, Cal?"

Calunoth was surprised by the Guardian's offer but was still reeling from his episode. He shook his head and replied, "Whatever you think is best."

Valthor nodded in response, then turned to Reil's body. Hoisting it up, he moved past Calunoth and Luca, and in a single motion, dropped it off the tower. He watched with Luca as it landed on the ground, avoiding passersby but startling several guards.

"I think it's best to avoid drawing unnecessary attention to Cal. We'll say that Reil jumped to avoid being arrested. The fall will hide the stab wounds. It's neater this way," Valthor announced. Motioning for them to follow him, the trio began the trip back to the throne room. On the way, still somewhat disturbed by Calunoth's rampage, Luca tried to occupy his mind by questioning Valthor about his delayed arrival, to which the Guardian responded with an exasperated sigh.

"It's very simple. Thomas gave me a map with bad directions. I followed it and ended up in the wrong place. I had to climb through a drainage system that was not the one that I had hoped for. I spent the rest of the time trying to get to the tower. I was well behind schedule at that point," Valthor replied casually.

"I guess that makes sense," Luca replied before pausing. "Hold on, didn't you draw your own map? Weren't you following one that you made?"

"Nope, definitely not my map. My mapping skills are actually good," Valthor replied. "Did Thomas survive? Do we know yet? I haven't seen any of the others since I left the group this morning."

"Valthor..." Luca didn't let the Guardian change subjects. "Did you get lost?"

"Of course not!" Valthor said with a snort. "Don't be ridiculous. I had bad information. It can happen to anyone." Valthor refused to speak further on the topic despite Luca's playful prodding.

When the trio returned to the throne room, Lauren enlightened them on the outcome of the battle after she ran over to see them. An exhausted Bleiz joined the group shortly afterward. They learned the fake guards had, to a man, been killed or captured. Captain Frederick had lost an eye in the battle, but as an experienced campaigner, he had taken it in stride, and once bandaged, had set about facilitating the restoration of the courtyard and entrance hall. Galen was nowhere to be seen, but it was not yet known if he was among the dead or merely in another part of the castle. Bleiz himself had escaped the battle only mildly wounded with a deep gash across his left hand and a shallow cut bleeding steadily from under his graying beard. He had surrendered his command of the guards to one of the lieutenants and, upon arriving, had fallen heavily down on the steps on the side of the throne room next to Cal and Luca, who were themselves exhausted from the day's labor.

The veteran viscount had expertly quelled the rioters when she had emerged on the balcony of the entrance hall and proclaimed an end to the combat. Although some of the younger members had it in their minds to continue their ransacking behavior, the uninjured real guards had immediately dissuaded them of the idea, and the city had fallen back into security almost as quickly as it had descended into madness.

Lauren had established an infirmary of sorts in a large storeroom close to the throne room. Here, she had assisted with the care of the wounded once it had been clear that Thomas's life was no longer in danger. She joined her companions on the steps of the throne room where they all sat together, marveling at the madness of the day.

As twilight began to fall, the viscount descended to her throne, the beautiful Sihleon priestess by her side, and declared the city safe and free once more, to the cheers of all Commerel citizens present. The battlefield would be cleaned up. The city sections destroyed by the riots would be rebuilt. And Commerel would once again know peace.

That was the message the viscount had hoped to give. But the celebrations were cut short when a sentry rushed into the keep from his post on Commerel's walls.

"Viscount Latoya!" the sentry cried. "An army approaches from the south, about four days away. They're flying the banner of the white rose!"

The viscount took the news coolly and bid the man to calm himself. "So, Byrant has made his move, has he? I daresay he will find Commerel a much harder target than he would have recently." The viscount briskly issued orders, mobilizing the fatigued guards into action.

Calunoth and his companions were largely forgotten in the ensuing flurry, for which they were grateful. Recognizing their exhaustion, Valthor directed them to a side room away from the throne where they could recover in peace from the day's exertions. Luca tried to protest, but Valthor shut him down.

"You've done enough for today. Leave the rest to us," the Guardian said before returning to the viscount's throne.

The companions were grateful for the rest but did not speak for several long minutes. The specter of civil war that had haunted them since they had left Crideir had now been made material, and the battle would be joined soon. They would have to face down an insurrectionist duke.

Calunoth sat quietly as he considered his next move. He would have to go to the capital first, that was certain. But he could no longer justify waiting. Lenocius, and Alistair, in their roles with PRIMAL would continue to breed treachery and sedition across the country. And while

Calunoth did not fully understand PRIMAL's goals, he knew the time for waiting had passed. They wanted his core, the Glathaous Pralia Core, and he wanted their lives as payment for the crimes they had wrought. It was time for the hunted to become the hunter.

Thoughts of his revenge and redemption swirled around Calunoth's mind as he rested. The Glathaous Core began to burn softly in his chest.

End of Book I

Chapter 16

The Road to the Capital

A heavy rain descended on the plains of the Central Steppe as Calunoth and his friends trudged along the road. They had left Commerel less than a week ago and were now within sight of their next destination, the Commandant's Bastion. Calunoth led the convoy alongside the Guardian Valthor, who seemed to take the rain in his stride. They were followed by Lauren and Luca, whose cheerful disposition uplifted the mood of the entire group as they marched through the downpour. The veteran Captain Bleiz took up the rear alongside the beautiful Sihleon priestess, Claere, who had decided to journey from Commerel with the group.

Their departure from Commerel had been, by necessity, abrupt and hasty. Though Commerel Castle had been reclaimed from the clutches of Duke Byrant's stooge, Reil, the duke's army on their doorstep had prompted the group had had to leave immediately to avoid being trapped in a siege. The viscount, for her part, had taken rapid steps to restore the prosperity of the city by imposing law and order, quelling the disturbed rioters, and reaffirming relations with the merchant class. Determined not to be removed again after so recently regaining her throne, the viscount also issued immediate orders to cut off supplies to Byrantia in the south and redirected them north and east to the king's primary force, the Holy Knights of Renderive. So too had she ordered the restocking of the armory, the fortifying of the walls, and the stockpiling of supplies in the city. She was prepared for a prolonged siege.

The viscount had also asked the Guardian Valthor to stay on and assist in coordinating the defense of the city, but the Hillman had refused, citing his obligations to coordinate the nation's strategy with the king and refusing to allow the only Pralia Core in the king's possession to be trapped in a besieged Commerel. He had, however, left instructions for the Commerel Guards to follow until the city could be reinforced by the Knights, and the group had departed the following morning. The incredible flatness of the plains meant Byrant's army had materialized despite being several days away, thus giving the companions enough time to escape the city.

Although every member of the group was aching and exhausted from the previous day's battle, they made no outward complaints as Valthor pushed them out the eastern gate. Claere had surprised them all by showing up at the gate before dawn, ostensibly, or so Calunoth had thought, to see them off. The Sihleon priestess had been an invaluable ally in the Commerel Coup, as the conflict was now becoming known, and Calunoth had been secretly excited when they had found her waiting at the gate. Upon their arrival, she had declared that she had to speak with the king urgently about matters relating to Sihleo, and Valthor had been happy to take her along. She had only been traveling through Commerel when Reil had staged his ill-fated coup and had been caught up against her will, being imprisoned while trying to protect the viscount. Her original destination now matched the group's current objective, and it was decided it would be altogether safer from them to travel together.

    The capital city and seat of the Kingdom of Renderive was in Deirive, over two weeks on foot from Commerel. Valthor planned to stop in the ancient fortress of Renderive, the Commandant's Bastion, colloquially known as just "the Bastion," and issue directives to the Knights stationed there. The fortress was now in sight, its majestic spires towering over the plains yet still bathed in the shadows of the mountain before which it stood. For the group, the cover of the fortress could not come soon enough. The rain had started two days ago and had been unrelenting, coming up from the southern Shellthrone Lake and barraging the group with thick slivers of water. Luca had maintained the rain was good as it would slow Byrant's army, but his optimism was curtailed when Bleiz pointed out that it was only raining on them; the skies to the south were clear of the roiling black clouds.

    The group had continued to wade through the misery, driven again by Valthor's relentless pace. Calunoth was beginning to grow close to all of his companions, their bonds forged by a common enemy and their experiences saving each other's lives many times over now. He had grown to respect them all, but he had come to hold the Guardian in even higher esteem. Valthor was relentless yet easygoing. Firm but fair. Strong, but less arrogant than many lesser men. He was an inspirational person to journey with. And yet there was something about him that stirred Calunoth's curiosity. Valthor was erudite, yet he had an air about him when he spoke that indicated a different source of strength. He gave Calunoth the impression that he knew secrets about the world that were obscured to all others. It was daunting but did not prevent Calunoth from enjoying the Guardian's company and speaking with him at length.

"Hey, Valthor, aren't you bothered by this rain? It's been going nonstop, and you don't seem to mind at all," Calunoth asked his friend.

Valthor laughed and shook it off. "You call this rain? In the Hills, this would be considered a light shower. Besides, I prefer the rain. It has a calming effect on the world. Everything seems more peaceful when it's raining. And I think the more peace we can have right now, the better off we'll all be."

"Do you think Commerel will be all right?" Calunoth asked. "Would it have been better for you to stay there? Bleiz could have led us to Deirive."

Valthor shook his head. "Commerel will be fine. The viscount was caught out by underhanded trickery before. She won't have any problems dealing with a direct attack. Honestly, I'm not even sure if there'll be an attack. We must have seriously disrupted Byrant's plans by retaking Commerel. If Reil had still been in charge, he could have just marched his army through the front gate and split the nation in half. As it is, he'll have to fight for Commerel, and if he does, he risks being trapped between the walls and the Knights. He may elect to fight the Knights on the Steppe instead and leave the cities out of it, which would be the best outcome for the citizenry."

"So, us retaking Commerel could lead to us defeating Byrant?" Calunoth asked.

"Quite possibly," Valthor replied. "If he had Commerel under his control, he would have been able to disrupt supply lines for the entire northern forces. In his position, taking Commerel would have been the logical first step and would have severely affected our ability to fight back. As it stands, he won't be able to take Commerel without a fight, and it's not an easy city to take. You've seen how those guards fight. When people fight for their homes, they become far stronger than when they fight for someone else's cause."

"It's strange, you know," Calunoth mused, "how I got involved in all this? I'm just a nobody, and now I'm helping defend a country from a civil war. I'm just a small piece, but it's good to know I'm helping how I can."

"You *were* a small piece of it," Valthor corrected him. "If you had died at Glathaous with your kin, you would have been a small part of it. But you've become more important now. You carry the only Pralia Core in the hands of the royalist forces now. We don't know how many Byrant has, be it one or a hundred. But you matter now. You helped resolve the terror of the Caerwyn Bogs. You discovered the origins of PRIMAL, to a certain extent, and you helped deliver a crippling blow to Byrant at Commerel. None of that would have happened if you had died at Glathaous, and any one of these achievements would be enough to make the life of any man. No, Cal, you are not a small piece of this anymore."

"I just want to kill the people who destroyed my home," Calunoth replied cynically. "I didn't want to be caught up in all this."

Valthor noted an odd tremor in Calunoth's voice as he spoke, almost as if he had held back a laugh, but made no mention of it. The young guard's eyes had taken on that dark glaze that had shrouded them ever since he had killed Reil at Commerel. "So? We, as humans, cannot be overly picky with what happens around us. But for what it's worth, I think the path you're currently traveling will lead you to Alistair and Lenocius. PRIMAL has clearly sided with Byrant, and eventually we'll have to fight them. I just hope that no one else gets to them first. For your sake," Valthor replied.

***

The next day, the rain subsided, and the group arrived at the Commandant's Bastion. There they were greeted by the commander of the Bastion, Calethor, Commandant of the Holy Knights of Renderive and leader of the Knight's Academy. Calethor was one of the most promising Knights in the order, with many believing him to be a future candidate for field marshal, the leader of the entire order. Tall and lean, with a bushy black mustache that outmatched his short, cropped hair, the commandant stood regally in his fastidiously polished armor to greet them. Only in his mid-thirties, he had enlisted in the Knights at eighteen and worked his way through the ranks quickly with his zealous attention to detail, sharp mind, and keen organizational skills. Though only an average fighter, he was an exceptional officer and took the job of caretaking the heart of the Holy Knights, the Commandant's Bastion, with all seriousness.

Calethor guided them inside the Bastion's central keep, giving a lecture on the composition of the fortress as he did so. Calunoth had the impression that the man was showing off to Valthor but said nothing and listened with interest. The Commandant's Bastion guarded the only major pass through the Galgre Mountains and protected the capital of Deirive from any invasion by land. The original keep had been constructed by the native populations before Renderive had existed, much like Caern Vaughn. The foundations of the fortress were nothing more than a hillfort designed to guard the pass, but over the centuries of Renderivean rule, the fortress had been expanded upon relentlessly by a succession of rulers obsessed with protecting Deirive from outside forces. As a result, the original fort had grown from a solitary set of walls on the southern mountain slope to an incredible fortress that spanned the length of the pass. The center of the pass was occupied by Bastion Keep, which stretched high into the heavens and acted as the primary base for the Holy Knights of Renderive. Stark white stone embodied the main tower, which was flanked on both sides of the pass by smaller towers of the same material. The towers were connected by three sets of walls, all three reaching across the long expanse of ground that made up the courtyards of the fortress. The walls themselves were layered, with the eastern and western wall connected by the northern and southern towers. Heavy steel gates combined with hardened oak portcullises guarded the roads and denied entry into the Bastion's grounds. The central wall stretched out from the main tower and connected to the peripheral towers. The fortress was considered impregnable and rivaled only by Thronegaard in the Legrangian Empire. It had never fallen to enemy assailants.

The courtyard was full of Knights, supply carts, and horses, all of which were being prepared for war. The group wound through the milling masses of the courtyard and were led to the guest chambers within the central keep. Rooms were made up for the Guardian Valthor, but he neglected to rest, instead electing to spend the remainder of the day in council with the commandant. This left the rest of the group with time to finally rest.

Claere was escorted to the ambassadorial suite, and she took Lauren with her. Over the last several weeks, Lauren had lacked for female companionship and was keen to have another woman to talk to. Due to the sensitive military nature of the fortress, Claere, as a foreigner, would not have been permitted to tour the fortress anyway. Bleiz took the opportunity to guide Calunoth, with Luca in tow, around the fortress. Calunoth was amazed at the sheer size and scope of the defensive capabilities of the fortress. Catapults lined the outer walls, interspersed with turrets from which defenders could release arrows from the cover of the stonework. The armory was massive, encompassing most of the Northern Tower, and stocked to the brim with weapons and armor. Calunoth had replaced his broken sword from the Commerel armory before leaving, but as he gazed around at the military-grade weapons employed by the Knights, he rather wished he had waited.

After several hours exploring the tower under Bleiz's guidance, the captain ushered them to the top of the tower. The room itself was small and circular. Sparsely decorated, windows opened up the room to a majestic view of Renderive. Calunoth could see both the city of Commerel to the west and what must have been the capital city to the east. Around the walls of Commerel, he could see a small force massing outside, though the distance was so great that it could have been a much larger force. It appeared Byrant's army had reached Commerel. They would be sorely surprised to discover that the gates would not open to welcome them as they had anticipated and that they would instead be met with a barrage of arrows and stone. Calunoth turned away to take in the room once more. The only furniture was a lonely pedestal in the center, upon which lay a single sheathed sword.

"What's this room for, Bleiz?" Calunoth asked the captain.

The older man had eyes only for the sword in the center of the room as he replied, "This is the Pedestal Room, where the Knights hold Relsarter, the only Holy Weapon currently in Renderivean hands. It was forged by the smith, Grayson, in the Schism Age. There are only four weapons of its equal in the world."

"If it's so important, why isn't anyone guarding it? We could just take it and run right now if we wanted to," Calunoth asked.

"Try it," Bleiz invited the former guard, gesturing at the sword. Calunoth stared at the man in confusion before accepting his offer. Stepping up to Relsarter, he marveled at the beauty of the sheath. It was beyond ornate. It was a work of art. The sheathed sword had an aura of mystique and power that caused Calunoth to hesitate before laying his hand on the hilt to unsheathe the sword. Calunoth instantly recoiled in pain as electricity bounced off the hilt, jumping back and holding his palm. The sword hilt had burned his hand! Calunoth's swearing was interrupted by a hearty laugh from behind them.

"I know it's a rite you Knights go through, but that doesn't change the fact that it's still mean, Bleiz!" Valthor said, walking in with Calethor. "We heard voices from the observation deck below and came to investigate. No luck drawing the sword, eh, Cal?"

"What good is a sword you can't even hold?!" Calunoth exclaimed, furious that he had apparently been taken for a fool.

"It can be held, just not by you," Calethor corrected him. "Relsarter was forged by the smith, Grayson, who forged his very will and soul into the blade. It can only be held by those whom the sword deems worthy, and can, according to the legends, only be drawn by the chosen hero of Renderive. Most men can't even touch it, but it's an informal rite of passage among the Knights to have new initiates try to unsheathe it."

"Can any of you touch it?" Calunoth asked the assembled group.

Bleiz shook his head. "I tried once and got the same burn as you. I can't imagine that's changed. The commandant can't hold it either, I don't know about Luca or Valthor."

"I've never actually tried," Valthor admitted. "Mostly because the hassle I'll get from the commandant if I manage to draw it isn't worth the effort."

"You should try, sire," Bleiz suggested. "Renderive could benefit from a hero right now. It would be good for morale if a royalist could draw the sword."

Valthor sighed before moving forward to grasp the sword. "I suppose there's no harm in trying," he said, wrapping his hand around the hilt. Unlike Calunoth, the Guardian was not immediately rejected by the sword, and he lifted it from its pedestal, marveling at the balance. Pulling hard, he tried to wrest the sword from the sheath. His muscles bulged, and his face contorted with the strain. But no matter how hard he pulled; he could not release the sword from the sheath. Shaking his head, he set the sword back down on its stand.

"Just as well," Valthor remarked. "It's already a pile of work being a Guardian. Throw on the extra work of being a hero, and I wouldn't have time to sleep."

Valthor moved back and Luca stepped forward to take his place. Calunoth looked on, expecting Luca to follow the same way that he had and recoil from the hilt of the sword. Instead, he watched in amazement as Luca tentatively took his turn touching the sword and did not feel the same shock that had struck Calunoth. Grasping the sword, he tried to pull the sheath off, but fared no better than Valthor, though he put in more effort than Valthor had.

"Well, well, young Draca," Calethor said to the youngest Knight. "Keep training, and maybe you'll wield that sword someday. Though Sentential knows, we could do with it now."

***

The group left the Bastion the next morning, grateful for the opportunity to have rested under a roof rather than on the ground. The journey to Deirive was much less difficult with the security of the Bastion at their backs and clear skies above. Even following Valthor's zealous pace, they could still relax.

Throughout the journey, Lauren had continued her tutelage under Calunoth during their nightly rests and was becoming stronger and faster all the time. Even Valthor begrudgingly praised her progress. Her training had been proceeding well but eventually stalled when she struggled to move onto the level required for fluid combat and sparring. As much as she was improving, Lauren was becoming increasingly infuriated with her lack of talent. Typically able to master anything she put her mind to, her consistent shortcomings were beginning to make her reconsider her stance. Perhaps Valthor had been right after all. It was at this point that Claere intervened.

The young priestess was around Calunoth and Luca's age and had similarly been trained from birth to fight. As part of the Order of the Sihleon Priestesses, she had been infused with Ynia formulae, engraved in ink across her bare skin, for years during her training and was as strong, or stronger, than many men without losing her slim and athletic figure. When she'd seen Calunoth trying to train Lauren using the methods practiced by his former Captain Oscar, she took to observing their bouts and training, watching silently as Lauren tried to master the awkward slashes of the guard's style. After seeing Calunoth disarm Lauren for the third time in succession, she strode over to their practice ground away from the campfire by the side of the road. Tying her long raven hair behind her head, she drew the long, slim sword she had recovered from the Commerel Castle treasury before departing.

Claere had been mostly silent for most of the journey thus far, keeping her interactions limited to short, terse conversations with Bleiz and Valthor. Calunoth himself hadn't spoken to her yet, partly because she hadn't spoken to him and partly because he found her intimidating. Accordingly, he was surprised to see her walk over and guide him out of the way.

"Your effort is admirable, Lauren, but you won't learn how to fight from Calunoth." Claere spoke coolly, ignoring Calunoth's protestations. "His style relies far too much on heavy blows and overwhelming opponents. It's fine for a larger man like him, but you'll never have the same success unless you change your style. Let me demonstrate." She pointed her sword at Calunoth and took up a position opposite him. "At your ready, Calunoth," she said.

Calunoth hesitantly raised his sword in return. He had seen her fight in Commerel and didn't doubt her abilities. Still, he had an internal problem with raising a weapon against a woman, regardless of their skill. He had overcome his doubts to train Lauren, but only because he knew he could hold back enough to not hurt her in any way. Claere could be a different story. She appeared far more delicate than Lauren but held herself with a grace that embodied her confidence.

Adopting his stance, Calunoth attempted a half-hearted horizontal slash at Claere's left shoulder. Because he hadn't moved in anger, he was not thrown off balance when his target disappeared, twirling away from him and leaving nothing but empty air where his target used to be. He recovered in time to block a sharp jab from Claere, who had spun to his left, then followed up with a downward slash at his shins. Because he was focused on the direction of the blade and compromised by having to move his blade awkwardly to cover his left shin, he was forced to try to shift to accommodate the motion. In doing so, he fell for Claere's feint rather than meeting her blade. Calunoth's sword sailed through clean air again, embedding itself in the soft ground and sinking two inches down. In the same motion, Claere reversed her strike and Calunoth found the cold metal of her blade at his throat. He had been completely outclassed.

"Do you see what I mean, Lauren?" Claere spoke over her shoulder. "Any contest of physical strength is one you'll lose. You have to use your brain and your agility to outwit your opponents. Calunoth was expecting me to hit back on his sword with mine. It's a common mistake for male soldiers, one that's usually fatal when facing me. This is a style that you can master."

Claere had to raise her voice over Bleiz and Luca's roaring laughter. They had just watched Calunoth be thoroughly trounced by the young woman. While Claere stayed with Lauren to teach her in more detail, Calunoth trudged, sulking, back to the campfire to sit by Valthor, ignoring the raucous laughter. The Guardian was reading through a notebook full of numbers and diagrams and comparing them to a map of the Steppe as he did so. Not wanting to disturb him, Calunoth waited until the Guardian had put away his notes to address him.

"Did you just get your arse kicked?" Valthor asked, watching Claere and Lauren engage in their own training.

"I didn't want to hurt her, that's all," Calunoth retorted. "She's fast though, I'll give her that."

"There's no shame in losing to a strong opponent, Cal, regardless of their gender. How much do you know about our Sihleon priestess?" Valthor queried.

"I know she's come from Sihleo to represent the Church of the One and that she was caught in Commerel during the coup. But that's about all," Calunoth replied.

"Is that all? Haven't you spoken to her yet?" Valthor asked. "She's quite something, you know. But then, all those priestess types are."

"How is she so strong? She can't be much older than me, but she acts a lot like you," Calunoth complained.

"Well, it's hard to give you a solid answer, but basically all of the members of her order are subjected to Ynium infusions when they're very young. The method is a closely guarded secret of the Church of the One, which is unofficially the governing body in Sihleo. In theory though, I think it's similar to the forbidden experiments performed on me at Akadaemia thirteen years ago. The Ynia infused into me was very concentrated though. I imagine the effect is similar but less extreme in Claere," Valthor explained. Calunoth thought he saw a dark shadow pass over the Guardian's face when he mentioned Akadaemia, but he dismissed it as a trick of the light.

"So then, does everyone from Sihleo have those infusions or just the priestesses? Could I get them? Would it make me stronger?" Calunoth asked, thinking about the possible strength of his nemesis.

"No," Valthor said brusquely, brushing the hair away from his left eye. "Everything has a price, Cal, power has a higher price in particular.

Only one in ten priestess candidates survive the ordeal, and what was put into me should have killed me. In exchange for that strength, priestesses lose much of their lifespan. It's rare to see one over fifty. They also can't bear children, and their mental function starts to deteriorate rapidly after forty. It's a heavy price to pay."

Calunoth was startled by the Guardian's revelations, and he pondered the graceful Claere as she continued her instruction. Then a second thought came to his mind.

"Wait, Valthor. If priestesses have a shortened lifespan due to the Ynium infusions, then does that make you the same?" Calunoth asked the Guardian directly.

Valthor gave a wry smile before answering. "Aye. It's much the same for me. I was sixteen years older when I went through those experiments, but again, the Ynia was much more concentrated. I've got ten years to live before my heart gives up for good. Give or take a couple years."

Calunoth was shocked by the Guardian's revelation. His strength and confidence was such that it seemed like he would live forever. Calunoth could only stammer out a hesitant, "Valthor, I ... I'm sorry," before being promptly cut off with a wave of the Guardian's hand.

"It was my choice. Sort of. But not one I'd recommend to anyone else. Those experiments have been banned in Renderive anyway, and unless you turn into a girl and age backward, you're not going to get the option from the Church of the One." Valthor shook his head. "Anyway, let's turn our attention to more pleasant subjects, shall we? There's a civil war going on. Maybe now would be a good time to forge some foreign relations. Why don't you go and chat with Claere yourself?"

"Well, she isn't interested in talking to me. I don't really see why I should go and talk to her. Besides, she seems pretty cold," Calunoth said, the glow of the fire obscuring the red tinge in his cheeks. Unfortunately for Calunoth, the glow wasn't enough to hide it from the Guardian.

"Ah, I see how it is," Valthor said, smirking. "Well, the priestesses are raised to be messengers of the One. They're very powerful in Sihleo. With all those responsibilities shoved on you at an early age, I can see how they can be viewed as cold. She can probably tell you more about that. But she's actually quite nice, if you take the time to talk to her. Do you want me to introduce you properly?"

"N-no, it's all right. I'm sure we'll speak more as we get closer to Deirive," Calunoth replied, now feeling distinctly isolated by the campfire and unable to count on a distraction from his companions to rescue him from his awkwardness.

"Okay, your call. I'll do it for you." Valthor replied, and before Calunoth could stop him, Valthor raised his arm and called over to the priestess. "Hey, Claere, could you come over here for a moment?"

"What? No, no, no, no, it's fine! It's okay!" Calunoth desperately tried to drag the Guardian's arm down, to no avail, and quickly sprung back into his place as the priestess walked over to the two.

Claere looked over, said a few words to Lauren, and then sauntered over. "Yes?" Claere asked, kneeling between Valthor and Calunoth.

"My friend Calunoth here was hoping you could explain more about your order. He's impressed by how you fought him and would like to know more about you," Valthor said. "I'll just go and talk with Bleiz about something. You can have my spot." Claere raised an eyebrow before shrugging and occupying the space Valthor had just deserted.

Calunoth made a mental note to try and kill Valthor after Lenocius was dead.

"I'm sorry, we didn't mean to disturb you. That was just Valthor. You don't have to stay," Calunoth said quickly.

"No, it's okay. You saved my life in Commerel, and I'm not sure if I ever actually thanked you for that in the commotion. So, thank you. I don't know how much longer we would have survived in there if you hadn't come. And you and Luca handled Reil and Jarl expertly," Claere said.

Calunoth shifted uncomfortably. "It was nothing. It was all Thomas's plan. I was just part of it. What were you doing in Commerel anyway? Why did you come to Renderive?" Calunoth asked, trying to keep the conversation interesting.

Claere smiled and said, "Learn to take a compliment. I came because I must warn the king about something. I'm afraid one of our ministers has gone rogue and is trying to undermine the Church of the One. Our latest intelligence has him active in Renderive. He's dangerous, and we think he might be involved in political matters here. I can't say much more than that. I could probably speak to Valthor, but the Speaker specifically asked me to relay this matter to the king as it would be deeply embarrassing if the details became common knowledge. What about you? I heard a bit about you from Bleiz, but you've stayed pretty quiet so far. What's your story?"

Calunoth hesitantly recounted his past to the priestess, explaining how the core in his chest had thrown him into the center of this civil war when all he wanted to do was avenge his home. He had recounted the story enough times now that he could recite it without thinking too hard about it, which made retelling it easier.

When he was done, Claere unfolded her legs and responded. "I can't imagine going through an ordeal like that. It would be like the entire priestess order being destroyed by a traitor in an instant. I'm sorry to hear this happened to you. This Alistair who stabbed you, do you know where he is now?"

Calunoth shook his head. "Alistair was the tool, not the mastermind behind the Glathaous Massacre. It's possible that he's running Glathaous through PRIMAL right now, but I think he's probably dead. No one should have survived that wound. If it turns out he's alive, then I'll deal with him next. But I have to take out the head of PRIMAL first. I know he's working with Byrant, but not much more beyond that. If I fight this war, I think I can get to him eventually."

"Well, whoever and wherever he is, I certainly hope you find him," Claere replied. "The Sihleon priestesses are raised together, selected every four years at the age of three, to be the messengers of the One. My cohort is the closest thing I have to family. We train together, live together, survive together. The Church of the One is overbearing at times. Unlike your Holy Church, the Church of the One holds significant political power in Sihleo. We exist to enforce the will of the One."

Cal furrowed his brow in distaste. "That sounds ... horrible. How can you be satisfied if your whole life is devoted to serving the Church like that?" Calunoth asked.

"The One gives us direction and meaning. Without the teachings of the One, we are but blind sheep stumbling around and succumbing to the evils of the world. Are you not an adherent to your Holy Church yourself?" Claere asked

"Well, not really. The Church in Renderive is invoked by every official, and while all our laws are derived from the holy books, it doesn't play a significant role in people's lives. At least, not that I know of. Religion is more common in the poor than in the noble classes."

"And you are of the noble classes?" Claere asked, her eyebrow raised.

"Well, no. But I grew up surrounded by the Glathaous nobles, so I guess some of it rubbed off on me. I'm just a nobody as far as the world is concerned. Luca's a noble though. You could probably talk to him about it more," Calunoth replied.

"Maybe later," Claere said with a smile and leaned back to lie on the ground.

Calunoth, in a bold move, mirrored her actions and lay down next to her, eyes skyward. Claere was reserved in her demeanor, but under that cool, alien shell was a person Calunoth felt comfortable speaking to. The person that the world had forced him to become seemed strangely compatible with the exotic Sihleon, and Calunoth felt himself becoming drawn to speak with her at length. He couldn't tell for sure, but he felt that the feeling was mutual, and they spent several hours before retiring discussing all kinds of thoughts Calunoth wouldn't have normally given voice to. The differences between Renderive and Sihleo, the nature of spirituality in the human heart, and the prospect of the Pralia Cores that was shaping the world around them. The two would continue to speak at length over the next several days. As it was, when the group finally reached the gates of Deirive, Calunoth had resolved not to kill Valthor for introducing him to the priestess.

Chapter 17

The Lines Are Drawn

The seaport of Deirive was one of the wonders of the modern world. Comprising the largest harbor in the world, an entire armada of ships connected the flourishing trade of Deirive with the rest of the world. Trade with the Chelian Isles flowed freely, with ships traveling to Draca, Revleir, and beyond. An outer wall covered the western side of the city, natural rock formations shielded the north, and soft sand guarded the south. Deirive had never been seriously attacked in its history because the terrain made an approach by land deeply unfavorable. And the sea provided the greatest natural defense for the city. So long as the harbor was not blockaded, supplies could flow freely in and out of the city, enabling the city to withstand any siege indefinitely.

With the Bastion blocking the only viable land route, the city was virtually unassailable, and had thus managed to thrive for centuries without being ravaged by war. Even with the threat of civil war ongoing, the people of Deirive lived comfortably, mostly uninterested in the prospect of war beyond the mountains. *It was a stark contrast to the spirited people of Commerel or the bustling Knights at the Bastion*, Calunoth thought to himself as the group followed Valthor through the city.

It had only been a couple months since Bleiz and Luca had found Calunoth. In that time, they had crossed the entire country and fought side by side together. Now they had finally reached their original destination, and Bleiz and Luca could at last proclaim that they had completed their mission.

Lauren would likely return to Akadaemia in the north, wiser now in the ways of the world. Bleiz and Luca would return to the garrison at the Bastion. Claere and Valthor would go on to act in their stately matters. Calunoth was the only one who had no idea what the future held for him. Would the king send him to Akadaemia to be studied on a slab? Calunoth would have liked to have stayed with his friends, but he knew there was no guarantee of that. With the war ongoing, each would have to do what they felt was needed. Calunoth just had to hope that his path would lead him to Lenocius.

Valthor led the group through the city streets to the royal palace. The palace was a relatively meager one. Although it was larger than the castle at Caern Vaughn, it was not nearly as attractive and settled into the mottled gray and black of the city effectively.

Valthor spoke brusquely with the guards, and soon the group was waiting outside the audience hall for the king to invite them in. Typically, audiences with the king were reserved many days in advance, but Valthor's rank gave him priority over virtually everyone else. Calunoth sat on a stone bench, talking anxiously with Bleiz while they waited. He had never met the king before and was concerned about the proper conduct.

Their conversation was interrupted when the massive door that closed off the audience hall swung slowly open, pushed by a tall and powerfully built man who strode out. The man bore a vibrant mane of fiery red hair echoed in a well-groomed beard. He wore armor of black steel and carried a broadsword across his back. The sword appeared to be almost as tall as Lauren. Emerging from the audience hall, he stopped when he sighted Valthor.

"Ah, Valthor! It's good to see you alive. That menace in the Caerwyn Bogs kept you busy, eh? I thought we were gonna have to replace you, you took so long." The large man spoke confidently, seeming to be completely at ease speaking with the Guardian.

"And you've lost none of that cavalier attitude of yours, Artair," Valthor retorted. "I was also kept busy fighting an underground terror cell and retaking a captured city. Although the matter in the bogs was the nastiest by far."

"Oh, really? I heard what happened at Commerel, but what went on in the bogs?" Artair asked, giving a cursory wave to the other companions as he stopped before them.

"I only have theories, but I believe the source of the concentration was a Selevirnian crystal saturating the living creatures of the bogs with Natural Ynia. The results were disturbing," Valthor replied, rising.

Artair crossed his arms and said, "Huh. You'll have to tell me more about it later. Will I see you at the Arms tonight?"

"I'll try and make an appearance. But I've got a lot to speak with Aiden about," Valthor replied, using the king's first name. Artair shrugged, then strode past the group and out the door.

"Who was that?" Lauren asked the Guardian.

"That was Artair Kaltrein. He's another Guardian. Last I heard, he was investigating a radical druid sect in Chelia. I'm glad to see he's on our side," Valthor replied. "He once cut a horse in half with that great bloody sword of his. Not someone you want to get on the wrong side of."

The doors swung open again, and an aide to the king beckoned them in. Calunoth stood with Luca and Bleiz and mirrored their actions as they followed Valthor into the throne room. Claere and Lauren followed behind. Calunoth followed Bleiz's directions as they advanced into the throne room. King Greshaun sat on a carved white marble throne high atop a dais. The king wore the winged crown that marked him as the Ruler of Renderive on his flowing gray hair. He was in his early sixties but maintained his fitness well. He bore a vicious scar across his left cheek and up past his eye that was a memento of his time on the front lines of the Third Schism War. His eyes were dark and heavy with deep bags, but he maintained a glowing air of regality.

Calunoth approached the throne alongside his friends, keeping his head bowed until he reached a charcoal mark in the stone that signified the appropriate distance from the throne. Calunoth bowed even deeper, in unison with most of his other companions, before kneeling before the marble throne. The companions strictly followed the protocol Bleiz had taught them, but the king paid it no heed. Valthor swept up the dais briskly, with no interest in formality.

"Aiden, it's good to see you again. We have much to discuss." Valthor was quick and to the point. Aiden gave the Guardian a weary smile before turning his attention to the group kneeling before his throne.

"Valthor, you are too hasty as always. You have brought new guests to my halls. Let us speak with them first, after which we can converse with each other at length," King Greshaun replied, turning his attention to the group. "I've received reports from Caern Vaughn and Commerel ahead of your arrival. I believe I must thank you for the assistance you have lent my kingdom in recent times. I am most grateful especially for your actions in Commerel. If Commerel had fallen, I fear this would have evolved into a much longer war." Then he remembered they were still kneeling. "You may stand easy."

"Of interest to you, Aiden, is the man named Calunoth Leiron, the only survivor of the Glathaous Massacre, who now bears our only known Pralia Core in his chest," Valthor told him before motioning Calunoth forward. "Cal, would you?"

Calunoth moved closer and removed his shirt, exposing the Pralia Core smoldering steadily away in his chest. Greshaun leaned forward, his steely gaze almost piercing through Calunoth as he examined the core for several moments before bidding Calunoth to redress.

"It was an incident most foul, young Calunoth. I understand you know of the individuals responsible for the massacre?" the king asked.

"Yes, Your Majesty," Calunoth replied. "The responsible parties are a Sihleon named Lenocius, who planned the attack, and Alistair Glathaous, who worked with him to expose the castle." Calunoth thought he heard a gasp behind him as he spoke, but he ignored it.

Aiden shook his head grimly and said, "To think Isaac's own son would turn traitor to his father. 'Tis an affront to the soul. Still, it is comforting to know that only demons most foul can turn my lords from me. From the reports I've received, Alistair Glathaous remains in Glathaous with Byrant's men. He hasn't been seen, but my spies tell me he has remained in the town ever since. As for this Lenocius person, I have only limited information about this individual that Cress, another Guardian, acquired from a member of PRIMAL, but I trust you and Valthor will update me accordingly."

"Your Majesty, if I may speak?" Claere stepped forward, and the king nodded his assent. "My name is Claere Heriong. I am a member of the Order of Priestesses, serving the Church of the One. I was asked to come here by the Speaker of the One. I believe I can tell you more about Lenocius. I had not realized my traveling companions had already interacted with this individual, and as such, I failed to make the connection to this PRIMAL group. Lenocius Velius is the second minister of Theoneria and has recently gone rogue. He has been attempting to subvert the will of the Church in favor of the government, the Politik, in Sihleo for several years now. He has been preaching that the One no longer has the right to rule our people, and thinks instead that humans should govern their affairs without the religious guidance of the church. We believe, and my companions have now confirmed, that he has fled to Renderive and is now working with Byrant. His motivations are unclear, but he is undoubtedly an extremely dangerous individual."

"What are his connections to PRIMAL? Is he their founder or is there more to this group?" Valthor asked the priestess.

"I don't know. We've only heard rumors of this group, but if he's involved, they can't be up to anything good. Lenocius rose to prominence by becoming the champion of Lekaia Colosseum before moving into government. He has always opposed the Church, and he has the support of many other Sihleons who have been disillusioned from the One. He should not be allowed to continue," Claere replied, brushing her long raven hair away from her face.

"And this Lenocius is the one supplying Byrant with these Pralia Cores? What does he get out of all this?" Aiden asked, directing the question at Valthor.

"We can't be sure yet. And I'm not sure that the Pralia Cores Lenocius is using are the real deal. The reports we found in the hills seemed to indicate they're close, but they hadn't perfected the formula yet. PRIMAL attacked Glathaous in order to obtain Isaac's work, the Glathaous Core in Cal's chest. I think they probably need the Glathaous Core to perfect their own. We should attempt to capture Lenocius, or other members of PRIMAL as a first course of action," Valthor said. Then he turned to the king and his voice turned hard. "Byrant has to die of course. But to be thorough, we will need to rob this rebellion of its teeth and take out this PRIMAL group as well."

"I agree," King Greshaun acceded. "But once we have the information we need, I see no reason why we cannot appoint the young Glathaous guard to be executioner. What say you, Calunoth? In exchange for your full cooperation with the military in matters relating to the Pralia Core recovered from Glathaous, I will ensure that you have the right to pass final judgment on Lenocius Velius and Alistair Glathaous. Is this acceptable to you?"

Calunoth nodded and thanked the king for his gesture. King Greshaun had the authority to order Calunoth to comply with anything, and more importantly, had the means to enforce that authority, but he had been king for many decades and had learned well the importance of treating his subjects with respect. A better outcome would always result when a subject wanted to serve and had a personal reason to do so.

Claere and Bleiz continued their individual reports to the king. He sat pensively on his throne, with Valthor standing beside him, listening without interruption. When they had finished, he clapped his hands together and spoke.

"I thank all of you. It is clear to me your journey here was not an easy one. But I must say it seems as though fate has given us the advantage in this fight if it has brought you all down the path to me. You are all dismissed. Captain Bleiz, report to the Knight Command. Luca, your father is currently securing supply lines from Draca to the Bastion, but his manor should stand free. Please guide our other guests there. Calunoth, I will appoint you a room in the palace for now. You'll be safe in Deirive, but I'm sure Sebastien will want to examine you at length. He'll send for you when he's ready. Valthor, stay here."

With that, the king waved them out of the chamber. They were led away to their respective destinations by two of the king's aides. As they left the room, King Greshaun beckoned his remaining aides to leave the chamber as well. The private conversations between the king and his Guardians were of the highest secrecy, and not even the king's own attendants could be privy to those discussions.

Once they were gone, Valthor procured a wooden chair from the shadows at the back of the chamber and pulled it up next to the king. Though they differed in rank, they relied heavily on each other and spoke as equals when ceremony was not enforced. With the chamber now empty but for the pair, the king gave a heavy sigh and held his head in his hands, his strong mask cracking before the Guardian.

"Val, I am truly relieved to see you again. You were missing in the bogs for so long, I grew greatly concerned for your well-being. I fear I need you now more than ever, my friend," Greshaun confessed.

"I've still got a few years in me. Probably not as many as you, Aiden, but I'm not going anywhere for a while. What of the other Guardians? Have any deserted?" Valthor asked.

"Two that we know of. Van and Relgar have sided with Byrant, saying his vision for the future is best for Renderive. You, Artair, and Cress are on my side. Xander's currently missing. I sent him to investigate reports of dragons in the northern Galgre Mountains and haven't heard from him in months," Greshaun reported.

"Dragons! Of course we have bloody dragons now." Valthor snorted. "They were supposed to have been extinct since the Schism Age. As if we didn't have enough problems! Anyway, Van I can understand deserting. He's always felt guilty about his own success, but what does Relgar get out of this?"

"He was most likely tempted by the power of the Pralia technology in Byrant's possession. Your companions did not bring much new information to me. How much did you tell them about the Pralia research at Glathaous?" Greshaun asked.

"I told them enough to satisfy them, but I left out most of the important details. The fewer people know about this the better. Especially that Sihleon. Calunoth will have to be told more, realistically. But the rest took my half explanation to be enough," Valthor replied. He shifted in his chair and added, "I imagine Sebastien is going to have a field day with him in his lab, and Cal's going to eventually discover the scope of what he's involved in now. He has sole possession of the only functioning Pralia Core in the royalist forces. Isaac's research appears to have been unintentionally successful."

"Unintentionally? What do you mean?" Greshaun asked.

"I've been thinking about this since I encountered that thing in the Caerwyn Bogs. I hadn't predicted I would find an ancient Pralia Core in that place. But there can be no doubt. That Pralia technology was reacting with the Life Ynia of the creatures in the bogs, somehow generating the Natural Ynia that formed that creature. The concentration of Life Ynia likely gave that construct its form. And yet as soon as Calunoth touched it, the core broke. So too did a shard of Pralia technology Byrant had given one of the traitor guards in Commerel. I'm not entirely sure how it works yet, but there is some reaction between Calunoth's core and Byrant's Pralia technology that makes Byrant's technology useless. We knew there was a connection between Life and Natural Ynia and the Pralia Cores, and Isaac wasn't basing his technology on ancient Selevirnian technology like Byrant and PRIMAL are. It was all his own work. In trying to create a source of Life Ynia for me, he inadvertently created a weapon that can be used to defeat Byrant," Valthor explained. "If it works against Byrant, it could also work against whatever the Legrangians are cooking up right now too."

"I see. So the boy could be the key to winning this war, and future wars," Greshaun mused as he slumped in his throne. "Can we remove the core? Give it to you instead?"

"I examined Calunoth at length on our travels. The wounds he received during the Glathaous Massacre were horrendous. You saw the scarring. I suspect that if we try to remove the core, his body will not survive. Seb will confirm this, but I believe that to be the case," Valthor said.

Greshaun shook his head mournfully. "I will not command one of my citizens to be harvested for the nation. A king who exploits his subjects is no king at all."

"If I may give my instincts voice, Aiden?" Valthor offered, waiting for the king's gesture to continue before doing so. "I feel like something is ... off with Calunoth. There's something about his core, how it seems to react to others, and how he himself seems ... haunted. I don't know what it is, I'm beginning to wonder if something in the core is affecting his mind. He could become unstable if we're not careful with him."

"Your instincts are usually worth attention, Val, but based on what he's been through, I don't think he's at risk of betraying us. I'll make sure an Upper Circle mage keeps an eye on him to ensure he doesn't succumb prematurely to instability," Greshaun said quietly before pondering for a moment. "Although I must say, I thought I saw something of Isaac in the boy. He was raised in Glathaous, so some resemblance is to be expected, but there's a gleam in his eyes similar to what Isaac used to have. Perhaps some of Isaac's mad genius rubbed off on him, in some form. If so, I pray that his strength surpasses Alistair's." Shaking his head to clear his musings, Greshaun continued. "But that's academic. For now, he is fully committed to the task at hand, which is suppressing this rebellion. You have done well, Valthor. Had Commerel fallen to Byrant, this civil war would have lasted much longer. As it stands, Byrant should be easy to defeat."

"What's your plan from here, Aiden? Byrant's men will likely engage the Knights on the Steppe and should fall back to Marston, then Byrantia. It would be suicide to attack the Bastion, and without Commerel, Byrant won't be able to maintain a siege," Valthor replied. "To be honest, I don't see any way to victory for him, even with PRIMAL's Pralia technology.

"He has to die. His ideas die with him then. But I suspect he believes he can capture the minds and hearts of the people enough to gain some concessions. Once that fire is lit, it will quickly spread beyond our control. He is a charismatic man, and the more time he has to spread his agenda, the more people will begin to believe in it. His sympathizers have already infected Akadaemia, among other institutions. If his beliefs continue to spread, then we could have a real uprising on our hands, one we cannot handle," Greshaun concluded.

"So we move aggressively. Can we take Byrantia from the sea? Hit the city from behind while his army is fighting on the Steppe?" Valthor wondered.

"The beaches will have been secured. And besides, they would make for a terrible landing ground. We'd lose too many men trying to take that beach. We can blockade the ports, but not take them. No, we fight them back to their cities and cut off their support. The Galgrenons could well decide the length of this conflict. They have yet to declare an allegiance, but they appear to be leaning toward Byrant, likely because of the technological edge he holds. We need to dissuade them of that."

"So we must obtain the loyalty of the Galgrenons. We'll have to give them a good reason. They've been alienated from you for a while now," Valthor replied.

Greshaun rose from his throne and strode to the back of the room to look through the stained-glass windows upon the colorful kaleidoscope of Deirive, pensive. Silence reigned for a time before he finally spoke with a sigh.

"Why do they rebel against me, Valthor? I have given them freedom and opportunity. The Knights enforce just laws. Never before has it been easier for a farmhand to become a merchant. An orphan can become the Knight's field marshal with enough dedication and work. Those born to dirt can die to gold by their own choices. Our borders are as secure as they can be. Poverty still exists of course, but it is a matter of action, not fate, in this country, unlike in Legrangia. Why then do they rebel against me? After I have worked to give them this country?"

Valthor rose and went to stand behind his king. "Although it may be for a greater cause, Aiden, freedom to succeed is also freedom to fail. Many people are scared of failure. They're more motivated by the specter of poverty than the dream of wealth. Byrant's ideals would seek to forsake both in favor of an equal outcome. That appeals to the people who live comfortably and see no reason for others not to do the same. It can never work, of course, until the hearts of men change form, but it only requires a belief to push change, regardless of how damaging that change might be. Do not feel offended. History will remember you as a just king for what you have done."

"I hope you're right." Greshaun grew quiet as he contemplated the fires that now raged in the hearts of Byrant's followers. His own citizens.

Chapter 18

A Reason to Fight

    Calunoth breathed a sigh of relief as the cool mountain air brushed his face, cooling him off. The southern portions of Renderive were known to be swelteringly hot during the height of the summer months. As the group had traveled across the foothills of the Galgre Mountains toward Galgrenon, they had been worn down by the humid warmth that had swept in from the southern coast and robbed their bodies of all moisture in concurrence with the blazing sun overhead. It had been as great a relief to feel the temperature relent and grow chillier as the air grew thinner higher up the mountain path as it had been to be journeying together again.

    Time had passed quickly for Calunoth during his stay in the royal palace at Deirive. Almost two months had passed since the group had arrived in Deirive. In those two months, Luca and Bleiz had returned to the Bastion, and Lauren had taken up work with the Upper Circle Mages and their leader, Sebastien, as they strove to understand the Pralia technology that was beginning to define this conflict. Valthor had left for the Commandant's Bastion to help coordinate the royalist war effort over a month ago. But Claere had maintained her ambassadorial role within the royal court and was the one member of the group Calunoth had spent time with.

    Left suddenly alone in the imposing city, the pair had taken to enjoying each other's company at length. The priestess spoke a great deal about her faith and experiences while Calunoth listened attentively, interested in learning what made the young woman so motivated. Then one day, the pair was walking in the palace gardens together when a messenger came from the king requesting their presence.

    The pair had hurried to the throne room and were pleasantly surprised to see their former companions lining the antechamber, having collectively been recalled by the king for the same purpose. Calunoth had spent the last month being poked and prodded by endless mages and researchers, so he had been thrilled to see familiar faces not wrapped in the red robes of the Upper Circle.

    There had been no time for reminiscing, however, as they had been beckoned into the throne room by a weary attendant. King

Greshaun had been terse in his exchange, but polite. The war effort had brought him a great deal of stress, and the deep bags under his eyes had belied the strength in his voice. Greshaun had not minced words, informing Calunoth that the Galgrenons were reportedly divided between supporting the visionary Byrant and the royalist Greshaun. Calunoth was in sole possession of the only Pralia Core in royalist hands, and news of the technology was spreading fast. As a show of faith to the Galgrenons, Greshaun had commanded Calunoth to act as his ambassador to Galgrenon, where he had hoped Calunoth could convince the rebellious Galgrenons to come back to the royalist fold, armed as they were with what was now being formally termed the Glathaous Core.

Calunoth and his companions had arrived in Galgrenon earlier in the afternoon and had been courteously received by the alderman of Galgrenon. Giric was the elected leader of the Galgrenon Council and served as the governor of the city and the surrounding lands. The city of Galgrenon itself was an engineering masterpiece. Nestled high in the Galgre Range, the mountain town had been carved out of a large basin in Mount Ferin and sat surrounded by the imposing peaks of the Galgre Range, decorated with the evergreen trees that dominated the lower peaks. Galgrenon was the capital city of the ethnic Highlanders and served as a testament to the brilliant, albeit occasionally unstable, minds that had emerged as a trademark of the highland people.

Unlike the rest of the country, Galgrenon did not follow the same nobility system that governed the lordships in other areas, instead maintaining an elected council of eleven members from various wards of the city and surrounding region. Giric had been in power for over two decades but now had to deal with the issue of war. Historically backing Renderive and officially being part of the country, the Galgrenons had always been considered a key component of the Renderivean army. However, with civil war ongoing, the people of Galgrenon were split on which side to support. Although there was a strong royalist component in Galgrenon, it was stifled by the much louder, if not larger, insurrectionists who supported Byrant. Most Galgrenons just wished to be left alone, but Byrant's vocal supporters had been pushing the city council mercilessly to declare support for the upstart duke, and the council had begun to bend. Coerced by rumors and reports of Byrant's powerful magical technology, many council members believed it would be advantageous to declare for Byrant, thereby saving their city from possible invasion.

That was the report that had been given to the king and had thus prompted him to send his own trump card, Calunoth, with his friends to influence the minds of the council toward siding against Byrant.

Giric was a royalist himself, having spent many years serving the king in the capital as a researcher before returning to practice his trade in Galgrenon and eventually leading the council. Now an old man, the alderman had lost none of his political awareness and welcomed with open arms the opportunity to sway the minds of the council. He himself was facing significant pressure to convert to Byrant's cause but had thus far resisted. While he continued to exercise his political acumen on the council, he had ordered the local embassy to be made ready for the group, and they now were forced to wait anxiously for an audience before the council.

As they waited, Calunoth had gone to the top floor of the embassy to take in the expansive mountain view. He was glad to be out of the capital city. King Greshaun had been a generous host, but the young former guard had spent most of his stay being observed and researched by the Grand Council and their leader, Grand Caster Sebastien. However, he had learned a great deal from them about the core in his chest, and he had also grown friendly with the mage, Alexander, who now accompanied them as a representative of the king's military research team.

Calunoth had learned what he had already subconsciously realized. The Glathaous Core in his chest was fundamentally interlaid with his own anatomy; if it was damaged, he would likely die. The core served to maintain the rhythm of his heart. The muscles around his heart were badly scarred but still functional. The Glathaous Core did not amplify Natural Ynia as he understood the PRIMAL cores did. Instead, the Glathaous Core had accelerated the regrowth of his body's cells in a similar manner to the experiments performed on Valthor, though to a lesser extent.

When he had been stabbed at Glathaous, the blade had pierced his heart, and he ought to have bled out there. Instead, the core had been infused with Natural Ynia, which had been converted, rather than amplified, into the Life Ynia that had accelerated the replication of his heart muscle cells to the point where they had been sealed. The result was not perfect, however. His heart had lost its ability to beat independently, and now the Glathaous Core was steadily drawing in Natural Ynia from his surroundings to keep his heart beating. Additionally, he had learned the core could heal his body if the technology was infused with Natural Ynia, but it couldn't fix complex cells. He now had a permanent lack of sensation in a minute portion of his lower back where the mages had cut into him to observe the healing process.

The mages had also shared what they had learned through reports and stolen technology. Byrant's Pralia technology was all based on the same flawed designs the group had discovered the remains of in the Llewyn Hills laboratory. Exactly how it worked was still a mystery, but they knew it was extremely dangerous, giving off far more energy than Calunoth's own core and powering all manner of strange technological defenses. While Calunoth's core acted in a unique manner, converting Natural Ynia into Life Ynia, PRIMAL's Pralia Cores seemed to have retained their designed function of amplifying Natural Ynia alone. But their technology had one fatal flaw: it was unable to survive a direct interaction with Calunoth. This made Calunoth an invaluable asset. The king had originally been inclined to keep Calunoth in the capital to be studied so the mages could eventually replicate the technology to defeat Byrant, but Valthor had convinced him to send Calunoth as his ambassador to meet with the Galgrenons instead. They were a proud people and sending anyone less than Calunoth might be seen as an insult.

Calunoth had been staring out at Galgrenon, pondering his role in this war and wondering how it could get him closer to Lenocius when his thoughts were interrupted by Alexander's arrival.

"Happy to be out of the capital now aren't you, Cal?" the mage said, his bright blue eyes shining with mirth.

"It's not the capital I'm glad to be away from, but the table and you mages poking holes in me," Calunoth retorted.

"Science requires sacrifices of us all, Master Calunoth," Alexander replied in his charming voice. A Galgrenon by birth, Alexander had studied the manipulation of energy through magic extensively and had risen quickly through the ranks of the Circles. He was now a member of the Upper Circle despite not yet reaching his thirtieth year. He carried around a tome containing many higher-ranking formulae that could be used to cast complex magical spells for both practical use and combat. Unlike Valthor, Alexander avoided using the short, terse phrases that did not require formulae on the basis that he found it too easy to let his mind wander elsewhere and create unintentional side effects. He viewed the formulae as a necessary limitation on his mind.

He waved a hand in the air, dismissing the sarcasm. "And I apologized for that about twenty times already. There aren't any useful muscles in that part of your back anyway. You'll never notice it."

Calunoth shook his head, smiling wryly. The mage had a slightly zany nature that didn't always make sense to the rest of them. "What are you doing here anyway, Alex? I thought you'd locked yourself in a room studying the light fixtures again."

"Those light fixtures were made by an esteemed professor of mine, and they're genius! I tried to explain it to you while you were on the table once. I think I can improve their efficiency by ten percent by utilizing concurrent Ynia sources. But no, I thought this would be a good opportunity to give you a tour of the town. You're our ambassador now, so it would be a good idea for you to learn more about the people you're trying to win over." Alex cocked his head and raised an eyebrow, his always tousled, mousy blond hair falling over one eye as did so.

Calunoth couldn't help but agree with the mage. He was a little eccentric at times, but his intelligence shone through, and he often offered a perspective many others would have missed. Following Alexander down to the main floor, Calunoth came across his friends on the way out and announced he was going to tour the town. To his delight, they agreed to join him. The air in Galgrenon was tense, and that tension could be felt in the air. Although they were staying in a regional embassy with every protection afforded them by law, there was every chance the common folk might decide to take action and would not be discouraged by those laws. Regardless, the group was escorted out of the embassy by Roy, one of Giric's men. Roy was a seasoned guard, and an intimidating presence given his size, and knew the town better than Alexander, who had spent the last fifteen years in Deirive, so he had volunteered to be both guard and guide.

Roy led the group through town, starting at the marketplace, then moving through the strange but wonderful technological sector, and finally touring through the residential sectors. The division in the air felt identical to the division and conflict throughout the country. Calunoth stopped frequently to speak to and learn the minds of the people in the street and was amazed at the stark differences between Galgrenon's sectors.

The technological sector represented the future of the world. This was where the innovation of the Highland people was put into action. The streets were lined with workshops and congregations of researchers and scholars all actively engaged in their own studies. The street was buzzing with energy and seemed inherently productive.

"What are all these people doing?" Bleiz asked, admiring an unusual catapult being assembled in a large, open warehouse.

"This is where a great deal of Renderive's innovations come from," Roy replied, "Almost all these workshops are funded by private donors, many from Commerel and Draca, who want to make money off of the brains of Galgrenon. Most workers here are fine with that though. Many just want to explore whatever their brains can think of, though they're usually well paid once they're established."

"So there's plenty of opportunity for the smart among them to wonder freely then? It seems like a great investment for the king," Luca observed casually.

"Only if you can prove it's worth his time," Lauren objected. "The king has a strict policy of only funding military and medical research that can justify public expenditure. Anything else he leaves to private donors, and they're only interested in what can make them money. So many of our best minds are wasted in work below their ability."

"It takes a great deal of wisdom to plow a field, even if the one plowing cannot read or write," Bleiz countered. "The opportunity to work in a lab is no different than the opportunity to work in a field. It's dangerous thinking to believe that any work is beneath you."

Calunoth felt himself agreeing with Bleiz over Lauren. In Glathaous, there were many intelligent people who worked in the forests who were wiser than some of the researchers in the castle, albeit in a different manner.

Stopping to talk at length with researchers in the technological sector, Calunoth and the entire group were regaled for nigh on half an hour by a researcher who espoused Byrant's ideas and how they would eliminate poverty and provide for all. Lauren listened with rapt attention while Bleiz quietly slid out of the conversation and carried on alone, forgoing the lecture to converse with a man operating a strange new type of grindstone that seemed to run without mechanical intervention. Calunoth's eyes started to glaze over as the researcher droned on and resolved to maintain the illusion of staying interested in the conversation while at the same time examining the surrounding sector. It was, Calunoth concluded, an exceptionally wealthy area.

Finally, the group managed to escape from the technological sector, dragging an enraptured Lauren with them. They moved on to the slums and Calunoth was astounded at the difference. While the technological sector had been abuzz with life and vibrancy, the slums were overtly downtrodden, yet vibrant with a different sort of energy. Calunoth stopped to speak with a young man helping to dig an irrigation tunnel to allow waste to flow away from the streets. He was dirty and thin but otherwise well built. In many ways, he reminded Calunoth of the loggers who used to cut down the trees outside of Glathaous.

"Hail, my good man!" Calunoth called to him. The young man rose from the hole, wiping sweat off his brow as he did so. Lauren kept her distance while Luca and Claere came closer.

"What's good, friends?" the dirt-covered young man replied in greeting.

"We hail from Deirive and have been tasked with soliciting aid from your beautiful city. We are keen to know your mind," Calunoth asked, hoping his formality would induce a more productive conversation. The effect was unanticipated.

"None a that tight talk 'ere, mate. We've a mind to 'elp the king, but you gotta talk like a man," the young man replied, prompting a snort of laughter from the usually serious Claere. Red-faced, Calunoth suppressed his annoyance and continued in a more casual manner.

"We've heard talk the Galgrenons want to support Byrant. What do you know, given that you actually live here?" Calunoth asked.

"I'll tell you what we want. We just want to be left alone," the young man said. "We've managed just fine under the king, and we don't want Byrant talking down to us like those posh pricks from tech sec. We'd prefer the king, if it comes to blows, but we don't want to do no fightin'."

"But you live in such terrible conditions!" Lauren exclaimed. "Why wouldn't you want to at least take a risk with Byrant? You wouldn't have to work so hard if he came into power."

"What's terrible about it? We don' sleep on goose-feather mattresses, but we get by a' right. I work hard so I can earn my keep and maybe convince a woman to make a better man out of me. If I have to dig a few holes and build a few dams to move up in the world, I'm a' right with that. We all are," the young man replied, putting his fists on his hips. "And when I do find a woman, she'll be with me by me own work, not by some prince's cast-offs from his ivory tower."

His response stymied Lauren, and Calunoth resolved to speak to her later about her hesitance. Given her Galgrenon roots, he could understand her interest in Byrant's ideals, which could be a problem in the future. Calunoth resolved to watch the young researcher closely from then on out. Calunoth thanked the man and the group headed back to the embassy.

His opportunity to talk to Lauren came later in the evening after the others had retired. However, she waved away his questions saying she had just been surprised by the man's response and there was no reason for Calunoth to worry.

Calunoth had to wonder otherwise.

***

Calunoth was delayed in his return to the embassy after being summoned to city hall to speak at length with Giric, so the rest of the group went on without him. After several hours of discussion about the best method to consolidate royalist support, Calunoth was left fatigued but emboldened. It was clear that Giric was a master politician, and Calunoth was sorely grateful he was on their side. With the moon rising in the sky, Calunoth finally returned to the embassy's abandoned common room. All but Lauren had retired to their beds, so after he had questioned her, Calunoth had attempted to retire himself, but after several uncomfortable hours of tossing and turning, he found himself unable to find even the half-sleep that haunted his nights. He climbed out of bed and returned to the common room, surprised to see Claere and Luca suffering from their own restlessness and conversing quietly over steaming teacups.

"What are you two still doing up?" Calunoth asked.

"We're trying to see who can stay awake the longest!" Luca replied cheerfully. "My record is four days."

"My record is six," Claere replied curtly. "But that's not what we were doing. We were just trying to figure out what the point of this war is. And what Sihleo has to do with it."

"I didn't know you could hold an intelligent conversation, Luca," Calunoth joked to his friend.

"Oh, I can't," Luca replied. "But I can look pretty and listen, and it turns out that ladies appreciate that far more."

"Stop it, you two," Claere chided them. "What about you, Cal? What are you still doing up?"

"I was just thinking about how different the people of Galgrenon are. They seem so divided, despite living in the same place. The rest of this country is divided along geographical lines, but the Galgrenons seem divided only by personality," Calunoth replied.

"You're basically where Luca and I were twenty minutes ago," Claere replied. "The wealthy and academic in Galgrenon love Byrant's ideals, but the poor, who would supposedly benefit the most, don't trust him at all. That man we met earlier only wants the chance to live his life freely, and he doesn't think that Byrant will give that to him."

"I'm a simple man, so I can understand that perspective. But it takes someone smarter than me to understand what Byrant's talking about. I get that he wants to help the poor, but from what I can see, they seem to be doing just fine by themselves. I think Valthor has it figured out, but I get the impression he'd jump at the chance to kill Byrant personally," Luca commented.

"I think Lauren would have a better idea of how Byrant's supporters think. Obviously, I would never hurt her, but I'm not sure how wise it would be to keep traveling with her if she becomes a liability. She's clearly sympathetic to Byrant," Claere spoke softly, hoping Lauren wouldn't accidentally hear their conversation if she came in now. "I can relate to the motivation to help, but all his ideas would only hurt the people he wants to help."

"What exactly are his plans anyway?" Luca interjected. "It's easy enough to get people riled up, but what's his plan if he actually takes power?"

Claere put her teacup down and shrugged. "Lauren would know all the details. She's studied Byrant's work in detail. I only know the bare bones of it. He intends to use the power of the throne to seize wealth and power from the merchant and upper classes and distribute it to the poorest in society. He wishes to push the poor up with the force of the ruling class. This opposes Greshaun's policy of enabling the poor to succeed on their own merit rather than circumstance. The problem with Byrant's thinking is that it doesn't create wealth, it only moves it around. It feels good to give a beggar a meal, but a better solution would be to teach him how to cook. It's an easy sell to people who want to help the poor but who only want to help them for their own gratification rather than to eliminate poverty. What about you, Cal? Where do you stand on Byrant's ideals?"

"I don't care about the politics or about poverty or about any of that stuff. I just want to kill Lenocius and everyone else involved with PRIMAL. If I have to fight all six Guardians to get to him, I will. Byrant is no different. If he's in my way, I want him gone. The king and Valthor have been good to me, and they'll help me get there, so I'm happy to fight for the king as long as that's the case," Calunoth replied.

Luca added, "I swore an oath on my honor to support the Crown of Renderive when I became a Knight. I know a couple of Byrant's men tried to sway the Knights by claiming Byrant as the rightful holder of the Crown, but that didn't get them very far. Besides, my father would hang me upside down from the battlements if I even thought about revolting against the king. Without my honor, or my family, I haven't got an awful lot left to live for."

The conversation was abruptly ended by an irritable Bleiz emerging from his room and telling them to shut up and go to bed. Although the man could only technically order Luca, Calunoth and Claere hastily followed the captain's orders.

And a despondent Lauren, listening to the conversation in the main room through her own door, did the same.

***

The call from Giric came early the next morning. The group had been summoned to meet with the council at their first sitting of the day. Not wanting to offend their hosts, the group donned their finest clothing. Calunoth wore a cloak of brilliant red that contrasted sharply with the forest-green cloak of the Sihleon priestess. Luca and Bleiz wore their freshly oiled armor and looked as sharp as ever while Lauren had chosen the formal robes of Akadaemia.

The royalist faction currently held four of the eleven seats firmly, led by Giric. The insurrectionists controlled the same number, led by the self-styled social scientist, Gordon. Gordon had been a highly accomplished instructor at the local institutions for many years and had swiftly gained a great deal of popularity among the young of

Galgrenon. Giric claimed much of the older voters. The remaining three seats were undecided, but the council was being forced to issue a formal proclamation from both Greshaun and Byrant to state their position, and the council needed at least six members in agreeance to do so. Either side needed two of the three remaining votes to decide the role Galgrenon would play in this war.

Byrant was represented by his own delegation, a trio of young Galgrenons led by a young man known as Leferte. The man spoke first to the council with a silver-tongued appeal to the sensibilities of the council before finishing with a thinly veiled threat regarding the fate of Galgrenon should it side with the king and lose.

Calunoth took the stand next. As he descended, Leferte bumped a shoulder into his. Calunoth did not possess the same persuasive speech as Leferte but spoke with the conviction granted to him by his experience. Although he could not explicitly tie Byrant to PRIMAL's acts, he could still allude to their nefarious actions, insinuating that one who consorts with such shady individuals could not be trusted as the moral leader of the nation.

The council listened and then sat in judgment. Ultimately, neither man's renditions proved moving.

It was here Giric revealed his masterstroke. His conversation with Calunoth the night before had allowed him to formulate his plan. If Byrant could be linked to PRIMAL, who by dint of the king's spy network were being blamed across the continent for the infamous Glathaous Massacre and the Commerel Coup, supporting him would become untenable.

"I would like to now bring the most recent reports received from His Majesty King Greshaun to the attention of the council," Giric announced through his flowing white beard as he brandished several sheets of parchment. "The organization of malcontents operating throughout the country responsible for the Glathaous Massacre and Commerel Coup have been associated with Duke Byrant! Operating under the name, PRIMAL, they have utilized every underhanded measure to overthrow our great country. And Duke Byrant is their main sponsor! How can we justify siding with such a man?"

Gordon replied by slamming his beefy hands on the table, his spectacles almost flying off his nose as he rose to respond. "Duke Byrant has no such associations with such an organization! This is simply misinformation spread by the king! Alistair Glathaous and the

Lord Steward Reil were responsible for these events! And no proof of such an organization even exists! It is fitting that someone as old and out of touch as you would fall for such a trick, Giric!"

"Is that so, Councilor Gordon? Well then, explain this!" Giric threw the papers down flamboyantly and pulled out a small piece of midnight-black cloth emblazoned with a strange insignia, a white "P" with its center enclosing a white eye. "This cloth was discovered at the Clern Ruins to the north. This insignia is not representative of any noble house in Renderive, nor is it the brand of any guild, band, merchant, or institute! I'd wager it's the garb of PRIMAL, on our very doorstep!"

"All you have is a piece of cloth! It could be a fabrication for all we know. It does not prove the existence of this PRIMAL organization, never mind proving an association with Duke Byrant!" Gordon retorted, though his voice wavered almost imperceptibly.

"If you're so certain, Councilor, then you will not oppose an investigation into the matter?" Giric demanded. "The Clern Ruins are of such age there is almost nothing left and is in the middle of treacherous wilderness. Why would anyone go there at all if not to establish a base for a terrorist organization like PRIMAL?"

Gordon's face contorted as he worked to hide the scowl that threatened to betray his true emotions before he relented, his face once again forced into neutrality. "Very well, if you are so certain, Alderman Giric, then I am keen to prove you a fool and a liar. Do whatever you see fit."

Giric nominated his own men, with the inclusion of Calunoth and his companions, to lead the investigation. Calunoth's experience with PRIMAL would be invaluable if they turned out to be active in the ruins.

This decision was opposed by the insurrectionists, and Gordon chose to abstain from voting. However, the insurrectionists were overruled by the royalists and undecided members of the council. The undecided's longed for a clear-cut reason to support one side over the other and were appropriately amenable to the investigation.

Giric delegated a collection of several of Glagrenon's guards, led by their grizzled Captain Craig, for the mission. Calunoth, for his part, leapt at the chance to pursue PRIMAL directly. So upon the dawn, the companions returned to the road again, the Clern Ruins of the Galgre Mountains their new destination.

Chapter 19

Traces of the Past

The path to the Clern Ruins as described by Giric was no path at all. While the journey to Galgrenon had been made far easier by the smooth and well-maintained road that had been hewn into the mountainside, the uncharted path the companions now traversed was only an amalgamation of slippery rocks and fallen trees.

That did not intimidate Bleiz and Claere, who forged onward without complaint. Bleiz's years of experience as a Knight of the Wilds and Claere's strict training in the priestess core meant the path would have to be literally untraversable before they would complain. Lauren too, had no trouble navigating the route, citing her frequent time spent navigating such terrain as a child in Galgrenon. Luca, Calunoth, and Alexander were less resilient than their companions. Alexander, who had spent most of his life in paved cities, was distinctly irritated by the slippery rocks and the overturned trees that kept catching the red cloak that marked him as member of the Renderivean Upper Circle.

Luca and Calunoth walked together, both of the same mood. The continuous lack of sleep had grated heavily on Calunoth's nerves, leaving him taut and irritable, and Luca's typically cheerful countenance was exasperated both by the young guard's mood and the sudden barrage of rain that had drenched the group just past midday.

Roy guided the group. He had taken on the mantle of navigator, holding the map that had been hand drawn by Giric's scouts in front of him as he looked for the milestones marked on the map. Although the path seemed meandering and winding, Roy assured Calunoth that they were heading in the right direction, and his confidence gave Calunoth the opportunity to admire his surroundings despite his foul mood.

The mountain scenery was both beautiful and vast, with the tallest peak of the Galgre Range, Mount Craggenoch, stretching up beyond the clouds to challenge the heavens with its reach. They passed waterfalls and gushing streams that trickled pure mountain water down the steep slopes into the grandiose Shellthrone Lake visible thousands of feet below. The air was thin and chill but refreshingly crisp after the smog that flowed from the steelworks in Galgrenon's technological sector.

The companions did not travel quickly as they had to carefully navigate the perilous route, freezing at one point as a large bear neared their group only to scamper away at the sounds of rattling scabbards. Their group was relatively large, much larger than Calunoth was accustomed to traveling with, consisting of his own companions, Roy, Captain Craig, and eight of Giric's men who were empowered to arrest and detain anyone considered unsavory.

After several hours of tracking through the wilderness, the group came across a worn goat trail that showed signs of activity. Heavy, booted footprints were ingrained into the dirt trail, with multiple bushes and branches trampled or swept aside unnaturally. They followed the trail for several more hours, and the sun was beginning to dip down over the plains to the west when they finally came to the place marked on the map.

Calunoth found himself looking at a wide valley that had clearly been conquered by nature. Tall pine trees grew high into the sky, towering over the stony floor of the valley, shielding it from the dying light of the sun. At first glance, the valley seemed completely inconspicuous, as remarkable as the rest of the mountain scenery and equally as unremarkable in its surroundings. But Calunoth could tell something was amiss here. The Pralia Core in his chest had begun to give off the warm glow that signaled the presence of another Pralia Core. The glow was hidden beneath his hardened leather armor, but he could feel it clearly on the skin of his chest.

As they descended into the valley, Calunoth began to see signs of habitation but only traces remained. Large stone pillars emerged, almost rendered invisible by the thick veneer of moss and vines that covered them even as they lay forgotten on the ground. Similar pieces lay scattered, all appearing to be ancient portions of the buildings that now lay in ruins in the otherwise verdant clearing. Sweeping away some of the moss on a passing boulder, Calunoth saw the blackened surface of the deformed rubble. Curious lines were etched along the fallen stones, detailing the architectural beauty that had been long lost.

"This is the place!" Roy announced to the group behind him. "The Clern Ruins stretch for miles around this valley, so we might have to do a bit of searching."

"We'd better make camp here for the night. We have enough people here, so we can run a double one-hour watch each, and the whole group can get some rest," Bleiz ordered. Even though he was not commanding a squadron of Knights, his automatic reversion to leadership was reflexive. "Are you all right with that, Cal?"

Calunoth nodded absentmindedly. His core was remaining warm, without increasing in temperature, as he walked around the valley. If PRIMAL was using Pralia technology in this place, they must still be far away. Signs of activity were plain to see, however, with a path cleared through the underbrush to the largest set of remaining ruins. The path terminated before what could have been a temple or a church by design, but the building was mostly hidden by greenery, and it was difficult to see much of the underlying design. The roof had collapsed in on itself long ago.

"What are you thinking?" Alexander asked Calunoth, coming up behind him. Lauren accompanied the red-robed mage. Technically, as a member of the Upper Circle, Alexander would be Lauren's commanding officer given she was a representative of Akadaemia. However, Alexander shirked this responsibility entirely. He was happy to guide, not to lead.

"I don't know how you can really call these ruins. There's barely anything left here. But there is *something* here. My core's heating up, which means that there must be another Pralia Core somewhere nearby."

"If there was a lot left, they'd be called the Clern Buildings, not the Clern Ruins," Alexander replied jokingly. "This is just one of several spots that make up the ruins. They've been studied before by the academics in Galgrenon, but there's so little left it was eventually decided it wouldn't justify further excavation. But I've wanted to come here for a while. There's still lots to explore."

"Do you want to take a look at that building?" Lauren asked, motioning to the largest section of ruins Calunoth had been eyeing. "It's getting late, but we still have enough light to see."

Calunoth nodded his assent, and they went to examine the collapsed building. As they approached, Calunoth felt a shiver crawl up his spine. Maybe it was the encroaching darkness or the mist that had begun to descend from the mountain top, but he felt as though a strange presence was pervading the valley. He felt like he was being watched.

Approaching the building, Calunoth saw that the entrance way had collapsed and been blocked by rubble. With the remains of the roof shielding some of the collapsed stone from the elements, it had survived the rampage of nature that had taken much of the surrounding rubble and lay only lightly covered by the mosses and small grasses that had sprung up around it.

"How long do you think this has been here?" Calunoth asked the others, who were studying the exposed stones furtively.

"No idea, several centuries at least. But I can find out. Stay here for a moment." Alexander said before hurrying back to the camp, where a roaring fire had now sprung up to provide warmth to the new inhabitants of the clearing. Alexander returned swiftly, clutching one of his massive tomes in his hands. "I wish I could have carried more of these, but I figured this book would be useful if we were looking for ruins."

Even in the fading light Calunoth could read the title, written in bright gold ink as it was: *Recognizing, Marking, and Recording Masonry and Steelwork*. "What is it, Alex?" Calunoth asked.

"It's a formulae book used in prospecting and archaeology. It should help me date these stones. Just give us a minute," Alexander replied and started leafing through the tome.

Calunoth had gained a functioning understanding of complex magic from his conversations with Valthor. Basic spells, such as the ones required to start a fire or pull water from the ground, could be managed with a simple phrase provided the concentration and willpower of the caster was sufficient to move the Natural Ynia through their bodies and into the caster's target. Highly accomplished spellcasters like Valthor or Sebastien could also conduct mid-level spells under those conditions, though the Ynia required was proportionally larger and far more likely to be diverted in unintentional directions. As a result, even accomplished magic users were hesitant to use that method to cast spells. Alexander was not at that level and only able to cast mid-level spells using the formulae books derived from years of research and development. Spellcasters inscribed the formulae in the air, guided by incantations that focused the mind on the correct movement of Ynia. Valthor had once explained that while mid-level spells had been developed by science and research, many of the most advanced spells had been recovered from ancient religious texts, the incantations often containing meaning and insights into the nature of the world that were beyond the understanding of the spellcaster.

Alexander could only effectively cast one advanced spell, which he reliably informed them could light up an entire city, but the Ynia that had to be channeled was of such magnitude that he didn't dare risk it unless his life depended on it. His Life Ynia would react to the Natural Ynia that passed through him and likely cost him dearly in the process. The spell that he was casting over the ancient stones was a mid-level spell that Alexander was comfortable with and confident casting. Calunoth watched on silently as the mage wove the intricate formulae signs into the air in front of him as he chanted quietly beneath his breath, careful not to break Alexander's concentration. After several long seconds, Alexander opened his eyes and banished the formulae from the air with a curt sweep of his hand.

"Well?" Calunoth asked the mage.

"This valley has been here for tens of thousands of years. I wasn't able to get a clear number, but that doesn't really matter. What matters is these stones. They changed form, meaning they were carved over two thousand years ago, which would have been before the New Age and likely well into the Lost Ages, pf which few records remain. It could be Selevirnian, but it could be something else. The Selevirnians are the only people we know of who existed in the Lost Ages, but we don't have any records left from that time to confirm if they were the only inhabitants."

"It would make sense if it was Selevirnian. I can sense Pralia technology somewhere nearby. If PRIMAL is active here, they'd likely be working with ancient Selevirnian technology, like they were in the Llewyn Hills," Lauren surmised, sitting on one of the moss-covered collapsed stones. As she did, she shifted slightly, aware this stone was colder than it should have been. Seeing her discomfort, Alexander motioned for her to move and examined the space where Lauren had been sitting. He frowned, then walked back to the campfire, returning with a burning log that doubled as a light.

"Be careful with that, Alex," Calunoth warned, "You could set this entire valley on fire if you're not careful."

"Don't worry about it," Alexander retorted. "There's so much water in this valley, I don't think I could start a fire here if I tried." Where were you sitting?" Lauren motioned to the space on the stone next to her where she had been sitting previously. Alexander approached the stone and carefully lowered the torch down onto the mossy rock, burning away the moss before stifling the fire with

Calunoth's help so it would not spread beyond the collapsed stonework. With the moss cleared from the stone, a dull placard appeared on the stone before them, so dirty and worn it was completely illegible.

"What do you think it says?" Calunoth asked Alexander.

"I can't tell, but I can bring the curvature of the lettering back, which should be enough. Here, hold this," Alexander replied, handing him the torch. Returning to his tome, he leafed through it again until he found the passage he was looking for. Collecting himself, he began to recite a second spell, this one far less complex than the first but one that still required the utmost concentration from the mage.

Calunoth watched in amazement as the placard began to shine with a pale light, and the engraved lettering suddenly shook off its ruined stature and shimmered like new.

"I can't really read these symbols. I recognize some of them—they're still used in Common—but there isn't enough in Common for me to read any of it. Although ..." Calunoth angled his head to the side, curious. "I think some of these might be Selevirnian. Lauren?"

Lauren knelt closer and said, "These are definitely some of the same symbols I saw on that PRIMAL technology in the Llewyn Hills." Lauren squinted as she examined the engravings. "'Welcome ...' something. I think this word is 'Jakert,' um, 'city of ...' ... something." She shook her head as she rose and stood back. "It's also the same language I saw in PRIMAL's notes. But I can't translate much more than that. It seems like there was a city here long ago, but the dialect is so old, we'd have to take it to an expert in linguistics. It's almost certainly Selevirnian in origin though." Lauren started scribbling notes on a sheaf of paper she had brought with her.

"Are you okay, Alex?" Calunoth noticed the mage swaying slightly, appearing dizzy.

"I'm fine, it's just …. That was just more Natural Ynia than I expected to handle. It drains you when you use that much," Alexander replied, accepting Calunoth's stabilizing hand.

"I think that's enough for tonight. Come on, let's get some food. We can check this place out more tomorrow." Calunoth helped the mage back to the camp where they rested for the evening under the watchful gaze of the stars as Lauren continued to examine her scribbling.

***

Calunoth's half-sleep was broken in the early hours before dawn by a distant rumbling as the ground began to shake beneath him, jarring him awake. Bolting upright, he reached instinctively for his sword and sprang to his feet with his weapon in hand. Looking around the clearing, he saw all his companions in a similar stance, rising from their rest to fight off whatever strange force had awoken them. Craig was the first to lower his weapon as he glanced sharply around the surrounding valley.

"Earthquake," he muttered, sheathing his sword, and going to check on the men.

"What was that?" Luca asked, remaining on his knees in anticipation of another quake.

Lauren answered him. "That was an earthquake. They're fairly common in the mountains. The earth is shifting beneath us. No one is quite sure why this happens yet, but they're usually limited to short, insignificant quakes like that. There's only been one major one in my lifetime, and that almost destroyed a mining village to the north of here."

"It's all right," Luca grumbled. "I didn't want to sleep anyway."

"We're so close to morning, we may as well just carry on," Claere informed him smartly.

Calunoth took the opportunity to explain what they had discovered at the ruins the previous evening, after which Claere pondered for a moment before announcing, "We should take a closer look at these ruins. It's lighter now, so we'll be able to see more clearly."

Calunoth guided the group over to the ruined building, pointing out the placard they had discovered the night before as he did so. His companions spent the morning crawling through the building, now illuminated by the light, while Giric's men began searching the other regions of the valley. Calunoth was beginning to lose hope of finding anything since his core remained resolutely warm without changing until he suddenly heard a grinding sound and Claere shouting out nearby. Clambering over the ruined rocks, he arrived beside Claere, followed closely behind by his other companions.

Calunoth felt the warmth in his chest rise a fraction as he gazed at the open cave Claere had unearthed in the side of the mountain.

"Where did this come from?" Alexander demanded. "This wasn't here last night!"

"I don't know," Claere replied. "I just leaned on this pillar and the entrance just opened. I think I triggered a switch somewhere." Claere pointed to a moss-covered stone pillar set into the mountain side, inlaid with what appeared to be symbols beneath the moss.

"We need to go down there," Calunoth reported grimly. "I can feel something, probably PRIMAL technology. Let's get the other men to come with us."

Calunoth called Giric and his men over, and the group converged around the entrance. The entrance was about the size of two doors and beckoned them onto a path descending toward the core of the mountain. The air smelled damp and musty, indicating that water flowed somewhere in the cavern. It was impossible to tell how far down the cave went.

"All right, everyone," Craig announced to the assembled crowd. "We'll leave two up here to guard the entrance. The rest of us will head in. Roy, take the girl and stay up here." He pointed at Lauren. "We'll only go as far as we can reach in half a day. Then we come out. We can map the tunnel as we go. Stay sharp everyone."

While Lauren and Roy stood back, Craig and Bleiz led the men into the cavern, with Luca and Alexander interspersed with Giric's men. Claere and Calunoth waited for the men to filter past them before following slowly behind. The tunnel was wide enough for the group to walk in pairs. Walking in, Calunoth noticed the wall was full of cracks and the tunnel seemed well traveled. The tunnel floor was dry and well marked, and the group passed frequent directional arrows on the walls as they went slowly further into the cavern. The caverns were clearly inhabited. Remembering the explosion that had rocked the cavern in the Llewyn Hills, Calunoth went to raise his voice and shout a precautionary warning to Craig and Bleiz at the front of the pack, but the words were jolted out of his mouth by a sudden violent rumbling. Glancing around quickly, Calunoth saw the cracks in the wall expanding rapidly as the earth began to shake violently, spilling dust from the tunnel and spreading more spiderweb-like cracks through the walls.

"AFTERSHOCK!" yelled Craig. "Everyone get out! Out of the tunnel!"

But the man's warning came too late. The cracks spread into the ground and caused the floor to split beneath them. Calunoth grabbed at Claere's hand and held on tightly as the floor collapsed beneath her. He was unable to help her, however, and he too was pulled into the new chasm in the floor after Claere, heavy rocks pelting down on him from above as he fell. Ahead of Calunoth, the remaining men had fled deeper into the cave as they had tried to avoid the collapsing floor, only to find themselves similarly engulfed by it, with Craig and Bleiz falling into another chasm, their men close behind them. With a heavy thud, Craig and Bleiz landed beside each other, with Craig promptly being squashed by a trailing Luca. The other men landed hard on the ground around them. Calunoth and Claere had no such swift landing, however, and instead kept falling deeper into the earth, sliding down the almost vertical slope that had appeared beneath them and landing heavily together on a stone floor deep in the depths of the cavern. Calunoth saw rocks beginning to rain down on them from above and instinctively threw himself on top of the winded Claere. His last thought before losing consciousness was a simple one.

I can't die here.

Chapter 20

<u>The Rot in the Roots</u>

Luca coughed heavily as the rising dust from the collapsed passageway engulfed him and his companions. Air swept past him deeper into the chasm they'd fallen into; rushing wind followed the reverberations that echoed down the passageway not far above. The passage itself was now cloaked in darkness, the torches extinguished by the rushing air, and the only indication that anyone had survived came in the form of groaning from the men strewn along the corridor. Regaining his feet first, Luca called out to his commanding officer and received a bright burst of light in response. Bleiz's torch erupted back into life, illuminating the hallway. With light now available, Luca scrambled up some of the fallen rubble and surveyed his surroundings.

The tunnel above them had completely collapsed, burying the previous fifteen paces under the weight of the hard rock of the mountain. Part of the floor remained cracked, but held, and carried the weight of the collapsed stone, blocking their path back to the entrance. Climbing to the top of the rubble, one of Giric's men found a small crevice, no larger than the man's own eye, that permitted a view to the other side of the wreckage. From his position, he announced that the floor had caved in on the other side. Even if they managed to clear away the rubble, the chasm that had formed on the other side of this pile would be untraversable. The way back was completely blocked.

Bleiz helped Craig to his feet, who then added his own torchlight to the tunnel so the damage could be properly surveyed. They had brought fourteen men into the tunnel with them, not counting Bleiz, Craig, and Luca, six of Giric's men and Alexander laying on the floor. Apart from a few cuts and bruises, the men were shaken, but otherwise unharmed. That left four people unaccounted for.

"Where's Cal? And Claere?" Luca asked, his heart in his throat as he scanned the tunnel for his friends.

"They were at the back of the group with two of Giric's men," Bleiz said grimly. "They either fell into the hole past those rocks, or they're somewhere underneath them. Either way, it doesn't look good."

"We have to find them!" Luca cried. "Let's start clearing this rubble. We have to get to them!" As he spoke, the young Knight ran up the rocks and tried to shift one of the smaller boulders. But even with all his immense strength, he could hardly move it.

"Luca!" Bleiz barked. "There's nothing we can do right now. It would take days to move all those. We'd starve before we moved them all given our supplies are back at the campsite."

"We can't just leave them!" Luca argued vehemently. "What do we do?"

"First, we calm down," Bleiz said. "You're a Knight. You know better than to let your emotions get the better of you." In the gloom of the tunnel, Luca could hear the restrained grief in Bleiz's voice, but the man was such a professional that the change in his tone was almost imperceptible.

Craig cleared his throat to interrupt the conversation. As the leader of the excursion, he was responsible for deciding the next course of action.

"This tunnel shouldn't have collapsed with a quake like that. Something else has been affecting the integrity of the tunnel. But that's irrelevant. The Knight is correct. It would take more men and time than we have to get through those rocks, and there's no telling who else is down here. Roy will have seen what happened, and he'll have gone back to the city to bring the miners here for us," Craig said.

"Should we just wait here then? We could try and shift some of the rocks ourselves and make the job easier for our rescuers," Bleiz suggested, silencing Luca's protestations.

"Without the proper tools, we wouldn't make enough of a difference for them to care." Craig admitted. "And we still have a job we came here to do. There's only one way for us to go right now. Forward."

Bleiz nodded, disquieted, accepting the man's rationale.

"What about Cal and Claere?" Luca demanded. "We can't just leave them!"

"They might have fallen through the floor as well. See how the rocks have slanted? If they did, then there might be other tunnels deeper in, just like this one," Craig pointed out. "If they weren't buried, we might find them if we go further in."

"So, let's go!" Luca commanded the group, all of whom had now regained their feet. Forging ahead relentlessly, Luca took the torch from Bleiz and marched into the depths of the cave.

***

"Stay down!" Roy barked at Lauren as he knelt, steadying himself on a fragment of the ruins. The ground shook around them with less urgency than before but enough to disconcert the young scholar. Unlike earlier, when the first earthquake had jolted them awake, she was fully aware of her surroundings and had been subconsciously expecting the aftershock. It felt more violent than the first but only by virtue of the fact that she had experienced it from start to finish. The surrounding stones vibrated, but otherwise seemed to weather the second earthquake well.

The noises from the open tunnel were far less reassuring. As the quake began to die down, Lauren could hear shouting echoing from down the tunnel, followed by a mighty crash and the sound of rocks falling. Lauren and Roy were both startled by the noises. When the shaking had stopped, Roy descended into the tunnel, emerging after some time with a grave expression on his face.

"The tunnel has collapsed. I don't know how deep it goes, but we're going to need to dig them out. We have to get back to Galgrenon and get help," he reported.

"Are they okay?" Lauren replied anxiously, her blond hair falling over her face.

"I don't know," Roy replied grimly. There's a pit that goes to the center of the earth on this side. They might have fallen down there or been trapped under the pile of rock beyond the pit. We need help. We can't possibly move any of this ourselves. We need the mining guild."

"Then let's go!" Lauren exclaimed, running back to camp and tearing through it, gathering her belongings. Roy followed close behind, and they began the short, arduous route back to Galgrenon. They moved quickly, nimbly jogging down their trodden path with more assurance than they had on their way into the grove. Even at their accelerated pace, it would be several hours before they returned to Galgrenon, and it would take time to navigate the mining machinery needed over the rocky terrain.

Roy struggled to keep up with the researcher, to his great chagrin, and resorted to slowing her down with conversation. Although he was confident he could outrun the girl over a distance, she was moving at a rate that would exhaust her and likely prolong their journey.

"Out of curiosity, Lauren, how did you come to travel with those people?" Roy asked the researcher, breathing heavily as he did so. Lauren slowed as her breath began to catch in her throat with her answer.

"My professor sent me to deliver the Glathaous Core to Akadaemia. After I'd met up with them, PRIMAL chased us out of town and into the Caerwyn Bogs. I've been traveling with them ever since," Lauren responded, huffing.

"Begging your pardon, but you seem to be the odd one out in that group," Roy noted. "You seem to be the only one who wouldn't kill Byrant on sight."

Lauren slowed substantially, her legs defying her heart as she continued to jog. "I guess I'm just more optimistic about him than they are. I learned so much about Byrant at Akadaemia. He cares for all people, regardless of their wealth. And he criticizes people who have done nothing to earn their wealth beyond being born while peasants have to break their backs just to get food. I don't think he's evil. I think he just wants to help those in need."

"You sound like many the young lads in Galgrenon," Roy replied. "They say much the same. Byrant would take from the wealthy who have excess and give to the poor who don't."

"Exactly!" Lauren agreed. "I don't want a war, but I do want to see the people get what they deserve for their work."

"If you want to separate a man from his inheritance, you'll have to do so by force. The only way those ideas are enacted is through conflict," Roy replied. "You could fight for that if you wanted to, but it would mean going against your friends, if they still live. Is that something you're willing to do?"

Lauren did not respond. Shaking her head, she dismissed the guard's words. "We don't have time to talk. We have to get back to Galgrenon." And with that, she resumed her blistering pace, but the guard's words stayed with her even as she ran along the rocky mountain path.

***

Luca led the way through the tunnels, sword in one hand, torch in the other, nearly jogging even as he kept his eyes peeled for signs of life. This tunnel was clearly inhabited. Lit torches decorated the walls, illuminating the cavern and negating the need for the group to bear their own lights. They were progressing quickly through the tunnel when Bleiz threw his arm in front of Luca, stopping him and the rest of the group in their tracks. Holding his finger to his lips, Bleiz bid the group to fall silent, and as they did, they could hear the heavy pounding of booted feet advancing through the tunnel toward them.

The tunnel curved sharply to the left up ahead, giving the group the advantage of surprise as they lay in wait for the figures to appear. On cue, two black-clad men appeared suddenly around the corner. The group did not give them time to raise the alarm. Bleiz and Craig moved expertly, dispatching both silently, allowing their screams to die in their throats as they fell to the ground.

As the group continued deeper into the earth, the light of the torches began to fade and was replaced by a familiar glow. Warm red light began to bathe the walls of the tunnel, and the sound of scuffling boots and barked orders began to permeate along the walls.

With the light quickly becoming as brilliant as the sun, it was apparent the tunnel tapered off to the right into a new space. No other paths had branched off to that point, so they were forced to continue going forward. Luca carefully crept forward and peered with one eye around the corner, unable to hide the shadow of his head on the back wall as the radiant light flooded the tunnel. Luca swallowed hard at the sight before him, then retreated to his group.

The tunnel had tapered off into a massive hall buzzing with activity, the walls lined to the roof with complex machinery and technology. The technology itself bore a resemblance to the technology they had discovered under the Llewyn Hills but on a different scale altogether. The room was filled dozens of people in black or white robes milling around the chamber. From what Luca could tell, only the black-clad ones were armed while the rest frantically darted between machines. A single, tall figure standing on a raised dais at the back of the room was issuing orders and directing the commotion below. The man's legs were obscured by what appeared to be a complex mechanical table. Luca couldn't distinguish anything else about the man from his position but detailed his observations to Bleiz and Craig, who surged into action.

Bleiz assumed command of the group from Craig as it appeared that a battle was looming and quietly organized the men into a combat formation. They were all stout of heart and able-bodied, but the men benefited from Bleiz's military instruction as he outlined the plan to spread out along the walls of the next chamber and move quickly to surround the armed, black-clad men. The men of Galgrenon were outnumbered three to one, but they were not outmatched.

Then, on Bleiz's command, Luca led the charge into the chamber, and the figure behind the mechanical table looked up at the intrusion. Luca surged into the battle, but for the briefest moment, he saw the long scar flowing down the man's face.

***

"Cal! Cal! Come on! Wake up!" Claere's voice seemed to come from far away but slowly grew louder until he could hear her right next to him. Calunoth couldn't see anything, but he could feel a heavy ache spreading around the back of his head and all down the back of his body. He could also feel firm hands shaking him awake.

"Ugh," Calunoth groaned as he shook his head and opened his eyes. He was lying face down on what felt like a stone floor. There was a faint blue light emanating from a singular blue orb in the center of the room that filled the chamber. The surrounding walls were not made of the same rock and stone that comprised the upper walls but instead seemed to be composed of metal, with long lines of glyphs running along them. The glyphs themselves glowed a gentle red, blending with the blue light of the orb to permeate the passage with an unnatural purple glow.

Sitting up, Claere's concerned face eased into focus. Her long black hair was tangled and escaping from the binding that had previously held it back. Her face was matted with dirt and grime, casting her bright, heterochromatic eyes in sharp contrast with her face.

"What happened?" Calunoth asked after another groan. "Are you all right?"

"I'm fine, thanks to you. There was another earthquake, and the tunnel collapsed. We fell through the floor and ended up here," Claere explained. "Some of the rocks fell down on top of us, but you shielded me. You've been unconscious for a while. I was starting to get worried."

Calunoth blushed and tried to hide it before realizing he was as covered in grime as Claere was, and his cheeks would not be clearly visible. "Where are the others?" he asked, changing the topic.

"I'm not sure. Everything happened so quickly, it was hard to see what happened. I think they got trapped on the other side of the rocks. But a couple of them might have been caught underneath as well."

"Actually, where are *we*?" Calunoth asked, looking around. They had fallen a significant distance, but he had no idea where they had actually landed.

"I don't know," Claere replied. "We fell a long way down. I cast a light spell, but these walls were glowing even before I cast it. This tunnel is far more refined than the others. The one above was cut by modern technology, but this one? I don't know how anyone could go add metal to the walls like they have down here. At least we should be able to follow this tunnel to an exit, though I don't know how far that will be. The good news, though, is that this tunnel shouldn't collapse."

Calunoth was grateful for Claere's cool head and demeanor. In the short time that he had known her, he had grown reliant on the priestess for the stabilizing effect she had on him. Even in a desperate situation like this, she always kept her head and acted with decisive logic and practicality. He accepted her hand, and she helped him to his feet before they began to make their way down the tunnel. They argued over directions at first, but Calunoth had the final decision, citing the growing warmth in his core as evidence they should head south.

Calunoth and Claere had not gone far when the tunnel ended abruptly, terminating in a hard metal barrier inset with a single, circular door. The metal was of the same strange composition as the walls. The door itself was barred tightly shut with a series of locks linked to a small, circular wheel in the center of the door. Shooting Calunoth an annoyed look, Claere went over to it and rotated the wheel. Perhaps it was a lack of strength on her part, but it was more likely due to thousands of years of decay rotting the mechanism that kept the wheel and the door firmly set in place.

"Gah, it's stuck!" Claere scowled at the door. "We'll have to turn back. I told you this wasn't the right way." She turned to start heading in the opposite direction.

"Hold on!" Calunoth said, moving to the door and holding his ear to it. "Do you hear something? It sounds like running water."

Claere's brow furrowed, and she moved to mimic Calunoth's actions. The rushing sound of water trickled through the door, barely audible through the metal of the barrier.

"All of the water from the mountains ends up in either the Southern Ocean or Shellthrone Lake," Claere murmured, remembering her studies. "If we can find the stream, we could follow it to an exit and hope that it comes out near Shellthrone instead of the ocean. But we can't get through here, so we'll have to look elsewhere."

Calunoth wasn't so sure. His core was becoming uncomfortably warm now, and for some reason he felt drawn to whatever lay beyond the door. He had to at least try. He asked for Claere's help, and they both wrapped their hands around the latch, gripping it tightly. They gave a mighty pull, and all the earlier resistance Claere had felt disappeared. The ease of the movement was so unexpected that Calunoth fell over in front of the door, leaving Claere holding a once more rigid latch.

Astonished, Calunoth regained his feet and tried turning the latch again. The same latch that Claere couldn't budge moved freely in his hands. Shimmying the latch through four rotations, the locks released, and Calunoth was able to pull the door open. It was amazingly light despite its size and composition.

"How did you do that?" Claere demanded.

"I don't know," admitted Calunoth. "Maybe it has something to do with my core. These are Selevirnian ruins after all. Maybe the door can only be opened by someone with Pralia technology."

Claere took that explanation to be sufficient and led Calunoth through the door. The duo found themselves in a beautiful, expansive room. The walls, floor, and ceiling were all made of the same light, strong metal as the door and were resplendent with glyphs radiating a gentle red light. The room was filled with strange metal devices similar to the ones in the Llewyn Hills but in far better condition. The chamber had only one entrance, with a large river flowing freely though the center of the room, driving a large waterwheel that seemed to be powering the surrounding machines, and down toward the base of the mountain. Calunoth and Claere crossed a small, elegant bridge over the stream, admiring the alien nature of the room.

"What is this place?" Calunoth wondered out loud.

"It looks like some kind of vault. But I don't see any gold or treasure or anything valuable. Just these ... machines," Claere replied, approaching and studying the strange devices. "Cal, try touching this. Maybe it will react like the door did."

Calunoth approached the strange console. His core was now burning, almost as much as it had in the Caerwyn Bogs. The console was decorated with strange switches and buttons, all centered around a strange pad in the center of the board. He had no idea what any of them would do, so he started by placing his hand on the center of the pad, hoping it wouldn't explode like the Llewyn technology had. Bracing himself to run, he instead felt a warm glow that bathed his hand in light, and the heat in his core subsided entirely. Several lights on the console flickered into being, and suddenly a person appeared above the device.

Startled, Calunoth and Claere both jumped back, reaching for their swords before they realized the person who was there wasn't actually there. They watched in astonishment as the image of the person appeared to flicker in and out of reality. Gingerly, Calunoth poked at the figure with the end of his sword and felt no resistance as the sword pierced the image. The figure did not react. It was as though he were stabbing through nothing but air.

Suddenly, the figure began speaking in a slow, mechanical tone in a language that sounded like Common but was so mangled it was nonsensical to the pair. Guarding himself against this strange apparition, Calunoth spoke uneasily.

"Who are you? We don't understand what you're saying," he addressed the image. The image responded by continuing to speak to them in the strange language, but the words began to grow steadily more coherent until they began to resemble the old Common, then finally the Common tongue now spoken, at which point Calunoth addressed him again. "We can understand you now. Who, or what, are you?"

The figure responded in the same mechanical tone. "I am the record of the Selevirn Union and the Free City of Jakert. I have analyzed your language and determined the natural progression of our language into yours. Who hath discovered the Pralia technology again?"

Calunoth answered hesitantly. "My lord, Isaac Glathaous, is responsible for the Pralia Core in my chest. However, an organization called PRIMAL has made their own discoveries of the technology."

"Place your Pralia Core on the central pad," the image instructed. Calunoth looked at Claere awkwardly for a moment before deciding to cooperate. Whatever this figure was, it didn't seem dangerous.

Stripping to the waist, Calunoth awkwardly positioned himself over the console so his chest lay on the pad. He felt a warm surge pass through the core, then, at the figure's direction, he removed himself from the machine and redressed. The figure was silent for several moments before speaking again.

"This is not the same Pralia Core that was designed by the Selevirnians," the figure announced. "Analysis shows that this core is converting Natural Ynia to Life Ynia. What other technology hath thou discovered?"

"We don't have any of PRIMAL's technology with us," Calunoth said. "But I can tell you what I know." Calunoth went on to recite to the strange apparition his encounters with PRIMAL technology in the Llewyn Hills and the shard in Jarl's arm at Commerel. Once he was finished, the figure fell silent again for several moments before once again responding.

"Then the time has come again. Sooner than anticipated, by several hundred years, but it has come again," The figure said. "This group called PRIMAL has discovered the true Pralia technology, the technology the Selevirnians left behind."

"I'm sorry, I don't understand. What are you? How do you know this?" Claere asked the apparition. The apparition did not move from its position above the console but addressed them both.

"I am merely a ghost, a reflection of the past, designed to recount the history of the Selevirn Union and warn future generations of its fall," the figure replied. "I am not alive, nor have I ever been. I simply exist to translate the records here for those who find them. Only those who have rediscovered the Pralia technology can enter this room. This machine is driven by the energy of water, attracting Pralia technology to it."

"So, you can tell us what Pralia technology does? How it works? We need to know how to stop it, so we can stop PRIMAL. They could generate an untold amount of energy to power their war if we don't know how to counter it," Calunoth demanded of the figure.

"It does not need to be stopped by its opponents. It will be stopped by its own limitations," the figure explained. "Pralia technology generates an extremely high amount of Natural Ynia, but Ynia cannot be created nor destroyed. Pralia technology is a product of humanity, and humanity cannot defy the fundamental rules of the world. It can only convert Ynia."

"Wait," Claere said slowly. "You mean the Pralia technology PRIMAL has isn't making energy? Only converting it? Converting it from what?"

"There are currently four known types of Ynia at the time of my storage: Natural, Gravitational, Cosmic, and Life," the figure replied. "Natural Ynia is the most useful but has the lowest potential. A great deal of Ynia is required to perform relatively little. Gravitational has far greater potential but is impossible to harness. Cosmic Ynia is theoretical only. Life Ynia is the only suitable source. The technology employed by your enemies works by converting Life Ynia into Natural Ynia. And because only a small amount of Life Ynia is required to create a huge amount of Natural Ynia, it *appears* to generate energy rather than convert it. However, your core seems to perform the reaction in the opposite direction."

"But wait, Life Ynia is what keeps us all alive. If you drain it and convert it into Natural Ynia, what happens to the person who loses that energy?" Claere asked the figure.

"As with all creatures, humans have a finite amount of Life Ynia in their body. Once it is depleted, they die."

"But then wouldn't you have to sacrifice people to use the Pralia technology?" Calunoth asked.

"And so you reveal the first sin of the Selevirnians," the figure replied. "The Selevirn Union was once the greatest empire in living memory. Our people came to Creidyl in the Glory Age from our faraway lands and dominated the landscape with our Pralia technology. It was truly utopic. But as always, the promise of that power was too much for many to resist. The rulers of the land started to demand more than what the people were willing to give and began conscripting slaves into the Pralia Reactors, sacrificing their Life Ynia to power their grand designs. The process was inefficient for hundreds of years, and more and more people had to give their lives for the union. The next advancement increased the efficiency of the process a hundred times over, but only for a short time."

"What happened?" Calunoth asked, fearing the answer.

"The second sin of the Selevirnians is thus revealed. In our greed and gluttony, we flew too close to the sun and sought to defy the laws of nature themselves. And so we were punished for it. We interfered with what we could not control. For at its highest capacities, the flaws of the Pralia Technology came to light. Even our strongest materials could not contain the unstable Life Ynia that was poured into the cores. As a result, on the Day of Reckoning, a surge of Ynia passed through the central grid that supplied Pralia-sourced energy to the entire union. The surge overloaded the reactors and caused them to release all the potential Life Ynia into the world as Natural Ynia. The results were cataclysmic. Every major city with a Pralia Reactor was immediately decimated, as was much of the surrounding countryside. The continent of Creidyl was spared much of the devastation as the Selevirnians had not yet cultivated the same civilization here as we had in our homeland, but all major cities and governments were destroyed instantly. Of the old Selevirn Union, nothing remained but the blackened, dead land afore and beyond the Faar Mountains. The remaining Selevirnians reverted to warring tribes, one of which left this record for their descendants to warn them of the dangers of the technology they had wrought."

Calunoth almost fell on the floor, staggered by the figure's revelations. All of the hope that Byrant had given to the people. It was all built on the hope of a technology that was never going to work, a technology that took human life and then destroyed it. Calunoth felt sick, and Claere had to grab his arm to stabilize him.

"Calunoth, this is the information we need. We can take this to the council and tell them. We can stop this, and PRIMAL. But you've got to hold yourself toge—" She was interrupted by a massive booming that seemed to reverberate even through the metal walls, and the air itself seemed to shift. From far away, they heard the sound of collapsing rock.

Chapter 21

<u>The Short Way Down</u>

 Luca heard his companion's footsteps as their heavy boots stomped across the hard stone of the cave floor. They moved swiftly and expertly, stalwart men all, and were soon upon their foes. The stale cave air carried the battle cries of the men as they attacked their black-clad opponents. The men were outnumbered, but with the element of surprise and the advantage of formation, they were not outmatched. Luca himself was in the first line of men that fell upon the melee.
 It was apparent in moments that the figures draped in white were not fighters. They weren't even armed. Quickly dispersing, they fled to the opposite side of the cavern where a great open gate loomed, allowing an escape. As they scrambled to flee, the white-clad figures attempted to collect various papers and boxes, with four carrying what appeared to be a heavy iron box between them.
 The black-clad men felt no such pressure to flee. Rallied by their commander, the robed man on the dais, they quickly organized into fighting formation and began to push back against their assailants.
 The initial chaos had allowed Luca and his comrades in the first line to cut down many of the black-clad men as they strove to disentangle themselves from their fleeing white-clad colleagues. Now, however, they fought with even numbers as Bleiz led his group of six men to press into the flanks of the assembled men while Luca engaged them from the front. While the black-clad men fought well and hard, they were ultimately outmatched by the tactical knowledge of the senior Knight, soon finding themselves surrounded and unable to break through. Seeing his men now cornered beyond hope, the commander on the dais moved to flee through the gate across the chamber, but his efforts were foiled by Alexander.
 The mage had turned to his formulae during the battle and wove the arcane symbols in the air with great efficiency, chanting the accompanying score under this breath. Luca could not hear what the mage was chanting, but he trusted him to be accurate in his spellcasting. Alexander finished casting his spell as the commander reached the gate and was about to join his fleeing companions. The

white-robed men were suddenly pulled into the floor, unable to move under the intense pressure the mage had created.

With the black-clad men handily dispatched, Luca followed Bleiz and Craig over to the immobilized men, with Alexander trailing behind breathing heavily. The spell was of an intermediate level only but had still taken a toll on the Upper Circle mage. Regardless of his ability, Alexander was still a relatively young mage, and the complex incantations and manipulation of Ynia required for combat magic put a significant strain on him.

"Stop right where you are!" Craig called to their opponents, rather unnecessarily. The fleeing white-clad men could not have moved even if they had wanted to. Alexander had cast a spell that had strengthened the pull of the earth around the area of the entrance, dragging the entangled captives into the ground with the gravitational force of planets. While the effect required no energy to maintain, Alexander would have to reverse the effect before the area would be traversable again. He shouted as much to Craig before the fiery captain could run afoul of his ally's spell.

Standing several paces back, in a spot Alexander pointed out, Craig unleashed himself on the captives from afar. His day thus far had consisted of being trapped in a cave-in, losing at least two of his men, and then losing an additional three in the fighting that had ensued in the cavern. The loss of five lives would be difficult for the young captain to explain to the council, and consequently, the hot-blooded soldier was eager to find an outlet for his growing ire.

"Who's in charge? And why are you acting without authority in Galgrenon Territory?" Craig demanded of the prostrate researchers.

The scar-faced man scowled darkly, his sallow features contorting as he attempted to push himself to his feet. However, try as he might, he could not overcome the gravitational force Alexander had summoned to pin him to the ground. Luca looked on warily as the man struggled for a moment before deciding to change his tactics. As it was, he was completely at the mercy of the men of Galgrenon. Ceasing to struggle, the man instead began to speak, and when he spoke, it was as if sweet honey flowed smoothly from his tongue. He spoke in a calming and melodious tone that belied his intimidating features.

"Forgive us, sir, but I am sure we are poorly met. This is merely a misunderstanding. Please, sir, release the spell that binds us, and we can converse in proper form as gentlemen are wont to do." The scar-faced man spoke coolly, appearing unintimidated by the dire circumstances in which he found himself.

"You'll stay where you are while we speak!" Craig responded harshly. "What misunderstanding is there here? You are operating a covert militant force without authority under our very noses, utilizing strange technology in hidden places. Who are you? Who are you working for? Are you here to attack Galgrenon?"

The scar-faced man appeared to quickly collect his wits and said, "We are simple scholars, sir, sent here by His Majesty King Byrant of Renderive to investigate reports of ancient technology in these hills, with the approval of Council Member Gordon Verl. I am the chief scholar, Lenocius, a simple researcher summoned to Renderive to assist King Byrant in his work here. King Byrant has nothing but love for the good people of Galgrenon and would never dream of offending them with military action."

Luca gave out a quiet gasp at the man's words, and he could hear the gasp echoed by his companions He glanced furtively over at Bleiz and saw the same recognition in his captain's eyes. While Calunoth had only given them a few details about the man responsible for engineering the Glathaous Massacre, the name was of such rarity in Renderive that it could not be a coincidence. This sallow-faced, silver-tongued figure laying on the ground before them was the man Calunoth had been searching for. Recalling the rampage Calunoth had committed on the Crideir highroad at the mere association with Lenocius, Luca was quietly grateful his friend was not present. He would have cut Lenocius to ribbons before they'd had a chance to question him.

The communication between Bleiz and Luca went unnoticed by Craig, who continued his tirade against the stricken minister, now posing as a researcher. "King Byrant? He is not king, and the Galgrenons' loyalty has still to be decided. Byrant has no jurisdiction to send men to this place without council approval, and Gordon has no such authority by himself! If you come in peace, as you claim, why do you have so many well-armed men at your disposal? And what of your colors? Last I checked, Byrant's men bore the white rose, not a deformed eye as their insignia," Craig said, pointing at the design on the captured men's cloak lapels.

Luca had failed to notice this insignia before, but on closer inspection of a nearby fallen soldier, he saw a crudely designed letter,

"P," with an eye in the circle. It was the same insignia Giric had brandished at Gordon at the council meeting. He knew now that the insignia belonged to PRIMAL, but he had once thought the group worked for Byrant. Even if they did so in secret, they would have no reason to show any colors beyond Byrant's. He moved to interrupt Craig's interrogation, but Lenocius answered before he could.

"These mountains can be dangerous for simple academics such as ourselves," reasoned Lenocius. "We have hired men with us for our protection, and they offered us their cloaks to ward off the cold. Nothing more." The lies flowed off the man's tongue effortlessly, and without prior knowledge, Luca might well have believed him such was the charisma with which he spoke. His musical voice had a strange effect on the men, many of whom began to doubt their resolve, even the irate Craig. However, Bleiz felt no such inclination, or at least if he did, he didn't show it. Taking the reins of the interrogation from Craig, the captain swung his sword forward, pointing it at the scar-faced man on the floor and standing as close as he could get without falling into the heavy gravity trap.

"Enough! Your words may sway the minds of lesser men, but you cannot hide who you are from us. You are the man responsible for supplying Byrant with Pralia technology, aren't you? You are responsible for the Glathaous Massacre and the Commerel Coup! I have a very reliable source who can attest to your crimes! And may Sentential protect you when he sees you!" Bleiz roared at the man.

Luca's head was spinning. They had encountered the man responsible for most of their woes where they had least expected him. But they could not kill him. It would result in a court martial and dismissal from the Knights were either Bleiz or Luca to slaughter a defenseless prisoner. And how they were going to keep Calunoth, if he was alive, off the man was an even bigger problem in Luca's mind.

Lenocius listened with razor-sharp focus to Bleiz's accusations and continued in his honeyed tones. "The blame for those terrible events lies solely with Alistair Glathaous and Steward Reil, if my lord informs me correctly, not with me. I am responsible for supplying King Byrant with technology, but that will enable him to not only win the war, but to usher in a bright future for all of Renderive. Surely you would not stand against the betterment of your people, Sir Knight?"

"Enough!" Bleiz bellowed at Lenocius. "Under my authority as Captain of the Wilds under the Field Marshal of the Holy Knights of

Renderive, I am placing all of you under arrest for the crimes of treason and insurrection against the Crown. You will be bound and gagged and transported back to Deirive to stand trial." Bleiz continued to conduct his arrest, his sudden imposition of military authority removing Craig from his usual role. While Bleiz recited his summons, Luca watched Lenocius wriggling on the ground, his white robe tangled around him and obscuring half his body. Unnoticed by Bleiz or Craig, Luca saw something shifting beneath the robe and moving slowly toward the heavy metal crate that had collapsed onto its side, exposing a light that shone through the cracks that had appeared in the surface. Realizing too late what was about to happen, Luca yelled out a warning to Bleiz but wasn't fast enough.

Lenocius had been able to surreptitiously move his hand beneath his cloak toward the collapsed container, even under the pressure of Alexander's spell. With a deft flick of his wrist, he pulled a pin from the base of the container, and the walls of the container collapsed outward, releasing the source of the light fully and blinding the unsuspecting group. Alexander gave out a strangled cry as Lenocius rose to his feet, now seemingly unaffected by the spell. With the container no longer whole, Luca could just barely make out the source of the light under his arm as he sought to block out the harsh light from his eyes. The light was coming from a large pulsating crystal that appeared to be inlaid with black veins that spiderwebbed up the length of the triangular prism. More than three feet in length and width, the crystal seemed to be giving off a dangerous amount of Ynia. Laughing cruelly, Lenocius now stood tall, completely unaffected by the gravity spell, and when he spoke again, he abandoned the melodious tones that had slithered into their minds so effectively. He now spoke harshly and arrogantly.

"You fools! You have no idea what you're dealing with!" Lenocius proclaimed. "You've come too late to stop me. But as a consolation prize, I'll let you be the first to be destroyed by my Pralia Core!" His voice wavered unstably as he laughed at them before he barked an order to disable them. "Invert!" Lenocius commanded, and he turned Alexander's spell back on them, channeling energy from the triangular Pralia Core. As Lenocius spoke, one of his white-clad colleagues gave out a gasp followed by a cry as his body shriveled up before them.

The effect of the spell was beyond what Lenocius must have anticipated. Instead of just releasing the spell holding his men and throwing the rest of them up to the ceiling, the entire cave seemed to tear itself apart. The heavy machinery that had been anchored to the ground crashed upward as the world inverted. The gravity spell slammed the equipment into the ceiling, followed closely afterward by most of the inhabitants of the room.

    Luca felt the most peculiar sensation of falling even though as he looked up, he saw the ceiling traveling toward him, rapidly. Then he realized the ceiling was not falling on him, he was falling into the ceiling. As easily as falling off a mountain, Luca and his companions slammed into the ceiling while Lenocius stood alone by the Pralia Core, himself occluded from the effects of the spell. That Lenocius had caught his own men in the spell didn't seem to bother him as he ignored their moans of pain as they landed heavily beside Luca.

    The next word from Lenocius was to be the final one, but he didn't have an opportunity to utter it. The machines that had been ripped from their foundations had begun to shine with the same bright red light that had emanated from the Pralia Core, connecting beams of light with their foundations in the floor. There was a loud grating, followed by the crash of thunder as a blinding wave of heat and light from the sundered machines bathed Luca as he lay against the roof before the floor disintegrated deep into the earth, and the cavern disappeared into blackness, taking all but Lenocius with it. Luca felt the normal effects of gravity restore themselves, and he plummeted downward into the abyss below. The air whistled past him, and he could hear nought but the screaming air and the sound of rushing water below.

***

    The ground shook even within the vault, jolting Calunoth and Claere off their feet. The room itself maintained its stable structure, designed as it had been to last unto the ending of the world, but the sudden reverberations were enough to unsettle the room's inhabitants. The river running through the room sloshed onto the cavern floor, rendering the surrounding metal slick and shiny as the water reflected the cool red light of the machinery.

    "What was that?" Calunoth asked, startled, as he lay on the cool metallic floor. Claere regained her composure first and helped the stricken former guard to his feet.

"It sounded like another cave-in," Claere answered. "I hope the others are all right. This whole mountain seems to be unnaturally volatile."

"But with this Selevirnian technology down here, there could be more technology somewhere else in the mountain," Calunoth pointed out. "And if PRIMAL is excavating without knowing how to properly mine, they could be weakening the stonework. I noticed in the Llewyn Hills that the tunnel we found was roughly hewn, probably created with tools instead of magic."

"How do you know so much about tunneling?" Claere asked.

"I read about it in a book once. There wasn't much to do back in Glathaous except read and practice with the swords," Calunoth said, shrugging. "If that *was* another cave-in, then we shouldn't stay here much longer. We need to get this information back to the council. If Byrant is messing around with this technology, then he could be putting a lot of people in danger right now. We should head back the other way, down the passage."

Calunoth and Claere set about examining the machinery for signs of a portable record they could bring with them. After cautiously pressing several buttons on the console, a series of flat metal disks less than an arm's length in width ejected from a slot in the base of the console. Upon closer examination, the disks were engraved with words from the Selevirn language. The language itself had been modified over millennia to become the common language now spoken across Creidyl, and while it was mostly unrecognizable, the occasional word and symbol resembled the modern-day language.

After careful examination by Claere, she declared that enough of the words were recognizable that they would serve as proof of their discovery, especially if they could find a scholar to translate all the disks. Neither had their packs with them, having anticipated a quick return to the campsite, so Calunoth, with Claere's help, used his belt to bind the disks to his back. When they started to slip, Claere added her own belt to the bindings. Her suggestion to do so had brought significant blushes to Calunoth's cheeks, but Claere assured him her plaited leather belt was mostly decorative.

The pair were leaving the vault with the hope of finding their friends and a way out when Claere suddenly stopped and turned to the river running through the cavern.

"Wait! Can you hear that?" Claere asked.

"I can't hear anything over the water," Calunoth replied, motioning at the rapidly running water, but then a sound trickled down the river, a noise that was jarringly different from the surroundings. A muffled noise. A human noise.

Calunoth and Claere looked at each other for a moment, bewildered, when suddenly the sound was muffled no more.

"Gyagh!" a voice suddenly yelled as a light brown head suddenly emerged from beneath the water, sputtering, even as the head was pulled along by the rapidly moving current.

"Luca!" Claere recognized the young Knight first and ran to the river's edge. "Luca! Grab my hand!"

Calunoth ran to the priestess immediately, his instincts kicking in belatedly. Claere reached precariously over the edge of the rushing water and managed to grab Luca's arm as he came whooshing around the bend in the river. Claere was stronger than most men, in no small part thanks to the magical modifications that had shaped her childhood, but the weight of the large Knight in combination with the speed of the current proved too much for her. Rather than letting go, however, she tried to hold onto Luca and instead found herself pulled into the river along with him. Calunoth reflexively grabbed her arm as she fell, steadying himself by using the bridge to lever himself on the bank. The weight of both Luca and Claere combined with the rushing current was too much to bear. Calunoth felt the sinews in his arms stretch, and he feared he would dislocate his shoulder before he could bring them both to shore.

He never had the chance. More bodies poured in from the northern source of the river—some thrashing desperately against the current, others lying as still as driftwood—along with several large rocks that had been caught in the current with them. Had it been Luca attempting to fish out Claere and Calunoth, he might have been successful. But Calunoth lacked the strength required to withstand the current and carry the weight of his two friends. So, with the remaining men and debris crashing into the largely submerged Luca, Calunoth felt his stabilizing leg give way, and he plummeted into the river alongside them, tightly gripping Claere's arm as he did so, refusing to let her go.

The water closed in around him, battering and bruising him as it flowed relentlessly through the room. The water flowed from a hole in the wall below the rocks into a similar tunnel on the other side of the room. With the tunnel rapidly oncoming, Calunoth took one deep breath above the water before being swept into the darkness of the cave's river, ducking his head under the water to avoid having it swept off by the rock wall as the water flowed underneath it.

He could hear nothing. He could see nothing. He could feel nothing but the cold mountain water rushing through the caverns, seeming to travel ever downward through the belly of the mountain, and the fading warmth of Claere's arm as he held on to her as tightly as he could. He could feel her hand on his arm in return, and though the darkness made it impossible to see, he could tell she was holding on to him as tightly as he clung to her, desperate to avoid being separated as they fell through the mountain. The river began to split as they made their way steadily downward, reaching speeds Calunoth had not felt even on the fastest racehorses.

After what seemed like hours but was likely only minutes, Calunoth felt his lungs about to burst just as he felt himself being dragged upward. Finally breaking the surface, he gasped, then inhaled deeply, and was immediately swept back under the water. Luca was dragging the three of them to the surface whenever it appeared. How he knew where that was in the darkness was beyond Calunoth, but the young Knight's efforts were keeping them from drowning.

After what seemed an eternity, light flooded into the river, and Calunoth felt himself being pulled up to the surface again. He continued to thrash about with his free limbs, but he couldn't reach the bank, even with what he could feel was Luca and Claere's coordinated effort. Looking around frantically, Calunoth could see they were now outside, the sun obscured behind overcast clouds and the droplets of rain falling steadily down from the heavens. The mountains were firmly behind them, and the Central Steppe was visible over the horizon. But most of his view was obfuscated by an enormous, still, blue sphere that seemed to stretch onward for miles just over a dip in the river ahead.

Calunoth rejoiced internally for a moment, recognizing the still waters ahead of them, but his celebrations were cut short by the realization that the dip in the river was no small dip but a cliff from which the river water cascaded down. Frantically, the three of them attempted to wade to the bank, but their momentum was too great, and Calunoth became aware of the water leaving him for the first time as they were propelled off the cliff. They fell heavily toward the base of the waterfall, the force of the falls separating them. Mimicking Claere's stance, Calunoth spread his limbs wide, turning his body so his head faced the water below, before clasping his hands together as he hit the water. Had Claere not shouted at him to follow her lead, Calunoth would not have had the foresight or reaction time to do so, but as it was, the three dove heavily into the frothing water, sinking dozens of feet into the pool at the bottom before finally emerging onto the surface.

    Calunoth, Claere, and Luca held each other as they clambered out of the water onto the nearby shore. Sputtering water and bedraggled, the three collapsed heavily onto the soft white sand, unaware of where they were or what had happened. The rain fell gently on them as they lay recovering from their endeavor, keeping their clothing unrelentingly drenched.

    After several moments of coughing up water, Calunoth was the first to rise to his feet. They had landed on a beach of soft sand on the edge of a massive lake. There was a city on the far side of the lake, but it was barely visible in the distance, such was the breadth of the water. The lake itself was beautiful even in the overcast rain, with its clean blue water framed by the misty Galgre Range behind it. They were not the only members of their company to emerge here. An additional four figures were stranded on the beach farther down, having dragged themselves there or been washed ashore where they now lay, unable to move after the tumultuous ride down the mountain.

    Checking on his companions, Calunoth attended to Claere first. Like him, she was soaked to the bone, her long raven hair spread all around her as she lay back on the sand coughing heavily. She was winded after having been knocked into a rock in the mountain river that Calunoth had somehow missed but appeared otherwise unhurt, beyond her pride at being washed up on a beach and left in a rather disheveled condition.

    Luca was in a far worse state. Calunoth was unsure of how much further he had fallen than he and Claere, but based on Luca's condition, it had been substantially further. The young Knight, typically so easygoing and cheerful, lay curled up in a ball, and was groaning precipitously. Calunoth moved to his friend, who was likely responsible for saving his life, but was forced to draw back when Luca retched, then vomited heavily upon the sand. The young Knight had been so egregiously tossed around that he lacked the strength to push himself back up and instead flopped into his own emittance.

"Luca!" Calunoth asked, pushing him onto his side. "Are you okay? Is anything broken?"

"Nnnggg …" was Luca's response. He rolled onto his other side, away from his recalled breakfast, and lay in the sand with his eyes closed. "Just leave me… I'll just die here …" he finally mumbled in response to Calunoth's probing.

Calunoth was deeply concerned about the extent of Luca's injuries, but then Claere came up next to him and assured him that Luca was merely suffering from a severe bout of seasickness and didn't appear to be egregiously wounded beyond that.

Leaving the stricken Luca to settle his stomach, the pair examined the other denizens of the beach. Alexander and Craig had washed up on the shore with them, plus one of Giric's men, who seemed to be the least affected by their trip down the mountain, and one white-clad PRIMAL member, clearly dead. The man's skin seemed to have been pulled tightly over his corpse, and he seemed to have been dried out despite the wet journey down the mountain. Chillingly, he looked like the prisoner in the cage hanging over the pit of bones Calunoth had encountered in the Llewyn Hills. There was no sign of Bleiz or the other men.

Craig stood without assistance, cursing fluently as he raged against the sky, taking out his frustration on the clouds. Alexander was nursing his left arm, having bashed it on a rock on the way down, but was able to walk after some recuperation. Of the survivors, Luca was in the worst condition, though Alexander joked that the deceased PRIMAL member looked to be in a better way.

No one attempted to explain what had happened. They were, to a man, battered and worn to the point of exhaustion. And the continued absence of their missing companions weighed heavily upon them. But with night coming shortly, they moved together silently, supporting each other as they walked along the beach to a nearby fishing village where the locals, seeing their sorry state, kindly put them up with fires and warm broth. By the time night did fall, Calunoth could stand the world no longer and fell into such a deep sleep that not even his demons could reach him.

Chapter 22

The Council Speaks

    Calunoth was awakened by the steady dripping of rain leaking down from the rafters of the small fishing hut. Looking up from the mat that separated him from the hard-packed ground, he saw through the small crevices, used to ventilate the hut of the previous evening's smoke, in the hut's latticework frame the early morning rain was slipping through.

    Glancing over at the embers, Calunoth shivered. Realizing he was wearing nought but his underclothes, he hastily rose and scanned the hut for his clothes. He saw them sprawled out on the opposite side of the fire with his tooled leather armor from Caern Vaughn. Thankfully, nothing was missing. Moving tenderly, he donned his attire, aware that it was still damp. The effects of falling through the mountain lingered not only on his clothing, but in his body as well. Examining himself, he noted several new bruises and lacerations that had not been there yesterday, but he sensed the worst injury was one he could not see, laced across the small of his back. Reaching behind with his hand, struggling with his lack of flexibility, he gently caressed the aching area and was unsurprised to feel several deep scratch marks marring his flesh.

    Grimacing, he pulled his top on, leaving the armor to dry out further, and ventured out into the small village they had found last night. They had been lucky to have landed so close to it. Small by design, it had been built to accommodate the local fisherman if they had to work too far away from their homes in Galgrenon or Marston. Most of the village was comprised of small, individual huts like the one Calunoth had awoken in, but the few permanent residents of the settlement lived in log cabins.

    It was from one of these cabins that the local matriarch, a plump woman named Lachina, resided. Having lost her husband in a boating accident over a decade ago, she had stayed in the outpost with her three sons, who had followed in their father's footsteps and become fishermen on Shellthrone Lake. When the watch had discovered the group the night before, they had brought Calunoth and his companions to Lachina first, where Calunoth had described their journey down the river in short form.

Lachina had been swift and generous in her response, immediately ordering the villagers to prepare food for the companions and instructing several of the locals to set out into the lake in darkness to try and recover the lost men. While many brave men would have refused to venture out into the deep waters of the lake without the sun's guidance, the men of the outpost were proud Highlanders to a tee and had wasted no time in wading out to the lake, experienced mariners all. So as Calunoth approached the matriarch, he did so with hope in his heart for news of his companions.

"How goes the morn, Calunoth? It does me well to see you walking so early in the morning after the state you was in last night," Lachina said in her booming voice.

"I'm still feeling the effects, but they are much-reduced, thanks to your kindness, Lady Lachina," Calunoth replied formally. "My companions and I are in your debt."

"Bah, think nothing of it! We're all under the same sky here. It would not do to turn away those in need," Lachina said dismissively. "Speaking of those in need, my boys found some of your companions. A couple young lads and an older man were dragged up in the nets in the night."

Calunoth's heart jumped. While he felt sorrow for Giric's men who had been lost on the journey, his own priority was Bleiz. Claere, Luca, and Alexander were accounted for. Lauren should be safe enough back at camp. That left only the grizzled old captain to find. Following Lachina, the woman guided Calunoth to one of the log cabins on the edge of town. This cabin belonged to her eldest son, Boyd, who had led the fishing trawlers on the previous night's excursion.

The interior of the cabin was as well decorated as the houses of Galgrenon, with a roaring fire in the back of the large central room. The retrieved figures were sprawled out close to the fire, all appearing to be sleeping soundly, slowly being dried out by the heat of the fire. Approaching them, Calunoth was relieved to see the slumbering form of Bleiz, seemingly unresponsive. The other two men Calunoth recognized as Giric's men. They all lay as he had, in nought but their underclothes, but they appeared to be breathing normally.

Bleiz was not in such a peaceful state. His skin was flushed a deep red. His breathing was shallow and rapid, and his body shivered regularly despite his temperature. His body was covered in the same contusions and lacerations as everyone who had made the short journey down the river, but the damage seemed less obvious, obscured as it was by his flushed skin.

"The two lads are all right," Boyd said, reading Calunoth's concerned expression. "But the other one was in the water longer than anyone else. It looks like he cut off most of his armor. We found some of it lodged in the nets with the straps severed. While the water isn't freezing at this time of the year, it's still too cold to swim in for long. And we only found him four or five hours ago, floating close to shore."

"Will he be all right?" Calunoth asked, concern evident in his eyes. It seemed cruel that Bleiz would survive the fall down the mountain only to succumb to fever shortly afterward.

"We'll have to wait and see. We've warmed him up, but now he's carrying a fever. I've seen it before. As it stands, he could go either way. We'll keep an eye on him here, but he's not going anywhere anytime soon," Boyd replied.

Calunoth thanked him and followed Lachina out of the cabin and toward the center of the village where they found Claere, Craig, and Luca awaiting them. None were wearing their armor, only the damp clothes that had been laid out in their huts. Claere appeared to be uninjured, and while Luca was unsteady on his feet, he was otherwise putting on a brave face.

"Where's Alex?" Claere asked as he neared them.

"I don't know. I haven't seen him yet," Calunoth replied.

"If you're referring to the mage," Lachina interrupted. "His arm was broken in the fall, and I stayed up late last night setting it. So he's likely still in bed."

"I heard they'd found others out on the water," Luca said quickly. "Did they find Bleiz?"

Calunoth told the young Knight about the condition of his captain. Luca's face grew dark as he listened, but he took the news better than Calunoth had been expecting. The young Knight went to see Bleiz and emerged several minutes later. He was equally concerned about the older Knight, but he had faith Bleiz would pull through.

With Alexander still resting and Bleiz out of action for the foreseeable future, the group retired to Lachina's cabin where she continued to pamper them with hot tea and smoked fish for breakfast. Alexander joined them halfway through, his left arm bandaged and wrapped in a sling around his neck. He was slightly irritable at the persistent dampness of his environment but was grateful to be alive.

With the group as reunited as they could be, they took turns telling their stories of how they had come to arrive on the shores of the lake. They left out details like the Pralia technology they had discovered and Lenocius' appearance, but otherwise hid no details of their bizarre journey down the mountain.

With that, the group decided to return to Galgrenon, approximately a day's march away, leaving Bleiz and the other incapacitated men to recover at the outpost. The companions thanked Lachina again for her hospitality and promised to return soon for Bleiz and the others. Then they gathered their equipment and set out for Galgrenon. The information was of such importance they had to share it immediately, which meant they were forced to leave Bleiz behind for now.

Along the way, Luca spoke quietly with Claere, detailing their encounter with Lenocius in greater detail. Claere disagreed with Luca about telling Calunoth about him, even when Luca warned darkly about Calunoth's previous reactions associated with the man. Luca had considered avoiding telling Calunoth at all in case he decided to immediately run off back into the mountain where, in his current condition, he would almost certainly die. With that in mind, Claere took it upon herself to tell Calunoth himself, waiting until they were far along the mountain road to Galgrenon before speaking.

"Cal? There's something we need to tell you. About what happened in the cavern above us," Claere began diplomatically.

"What is there to know?" Calunoth asked wearily. "Luca and the others found a PRIMAL lab, and the technology went haywire and blew a hole in the floor. What more is there to know?"

"Most of the PRIMAL members are probably dead, but there's one who almost certainly survived. He ran off with what he called his Pralia Core," Luca announced, braving Calunoth's ire by venturing into the conversation. Claere was prepared to speak, and he'd be embarrassed if a woman, even one as capable as her, was braver than he. "A scar-faced man with a voice that could charm snakes out of the grass. A man named Lenocius."

Calunoth stopped dead in his tracks, suddenly breathing heavily. His eyes narrowed, and he turned his accusatory gaze on Luca.

"Lenocius was running that lab? Why didn't you tell me sooner? Come on! Let's go! If we get there quickly, we might still catch him!" Calunoth started to break into a run before stumbling and falling. His body was exhausted after many weeks of travel, and the recent bludgeoning he'd taken in the river hadn't helped. He quickly regained his feet, however, and ran forward again, a red mist clouding his vision as he pushed through the pain. He gave out an involuntary giggle as he pulled himself through the mud. He knew where Lenocius was. And he was close.

Then he felt Claere's cool hand on his shoulder. Calunoth didn't know what strange magic she used that cleared his thoughts, but she could always restore him to lucidity when he would otherwise be consumed by madness.

"Cal! Don't be crazy! He'll be long gone by now, and even if he isn't, there's no way to get back to that cavern. The entrance collapsed, remember? So unless you want to try swimming back up that river, I suggest you control yourself better." Claere scolded him.

If Luca had said that, Calunoth would have punched him, but the measured tones and the scolding nature of Claere's voice brought Calunoth to reason.

"If we can't go after him now, we'll have to go back to the cavern with the miners. Craig said they'd be sending miners to dig us out. We'll have to go with them," Calunoth said, slightly embarrassed now at his fall.

"We need to report to the council first," Craig replied. "They're going to have questions about the men we've lost. But hopefully Roy will already be there and have sent people out. Losing so many men in a single exploratory operation is unacceptable, and I suspect the council will be fully behind a manhunt for this Lenocius character. You'll be welcome to tag along, I'm sure."

"What about the war effort? Will this incident cause the Galgrenons to support the king?" Alexander asked the red-haired Galgrenon captain.

"I can't say for sure. The young and the elites are set on Byrant. I suspect this incident will unnerve some of the elite types, but the young are not so sensible. They may view people like Lenocius as a requirement for the greater good. And unfortunately, many of the council members are beholden to these people. We'll just have to wait and see. I'll make the report, with your assistance, but I can't make political judgments in my report. While I'll have to note that Lenocius named Gordon as a conspirator, I can't decide his fate. That will be up to the council to decide." With that, Craig grew quiet and despondent, pondering the ramifications of his upcoming report. Although he had preached that he would not make a political statement, the nature and presentation of his report could determine the future of Galgrenon. It was a heavy weight for a relatively young man's shoulders to bear.

It was times like this that the experienced head and hand of Bleiz was most sorely missed. A professional to the core, he would have known exactly how to relieve the young man of some of the burdens of his duty, or rather, how to help manage them. Even with Lenocius in the offing, Calunoth thought he would have to return to the outpost for the captain first. He felt guilty for leaving him in the first place, but it couldn't be helped. They wouldn't accomplish anything by waiting around his bedside.

Luca in particular had been adamantly against leaving the captain at the outpost, but Craig had assured him that Bleiz was in the care of the most experienced people and personally reassured him that once in Galgrenon, Craig would have a doctor sent to the village to look after him and the other men.

As it was, their arrival in Galgrenon that evening was greeted with exclamations and surprise. Most had heard about the cave-in and were astonished to see any of the companions walk through the southern gates. Lauren and Roy had arrived yesterday, and Giric had immediately dispatched a team of miners and engineers to extract them from the cave. After a short meeting with Craig, Giric assured them the council would convene on the morrow and bade them return to the embassy where they would await the dawn.

***

The air in the streets of Galgrenon was heavy with tension the following morning. The news that Craig and Roy had returned had spread quickly, and a decision on Galgrenon's place in the war was expected later in the day. The king's representatives left the embassy at midday and were escorted by the city guard to the council hall where they took their place in the stands while awaiting their summons. The emergency meeting had been deemed a private affair due to concerns that civil displeasure at the decision that could sway the hearts of the councilors.

Calunoth sat in the stands with his companions as he listened to Craig recite the details of their excursion before an elevated semicircular table behind which sat the councilors. His report was detailed, but he was forced to stop repeatedly to address questions raised by the council members on matters relating from everything from the Pralia technology in the lab to the structural stability of the mountain. Several of the eleven council members shifted uncomfortably as Craig described the encounter with Lenocius. The captain capably answered all the questions; however, he was loudly interrupted upon naming Gordon as a conspirator of Lenocius.

"How dare you impugn me honor?!" Gordon shouted, erupting from his seat. "I would no sooner work with dogs as I would with that man!"

"Gordon, restrain yourself!" Giric barked, exercising his authority as the governor. "You will have your chance to defend your actions, but let the man finish his report." And Craig did so, without interruption, before bowing out.

Gordon seized the opportunity to vehemently deny his involvement, and the council swiftly descended into a frenzied shouting match, his supporters rallying around him. "You have no proof!" Gordon roared at Craig, who stood stoically at the back of the room. "You can't prove any of this! You're just trying to hide your own incompetence!"

Calunoth found Gordon to be an abrasive and blustery figure, but he was right. They had originally only had the captain's word to go on, and given the political dynamics at play, that wouldn't be enough. Fortunately, the captain's word paired with the silver disks recovered from the Selevirnian apparatus and the dried-up husk of the PRIMAL member would support the captain's word. Even if it proved impossible to fully implicate Gordon, they could still turn enough of the council against Byrant.

Eventually, order was restored, and the council debated at length for almost an hour before Giric banged the gavel before him and summoned Calunoth to submit to questioning. He was nervous, understanding the importance of his mission, but if he wanted to get to Lenocius, then he would need Galgrenon's help. Standing proudly, but not arrogantly, Calunoth stood in the center of the room, mentally reciting his prepared words. He had spent much of the previous evening formulating what he was going to say, at the expense of even his half-sleep, but he felt confident he could convince the council to help.

Giric began the proceedings. "Master Calunoth Leiron, you have been summoned by the council of Galgrenon to testify regarding matters of specialized technical knowledge and reconnaissance of militant activity within Galgrenon jurisdiction. Do you swear to answer all questions asked by the council honestly and in their entirety?" Calunoth assented and Giric continued. "Then allow me to begin." The governor leaned back in his seat as he surveyed the council room.

"You came here as a representative of His Majesty King Greshaun, who seeks our assistance in combating the uprising led by Duke Byrant in the south. Many of our members are sympathetic to this cause, but you have stated that to associate with the duke over the king would be hazardous to the interests of the Galgre people. While Captain Craig's report detailed your adventures in the cavern, and while PRIMAL's presence without authorization is troubling, you have stated to me privately that they are not the true reason why an alliance with Byrant is not in the best interest of our people. What say you to that?" Giric asked, reciting the lines he and Calunoth had agreed to privately in the early hours of the morning.

Calunoth was aware of Gordon's withering stare as he spoke but refused to be cowed by it as he answered the governor.

"Governor Giric, by virtue of his association with the organization known as PRIMAL, led by a man whose crimes are an offense to the earth itself, Duke Byrant has shown he is interested in power more than people. The crimes committed by PRIMAL are evidenced in these documents, signed by their leader, Lenocius, we procured from an excursion into the Llewyn Hills. As you can see, the destruction of Glathaous Castle, my home, was a direct result of PRIMAL's efforts to seize Lord Galthaous' Pralia technology to perfect their own." Calunoth submitted the documents they had brought from Deirive to the council. "Additionally, PRIMAL and Byrant were responsible for organizing a coup at Commerel and for imprisoning Viscount Latoya for weeks as they attempted to steal the city from under the nose of the king. This cowardly act, coupled with the subterfuge of putting unauthorized militant forces in your area, speak to the character of the man you would ally with."

Calunoth was interrupted by Leferte. "While these actions may not reek of honor, they are a necessary reality of war. Duke Byrant may have unconventional methods, but any who doubt his motives are clearly deluded. Byrant can do more to bring this country forward than the royal family ever could. The technology Craig spoke of is proof of that."

"That technology is an extension of PRIMAL's obsession with power," Calunoth countered. "Which leads me to the evidence that Craig was unable to reveal in his reports." Calunoth motioned to Claere, who brought over the silver metal disks they had recovered in the vault. One had been dented badly in the journey down the river, but the engravings were otherwise undamaged. Holding up the disks, Calunoth recited his indictment. "The information contained on these disks was procured from a machine left behind by the Selevirnians. It is a record of their time and of the Pralia technology Byrant and PRIMAL are attempting to revive. Recorded on these disks is the history of the fallen Selevirn Union. As many of you know, the Selevirn Union, once believed to have spanned the entire world, disappeared almost completely from the histories a little over two thousand years ago. The information we received shows that the Pralia technology being studied now, and advocated for by Byrant, has two major faults. The first is that it does not, despite modern belief, create Ynia. It only converts it, and all the technology utilized by the duke converts Life Ynia to Natural Ynia, requiring that life force be sacrificed to power their devices. The body recovered from the beach proves this."

William Rankin, the councilor for the engineering section of the city gave out a heavy sigh at the end of Calunoth's speech, drawing attention and raised eyebrows from the other councilors. Addressing them, he said, "I knew it was too good to be true. When Byrant came to us with the diagrams for this technology, we believed it could create Ynia, or possibly even draw from Cosmic Ynia in the atmosphere. But to do so would require a violation of the laws of nature. This answer, I regret, is far more consistent with what we would expect." This was a welcome boost to Calunoth. Rankin carried a great deal of influence in Galgrenon, despite his eccentricities, and his condemnation of Byrant's Pralia technology boded well.

"Thank you, Councilor Rankin. Now we must let Master Leiron finish," Giric replied, acknowledging the engineer. "You mentioned a second fault in the Pralia technology, yes? And what is that?"

Calunoth stood taller and clasped his hands behind his back as he answered. "The second flaw of the Pralia technology has been recorded in at least two places in our time and is evidenced by the presence of The Wastes of Legrangia. According to the record, the Ynia once contained in the Pralia Reactors, large-scale monoliths that once converted Ynia, was inherently unstable. If that energy, in anyone's possession, goes even remotely out of balance, the Pralia technology fails, and the energy stored is released into the surrounding area in an explosion. According to the disks, the fall of the Selevirn Union was brought about by a simultaneous overload of the system, which caused every connected Pralia Reactor to shatter and release its energy. In other words, they all exploded. In the most heavily concentrated area, this resulted in the creation of The Wastes and the Forsaken Land past the Kreil Peaks. The same type of explosion, though on a smaller scale, leveled Glathaous Castle and destroyed a PRIMAL laboratory under the Llewyn Hills. The technology that Byrant markets as a savior is dangerous and unstable. For these reasons, Galgrenon would be in danger under Byrant's banner." Calunoth concluded.

The room was silent for several moments while Giric expertly let Calunoth's words fester in the minds of the council. After an uncomfortably long time, during which Calunoth's legs began to ache from standing for so long, Giric at last spoke. "As chair of this council, I would now like to thank and dismiss Master Leiron. The council will now proceed to private deliberations unless another member of the council wishes to offer anything else to the proceedings?" Giric asked through his flowing beard, looking around. Gordon maintained his scowl but made no comment. Seeing no official objection, Giric thanked the assembled companions and motioned for them to leave.

"Do you think Giric will be able to convince them?" Calunoth asked his companions.

"If he doesn't, it won't be for lack of trying. We did all we could. Now all we can do is wait," Claere replied.

The debate stretched for several hours before the doors to the council room finally opened and Giric emerged, stone-faced. The sprightly old governor was quickly accosted by the companions eager to discover the results of the debate. Giric sighed heavily and stroked his beard before speaking.

"We did all we could, but the radicals on the council weren't swayed away from Byrant. Gordon argued that all progress requires sacrifice, but while that might appeal to his constituents, it's a deadly argument for the rest of Galgrenon. I have no doubt of his guilt, but it is no small thing to arrest a sitting councilor, particularly one in line to be governor. The four royalists voted to assist the king, the four radicals voted for Byrant, and the three moderates were split. We got one to support us against this madness, but Councilor Ainsley caved to the radicals. Her district has many young voters. She's rational, but I think she's scared of her own constituents. Councilor Garag refused to cast the deciding vote, and we were forced to table a different motion that passed nine to two, myself and Gordon voting against it," Giric reported.

"And what did you decide that gained such widespread support?" Alexander asked.

"The motion proposed by Garag stipulated that Galgrenon will remain officially neutral in this fight. I wish it were not so, but we cannot force our people to fight for a cause they do not believe in, and we will not tolerate in-fighting within Galgrenon itself. So, the official decision of the council is that we will continue to trade as normal with both the king and Byrant, but we will refuse to offer any military aid, supplies, or relief to either side in this conflict. We will weather this storm and hope the victor takes mercy on us."

"What?!" Luca exploded. "Have they lost their minds? How can they possibly still side with Byrant knowing what he's doing?"

"The radicals believe we can succeed where the Selevirnians failed," Giric replied. "It is a fool's notion, but it's what they believe."

"This isn't a complete failure," Alexander interjected. "We don't have the Galgrenon's support, but neither does Byrant. He needed it more than we do. This way at least, we won't have to fight the Galgrenons, and Byrant's lost the support of the Highlanders. The map just got a lot smaller for Byrant. Unless he can find help elsewhere."

"That seems unlikely. Although it will result in more death for the king's men and will not endear us to the rest of Renderive, this decision is likely the beginning of the end for Byrant," Giric agreed. "Now, if you'll excuse me, I must make an announcement to my people. I hope they will accept this result." Shaking his head, he went to address his people from the elevated balcony overlooking the aggregated crowd in the town square.

"We should return to the embassy. We need to relay our report to the king and determine our next step," Alexander said. The companions agreed and the group retired to the embassy for the day.

It was a fortunate location for them as they ended up being in the most secure building in Galgrenon that evening. The council's decision was rejected outright by many of Byrant's sympathizers, and they responded with protests at city hall that soon devolved into violent riots. The night was a sleepless one, with the cool night air routinely punctuated with screaming from the streets and smoke from the fire as the rioters torched buildings on the main street before finally being subdued by the militia in the early hours of the morning.

The tumultuous atmosphere that pervaded the air was not obstructed by the thick walls of the embassy. The noise from the riots rose up from the streets, permeating the embassy and banishing the dominion of sleep from the place. While the companions tried to rest, they found themselves tossing and turning, unable to drift off, with the score of chaos proving an unsuitable lullaby.

Lauren's rest was far more disturbed by her own thoughts than by the noise outside. She rose from her bed in the room she shared with Claere to find herself alone. The strong Sihleon priestess had been a source of inspiration to her ever since they had met in the dungeons of Commerel. Perhaps she could present the answers Lauren could not find.

Leaving her room in search of Claere, Lauren saw the common room was deserted, save for the mage, Alexander. Alexander sat in flowing red silk robes, his broken arm cast in a sling, writing awkwardly with his left hand as he tried to scribble out a report for the king. Lauren had spent several hours talking with Alexander since leaving Deirive. The mage was prodigiously advanced in his career for his age, and Lauren benefited greatly from their academic discussions about complex Ynia research that too often flew far above the heads of her other companions.

"Can you not sleep either, Alex?" Lauren asked her superior, descending the spiral stairs that linked the upper rooms to the common area.

Alexander winced as he looked up, shaking his unbound hand. "Oh, hello, Lauren. No, I couldn't lay comfortably with this accursed thing on. So, I've been trying to fill out my report to the king, but I'm not right-handed. You never realize how weak your off-hand muscles are until you have to use them. Still, I'm hopeful the king will be able to decipher these chicken scratches I've managed to jot down." Alexander put down the quill he had been using and rested his hand on the arm of the seat. "Actually, while you're here Lauren, I could use someone to bounce a couple of my theories off. Would you mind?"

Lauren was slightly irritated by the request, as her mind was quite occupied in other matters, but she could not refuse the Upper Circle mage, and so she sat down next to him.

"What did you have in mind, Alex?" The young researcher asked.

"Well," the mage replied, "I've been thinking about the Pralia Technology that PRIMAL is using. I've noticed that they seem to have more control over the technology than maybe we give them credit for. You were the only other capable person who saw the technology that they had unearthed in the Llewyn Hills, apart from Valthor, and he's not here, so I thought you might be a good source. When we spoke before, you mentioned that Valthor wasn't able to cast magic in the vicinity of the equipment?" Lauren nodded, unsure of what the mage was thinking. "Also, that equipment seemed to drain the Life Ynia out of the livestock in the area. But Valthor would have been using Natural Ynia to power his spells. Also, why didn't we see the same effects near the Clern Ruins? It doesn't quite add up."

Lauren gave a start as she realized what the mage had detected.

"When we were in the Llewyn laboratory, we weren't adversely affected by the machinery even though we were in very close contact with it. Actually, come to think of it, Cal said he was feeling even better than usual." Lauren's heart quickened as she rushed to her conclusion, "Maybe PRIMAL has discovered a way to use the Pralia Cores safely? Maybe they've advanced the technology enough to actually generate Natural Ynia!" Alexander shook his head.

"No, that's not it." The mage replied sharply, "the principle is the same. The Pralia Cores require Life Ynia, there is no physical way around that. You can't *make* Ynia. But I think you're right in saying PRIMAL have developed the technology further. I suspect that the machinery they used in the Hills was excavated and used to make a Pralia Core, but the machinery was still dysfunctional. The work they did in the Clern Ruins was using technology that they built from scratch using data from the excavated machinery. I suspect they refined the core they made in the Hills in the Clern laboratory so that it could be put to more militaristic purposes."

"But if that's true," Lauren pondered, "Then it would suggest that the equipment they have is much more stable. Or at least, less liable to implode."

"It's still too dangerous to use. You weren't there in the cavern." Alexander responded, "Those machines exploded when broken just like the ones at Glathaous and the Hills did, just to a lesser extent. But I suspect that a huge amount of Natural Ynia is required to make a Pralia Core, and that's what the old machines in the hills were doing. While PRIMAL was experimenting with their core there, the core was draining the Life Ynia from the area and the prisoners to power the machines. When it was removed, the machines pulled all of the Natural Ynia from the area into them instead. That's why Valthor wasn't able to cast any spells. The Glathaous Core converts Natural Ynia into Life Ynia. I imagine the Glathaous Core was pulling in Natural Ynia away from the old machines that Valthor couldn't manage. It also explains why Calunoth felt stronger when close to it."

"Which means that if Calunoth is close to PRIMAL's machines, he'll be much stronger because of the glut of Natural Ynia around the machines." Lauren concluded.

"I think that would have been the case, but I believe PRIMAL have made advancements to focus their Pralia technology. I was able to cast spells in the Clern Ruins, even when in the same room as the machines. PRIMAL have made advances that can better direct the flow of Ynia so that it's more controlled. The Glathaous Core should still be able to destroy them, but I think that PRIMAL's control over the technology has increased enough that we can't count on it blowing them up without us interfering."

"So in the end, Byrant will still be sacrificing his people for this war? There's no way to make this technology work for us?" Lauren asked, glad for a window to return to the framework of her thoughts.

"If the Legrangians invade in force again, it would be useful trump card, but beyond that," Alexander scratched his chin, before sighing, "between you and me Lauren, I want this technology to work as well. But the moral cost is too high. And if the closest that our best, Isaac Glathaous, could get is with the Glathaous Core, I think we just have to accept that this technology is just not the future of our people." Alexander went to pick up his quill again and gave a sharp curse as he pulled on the sling binding his arm. Seeing his grimace, Lauren's clouded thoughts were cleared for a moment by concern for the mage.

"Surely there are medics who could have healed your arm more thoroughly?" Lauren asked. "Most doctors can use at least some Ynia-based medical techniques which would accelerate your healing."

"Yes, but they were all busy. One of the outer mines collapsed in the same quake that trapped Cal and the others. Combine that with the damage being done by these riots, and there's a lot of people getting hurt out there. I couldn't justify asking a doctor or medic to waste their energy on me when it can heal by itself. You know how much Ynia it takes to cast medical spells. I figured I shouldn't waste their time for my convenience," the mage replied, scrunching up the paper he had been writing on and throwing it in the fire burning in the center of the room.

Lauren shifted closer to the mage and said, "I suppose that makes sense. But it will take weeks to heal properly by itself, and we might not have that much time. Give me your arm," she ordered, her voice firmer than usual.

Grimacing, Alexander used his free hand to pull his injured arm from the cloth sling wound around his neck. Lauren drew back the silk robe of Alexander's sleeve to reveal the mottled bruising that had settled in since the fall down the river, turning his pale skin an unsettling tinge of yellow and black.

"Stay still," Lauren commanded and started weaving the formulas she had been studying while working at the Deirive Laboratories after Commerel. Her eyes narrowed as she wove the signs in the air, setting her hand gingerly on the injured mage's tender arm. Once she completed the spell, she felt a great rush of energy leave her body, and she was left exhausted by her exertion. Her reward though, was watching the yellow-and-black bruising fade to a red-and-white tinge that reflected a far less severe injury. Alexander began moving his injured arm slowly, wincing as he did so but with far less grit in his teeth than before.

"It's not perfect. You shouldn't be doing any exercises with it, but your arm should be completely healed in about a week now." Lauren's eyelids fluttered with fatigue as she lay back against the wooden bench on which they sat.

"I didn't know you could use healing spells," Alexander said. "Usually students in Akadaemia don't start learning these spells until they're much older."

"I learned the basics in my first year there. The rest I've picked up in the past few months," Lauren replied tiredly.

"You've only been learning for the past few months, and you can already heal severely broken bones? You've a talent for this, Lauren."

Alexander looked at her incredulously before shaking his arm again. "But thank you, truly. I can write now, so at least we won't lose the war due to my bad handwriting."

"Have you seen Claere anywhere, Alex? I wanted to speak with her," Lauren asked.

"I saw her heading to the balcony about half an hour ago. As far as I know, she's still out there. I think she's alone unless Cal's grown the guts to spend some alone time with her," Alexander said jokingly, gesturing up at the closed doors on the exposed upper hallway.

Lauren thanked him, and after taking a moment to regain her strength, journeyed back up the stairs and through the closed doors that blocked the balcony from the rest of the common area. Alex was proven correct, and Lauren saw the exotically beautiful Sihleon priestess's flowing raven hair fluttering in the breeze. She leaned comfortably over the balcony railing observing the chaos in the city below. Hearing the doors open behind her, the priestess turned to see who had intruded upon her vigil of the burning city.

"Lauren? Well, I suppose it's a lot to ask for anyone to sleep with all the chaos outside," Claere observed coolly, turning to address the young researcher. "But this is probably the safest place in the city right now. I don't think you need to be concerned."

Lauren shook her head and said, "It's loud, yes, but it's not what's keeping me up. I was wondering if I could ask for your advice?"

Claere looked at her and raised her left eyebrow. "You're intelligent yourself, you know, Lauren. More so than me, honestly. What can I help you with?"

"You're far stronger than I am. I … I'm having a hard time trying to figure something out. I'm confused. Since I started traveling with Cal and Luca, I've always wondered if maybe I was on the wrong side. I don't support using these flawed Pralia Cores, especially not if Byrant's using his own people as a source of Life Ynia. But if it's temporary and means that the people who need help receive help, then maybe's it worth it, at least for a little while. But even then, I can't stand the idea of just sacrificing a human life for it. It's … it's hard to justify, even if the ends are good."

"Have you ever had to kill anyone, Lauren?" Claere asked her.

Lauren averted her eyes and fidgeted as she answered haltingly. "Once … in Commerel. We were attacked at the inn, and I had to save Bleiz. But it made me feel so … so unclean. It still bothers me. I can still see his face when I dream. A life that I ended, even if it meant saving my friend." Lauren's voice took on a dark tone as she spoke, her voice almost a whisper. "I don't know if I can take a life like that again. Not that I even could," she added as a bitter afterthought. "I got lucky that time, but I'm useless in a fight, especially compared to you. I just, I don't know if it would be better for me to just stay in Galgrenon and go back to the lab where I belong." Her voice held resentment as she spoke, and she still had yet to look the priestess in the eye. The doubts that she had been carrying for so long had finally spilled out.

Claere shifted from her position leaning against the balcony to put her arm around the younger girl. Despite being close in age, Claere's experience and training gave her a far older disposition. "Now you're just being a fool. You've been invaluable throughout this journey. If I recall correctly, the only reason we're all here is because you saved everyone in Glathaous. We can win this war thanks to what you did. That doesn't sound like someone who belongs in a laboratory."

"But I can't fight. I'm scared to kill. Even with you training me, I'm still useless on the battlefield, especially when I'm next to you," Lauren protested, tears starting to form in her strong eyes.

"You shouldn't compare us, Lauren. It's not a fair comparison. Comparing you and I is like comparing Cal and Valthor. You won't ever be able to be as strong as us no matter how hard you train. With your training, you can least defend yourself, even if you can't be on the front lines with the rest of us." Claere paused before continuing. "You are far more intelligent than anyone else here, and that's the weapon you should focus on developing. And if you need to fight someone, you might not be a help, but you won't be a burden. Your strength exists outside the fighting anyway."

"How do you do it, Claere?" Lauren asked, burying her head in her hands, her long hair flowing around her face. "You say I'm smarter than you, but you seem so perfect. You don't spend the nights crying over a random stranger, a murderer who deserved to die. I can't think my way past that! And I'm not even sure if I'm fighting for the right side! What should I do?"

Claere sighed and hugged the young researcher comfortingly. "Well, the first problem I deal with by telling myself that killing a bad person is no different than saving a good person. The result is the same to me, so maybe that rationale will appeal to the logic of your mind. As for the second one, I have an obligation to the One to stop and punish evil. I believe the Pralia Cores are evil. That's all the justification I need. But you need to find your own reasons."

Extricating herself from Claere's embrace, Lauren wiped her tears from her eyes, shaking her head. "I can't run from this decision anymore, can I?"

Claere shook her head solemnly. Lauren turned her gaze to the sky, obscured by the polluting light and smoke emanating from the city. Setting her jaw firmly, she leaned against the railing and resolved to find her answer before leaving that terrace. "Thank you, Claere, for everything you've done to help me." Lauren said, truly grateful to the powerful, exotic priestess.

Claere smiled warmly, breaking from her usual cool aloofness. "It's part of the job. Even if we end up on opposing sides, you can still call me your friend." Then the priestess was gone, leaving Lauren alone on the balcony.

***

In the common room below, Alexander had concluded writing his report in his halting script. He would send it away in the morning when he could leave the embassy and head to the town hall. One of the five arcane circles in Renderive that could transport matter was located in the Galgrenon Council Hall. Alexander would be able to relay back their report to the king using the circle, causing his report to disappear and then reappear dozens of leagues away. It would be sent to a sister circle in the Royal Palace in Deirive, materializing in the arcane room designed to receive such reports.

And while the rest of their companions finally retired to their sleep, Lauren looked out, despondent, over the burning city, watching her home fall to the chaos, finally ready to commit to her decision.

Chapter 23

To War

  The once clear mountain air was now contaminated with the smoke of the fires set in the city the night before. The high altitude made the air feel thin and chill, and the remnants of the smoke wafted loosely upon the breeze. The decision of the Galgrenon Council to remain neutral in the ongoing civil war had caused consternation in all corners of the city, leaving few satisfied. However, the youth supporting Byrant's cause had taken the news most poorly, choosing to hide their faces and head into the streets to express their disdain for the decision. With growing discontent among the people, the council had, overnight, authorized the local militia to disband the growing mass, causing the conflict to escalate into a minor skirmish. The passion of youth was no match for the experience and courage of the local militia, however, and though several fires were set and the main street shops lost some of their wares to looting, the rioting radicals were suppressed and dispersed expediently, with the fires being doused by morning.

  Calunoth gave out a low chuckle at the scene. *It seems I'm not the only one who'll burn down heaven and earth to achieve my goal,* he thought as he viewed the city.

  Preoccupied with his thoughts, Calunoth failed to notice Alexander coming up behind him, joining him on the balcony. The embassy was the second most protected building in Galgrenon, behind city hall, and as a result, had been unaffected by the previous night's riots. While the physical security of the property had been preserved, the noise and the smoke of the evening had not proven conducive to restful sleep. That was doubly true for Alexander, whose broken arm had magnified his discomfort even with Lauren's assistance, so he had been unable to seize even the few hours of sleep that Calunoth had been partial to. To compound his misery, he had also acquired a cold.

  "Everyone still alive? The city didn't burn to the ground in the night?" Alexander asked.

  Calunoth smiled wryly in response and said, "It looks like it's all still there. It'd be a real pain if we'd gone through all this hassle and lost the city anyway."

"Honestly," Alexander said with a snort, "those inspired by Byrant should tell you all you need to know about the man himself. He's delusional. A delinquent. And he's going to get a lot more people killed before this war is over."

"We'll stop him. And Lenocius. We have to because if one of those Pralia Cores explodes in a city, a lot of innocent people will die. It's more important now than ever," Calunoth replied.

"Speaking of which, there's something I wanted to speak with you about. Regarding your Pralia Core," Alexander said.

Calunoth had been expecting this conversation. Ever since learning about the true nature of the Pralia technology, the same problem was looming in his mind. Was he a ticking time bomb? Would his core also lose control and explode? Would he be responsible for killing his friends again? He had spent the waking hours of his night considering his fate, so he shared his thoughts. "I don't know if my core will react in the same way as PRIMAL's. Mine works in the opposite direction, converting Natural Ynia to Life Ynia. So it's possible mine doesn't have the same defect. PRIMAL was willing to raze Glathaous Castle to the ground to get this core, so I guess that means it's worth a lot to them," Calunoth replied.

Alexander shifted in his discomfort. "But what if it does have the same defect? You certainly wouldn't survive."

"If I die, I die," Calunoth replied, shrugging. "I'm already on my second life. I should have died at Glathaous. Anything more than that is just a bonus. As long as I survive long enough to kill Lenocius, I won't complain."

"Well, if that works for you. It's your life," Alexander said with a shrug in return. The conversation was cut short by Luca and Lauren.

"I think they forgot to deliver breakfast," Luca reported, his stomach growling as he spoke.

"If it weren't for the guards, we'd have been cooked ourselves, so get over it." Calunoth grinned at the young Knight. Luca smiled in response and begrudgingly agreed.

"What's our plan now then? Is it safe to leave the embassy now?" Lauren interrupted. Her eyes were marred with deep bags from recent sleepless nights, but now they shone again with the resolution that had brought her into this journey with them.

"We need to get back to Bleiz," Luca replied resolutely. "It's up to Cal what we do after that, but we need to go and make sure he's recovered."

"I agree, but after we check on Bleiz, we should follow Lenocius," Calunoth said. "I know it's been a couple of days, but we should still try to pursue him. If we can stop him from getting to Byrant, we can stop him from ever using the Pralia Core."

"Cal, I hate to be the bearer of reality here, but that's a terrible idea." A musical voice floated up from the stairs behind them, and Claere emerged, fully refreshed onto the balcony. Her long raven hair, freshly washed, shone radiantly as she walked toward them in her usual military gait. Reaching the balcony, she continued her criticism. "Bleiz was incapacitated last we saw him, and even if he's recovered enough to travel, he'll be too weak for the fight. Alex has a dead arm, so he can't cast anything beyond basic spells, and even if we were to travel night and day to try and capture Lenocius, we have no idea where to look, and there's a lot of contested ground between here and Byrant's army. Add in the fact that you look like you're about to drop yourself, and you're going to get us all killed."

Her stinging words made Calunoth wince, but he knew she was right. The last several days had taken a heavy toll on the companions, and an attempt to catch Lenocius now would likely end in disaster.

Clearing his throat awkwardly, Alexander offered a solution. "I agree that chasing Lenocius right now would be foolhardy, but we can go and retrieve Bleiz. I sent a message to the king, and I expect to be updated in a couple days. He'll likely have more orders for us. So, we have time to get Bleiz then return here to discuss our next course of action when we know more. Giric will not begrudge us our continued presence in the city, I don't think, and it is as fine a spot as any to rest."

The rest of the group agreed, and after finishing Luca's much coveted breakfast that had finally arrived, Calunoth led them out of the damaged city and back to the fishing outpost nearly a day's walk down the trail. The return trip was much faster than their previous journey without the exhaustion and injuries of their fall through the mountain slowing them down. Lachina greeted them heartily when they arrived and led them to the hut where Bleiz was recovering.

Once inside, they were gladdened to see Bleiz sitting up and talking with his fellow patients, with the doctor sent from Galgrenon occupying a chair close by. On closer examination, Bleiz was still flushed, but his fever had gone down, and he was no longer shivering. What could be recovered of his armor had been laid out on the floor in a corner of the cabin to dry. The moment he saw his friends, he pushed himself to his feet and went to greet them, stumbling slightly but fighting through the pain.

"You kids didn't think I'd be done in that easily, did you?" he demanded with a laugh as the companions greeted the grizzled old captain. The companions spent some time quizzing Bleiz about his condition and their next course of action. Bleiz was weak but stubborn and informed them in no uncertain terms that he would be returning to Galgrenon with them, even if he had to crawl.

***

After returning to Galgrenon more slowly the next day, with Bleiz soldiering on despite his condition, they arrived to a message from the king. The Holy Knights had seized the advantage over Byrant and were in the process of besieging Marston. With the city projected to fall within the next week, the king ordered them to escort relief supplies from Galgrenon via Shellthrone Lake. Because the supplies were destined for the citizens of Marston, Giric had procured the supplies without violating the agreement of the council and ordered a ship to be readied at the Galgrenon docks.

The companions rested in Galgrenon for three more nights while the supplies were gathered and loaded, during which Bleiz recovered to full strength and had his missing armor replaced. On the dawn of the fourth day, the companions boarded *The Maelstrom*, one of three supply ships Giric had procured, and set sail across Shellthrone Lake. The journey across the lake would take three days, given the current wind conditions, which was favorable to the convoy. It was expected that Marston would surrender by the time the group reached their destination, and the problems associated with landing in a besieged city would be abated.

On the third night, the burning city of Marston came into view. The local citadel still flew the white rose of Byrantia but did so against a backdrop of fire and smoke. The city itself had been under bombardment from the Knights for over a week, and the city's walls had not been designed to withstand the full force of the eastern army. It was likely that when declaring their allegiance to Byrant, the

Marstonians had done so believing they would not be attacked because they expected Byrant to take Commerel and Galgrenon. They had assumed they would serve primarily as a supply city. However, with the group thwarting Byrant at Commerel and Galgrenon failing to commit to Byrantia, Byrant's strategy was collapsing rapidly, and Marston was now the last line of defense before the city of Byrantia itself.

As *The Maelstrom* lay anchored offshore, Lauren chose to avert her gaze from the burning city; instead, she lay on the deck and gazed up at the stars away from the city and back toward the mountains. The sky was clear from her perspective, with the smoke blowing away from the mountains over the plains, and she could see the glimmering light of faraway stars in the distance. It had taken her a long time, but she now had an answer to Calunoth's question.

Rising from the listing deck of the ship, she spied Calunoth standing on the prow, his gaze on the burning city, the flames reflecting in his eyes. He appeared to be speaking to someone to his right, yet he stood alone. Dismissing it as a trick of the light, Lauren went to speak to Calunoth. He had become the de facto leader of their strange little group. His determination drove them all forward, and though they were all motivated by different reasons, he pushed them along and gave them a cause to fight for. He seemed to be a natural leader, despite his insecurities.

Approaching him, Lauren cleared her throat to draw Calunoth's attention. The young guard looked over at her, and she noticed an odd glaze in his eyes, possibly from watching the fire for too long, but Lauren thought she sensed something darker in his deep-green eyes. For all the time she had known him, he had carried a great weight on his shoulders. He was not yet relieved of it, and it seemed the more he grew accustomed to it, the more cumbersome the weight became.

"What is it, Lauren? Did you want to train? I would rather conserve my energy in case we have to fight tomorrow. Maybe Claere could help you instead," Calunoth said, but Lauren shook her head in response.

"I've been thinking a lot about this war. I know we all have. You once asked me if you could trust me, if I would side with you or fight for Byrant for his ideals. I wanted to tell you what I'd decided," Lauren explained, leaning against the rail.

"You believe in him, don't you? I don't want to hurt you, but I won't let anyone get in my way," Calunoth warned her quietly.

"You won't have to," Lauren replied. "I've been thinking about what you said, what Bleiz has said, Roy, and even Valthor. I still believe there's a better way to live than the way we do now. I've seen enough on our travels to know that. Bleiz and Valthor are content with the world. I know it can be better. But …"

"But?" Calunoth pressed her.

"But Byrant isn't going about it the right way. He wants to tear down the system and rebuild it into something it can't be. In the same way that I can never be a true fighter, this world can never be the utopia he wants it to be. I'm not Claere, and he's not the king. And no amount of wishing will ever change that," Lauren continued, answering resolutely.

Calunoth was surprised by her answer, and turning to look her in the eye, pushed her on it. "Your training progressed better than many of the guards at Glathaous, so I know you're strong and determined. I'm being driven on by willpower alone. What makes you so convinced that you or Byrant can't do the same?"

"Because people can't be forced to change who they really are. They have to do it of their own accord. This world wants to force me into becoming a warrior. Byrant wants to force people to put others first. But that's not who I am. And that's not what people are." Lauren's voice began trembling as she spoke. "I've only ever killed one person, at Commerel, and it still haunts me. I can't take life. I won't."

"And what about me?" Calunoth interrupted her. "I didn't choose to have my life destroyed. The person I have to be was forced on me by fate."

"Was it fate or choice?" Lauren asked him quietly. "I can't answer for you. I can only say that the person you are is a person worth following."

Calunoth was silent for a while before replying, "So you won't fight anymore? And you won't support Byrant? Then what will you do? Do you still want to travel with us, or do you want to return to Akadaemia?"

Lauren shook her head resolutely. "You're stuck with me for now. I can't let you go off and get yourself hurt now. I can't kill our enemies, but I can heal our friends. I've been learning healing techniques from Alex and Claere. And the theory behind Life Ynia manipulation is easier for me than learning how to swing a sword. I want to be a person that helps the world and the people in it."

Calunoth stared at her intently. They had become close friends over the course of their journey, they all had. And just as Lauren did not see the same frail man she had met in Glathaous, Calunoth did not see the obnoxious rebel he had met at the same time. A rare smile graced his face.

"All right, well you should probably check in on Luca then. He might still be feeling the effects of the waterfall now that he's back at sea," Calunoth suggested. Lauren smiled back, put a hand lightly on his arm, and went to go find the young Knight. Before she disappeared below deck, she heard her name. Looking over her shoulder, she saw Calunoth looking at her.

"Lauren, thank you for believing in me," Calunoth said softly. Lauren nodded, happy that she had finally found her answer. Calunoth turned his gaze back to the burning city. He would not sleep this night.

***

Finding the young Knight in conversation with Bleiz and unwilling to disturb them, Lauren returned to the deck and gazed up at the stars again, marveling at how the events of the last half-year had shaped her.

Luca interrupted Lauren's reverie. He trod quietly over to her and lay down on the damp wood next to her. There they spoke at length about Lauren's new resolve and how she now realized her ability to change people's lives came from healing, not hurting. Blushing heavily, she curled up closely to the young Knight, who was thankfully not suffering seasickness again, and they conversed quietly for the rest of the night.

***

By morning, Marston had surrendered, and Calunoth and his companions could access the city. They stayed for three days helping to secure the city with the Knights, answering to General Volym, who commanded the eastern army. As they worked, they learned that Byrant's forces had retreated across the Steppe and now waited for the Holy Knights to converge on Byrantia, where he would either break the king's armies or make his final stand.

Calunoth and his companions spent the next week marching across the Steppe to join the central army now camped outside Byrantia. After several days of marching, the vast plain gave way to the lowlands of Byrantia, and the city came into view, heavily fortified and with the full force of the Holy Knights of Renderive encamped outside it. The end of the war was nigh.

***

"So, this is the perfect Pralia Core that will grant us victory, is it?" The rebellious Duke Gerald Byrant surveyed the large metal box brought forth by the honey-voiced Sihleon minister.

"Inside the box, yes," the scar-faced Lenocius replied in his melodious voice. "The box is lined with a heavy metal that inhibits the core when it's not set into the apparatus. Without that box, it would drain the Life Ynia out of everyone in this room."

The pair stood in the War Room of Byrantia Castle, surrounded by clusters of generals, officers, and strategists who milled about the large room, holding low discussions over detailed maps and cursing over reports received from the field, all the while casting dubious glances at the white-robed minister.

Lenocius had arrived at the gates of Byrantia yesterday, alone, bearing the strange metal box that now sat on the oaken table in the middle of the room. The minister's silver-lined hair was matted with mud and dust, and his white robes were stained with the wear of days of hard travel. He had arrived only hours before Byrant's forces had returned, driven back after their defeat by the royalist forces in the Battle of the Steppe. The bedraggled minister had immediately been brought to the council by Duke Byrant only to collapse during their initial meeting. Bearing the Pralia Core alone, even with the protection of the metal lining of its container, had proven too much for PRIMAL's leader, accomplished even as he was.

"It's a shame that progress requires such sacrifice, but no true change can be made without the blood of heroes being spilled to overthrow the old guard. How much Life Ynia will be required to generate the Natural Ynia needed to sustain our defenses?" Byrant asked, his neatly trimmed black mustache bristling as he spoke.

"The barrier will require several hundred citizens. Even with the huge potential of the converted Life Ynia, we need our Ynium barrier to withstand reasonable force, and that will require many sacrifices. The weapons we've designed will require less, and that Ynia will mostly be derived from their wielders and the surrounding citizenry. The weapons aren't nearly as complex as the barrier," Lenocius replied. "If we had held Commerel, we could have used the captured guards as the source as we originally intended. As it is, we have no choice but to use what's available."

"Indeed, but it's a worthy sacrifice to overthrow such a corrupt system. Many of the poorest of our citizens would lose their lives to hunger or disease if we failed anyway. So, we'll use them for their Life Ynia, such that their deaths, should it come to that, will not be wasted. How confident are you that this technology will be successful, Lenocius?"

Leaning casually against the table, the minister replied confidently, "Completely. The king's forces have been lucky so far. Losing Commerel was a blow, but not a critical one. With this Pralia Core supporting our defenses, every soldier we lose will cost the king five. And once Greshaun is deposed, I expect you to honor our agreement."

"As I promised, when I am king, I will give you the military support you need to overthrow the Church of the One in Sihleo," Byrant replied dismissively. "In many ways, you and I are alike. You see the corruption, the totalitarianism of the Church as I see the totalitarianism of our wretched system. Both must be torn down for the sake of progress."

"Indeed, we cannot rebuild the world while the old systems remain, my friend, and when I assume full control of the Sihleon government with your help, we will have half the continent prepared to embrace a new age of progress." Lenocius smiled his charming snake-oil smile as he spoke. "Now, I trust all the arrangements I requested have been made?"

Byrant nodded and said, "They have," as he beckoned forth a black-clad soldier from his post in the corner. "In the turret of the Central Tower, your men have completed the construction of the machinery you designed. You should have a commanding view of the city from there. The cells in the dungeon have been fitted to accommodate the required sacrifices, so you should have everything you need. We expect the king's army to be here within the week. You should go and make your preparations. Your man here can show you the way. I have much to do here." Byrant dismissed the Sihleon with an easy wave of his hand. Despite the seemingly impossible odds arrayed against him, the duke was a true visionary and would not be cowed by hopeless circumstances.

Once Lenocius had exited the room with his PRIMAL warrior, one of the few remaining in Renderive following the calamities that had dogged the minister, his charming smile reverted to a scowl. As he walked with the black-clad man, he ranted, continuing until they reached the Central Tower.

"That man is insufferable. It's a good thing nobles are born into their roles in this rotten country, or they would be cast down as witless morons before they ever claimed power. That fool is so much easier to manipulate than Greshaun ever would be." Shaking his head, the minister sighed and addressed his man. "Anyway, as long as we can use the Pralia Core, we'll only have to deal with him until I take control of Sihleo. We can arrange to have someone else take power in Renderive after, someone more intelligent and tolerable. What news do we have of the Glathaous Core? The last report I heard said the king had sent it to Galgrenon. Do we know who has it now or where it is?"

"Nothing certain, sir," the PRIMAL soldier replied. "We believe the Archmage Aaron escaped from Glathaous with it and happened upon the Guardian Valthor Tarragon after being pursued into the Caerwyn Bogs. It arrived in Galgrenon in the hands of some Upper Circle mage as part of an ambassadorial envoy." The soldier opened the heavy wooden door to the tower for his leader.

"The Glathaous Core is the key to this whole project. It can destroy our technology, or perfect it if my theory is correct and the papers Alistair stole from the Glathaous laboratory are accurate. The core I gave to Byrant isn't perfect, though I need him to believe it is. If the men who took Glathaous Castle hadn't screwed up so badly, we wouldn't have this problem. As it is, we will have to be on the watch for the mage and the core. If I had to guess, I suspect Guardian Tarragon will be in possession of it. By all reports, he'd had the most contact with Isaac Glathaous during its development. I want eyes kept on him and the other Guardians at all times. I doubt they'll even breach the barrier, but we shouldn't underestimate our opponents," Lenocius ordered as he entered the room Byrant had set aside for him.

Eyeing the complex machinery he had developed, Lenocius let out a low chuckle. "I almost want to see a Guardian in here. With this technology, I could cast down the One himself."

Then the white-robed minster busied himself with the myriad metal consoles in the room, checking the tubing powering the machine and muttering to himself as he prepared for the debut of his ultimate work.

Chapter 24

The Night Before

The march to Byrantia had gone as smoothly as the companions could have hoped. Wisps of cloud had stood a constant vigil against the beating rays of the sun, masking the plains from the full heat of the star. The slowly dying grass of the plains had crunched softly underfoot as the eastern army had marched across the Steppe, carrying with them provisions from Marston and water siphoned in great vats from Shellthrone Lake. The army was over fifteen thousand men strong and comprised of men from all over the country. While the Holy Knights made up the backbone of the force, some ten thousand all told, the entity was augmented by defecting Galgrenons, some Hillmen from the north, and the fervent working-class men of the capital, all seeing this war as an opportunity to raise themselves from their station to higher glories. Many of the young assisted the Knights in whatever manner they could, eager to impress and earn a position in the Knights themselves.

The Holy Knights of Renderive served as the primary military force in Renderive, operating out of the Commandant's Bastion, under the command of the field marshal. Highly disciplined and exceptionally well-trained and equipped, the Knights were widely respected and trusted by the populace of Renderive. The process of becoming a Knight was an arduous one and typically required several years of squireship to a senior Knight as a boy before being recommended for induction into the order by their superior. While that was the most common path to Knighthood, any Renderivean citizen could be inducted at the recommendation of a superior provided they demonstrated the requisite Knighthood ideals of patriotism, courage, and honor.

For many working-class men, that was their escape from their roots. King Greshaun had issued a decree after the Third Schism War declaring there were to be no class or income requirements to join the Knights, and completing one's training resulted in a well-compensated career in exchange for risking one's life to defend the land underfoot.

Most of Byrant's forces were comprised of the southern army, the largest subdivision of the Holy Knights. While most Knights had sided with the king, the southern army was based in Byrantia and had felt their allegiance to the country was best served by following Byrant. The southern army was supplemented by common folk subsidized by the funding of the wealthy elite. While lacking formal training, most of Byrant's men—beyond the Knights—believed religiously in their cause, and a zealot was always a more dangerous opponent to face.

The eastern army had spent the journey across the Steppe trailing behind the central army, which had engaged the bulk of Byrant's forces in the Battle of the Steppe, as it was called by the men now. The central army, through rumors spread by messengers, had spun the battle into a glorious tale of blood and gore that had seen the pretender king driven back. Bleiz however, as a Captain of the Wilds, had had the opportunity to view the official messages and had grimly reported the truth of the matter to the companions. Though his rank entitled him to a battalion of men to command, Bleiz had instead requested command of a guerilla commando unit, namely his friends. Bleiz may have held a relatively low rank in the Knights, but his previous experience as a Commander in the Knights of the Wings afforded him influence that far outstripped his rank. General Vordym had agreed readily. His command structure had been established well before the battle of Marston and did not account for the addition of the Wilds Knight into the hierarchy. Though officially reporting to an incompetent lieutenant named Caldwell, the only available officer, Bleiz could direct his band without any significant oversight, with the exception of participating in briefings with the other officers, which allowed him access to the reports.

While the central army had successfully driven back Byrant's army, they had sustained heavy casualties, almost rendering their victory pyrrhic. The battle had taken place over a week ago in the plains to the south of Commerel, but heavy rain and the imprints of the army on the earth had bogged down the Holy Knights, heavily impeding their progress and leaving them unable to pursue Byrant's retreating army quickly. With the advantage of their supply lines, Byrant and his forces had retreated quickly across the plains, abandoning the indefensible towns of Coleir and Berren to expert teams of guerilla forces that would slow down the army, but couldn't possibly stop it, seizing from them additional supplies and recruits in the process.

Knowing the central army had been heavily weakened, Byrant's forces might have held Coleir and engaged there, but with the addition of the eastern army and a large portion of the western army detaching from Asta's Gate to encircle them, Byrant had instead decided to retreat to the strategically defensible Byrantia. The combined force of the Renderivean armies was now coming to bear on the capital city of Southern Renderive, and the battle was expected to be bloody.

As they had journeyed, the eastern army had been supplemented by a large contingent of Knights of the Waves and Mariners from the Chelian Isles and Draca. Although the Waves were the second smallest contingent of the Knights, ahead of only the Willow Knights, and were unused to fighting on land, the infusion of troops and supplies provided a significant morale boost to the wearying eastern army. More importantly, the reinforcements had seized the port of Revleir, so the royalists now had a steady flow of water and provisions from the Southern Ocean to the army.

With Byrant's port seized and the walls closing in around him, he had no choice but to retreat to the heavily armed fortifications of Byrantia's city walls. As the unofficial capital of Southern Renderive and the second most dominant city outside of Commerel on the plains, Byrantia was a major stronghold for Renderivean assets.

Having marched through the night to reach and resupply the central army in time, dawn was breaking when the city fortress of Byrantia appeared before the eastern army and the companions. As one of the youngest Renderivean cities, having only been founded four hundred years ago, Byrantia lacked the archaic and sprawling structures that defined the capital, and to a lesser extent, Commerel. But benefiting from the wealth its southern monopoly had acquired for its wealthy inhabitants, the city was well maintained and tidily organized. Paved streets were laid out in structured rows, neatly dividing the city into banks of buildings, with an inner road running alongside the inside of the outer wall allowing easy access around the city.

Unlike the centrally located Commerel Keep, Byrantia Castle was located on the southernmost side of the city, with the southern wall performing double duty as both a city and castle wall. The castle was made of clean, gleaming white flagstone and stood an imposing eighty feet above the ground from the top of the tallest spire. The castle was additionally guarded by a low, ten-foot wall designed more for privacy than defense.

The man-made defenses were supplemented by the natural curves of the uneven lowlands, with brief dips of elevation outside the walls that left invaders facing an upward climb. The surrounding uneven area was also well irrigated, with freshly harvested crops dotted around the hillscape, their product likely procured by Byrant and stored inside the city away from the seeping waters that came with the spring thaw.

All of these defenses had been anticipated and discussed by the Renderivean royalists beforehand. What they hadn't anticipated was the strange red light now emanating around the city. The light seemed to form a protective cloak, eerie and unnatural against the rising light of the dawn. It was matched by small bursts of light sprinkled periodically around the city, centered around the walls and the open town squares. Calunoth didn't need the scouting party to tell him what it was. The Pralia technology had made it to Byrantia, and from what he saw, had been developed far more extensively than Lenocius' notes in the mountains had made it seem.

Calunoth watched in awe as siege engines swung into action across the field, hurling rocks at the city gates. The large boulders, extracted from the earth and bound together with magic, should have cracked the stones and crushed any poor soul who found themselves under them. Instead, the rocks clattered against the light cloak with a sound like crashing thunder but disintegrated as they collided, unable to breach the light surrounding the city.

The barrier was immune to smaller projectiles as well. Scouts flung arrows, cautiously testing the limits of the barricade. The barrier sparked as the missiles crashed into them, but the inhabitants behind the dome didn't blink. Whatever technology Lenocius had conjured to power this shield was substantial.

With the encamped central army only able to take potshots at the barrier, the king's forces had marshaled themselves into their respective battalions as they formed the camp that stretched out for miles across the lowlands. Although the magical barrier was deterring the attackers for now, the signs of war that stretched out beyond the walls must have been far more demoralizing to the inhabitants of the besieged city.

When he arrived in Byrantia, Calunoth was surprised with a summons from the central command tent. Following Bleiz's lead, the companions worked their way around the encamped soldiers' tents. The scent of cooking food wafting from the fires made his belly rumble, and the warmth of the fires beckoned him to leave the chill autumn air. Bleiz, in his recently replaced armor, drew murmurs of respect from passersby, and Calunoth couldn't help but notice the number of stout Knights who gazed after the silky raven hair of the Sihleon priestess who accompanied them. Claere paid them no heed, however, maintaining her brisk military walk alongside Calunoth.

"You seem to be drawing a lot of attention. Will we be okay staying here?" Calunoth murmured to Claere, and at her baleful glare in return, immediately regretted it.

"Don't worry. If they want to hurt you, they'll have to go through me first," she replied caustically, clearly unimpressed by his concern. Behind them, Calunoth could hear Luca and Alexander snickering.

The companions moved hastily through the camp, arriving at the heavily guarded central command post in short order. The post consisted of a wide dark-red pavilion erected using spun fabric and collapsible metal posts. It's single entrance was blocked by six men of the Royal Guard. The Royal Guard was the king's personal detachment and guarded him wherever he traveled. They were the finest of men, selected carefully from Knights who had served with honor and distinction. It was a post of the highest honor, and they took their duties seriously.

Upon their arrival, the group was searched thoroughly and relieved of their weapons. The formality would have passed without incident, but the guard searching Calunoth discovered the glow from his chest as he inspected Calunoth's armor for hidden weapons. Without hesitation, he threw himself upon Calunoth, tossing him heavily to the ground and suppressing him. The man was over six feet tall and, combined with the thick red armor he wore, had no trouble pinning Calunoth to the ground as he awaited orders from his captain, ignoring Bleiz's protestations.

Calunoth feared that he was going to be arrested, but the shouting and commotion brought forth interest from inside the pavilion. Unable to see anything but red armor and overcast skies, Calunoth was relieved to hear a familiar voice break through the cacophony.

"All right, lads, what's all this noise about? Who have you accidentally killed this time?" The familiar voice had a lyrical lilt to it, and he continued speaking when he recognized the captain. "Ah, Bleiz! What's the problem? Where's Cal?"

"Valthor!" Calunoth called out, his voice muffled by the guard. "I'm here!"

"What are you doing, man? What's the issue?" Valthor asked the guard.

"Sir, he's carrying a magical device in his shirt. It might prove dangerous to the king," the Knight responded as he pinned Calunoth heavily to the ground.

"That magical device might be our best weapon here. Unhand him. He's no threat to the king. Besides, we've got three Guardians in here as well, so if he can take us all out, we're properly screwed anyway."

The guard grudgingly peeled himself off Calunoth. Although they answered directly to the king, a Guardian's authority was not to be questioned. Calunoth gratefully accepted a hand up from Valthor, who scanned him for injuries as he rose.

"You seem a little the worse for wear, but I'm not seeing any major injuries. You got along all right in Galgrenon?" the Guardian asked.

"Bleiz was taken ill after we fell down the mountain through the river, and Alex broke his arm at the same time, but everyone's recovered well enough to fight," Calunoth replied, dusting himself off.

Valthor let out a hearty laugh and said, "Yes, I read about that in Alex's report. That was a bold move, but clever. All of the tributaries of Shellthrone Lake come from the mountains, so just following one would have gotten you out eventually."

Calunoth realized then that Alexander may have glossed over some of the finer details of their endeavor, including the part where they had almost drowned by accidentally falling into the river. "You'll have to tell me more about it sometime, but Aiden's been expecting you, and I don't think we should keep him waiting." Valthor held the flap of the pavilion open and beckoned the group inside.

Calunoth filed inside the tent, surprised at how spacious the room was. As the army's central strategic hub, the room was centered around a single, massive oak table, around which several generals were clustered.

When all the companions had filed into the tent, Valthor guided them over to the table, upon which were sprawled maps, supply chain reports, scouting assessments, and a whole host of related documents. Calunoth did not recognize all the people at the table, but he did recognize some. King Aiden Greshaun sat at the head of the table, the only one sitting, while his generals stood around the edges. Calunoth recognized Guardian Artair, the monster of a man he had met in Deirive, and Lord Berwyn from Caern Vaughn. Grand Caster Sebastien stood next to a shorter woman with coal-black hair and wrapped in dark robes. Valthor took up a position between the dark-robed woman and Artair before beckoning the companions to file in, at which point they were greeted by King Greshaun himself.

"Good tidings, Master Calunoth. It does my heart well to see you and your friends unharmed. I trust you found the march here to be none too taxing?" Calunoth shook his head, responding politely to the formalities. "Good," the king continued. "I have read the results of the envoy to Galgrenon from the report, but I would like to hear your story in full, if you would."

Calunoth assented and retold the story of their adventure in Galgrenon, detailing the dealings with the council and the escapade in the mountain. Bleiz interjected periodically to fill in the gaps Calunoth missed, including their encounter with Lenocius, but otherwise left the young former guard to explain the story.

When he was finished, Calunoth apologized for failing to bring the Galgrenons on board, but the king waved his hand dismissively. "Bah, think nothing of it. It would have been easier to have their technology and engineers on our side, especially given what we're up against, but keeping them out of the war entirely is a much bigger blow to Byrant than it is to us. You did well, Master Calunoth, and indeed, your tale completes the puzzle we were trying to decipher."

"This information about the Pralia technology being dangerous," Artair mused. "I had been under the impression it was the next great advancement in magitechnology, but it seems to be the opposite. I wonder, does Byrant know what he's unleashed here? It might not be a bad idea to just wait him out."

"Forgive me, sire," Bleiz interrupted. "We have not yet been briefed about the situation on the ground. Given our experience with this technology, we may be able to offer insight into the situation. What's going on?"

Valthor explained the situation for the king. "As it stands now, Byrant is holed up in his city. He has two Guardians and the southern army's general commanding his forces right now. The walls of Byrantia are tall and strong but not insurmountable. We have the combined force of the central and eastern armies, with reinforcements from the western army, who chased some of Byrant's men out of the north. We also have support from the Chelians and a decent flow of supplies. If we attack as we usually would, we'll lose many good men, but we would inevitably succeed. However, there's a catch."

At Calunoth's raised eyebrow, he explained. "You saw that barrier that's been erected around the city? Thus far, it's proven impregnable. We've thrown boulders and arrows at it, and the Grand Council brought lightning down on it early this morning. The lightning broke through, but only for a moment. The physical projectiles were useless. They disintegrated on impact."

"This barrier glows the same color as the other Pralia technology did," Alexander noted. "It's likely powered by the core Lenocius escaped with. If it works like it's supposed to, it's converting the Byrantians' Life Ynia into Natural Ynia to power the barrier. Someone has to be maintaining the spell though. Probably Lenocius himself. We aren't going to be able to break through it with any human measure of strength, magical or physical."

"I studied the barrier with members of the Grand Council myself," Valthor replied. "I believe it can be broken, but it would require a sustained and massive force so that we can break it all at once. The amount of energy required to destroy it would be astronomical. It's impractical to try to force it open unless we have no other choice."

"Do we even have to attack?" Bleiz posited, examining the map. "We've cut off their supply lines, and Byrant has no allies left to send him relief. We could just lay siege to the city and starve him out."

"We thought about that," Artair replied. "But the seasons are changing soon, and it would be ill-advised to wait out our opponent in the snow and ice. We could manage for a few weeks, but going through the winter would be suicide. We'd have to retreat. And Byrant has enough food and water stockpiled to outlast us in these circumstances. If we were in the spring months, I would suggest that, but realistically, we have to deal with him now."

"So, what can we do?" Calunoth asked, lacking the same tactical experience of the other members at the table.

"We have to get past that barrier. Once we do, Byrantia will fall, but we can't go through it, or around it, or above it. But we can go under it," the dark-robed woman announced. "Earlier today, a peasant, a young boy, from within the city came into our camp claiming to have a secret way in and out of the city. I investigated myself and found it to be accurate. The boy knows of a tunnel that leads under the walls of the city and emerges in the financial district. He's willing to guide a team in."

"Cress, that sounds like a trap for our best commando units," Artair interjected. "If we dug our own tunnels, it would leave us pressed for time, but at least they would be trustworthy."

"The ground here is hard-packed clay below the mud," Cress replied. "Tunneling would take weeks, maybe months. We don't have that luxury of time."

"So, we need to send a team in to disable the barrier from the inside," King Greshaun mused. "It would be ideal if you led this team yourself, Valthor. You've dealt with this technology before, at least in part, so you should be able to find a way to bring the barrier down."

Valthor shook his head. "I don't think so, Aiden," referring to the king by his first name again. "I could lead a team in, but the success of this mission hinges on the element of surprise. I'm a high-profile Guardian, and Byrant's spies are going to be watching for us. If a Guardian goes missing, it would be highly suspicious. If anything, I should be a distraction."

"Then who should we send?" King Greshaun replied. "I could send some of the Knights of the Wilds in. They're the most skilled at moving stealthily, but they won't be familiar with the technology. They might not even know what to look for or where to start."

Artair interrupted with a hefty cough as he cleared his throat. "We have agents in the city sending us reports through the barrier. That's how we know the field only stops things in one direction, so Byrant's forces can still shoot arrows and boulders at us from behind their shield. We also know from Calunoth that the barrier is likely supplied by this Pralia Core Lenocius brought into the city. The agents mentioned a box was transported through the city a few days ago, before the erection of the shield. It's most likely enshrined in the castle somewhere with Lenocius. So, any team we send in will have to breach the castle itself, without support from the army."

"It sounds like a suicide mission," the king mused disquietly. "Even if we could get a team in to destroy the core, they would almost certainly draw the attention of the garrisoned soldiers. We would have no way of extracting them."

There was a long silence around the table as the king mulled over the difficult decision of who to order to the task. As King of Renderive, he had an army of Knights who would happily give their lives to defend the country. But this was not as simple as ordering Knights into battle where they shaped their own destiny. This was akin to ordering an execution.

"I volunteer."

Calunoth broke the silence and grimly spoke the words, ignoring his shaking knees. "The core Lord Glathaous put in my chest can destroy the ones developed by PRIMAL, and I owe Lenocius for what he did to my home. I'll infiltrate the city and destroy the core."

Valthor nodded in agreement. "It makes the most sense for you to go. The Ynia required to destroy the core conventionally could only be maintained by a Guardian or one of the Grand Council. You can do it just by touching it. And this gives you a chance at Lenocius. But you shouldn't go alone. We'll find some volunteers to go with you. Not many. A big group would draw too much attention, but we need to give you some support."

"Sire, I also volunteer." Bleiz stepped forward. "I've come to count Calunoth as my friend. I will not let him walk into this alone."

"Me too," Claere said, also stepping forward. "Sihleo is responsible for Lenocius. I am obligated to help you stop him."

"I'm not going to sit back while my friends run into danger," Luca said resolutely. "I'll go too."

"If anyone gets injured, they'll need my help. I'm going with you as well," Lauren added.

Alexander, left as the sole companion, shook his head wryly. "You people are insane. All right, well, I suppose it was asking too much to die in my bed. I'll come too."

Valthor and Artair exchanged a glance before Artair responded. "I would prefer to send a squadron of the most experienced Knights on this mission. Bleiz, I accept, but forgive my doubts about the rest of you, given the importance of the challenge."

"Nonsense!" Lord Berwyn boomed, pounding the table with his fist. "They served us well at Commerel, and at Galgrenon. They have earned the right to fight this battle. Why, were we twenty years younger, Aiden and I would be riding in alongside you. There's a strength in trusted comrades that puts the lie to experience. I say we trust them."

"I agree with Berwyn," the king proclaimed. "We needed volunteers for this mission anyway, and I can think of no finer companions for Calunoth than those who have walked this path with him already. Spend the rest of the day getting ready. What equipment and supplies you need are yours. And sleep well. We'll send for you at dawn."

At that, Calunoth bowed to the king, his companions following his lead, and left the tent.

***

The night air was cool, and the fatigue of months of travel weighed heavily on his body, yet Calunoth could not sleep. He rose from his cot on the far side of the camp and wandered outside. The campfires that provided warmth and light and the glow from the city kept the stars hidden in a shroud of darkness. The camp itself was quiet, save for the rustling of the guards as the army rested, preparing for battle the next day. The entire war effort now came down to him, and the magnitude of the occasion was not lost on him. If Calunoth could not destroy the Pralia Core, then the army would freeze here and be forced to retreat. Byrant would make up the ground lost, and the war would last through the winter, maybe for years. This was a chance to end the war before it truly consumed the country.

Walking through the camp, he passed others in a similarly sleepless state. Many men clasped their hands in prayer while others fastidiously polished their equipment, occupying their hands more than their minds. Coming to the edge of camp, Calunoth found himself standing on the hill overlooking Byrantia. The steep slope had made it impractical to establish a base here, and the hill stood bare as Cal looked out at the city and the starry sky beyond. Lying down on the moist grass, Calunoth contemplated the city and his journey thus far. It seemed like an eternity ago that he had been stabbed at Glathaous and implanted with the core that now made him a major player in the war. In the half-year since that fateful night at Glathaous, he had been tortured by the demons of his dreams, of his past, blaming him for the massacre. And they were right. He had failed in his duty. He had fallen where stronger men would not have. And now he had the opportunity to repay his debt to the fallen by slaying the architect of the Glathaous Massacre and destroying the Pralia technology that risked the lives of so many, the technology that Isaac Glathaous had given his life to stop.

Calunoth shook his head to clear his mind. The demons that had haunted him since Glathaous had not relented in their torment. Even now, he could hear them whispering in his ears and see them dancing in his periphery. They had prayed on his mind and his soul for months. It was almost a shame that they seemed to be losing their power now. He could still feel them, but he didn't care anymore.

So deep in his thoughts was he that he failed to hear the soft footsteps that approached from behind, and he only realized he had company when a flash of raven hair eased into his vision with the scent of juniper on the air as the Sihleon priestess lay down next to him.

"Couldn't sleep either, Cal?" Claere asked him softly, deviating from her usual coldness.

"I've had a lot of sleepless nights since the massacre. But this is different. I can end it all tomorrow. Everything that Lenocius has done can end tomorrow. Whatever the cost, I've got to finish him," Calunoth replied.

"You're not the same man who left Glathaous. Even in the time I've known you, you've become different, stronger. I don't think the man at Glathaous could succeed in this mission. I think that *you* can. That *we* can," Claere said.

"Claere, why did everyone volunteer to come with me? This could be a one-way trip. It probably will be. Why would they do that?" Calunoth asked.

"Everyone has their own reasons, but they all have one thing in common. They trust you. Whether you like it or not, you're a natural leader. Your drive and passion motivate them to be the best versions of themselves. Versions willing to sacrifice themselves for this cause," Claere explained as she looked over at him.

"And what was your reason?"

"As I said at the meeting, Lenocius is a Sihleon problem. As a representative of Sihleo and an envoy of the One, I should be part of the solution," Claere answered coolly.

"Is that the only reason?" Calunoth asked, looking right back into her bright eyes.

In the limited glow of the stars, Claere's blush was almost imperceptible, and she hastily looked away from Calunoth's gaze. "The Church teaches us to guide those who are lost to the light of the One, so that they may be purified and know salvation. I ... I think you might be in danger of losing yourself, and I'd like to see who you are without the rage that fills your soul. There's something about you that I just can't figure out. Something ... off. So, if killing Lenocius and Alistair relieves you of that rage, I want to help you. That's all."

"If this mission goes south tomorrow, you won't get to see me after all of this, at least not in this life," Calunoth remarked offhandedly.

"I have no intention of waiting around in the next life for you, Cal. So if you want to see me after all of this, you'd better survive. I don't want you trying to sacrifice yourself for something as stupid as revenge," the priestess said, laying her head on Calunoth's shoulder.

"Claere ..." Calunoth said, choking on his voice, unable to answer the priestess as her cool touch drove the demons from his sight.

Calunoth was spared the embarrassment of his response by another interruption, one of which he was only partially grateful for.

"I hope I'm not disturbing you two lovebirds, am I?" Valthor asked smoothly, coming up behind them.

Claere bolted upright and snorted derisively. "I don't know what you're talking about. It was just more comfortable to lay than to sit."

"Of course, madam priestess, forgive my transgression," Valthor responded, his serious demeanor from the earlier meeting now replaced by his usual easygoing nature. "I thought I'd come and give Calunoth a motivational kick, but I see you've beaten me to the punch."

"What do you think of our chances tomorrow, Valthor? What happens if we fail?" Calunoth asked the Guardian.

"Well, if anyone can do it, it's you. You have a habit of achieving the impossible, even without my help. As it is, if you fail, we do have a back-up measure. Most of the advanced magic we've tried so far hasn't done more than damage the barrier. But we have some texts the commandant sent from the Bastion that were hidden in the Willows vault. Because the Willow Knights were the first branch of the Holy Knights established and they represent the Church, many of the ancient spells are transcribed into scripture only they have access to. Most of the ancient spells in those scripture books can probably only be cast with the assistance of Pralia technology, but we can try to use one ourselves if the reaper comes calling for you." Valthor hesitated before adding, "Using magic like that would probably kill me, the Grand Council, and all the Willow Knights combined. So try not to die. It would be a real pain in the arse if you did."

Calunoth couldn't help but smirk at the Guardian as he sat down next to them. Changing his tone, Valthor turned to Calunoth. "You'll be pleased to know that Glathaous was liberated from PRIMAL last week. A garrison of Knights from Asta's Gate drove them out. As it was, they fled across the plains. They would have arrived in Byrantia shortly before the central army. It's likely Alistair is with them."

Calunoth responded carefully, noting Valthor was watching him closely. "Good. If I see him, I'll kill him. I guess I didn't finish the job properly the first time."

"No, I don't suppose you did," Valthor mused quietly before shaking his head. "Regardless of what happens to Alistair, or even Lenocius, you need to take out the core. That's your priority. If you can take them out along the way, then great, but the core comes first."

"I know," Calunoth said quietly. "But if the opportunity comes to strike, I will not hesitate."

"Nor should you. But remember something, Calunoth," Valthor said, his voice maintaining its new, uncharacteristically serious tone. "Killing Lenocius will not quiet your nightmares. Your redemption can only come from within and the judgment of your god. And I would prefer if you did not receive the latter prematurely. You've got a lot of potential. Don't throw it away recklessly."

With that, the Guardian rose to his feet. "I still have some preparations to make myself. I'll be stationed with Seb and the rest of the Grand Council while Artair leads the ground forces. Gods be with you, Calunoth, and with your companions."

Valthor began to walk away, then stopped and turned.

"And Calunoth, Isaac would be proud of you." With those last words, the Guardian disappeared into the night, leaving Calunoth and Claere alone to contemplate the stars before the tides of battle swept them up one last time.

Chapter 25

<u>Assault Initiation</u>

 The dawning sun was obscured by the metal-gray clouds that had rolled into the skies overhead from the Southern Ocean, casting the world into a pale mist of despairing drizzle as if the heavens themselves sought to deter the upcoming clash from its earth.
 Calunoth stood on the hill that he had abandoned only a few hours ago, looking out upon the city he now sought to conquer. He stood surrounded by his companions, who likewise had their gaze grimly set upon the white city. Valthor had asked them to meet there. Although he would not accompany them, he was responsible for organizing their infiltration and had taken it upon himself to personally concoct their method of attack. Last to join the group was the boy, Aelrin, who had escaped from the city through the passageway he would now lead the companions through.
 Aelrin was no more than sixteen, scrawny and small. Calunoth had initially been paranoid about following the boy into danger, but Valthor had assured him the passageway was secure and the boy was trustworthy. Aelrin was the son of a local cobbler Byrant's guards had killed and made an example of after refusing to give away his stock at a price below cost. Despite his dirty skin and his skinny body, Aelrin's eyes burned with a resolute desire that reassured Calunoth his intentions were good. Valthor welcomed them all to the hill and delivered their mission brief.
 "Your objective is to infiltrate Byrant Castle and disable the Pralia Core powering this barrier. Once the barrier is down, you are to hide, or batten down where you can, and await rescue while the army moves in. We'll have our advance units looking for you, so we'll get to you as quickly as possible. If you want to join the fighting afterward, you're free to reinforce whichever unit you judge to be needing assistance." He looked at them each in the eye, so he was certain they understood. "Now, you will enter through a passageway about a mile from here that will take you under the walls and into the basement of a local wine merchant. The boy, Aelrin, will guide you through town, but he has been told to flee if trouble arrives, so you will not need to defend him. If there is no change in the barrier's status by sundown this evening, we will assume you have failed and will modify our plans

accordingly. Any questions?" Valthor finished reading from the paper he had brought with him.

"Sire, how will we get into the castle?" Bleiz asked. "It's likely to be on high alert, and a group not wearing Byrant's insignia is likely to raise a commotion."

"I've thought of that. I've got a couple spare breastplates from the southern army for you and Luca. They'll present the rest of you as prisoners. Insist that you report to Lenocius and you might be able to get the whole way to him. Regardless, these should get you in the gates," Valthor replied. A pair of squires ran up beside him with the breastplates. "Sorry if they're a bit tight. I had to guess your sizes."

"Fits perfectly," Bleiz said, donning the plate engraved with southern army's initials. Luca's was marginally too tight for him, but he bore it without complaint, saying it was rare to find armor that fit him properly anyway.

"What will you be doing, Valthor? Are you going to be on the front lines with the Grand Council?" Calunoth asked the Guardian.

Valthor shook his head. "No, I wish I were. I'll be setting up here with the Grand Council. When the barrier comes down, we'll provide strategic magical support from afar. We've got a few of the ancient texts here as well if we need to use something really nasty. Artair will lead the frontlines and will deal with Byrant and his Guardians himself. Cress is guarding the king. Truth be told, she should lead the council since she's the best mage on the continent, but somehow the job fell to me."

"Will Artair be able to manage going up against Byrant's Guardians by himself?" Luca asked Valthor.

"He'll be all right," Valthor answered. "Only Van and Relgar have turned, and Artair can handle Van one on one. Relgar might be a bigger ask, but they're unlikely to fight side by side. If worst comes to worst, we can attack with magic from afar, but we're probably not going to be able to target accurately from this distance. Our job is to cause chaos more than real damage."

Calunoth sighed and steeled himself. "Okay, well, it's time for us to go," he announced. Valthor gave them his blessing before retreating to the top of the hill where Sebastien, Grand Caster, and leader of the Grand Council, awaited him.

Calunoth and his companions followed Aelrin to a small, abandoned farmhouse on the northeastern border of the city. The land had been harvested of its seed before the army's arrival and all of the bounty had been collected and stored within the city walls. The chill air of fall whispered across the plains and into the lowlands, mixing well with the light rain to banish the warmth from the bones. Inside, the farmhouse was scarcely decorated beyond the simple accessories a farmer requires to function. A small table, a wood-burning fireplace, and a cot stuffed with hay decorated the otherwise bare single room.

    Calunoth was wondering where a hidden entrance could possibly be in this tiny place when Aelrin moved the cot, with Luca's help, revealing a small trapdoor leading underground. Climbing down, they discovered what was ostensibly a cellar used as a small slaughterhouse, with clean hooks decorating the wall and shaved chicken carcasses on the dirt floor. While navigating the small cellar, Aelrin explained the personal slaughterhouse allowed the farmer to increase his profit without deputizing the local butcher. The boy then revealed a dirt-hewn passageway that he said led into the center of the city hidden behind a large cow carcass.

    The passageway was short and narrow but not unreasonably tight. The companions had to follow Aelrin single file down the passageway, and Luca had to keep his head down to avoid banging it on the ceiling. The passageway looked suspiciously well traveled to Calunoth, the imprint of recent footprints in the dirt causing him to raise his concern to Aelrin. The boy explained that this passageway was used to smuggle goods out of the city to avoid the high tolls leveled on all goods leaving Byrantia. The passageway was well known by the city's dwindling merchant class but had not been leaked to the authorities, who would have closed the tunnel immediately and likely seized the property and life of both the farmer and the sommelier on either end of the tunnel.

    The companions traveled for over an hour in near darkness, the torches Aelrin and Bleiz carried the only source of light. They walked in silence, the heavy underground air pressing down on them. Calunoth had begun to grow anxious as the quality and availability of the air diminished, and adrenaline began to make up the difference. His thoughts became so rapid he began to hyperventilate, only to feel Claere's reassuring hand on his shoulder. This was not her first high-risk mission; she had the advantage of experience Calunoth lacked, and she transferred her cool demeanor to him with that one firm touch of her hand. Calunoth collected himself just in time to stabilize his breathing as Aelrin stopped suddenly, almost causing Calunoth to walk into him.

Aelrin raised a hand, then knocked on a wooden panel in the ceiling. When he heard only silence within, he pushed the panel open, allowing candlelight to flood the tunnel, blinding them as their eyes grew accustomed to the light. Handing his torch back to Calunoth, Aelrin grabbed the edge of the floor above and pulled himself up, reaching down a hand to relieve Calunoth of the torch as the former guard followed suit.

Peering around at his new surroundings, Calunoth noted he was a in a cool, well-lit wine cellar, with racks of bottles stacked neatly in latticework stands filling the room and lining the walls. The room had the appearance of being well maintained, but dust had begun to settle on the bottles lining the far wall, perhaps on purpose to add an air of exclusivity to the finer wines in the sommelier's inventory.

"Aelrin, who owns this place? Are they friendly, or are we going to have to subdue them?" Bleiz asked, emerging from the panel in the floor.

"The owner was arrested for trying to avoid a recently imposed liquor tax. His wife is running the shop, but she's no friend of Byrant. She knows me. I'll talk to her first and warn her. She shouldn't be a problem," the young boy assured him.

With those words, he disappeared up the stairs, and the companions heard a muffled gasp followed by a whispered conversation. Bleiz kept the panel in the floor propped open, with the intention of keeping their escape route clear if they needed to make an expedient getaway.

Fortunately, no such movement was required. Aelrin darted back down the stairs to the cellar, and called the rest of the group up, beckoning for them to be silent. The companions stealthily followed the boy as he guided them through the back door of the shop and into the alleyway behind.

The sun had risen higher in the sky by now, but the gray clouds continued to obscure it, casting a pale shadow over the white city streets. Peering out from the alleyway, Calunoth saw the streets were almost deserted, their only inhabitants the soldiers who patrolled them regularly, watching carefully for any who might cause trouble. The tension in the city was palpable, and the air felt like it could be cut with a knife.

Calunoth cursed under his breath. The companions had emerged near the largest and most luxurious buildings, and the gleaming white stone of Castle Byrant towered behind. They were much closer to the castle than Calunoth would have anticipated, but the emptiness of the streets combined with the patrols would make it almost impossible to get to the castle undetected.

"Why is it so quiet here?" Calunoth hissed to Aelrin.

The boy pursed his lips before answering, "There aren't any rules about moving about if you're a citizen. It's just that right now, no one wants to leave their homes. But I know a way in."

Calunoth noticed Aelrin was now quite pale and had a mild tremor in his voice.

Bleiz put his hand on the young boy's shoulder, trying to reassure him. "Easy, lad," Bleiz said. "Just relax and tell us what to do."

"You'll have to split up. The Knights will go alone. It would draw attention to have Knights wandering around with civilians. We can go separate ways, and you can meet up with us closer to the castle," Aelrin said nervously.

"If we pull the prisoner ruse now, we may end up with additional Knights joining us, and that would complicate our job," Bleiz surmised. "So, we'll have to act like we're on patrol, and everyone else just walks openly in the street as citizens. Risky, but then I suppose this whole operation is risky."

"There's a tailor shop with an alleyway behind it just outside the castle," Aelrin suggested. "We should meet up back there."

The group agreed to the meeting place, then split off down the street in different directions. Their faces hidden by their helms, Bleiz and Luca walked with their heads held high, blending in superfluously with the other Knights patrolling the city. Calunoth and his group had to be more discreet. They walked hurriedly, heads down, attempting to pass as townspeople.

The ruse was successful for several streets as they neared the tailor shop. They were not questioned by guards, despite a few suspicious glances sent their way. Calunoth led the way until the shop came into sight, and he slipped into the alleyway behind, suddenly aware that his party was short one member. Aelrin was missing.

Panic struck his heart as he realized the boy had vanished. Had he betrayed them? Or been captured? Had he simply lost his nerve and fled? His answer came with the sudden emergence of eight Knights, who marched solemnly out of the darkness that obscured the ends of the alley. Calunoth cursed. They had been walking into a trap all along.

The Knights had blocked off both ends of the alleyway, trapping them. Alexander had been acting as rear guard and now found himself with his back to Lauren as he faced four Knights at the entrance of the alley. Calunoth and Claere were similarly held with their backs to Alexander's, facing four Knights of their own who now strode forward from the dead end of the alleyway. Drawing their swords, Calunoth and Claere moved to defend themselves, with Calunoth circling back around the group to cover Alexander. The mage could use the small dagger he carried at his waist, but against the superior skill and training of the Knights, his true use lay in his magic.

"Claere, hold them here. Lauren, support Claere. Alex, I'll hold them off on this side. Use your magic to support me," Calunoth ordered the companions, hastily formulating a defense. Whatever the outcome of this fight, he had no intention of surrendering.

The Knights struck at Calunoth first, warily encircling him, calling on him to surrender. Calunoth responded by leaping to the side and lashing out with his blade at the Knight on his right. He was met with the reflexive shower of sparks as his blade crashed against the Knight's before leaping back to his initial position in front of Alexander. He could hear the mage chanting behind him, with the unnatural push of air at his back indicating the weaving of the formulae.

The Knights were experienced fighters all and moved rapidly to counter the threat Alexander posed to them. Calunoth prayed Alexander could keep his focus as the former guard stood his ground and deflected the strikes of the incoming Knights, managing to parry two blows with one. The Knights were more skilled than Calunoth was, and he knew that he could not hold them off indefinitely, but fortunately, Alexander was able to complete his spell.

"Close your eyes!" Alexander barked from behind, advice not typically recommended in the middle of a melee, but Calunoth had learned to trust his companions, and he duly obliged. He was glad he did. Even beneath the lids of his eyes, he could see the blinding flash of light that briefly lit up the entire alley. Opening his eyes again, Calunoth moved quickly, striking down two of the Knights with neat cuts to the throat after finding the gap in their armor. The light had disoriented them momentarily, but not enough for Calunoth to finish the remaining two. He was surprised to see Claere's graceful form rush past him, following his lead and deftly executing the remaining two Knights in the clearing. Astonished at how swiftly she had dispatched her own opponents, Calunoth turned his attention to the dead end of the alleyway and saw two of the Knights laying dead on the ground and two remaining Knights coolly sheathing their swords. He went to jump in front of Lauren who had leapt to the side but stopped short when he realized who the Knights were.

"Luca! Bleiz! What were you doing with them?" Calunoth asked, surprised at his companions' appearance.

Lifting the visor of his helm to expose his eyes, Luca grinned at the young guard. "We're here to ambush you, I guess. We got here first and found the other Knights here. We asked to assist them, and they seemed happy for the help. Probably wish they didn't have us on their side now. I'm so bad with a sword, I accidentally decapitated one of my own squadmates." Luca shrugged. "Oh, well."

Claere interrupted them as she grappled with a struggling Aelrin in her arms.

"I found him waiting just outside the alley," she reported grimly. "He'd been told to wait for us to be arrested before going back to the castle with the Knights."

"So, the boy betrayed us after all," Bleiz said, somberly shaking his head. "It leaves a bad taste in my mouth, but we should have expected the worst. I thought that this was going too well. What should we do with him, Cal?"

"We should take him with us," Alexander suggested. "They'll be expecting him at the castle, and he can add some credibility to our entrance. Bleiz and Luca can still take us prisoner, and we can claim the rest of the Knights, including the real Bleiz and Luca died in the struggle. It makes the most sense."

"No," Calunoth replied, his mind clouding over. "Give me the boy." He reached out his hand, and took the struggling Aelrin from the priestess.

"I'm sorry. Please don't hurt me! They have my dad. I just wanted to help him!" Aelrin pleaded with Calunoth, who raised his sword to the boy's throat.

"And you thought this would bring him back? Bringing us here to be slaughtered and captured? We trusted you!" Calunoth threatened Aelrin, who was now utterly terrified.

"I can come with you. You're going to the castle, right? We can save my dad. He's in the prisons. I'll help you. Just please don't kill me!" Aelrin wailed.

The rage that Calunoth had subsumed within himself smoldered quietly now, stifled by the strange voices that dominated his mind. He had no intention of bringing the boy with them. Once a traitor, always a traitor. And there was only one price that he would accept as penance.

Removing his sword from the boy's throat, Calunoth reversed his strike, aiming to plunge the blade deep through Aelrin's heart.

With a mighty clang, he found his strike diverted by Bleiz's swift interception. "What are you doing, Cal? He's just a boy!" Bleiz demanded of Calunoth, but he did not seem to hear the captain's protestations.

Turning his wild-eyed scowl on Bleiz, he said, "It doesn't matter. Traitors deserve death. There can be no exceptions," Calunoth growled at the elder Knight before parrying his blade and moving to finish his strike, his mind shrouded with shadows.

Then the dark fog of his mind cleared as he felt a cool, familiar hand on his shoulder—and a second grasping his sword hand. Coming back from his trance, Calunoth arrested his strike and turned to face the clear, heterochromatic gaze of the priestess holding him back.

"Cal, what's wrong with you? This boy is a victim like you, not an enemy. Do not fall to the level of our enemies," Claere spoke directly to him, her smooth hands holding him tightly.

Calunoth stared back at the priestess and felt the demons retreat from her holy touch. Sheathing his sword, he shrugged her off but whipped around and knocked Aelrin unconscious with a firm blow to the head.

"Just bind and gag him, Luca," Calunoth muttered before adding under his breath, "I'm not a victim. I'm the accused." Once Luca had bound and gagged the young boy and hid him out of sight at the back of the alleyway, Calunoth cleared his throat and announced they had to continue to the castle.

Calunoth's companions shared a concerned look before following Calunoth out of the alley toward the open gate of Byrant Castle.

Bleiz took point after he and Luca had confiscated their companions' weapons, with Luca following up the rear. The group walked through the castle gates, garnering the attention of the captain of the gate. Bleiz played his role brilliantly, citing the beaten companions and his own bloodstained armor as proof of their struggle. The captain was excited and insistent on accompanying them through the castle himself. Fortunately, his men talked him down. They needed him to remain at the gate.

The Knights and their prisoners were rushed inside, hurriedly, with the local guards keen to see them on their way; they had more urgent matters to attend to. The lower courtyard was bustling with activity as Byrant's amassed forced milled around, preparing for battle. The activity was not what would be expected of a besieged army. Rather than entrenching themselves and fortifying defenses, they were gathering weapons and modifying artillery for range and accuracy. When Calunoth suddenly realized why, his heart flashed ice cold.

They were preparing to attack.

***

"Do you think those kids can do it?" Sebastien asked Valthor, pensively staring out at the sprawling city from the hilltop perch that the Grand Caster had commandeered for his followers. As the head mage of Renderive's Grand Council, and through that authority, every mage in the kingdom, he had decided to centralize all of the army's magic users on the lofty heights of the hill. Given the high risk posed to mages engaged in ground combat, he had instead elected to keep his forces at a distance and utilize long-range general strikes over integrating the mages within the various Knights' platoons.

"They're not kids, Seb. You're just a fossil," Valthor replied with a snort. "Calunoth will tear down heaven and earth to get to Lenocius. He had to go. The rest were just the best people to support him."

"If they fail, we need to have a plan in place. That barrier could be the end of us. The troops might not know, but we do. We barely have enough supplies to return to the Bastion, so we have to attack in the next two days if we're to take the city."

"Well, I have a few ideas in mind, but nothing concrete, short of using the ancient spells." Valthor crossed his arms.

"I take it none of those ideas require using the ancient spells? You know we can only cast them using Pralia technology. We've spent years trying to determine how the Selevirnians could cast spells with such colossal energy requirements," Sebastien said, his words muffled by his long gray beard. "Casting any of those spells using modern methods would probably kill us all. And we're not even sure if we'd be able to target them properly."

"I was thinking a concentric bombardment of—" Valthor's reply was cut off by the arrival of a messenger, who cried out to them as he reached the base of the hill. Jogging down the slope, the Guardian met the messenger halfway as he tried to climb as swiftly as his legs would allow.

"Guardian Valthor, sir! News from the north! The Legrangian Empire has attacked Caern Porth! They're requesting assistance. The king has asked for you immediately!" The man panted out his message.

"Damn!" Valthor swore explosively. "They knew we'd be vulnerable with us at each other's throats down here. Get the king over here. We can't abandon this position right now."

The messenger took a deep breath, his hands on his knees, then saluted and ran back to King Greshaun's pavilion. Valthor strode back up the hill to relay the news to Sebastien, but he was met by a pre-emptive curse as the Grand Caster looked out at the gates of the city.

"What is it? What are you swearing at?" Valthor demanded. Following his friend's gaze, he saw what had drawn his ire, and with the subject sighted, he heard the screams accompanying it.

Large rocks had begun raining down on the entirety of the Knights' armies, even as they stood arrayed in formation, ready for the assault. The boulders were followed by arrows that peppered the lines of troops and a sudden flood of water magically conjured from the earth. The projectiles came in focused waves from within the barrier itself. The Knights below were mired in the thick mud that had formed at the base of the lowlands, preventing rapid retreat.

"What?! They're out of range! They shouldn't be able to hit us!" Valthor exclaimed.

"Well, maybe Byrant's gotten something more than just that barrier from Lenocius!" Sebastien replied. "We have to move the troops back. They're getting slaughtered as it stands."

"We can't! If they break ranks, they'll trample each other in that mud. And even if they didn't, they wouldn't be able to reposition in time to counterattack. We can't move them!" Valthor said urgently.

"And those missiles are going straight through the barriers they erected on the front lines," Sebastien noted, crossing his arms and furrowing his brow. "We can't defend against this attack."

"Then we have to go on the offensive," Valthor replied. "Send word to Artair to march on the front gates. We'll have to disrupt that barrier now—concentric lightning and earth bombardment on the gate. We don't have to break through it permanently, just long enough to get troops inside."

"That won't work! The few men we might get in will be slaughtered. We have to bring down the barrier now!" Sebastien argued back.

The air grew nearly silent even as it was permeated by the screams of the dying Knights in the lowlands below as both men realized what they had to do. Sebastien nodded grimly and bade one of his staff to bring forth one of the ancient tomes.

"I'll lead the formulae. Cress has to stay with the king," Valthor said resolutely, standing taller and fortifying his resolve. "It's my responsibility. Get the rest of the council and your mages to feed all the Natural Ynia that they can muster toward me, and I'll act as the primary conduit."

The staff returned with an ancient leather-bound tome that carried the weight of the ages in its pages. Taking it in his hands, Sebastien began to fervently skim through it.

"These are all exceedingly dangerous. We need one that can destroy the barrier without destroying the entire city and countryside," Sebastien muttered to himself as he flipped through the sheaves. His old, knobbly fingers moved nimbly until they at last settled on a page replete with formulae that had not been cast since the Breaking Age. Handing the book to Valthor, Sebastien sought his affirmation. Valthor scanned the page, briskly analyzing the complex and archaic symbols until his eyes fell at last on the translated effect of the spell.

Raising his gaze to Sebastien, the Guardian spoke in a low undertone. "Are you serious?" Valthor asked.

"Whatever you do, don't miss," Sebastien replied gravely.

***

The excitement and fever pitch of the oncoming battle radiated throughout the courtyard of Byrant Castle. The army had been beaten sorely at Marston and on the Central Steppe, but now they had the technology and opportunity to take the fight to their opponents, and many were gleeful for the opportunity.

The courtyard became a mess of men that cheered as mechanical catapults, emitting the light of the Pralia technology, fired their wreckage at the encroaching Knights. The boulders were joined by a battery of arrows fired with strange composite bows that carried such weight that no one man should have been able to fire them. Yet the soldiers were firing them with ease, and the damage they wreaked on the encamped Knights was plain to hear.

The companions increased their pace, their movement shielded by the throng of soldiers milling about the courtyard even as the group ran toward the exposed entrance to the castle's Western Wing. Reaching the entrance, they paused as a strange pall of darkness fell upon the courtyard. The limited light that had filtered through the overcast clouds had now filtered to nothing, blanketing the castle in a strange darkness. It was still daytime, but the lack of light created an eerie perception of twilight even as the sun reached its zenith in the sky.

The companions stopped at the sudden change in conditions. Around them, the bustling men, their battle lust raised to a fever pitch, also stopped short, gazing at the sky.

Following their gaze, Calunoth cast his own gaze to the sky above. Valthor had told them that if they failed, they had a back-up plan, one that was dangerous, and life-threatening, and one that would only be used if the worst came to pass. And so the worst had come to pass. The rain had stopped. Calunoth watched in awe as the full power of the Guardian Valthor, supported by the Grand Council, came into full display.

Valthor had called down a mountain from the heavens.

Chapter 26

The Battle of Byrantia

The entire world had grown silent as the clashing armies gazed up at the sky. The demons that drove men to combat were stilled in awe at the incredible display of power conjured by the Grand Council. The barrage of arrows and boulders ceased, as did the flight of royalist forces as they stared, mouths agape, at the oncoming devastation. The shadows that passed over the land became steadily more concentrated until at last the meteor burst through the clouds, scattering the heavens as wantonly as specks of dust, allowing light to flood around the falling colossus.

Upon the hill overlooking Byrantia, the Grand Council sat arrayed in formation with every mage in the army arranged in concentric circles around the central caster of the spell, the Guardian Valthor Tarragon. The Lower Circle mages made up the outermost ring, followed by the Upper Circle members, then the seven members of the Grand Council, and at the heart of the circle stood Valthor. Tasked with casting the spell in its entirety, the Guardian's eyes remained firmly shut as he weaved the arcane formulae needed, chanting the words in the Ancient Selevirnian Tongue, knowing not what he said but feeling the weight of power pulsing through the words he spoke.

"*Eskiv erlin feren dvete re ecalione heloions aend vatr keligarn, eskiv herlin ute eon perlioneser, xts reokern cor serner.*" Valthor grunted out the words of the spell he had memorized from the book, simultaneously weaving the formulae in the air as he cast his mind up to the heavens. He was already exhausted. The spell had required him to cast a tendril of Ynia beyond the sky to the outer atmosphere, stretching it molecularly thin as he searched for a suitable target for the spell. The surrounding magic users had long since drained the surrounding area of Natural Ynia to reach the space rock, leaving the earth on the hill dry, browning, and cracked. With nothing left to draw on, the mages had begun stretching even further into the earth, their own Life Ynia reacting violently to the spell as they funneled the Natural Ynia through themselves to Valthor. Then, unable to break away from the spell, they felt their own Life Ynia being inefficiently drained to support the Guardian.

With the target discovered, Valthor began the second, and most draining portion of the spell: bringing the meteor out of orbit and toward its intended target. He could feel his face contorting and twitching as the strain of the spell began to take its toll. The spells from the ancient tomes had been designed to be cast only with the assistance of a Pralia Core. Valthor was casting them using nothing but the energy of the surrounding earth, conjured up and maintained by sacrificing the Life Ynia of the mages around him.

The boulder had refused to shift from its path as it had traveled around the earth, resisting the pull of the magic from the Guardian until Valthor had finished the incantation, and with a guttural cry and an overwhelming surge of energy, ripped the meteor from its dance around the planet and brought it hurtling toward the earth.

Valthor was now engaged only in controlling the flow of the magic. The spell had been cast. The strike was on its way; there was no stopping it now. All he could do now was direct it to its intended target, regardless of the costs or consequences.

The costs of the spell were astronomical. As Valthor channeled the dozens of Ynia streams with his mind, the Ynia flowed through his body at a rate he had never before experienced. He guided the missile down, using the Ynia to shift the missile only degrees at a time. He felt several Ynia streams begin to fade as the Lower Circle mages gave their last life energy to feed the spell. Then two disappeared completely as their rivers of Ynia diminished into streams, then into rivulets, then into their last drops, and then into nothing as they gave their last bit of strength, unable to break from the spell they had cast and giving all their energy to Valthor.

Valthor's mind was overwhelmed. His body was overwhelmed. As the missile came ever closer, hurtling toward the ground at an ever-increasing velocity, the energy required to maintain its course became ever greater. He could feel fewer and fewer streams of energy moving through him as he moved to cut off the dying streams himself. The additional strain of cutting off the streams pushed his body past its limits, but it meant saving the lives of the surrounding mages, who otherwise would have given their life energy until they had no more life to give.

With the meteor now within striking distance, Valthor opened his eyes to check its trajectory. As it stood, it would strike the front lines of his own army. He had miscalculated. The degree of difference three hundred miles above would manifest itself in a strike on his own forces, and surely the end of his king's reign.

Valthor refused.

The Grand Council members could see what was about to happen and followed Valthor's lead, understanding that they were now the difference between winning and losing this war. Valthor cut off every energy stream but the steady and reliable flow of Natural Ynia flowing from the Grand Council members. With their skill and experience, they had been able to extract Ynia from reaches beyond that of the Lower Circle members, pulling Natural Ynia from the atmosphere and earth further away than what their pupils could muster. But now, that proved insufficient.

So Valthor tapped into his own Life Ynia and could feel the Grand Council members around him doing the same, preparing to unleash a veritable flood of energy through Valthor. The rush was beyond anything anyone could handle.

"Gyagh!" Valthor screamed as the Ynia exploded through him, triggering the condition that had come at the price of his power. His chest seemed to explode as the strain shocked his system and brought his heart to a jarring stop.

No! Not now! Not here! Valthor thought. *So ...close ...*

The Guardian fell to his knees. The Ynia rush was overwhelming, debilitating, devastating. The meteor was shifting toward its intended target, but time was running out, Ynia was running out, and Valthor's strength was running out.

No! I won't ... let ... it go .... Valthor's Life Ynia flowed toward the meteor. He could feel three of the rushing streams flicker out as members of the Grand Council fell around him, their lives spent. His heart had failed. His body had been devastated. His mind was on the brink of darkness.

I'm ... not ... done ...

"GYAAGGHH!" Valthor screamed as he set the last formulae free into the air and his last burst of Ynia exploded out of him. With the caster incapacitated, the spell was released, and the meteor was now firmly set on its final collision course, accelerating toward the front gate obscured by the barrier.

Collapsing forward, Valthor saw the meteor mere breaths from the gate, obscuring the city, but did not see the impact. Falling on his chest, his body destroyed by the force of the spell, he passed into oblivion.

Calunoth ... the rest is ... up ... to you.

***

The falling star was not of the immense size that it had appeared to be when it first cast a shadow over the world, but the impact was devastating nevertheless. The meteor crashed through the barrier, overwhelming the force that had sustained it, and shattering through the light into the front gatehouse and surrounding wall. The ground shook violently, and shockwaves radiated throughout the city and surrounding landscape, shattering windows and unsettling foundations.

Many of the royalist soldiers surrounding the city were swept off their feet by the force of the impact, but most quickly regained their feet and took in the damage wrought by their Guardian and Grand Council. The meteorite had shattered on impact, with pieces of rock and metal littering around the area, bouncing away from the impact site. The barrier had been obliterated, absorbing most of the impact before failing. The front gatehouse and surrounding walls lay in ruins, and the defenders lay strewn about the streets and the surviving battlements, many dead, even more too wounded to move.

This was the opportunity that the Knights had been waiting for. Quickly rallying the men to their feet, the Knights marched into the city, clambering over the smoldering ruins of the gatehouse and moving to engage their foes.

Calunoth and his companions were among the few who had maintained their feet as the shockwaves rolled through the city. Shielded by the low curtain wall of the castle, the effect hadn't been as jarring to those in the castle, and many were able to stay on their feet. After the impact, silence reigned as the dust from the ruins of the gate and wall settled.

Calunoth regained his composure first just as the courtyard descended into anarchy. The assembled military began running out into the city to meet the wave of incoming Knights. The battle would be joined in the town. Calunoth seized on the confusion to pull Claere and the rest of his companions into the Eastern Tower, where they ducked under a staircase to plan their next move.

"What the hell was that?" Luca whispered quietly. "Do we even need to keep going? Or should we go back to join the fighting in the city?"

"The barrier is down, but you saw those weapons. The Knights will be at a disadvantage against them so long as the Pralia Core is active, even with the barrier down," Bleiz replied.

"And we have to take out Lenocius. We can attack their command here," Calunoth added. "How guarded will the keep be now? Do we know?" He looked at the experienced Bleiz for guidance.

Bleiz shook his head and said, "I can only guess." The veteran captain went on to explain. "This castle isn't as defensible as the outer wall. Most of the fighting is going to be in small pockets in the city. Byrant's forces might be driven back here, but they're most likely going to try and make a stand in the streets first."

"We actually saw Byrant on the way here," Luca announced. "It looked like he was heading to the town square with his entourage."

"He is the sort of man to lead from the front, from what I've heard," Lauren said.

Luca looked up at the staircase and said, "Well, I can respect him for that at least, but it means that the castle won't be as well guarded. We should be able to move through it without too much resistance."

"What about the Guardians?" Alexander asked. "Relgar and Van both defected. Did you see them with Byrant?"

Bleiz sat on the first step, taking advantage of a moment to rest his older bones. "I recognized Van. He was walking next to Byrant. Byrant wears golden armor, so he's easy enough to see. I didn't see Relgar though."

"Did you just miss him?" Lauren asked, but Bleiz shook his head in response.

"Relgar's massive. He's bigger than Artair. If he was there, I'd know. I'm hoping he was at the gate, personally. He's the last person we want to be seeing," Bleiz replied.

"It doesn't matter where he is. We have to get to the Pralia Core anyway," Calunoth interrupted. "Alex, you were studying maps of the castle last night. Where should we head?"

The mage looked around grimly, matching their current location to what he remembered of the map. "We're at the base of the Eastern Tower right now. Our intel stated the Pralia Core was located in the

Central Tower, close to the top. It makes sense. If Lenocius is using it, then he'd have to have a high vantage point."

"All right, then let's head there. We move quickly and kill anyone in our way. We'll do better with the element of surprise than with trying to bluff our way through the castle, especially with everyone on edge right now," Calunoth decided. "Let's go. We're finishing this war."

Bleiz rose, and together, he and Luca handed their companions' weapons back now that there was no more need to continue their prisoner charade, and they started moving rapidly through the halls. The castle's interior was of the same glistening white stone as the exterior, almost blinding the companions when the sun shone through the windows and reflected off the glaring rocks. The castle was luxuriously appointed, far more so than Commerel since this castle was primarily residential rather than militaristic. Long flowing rugs swept down the corridors, and artisanal paintings decorated the walls.

It seemed odd to Calunoth that a man like Byrant would preach about the poor while living in such a well-appointed manor, but his musings were interrupted as the companions encountered their first opponents. A group of four men-at-arms, brought in from the far-flung reaches of the country and drawn by the prospect of improving their fortunes in the fires of war ran up, swords drawn. They were no match for the skilled companions. Calunoth and Luca led the charge, with the skilled priestess and veteran captain falling in behind. Alexander didn't even bother to ready his spells. Primarily with the group to provide magical support, the mage wouldn't have had the time to weave formulae before his companions concluded the skirmish.

The group traveled as quickly as they could through the castle after that, aware of the sounds of the battle floating in through the windows. The buzz of noise outside was frequently punctuated by a sudden onslaught of combat as the group fought their way through the castle. With most of the veteran separatist Knights facing their opponents in the streets, there were few skilled opponents left to defend the castle, and no group or single fighter they encountered could outmatch the companions, who now worked seamlessly together.

The distance was not far, but the frequency of the fighting slowed the group down considerably. Calunoth briefly wondered if moving covertly would have been the better course of action but dismissed the idea. For good or ill, they were committed now. They would stay their course.

The group soon arrived at the tall staircase that marked the Central Tower steps and found it guarded by two Knights, who stood at their posts resolutely despite the cacophony of noise emanating from outside. As they had not been detected yet, Alexander took the opportunity to flex his own muscles, weaving several basic formulae in the air and whispering verses of a spell. Calunoth thought to ask him what spell he was casting before he started, but Alexander merely winked and whispered, "You'll see."

Calunoth wished he had exerted more pressure on the mage as the white stone of the hallway suddenly exploded with red light, reflecting the noise and light of the ball of fire that Alexander propelled toward the vigilant Knights. The spell was effective but had an unfortunate side effect.

"ALEX! I can't see anything!" Calunoth cursed at the mage. In a dark hallway, the effect would have been reduced, but against the bright white stone of the castle, Calunoth was blinded. It was a grim positive that the victim Knights wouldn't have seen their impending doom.

"Worse, you've just told every man within a hundred miles we're here!" Bleiz yelled.

Shielding his eyes from the aftereffects of the fire ball, Calunoth ran past the charred corpses of the guards and up the stairwell with his friends in tow. Along the way, they encountered three more Knights who had been alerted to their presence by Alexander's spell. This battle was not as smooth for the companions, with Calunoth receiving a sharp cut across the back of his hand and Claere receiving a shallow gash along her forearm while dispatching their foes. The battle won, the group stopped only long enough to let Lauren tend to Claere's cut. Calunoth refused her help, telling her to save her strength.

"This tower is far more well guarded than the rest of the castle," Bleiz observed.

"It means that there's something important here," Claere deduced. "Byrant wouldn't waste his best men here if there wasn't."

The companions continued to climb the stairs, encountering more resistance, but always pushing forward. It had now been over an hour since Valthor had brought down the front gate, and the battle outside now raged in earnest. Calunoth briefly sighted the chaos from a window cut into the side of the tower that granted a commanding view of the city. The Pralia-enhanced weaponry allowed the defenders to stand fast against the overwhelming numbers of attackers, even with the losses they had taken at the gate. The core of the battle now seemed to be centered in various hot zones around the city: in the market, the slums, and the western wall. But the heaviest concentration of fighting was in the central square.

Calunoth continued to climb the stairs, his mind ignoring the protestations of his body. He was close now. Closer than ever before. This was his opportunity to kill Lenocius and excise the demons from his mind for good. As he neared the top, there remained only two ways to go: to the top of the tower or through a side door manned by a single guard. The group had no need to make a decision because they divided and conquered. Calunoth dispatched the guard, and Luca ran up the rest of the steps to scout out the tower. He returned quickly.

"Nothing but Byrant's office up there. No guards, nothing suspicious," Luca reported.

"I could've told you that!" Calunoth snapped at him. "It's this way. I can feel it. My core's burning up right now." Shifting the dead guard's body out of the way, Calunoth pulled the heavy oaken door open and rushed into the room, followed by his companions, only to stop dead in his tracks.

The room they were in was large, and empty, but it was tiny compared to the man who blocked the way, standing in front of the stairs that led to the solitary turret attached to the Central Tower.

"Relgar," Bleiz breathed, and Calunoth was startled by the note of fear in the captain's voice.

Relgar had been sitting on a stool in front of the opposing door, acting as the final guard to the Pralia Core. Seeing the companions rush in, he rose to his full, towering height. Well over seven feet tall and built like a brick wall, the man could avoid fights with just a glare from his pitch-black eyes. He had a long mane of silver hair that belied his age, framing a heavily bearded face. In his left hand, he held what appeared to be a large scythe almost as tall as he was.

"So, you're the team the boy tried to smuggle in?" Relgar's voice was deep and ominous, a reflection of the chest it emanated from. "You came for the Pralia Core, I suppose? You must be since it's your only chance of winning this war."

"Look outside, Relgar!" Bleiz yelled before regulating his tone, ever the diplomat. "Your armies are crumbling. Surrender the core to us, and we'll speak favorably for you when the battle is won."

"I would disagree with you, Knight of the Wilds. As long as Lenocius can stream our men's Ynia through the core, our defenses will hold. We only need a few more hours to re-establish the barrier. Though I admit that meteor was something. I'm guessing you can only do that once. That must have been Valthor, yes? No one else is stupid enough to try something like that," Relgar responded.

"Why aren't you out in the field?" Luca asked. "Your men are dying out there. You should be fighting with them!" Luca's appeal to the man's honor was ineffective.

"I can do more to honor my men by defending the source of their power, which now I must defend from you. Prepare yourselves! You will never reach Lenocius!" Relgar swung his weapon and advanced on the group.

The companions scattered, drawing their weapons as Relgar surged toward them. Calunoth, Claere, Bleiz, and Luca dove to opposite sides, narrowly dodging the first sweep of the scythe, then diving back to the corners of the room to avoid the second fluid sweep. The Guardian was not as fast as Valthor, but he was far stronger. He would only need one good hit to land to strike a fatal blow.

Unfortunately for the companions, Relgar was not just strong, he was intelligent. Alexander and Lauren had stood behind the group and hadn't needed to dodge out of the way of the enormous blade. In just his first two sweeps, Relgar had dismantled the protective layer that the vanguard had given their magic-using allies, leaving them exposed to the Guardian's sweeping scythe.

Without the time to cast formulae, Alexander was at Relgar's mercy. Using his own intellect, he jumped forward, beyond the path of the sharp blade. Though his maneuver had kept him out of the path of the blade, it had brought him closer to Relgar and allowed the scythe's hilt to crash heavily into the mage's outstretched hand. That brief moment of resistance gave Lauren enough time to follow Luca to the back of the room, even as Alexander was thrown to the far wall by the force of the scythe, slamming heavily into the white stone and landing on the floor, severely winded.

With Alexander temporarily disabled and the threat of their magic user neutralized, Relgar turned his attention back to the warriors who now encroached upon him. Luca attacked first, swinging his sword downward, only to find it met by the steel handle of Relgar's scythe, then quickly repelled as he was forced back by the strength of the Guardian. Bleiz and Calunoth followed behind, launching simultaneous attacks on the Guardian, attempting to flank him while Claere moved in, aiming her weapon through the center of the gap they had created.

Relgar was having none of it. He swung his massive weapon with the ease of a pitchfork, spinning it over the back of his hand as he whipped the blade around the room, imperiling them all as they ducked under the blade. The companions tried to attack Relgar, now in the center of the room, from every angle, but they were thwarted by the sudden appearance of his black metal blade at every attempt.

Relgar had earned the title of Guardian. And he proved it in earnest as he fought even handed, outnumbered six to one, against his capable foes, even pressing his advantage against them. Surrounding the Guardian, the melee combatants of the group attempted to poke and prod at Relgar, trying to keep him in the center of the room, or at the very least, away from Alexander and Lauren.

Lauren had been tending to Alexander, who had recovered enough to speak, although he did so with difficulty. He now regained his feet, clutching his ribs. Grimacing, he began to recite incantations and cast formulae with the intention of disabling Relgar for long enough for one of his companions to land a finishing blow. But Relgar was wise to the mage and broke free of the circle with a vicious lunge, shattering the mage's concentration and interrupting his casting. Alexander dove back behind his armed companions, and they provided cover from the sweeping blade as they moved to intercept the Guardian.

Luca began to attack in earnest, being the closest physical match to Relgar, and attacked with such ferocity that it put the Guardian on the defensive. Luca's onslaught also gave the companions time to retreat and strategize.

"We need Alex or Lauren to attack him at range. We can use that opportunity to finish him off," Calunoth panted on one knee.

"No," Bleiz replied grimly. "He's too sharp for that. We can't beat him as it stands." Sweating profusely from the exertion of fighting a Guardian for so long, the captain watched Luca battle. "All we can do is distract him as long as we can. We have a mission to complete. Cal, get to the core. We'll stay down here and keep Relgar busy."

"But Bleiz!" Calunoth began, but the old captain couldn't hear him. He had already jumped back into the fray.

"Cal! Let's go!" Claere grabbed his arm and pulled him away and up the open stairwell, running past Alexander and Lauren as they tried to cast formulae but struggled to complete them with the barely supressed Relgar looming. Luca and Bleiz doubled their efforts, and Relgar was unable to intercept Calunoth and Claere as they ran up the stairs.

Calunoth despised leaving his friends behind to face the fearsome Guardian, but he felt like he had no choice. They were running out of time. And every minute they waited, more of the king's men would die at the hands of the Pralia technology. The pair ran quickly, finally reaching the top of the turret and coming to a heavy oaken door sealed with magic.

"What is this?" Calunoth asked, attempting to open the door without success.

"It's a Sihleon locking formulae," Claere answered. "I can remove it, but I need some time. Watch my back!" Calunoth did as the priestess commanded, and as he did so, the red rage that had given him purpose rushed to the surface. All that was separating him from Lenocius was this single oaken door. He could hardly wait a second longer as Claere murmured the incantation to unlock the door.

Claere spent several minutes unlocking the formulae and had just completed it as a guttural roar sounded from below. Startled, Claere almost ran down to check on her friends, but Calunoth stopped her, shaking his head.

"We can only go forward now," Calunoth said. "As fast as we can. We need to get to Lenocius before Relgar comes after us."

Claere was about to protest when she was interrupted by the appearance of a blood-soaked Luca, who wore a grim smile as he ran up the steps. Alexander appeared behind him, with Lauren assisting a grimacing Bleiz.

"Are you all okay? Where's Relgar?" Claere asked her companions.

"Dead," Luca reported. "thanks to Lauren's quick thinking. Bleiz took a heavy blow to his arm, and Alex has a couple broken ribs, but apart from that, we're okay."

"Bloody quick thinking it was too!" Bleiz exclaimed. "Using a medical spell to accelerate Relgar's strike! Medical spells are supposed to heal not hurt!"

"It was nothing," Lauren replied sheepishly. "I just thought if he gained more strength in his dominant arm, then he wouldn't be able to account for the weight of his attack. I threw him off balance, but Luca gets the credit for the final blow."

"Enough talk. Let's go!" Calunoth pushed the door open and stormed into the turret room, pausing for a moment. The room looked like a different world.

The room still sported the white stone of the rest of the castle, but it was overlaid with a complex mesh of metal wires and pipes, all of which emitted the strange red light of the triangular Pralia Core housed in an apparatus at the back of the room. The turret room offered a commanding view of the city, but was relatively small, occupied only by the machinery and a single solitary figure cloaked in white standing before the Pralia Core.

"I see Relgar has failed me," a voice of honey said without turning around. "Not to worry, I can handle myself."

"LENOCIUS!" Calunoth roared, sprinting across the room ready to deliver the death blow to the architect of the Glathaous Massacre.

"Away!" Lenocius commanded, sweeping around to face them, waving his arm, the magic of the Pralia Core powering his spell.

A strong gust of wind pummeled Calunoth's chest, reversing his momentum and sending him and his companions flying against the wall.

"Bind!" Lenocius continued, and Calunoth alone fell to the floor, feeling an infusion of strength from the core in his chest. His companions had been bound by magical chains to the far wall, immobilized by the magic. They struggled as Lenocius considered them, his eyes narrowing as he realized Calunoth had been unaffected by his spell. He examined Calunoth for a moment.

"What is this trickery?" he wondered aloud before his eyes widened in recognition, and he let out a sigh of understanding. "Oh! Of course. The pieces finally fall into place. I thought you were hiding, boy. I thought that the rumors of someone taking your name would bring you out, and I see they have. Do you have the Glathaous Core with you? Or is that pesky mage, Aaron, on his way here as well?"

"Aaron's dead. It just me, you bastard!" Calunoth growled, resuming his feet. "I'm going to make you pay for what you did. You destroyed Glathaous Castle! You killed all of them! All for this stupid core! It's time for you to answer for what you've done!"

"My dear boy, I thought we had an understanding? If my agents had been able to retrieve the core as planned, that whole nasty accident could have been avoided. Isaac must have overloaded the machinery, causing the explosion. I had no intention of letting Glathaous Castle be destroyed like that. You must believe me," Lenocius replied calmly.

"You lied to me! You said they'd be safe! You said they would all be safe! Your men slaughtered everyone in the grounds!" Calunoth bellowed, the rage making his voice hoarse.

"There were more casualties than expected, but sacrifices are made in war. Your family would have been safe if you had done your job properly instead of disappearing into the night with the core." Lenocius tried to reason with the almost incoherent Calunoth. "But look at what I've done even without the Glathaous Core!"

Lenocius gestured around the room. "This technology will not only win the war for Byrant, it will help me retake Sihleo from the Church of the One! It will take humanity further forward in the next ten years than we have advanced in the past two thousand years combined! It's not too late my boy! My offer still stands. Give me the Glathaous Core, and with its unlimited potential, we can build a future without war and suffering. We alone can cast down the gods! What say you? Will you strike me down and send us all back to the dark ages? Or will you stand with me and together usher in a future brighter than ever before? Or will you die here trying to stop me like the rest of your family? What say you, Scion of Glathaous?"

Reaching for his longsword, he drew it and pointed it at Calunoth. "What say you, Alistair Glathaous?!"

Chapter 27

The Debt Comes Due

"You took everything from me!" Alistair screamed at the white-robed minister. "What say I? What say I? I'll tear you to pieces!" And with that guttural roar, Alistair sprinted across the room, slashing his sword at Lenocius in a savage strike across his torso. Lenocius held his ground and easily blocked the blow, parrying the blade away and sending Alistair reeling back. As he was knocked off balance, Alistair backpedaled before spinning around and slashing horizontally at Lenocius from his opposite side.

Luca watched on, unsure of what to do, as Alistair attacked fervently, madly, recklessly. Any desire to survive had deserted Alistair as he ducked and wove, smashing back at Lenocius with murderous intent. There was no one to hold him back anymore.

Luca's head was spinning at the revelation of Calunoth's real identity, but he couldn't afford to contemplate it now. He yanked his hands from the wall with all his strength, but the magical manacles cut deeply into his flesh. He strained with all his might, but the manacles held. His companions were similarly bound and could do nothing but watch as their friend—was he even their friend?—dueled his mortal foe.

Lenocius was a skilled duelist, going through his paces with moves that bore several similarities to Claere's style, but there was more to his ability than just skill. He moved faster than a human should and seemed to strike harder than a human should be able. He wasn't as strong as Valthor or Relgar, but he fought on the same level as a Guardian candidate. As he watched the blur of their forms and the sparks of their blades, Luca remembered fighting Jarl in Commerel. He had been augmented with a shard of Pralia technology. That technology had made Jarl so strong he had been able to shatter Calunoth's sword. Jarl had been an amateur fighter to begin with, so even with his augmentations, he had not been strong enough to defeat Luca and Calunoth combined. Lenocius was a different opponent. He was older than Jarl but far more skilled, and Alistair found himself slowly being driven back.

Lenocius maintained his calm demeanor even as he fought, slipping his blade past Alistair's guard on multiple occasions, needling his body with small pricks and scratches. The power of the Pralia technology gave Lenocius the advantage, but he was almost matched by the unchecked rage that burned through Alistair. The minister's heightened strength was matched by Alistair's hatred, which passed through their blades with every strike. And the minister's speed was countered by Alistair's abandonment of his own safety.

Their blades danced up and down, creating a cacophony of clanging that mingled with the noise of battle rising from the city. But Lenocius was slowly emerging as the victor, even as he was pushed to his limits. Alistair could not compete with the raw energy of the Pralia technology that powered Lenocius' onslaught. Alistair had only the power granted by his rage; his life alone sustained by the Glathaous Core. Lenocius had the Life Ynia of the citizens of Byrantia to power his strikes.

After several frenetic minutes of frenzied sparring, Lenocius finally made a strike tell, feinting to his left, and then reversing his strike, he slashed through Alistair from hip to shoulder, severing the straps that held his leather chest guard in place and sending him spiraling backward onto the floor, his armor fluttering off his chest. Lenocius would have jumped forth to finish the job, but he was forced to retreat to his defensive stance as a glaring light erupted from beneath Alistair's chest.

The Glathaous Core shone a radiant white, as close as it was to a fully active Pralia Core. Previously held in check by Alistair's armor, it now emitted both heat and light, blinding his opponent. Rivulets of blood slowly dripped from the long, shallow cut he had sustained along his torso. Lenocius held back for a moment, cautious of this new threat, as he waited for his eyes to adjust. Alistair used the brief respite to regain his feet, panting heavily, but not yet depleted.

Lenocius eyed the disgraced noble warily, his pupils dilating even in the face of the bright light, his mind working quickly.

"How did you do that to the core, Alistair? It's not sustainable implanted in a living being like that," Lenocius asked, carefully calculating the new threat.

Alistair let out a cackle, the demons inside him now given full reign.

"How did I do it? I'll tell you how I did it! I killed the guards protecting my home and got stabbed through the heart in return! My father thought it was some sick joke to put this core into my chest when I should have died at the gates!" Alistair replied, his eyes glazed over, a sickly grin plastered across his face. "This thing keeps me alive. At least it will long enough to kill you!"

Lenocius stared at the shining core in disbelief before he scowled and growled, his honeyed tone disappearing. "Then I'm afraid I must rescind my offer. I'll cut that core out of your chest myself!"

Alistair threw back his head and laughed wildly. "Come and get it! I sure as hell don't want it!" he replied, laughing.

"Cal! Look out!" Claere's voice rung out, breaking Alistair from his mad stupor as Lenocius jumped the difference between them.

Alistair allowed Lenocius to close the gap between them, waiting until the last moment to move, shifting ever so slightly to avoid the flashing steel of the longsword, missing death by inches. Then he struck back, swinging wildly. The dynamic of the fight had changed. Lenocius had, initially, been aiming to subdue Alistair, even as he was consumed with rage. Alistair's death could have meant losing the only known information about the Glathaous Core in his chest, which Lenocius hadn't been prepared to risk. But with the core now the prize of the duel, Lenocius fought to kill.

Alistair had forsaken the promise he had made to Claere to overcome the darkness in his heart, instead being consumed by it, and attacked with an energy beyond rage. The guilt that had been weighing on his mind, beyond even the weight of the world, had taken its toll, and the damage was done. His eyes grew vacant, his mind was in a different place. He attacked clumsily, cackling. Lenocius was unnerved by this sudden change in Alistair, but he had his goals set. He needed the core; all he had to do was finish the job he had begun and kill Alistair.

Lenocius struck again, repeatedly jabbing and stabbing at Alistair, landing more hits than he was missing, slowly wearing him down. Alistair responded by swinging his sword crazily, severing some of the metal pipes feeding into the Pralia apparatus at the end of the room, before striking back at Lenocius again. He laughed madly even as blood oozed from the many small wounds Lenocius had inflicted upon him until they were back at the beginning, with Lenocius facing Alistair, just as they had faced each other in Glathaous Castle on the day of the Spring Dawning. Lenocius' back was to the Pralia apparatus.

Lenocius had been measuring Alistair's rapidly deteriorating form and prepared to finish him. Alistair gave a triumphant roar and surged forward, leaving himself exposed to a fatal strike. It was not an opportunity Lenocius would waste, but in seizing it, he made a critical mistake, a mistake made by fighting an opponent who had no care for whether he lived or died.

Lenocius shifted his stance, and in a single smooth motion, drove his sword clean through Alistair's chest, piercing his torso just below the Glathaous Core and thrusting out through his back. But in doing so, he could not arrest Alistair's momentum, and with his own sword embedded deep within Alistair, he had no time to recover.

With a sputtering, bloody gasp, Alistair drove his sword through Lenocius' heart, crashing into him as his own body was penetrated and carrying them both backward where they collapsed onto the Pralia apparatus.

Lenocius' eyes widened in pain as he stared dumbly down at the hilt of Alistair's sword buried in his chest, then up at the demonic smile that illuminated Alistair's face. Lenocius was finished, and he knew it. The Glathaous Core burned with an explosive energy as it came into contact with the Pralia apparatus, and Lenocius realized what would happen next. He coughed up blood before staring into Alistair's madness-tainted eyes, the eyes of the man who had slain him.

Lenocius gave a heavy sigh, then a small smile. "This fight's... not over, my boy." The minister's breathing was shallow and rapid. "PRIMAL... will endure. We will... be bound by our gods no... longer. You...are my proof... of that." Then he slid down to the base of the Pralia apparatus to lay on the floor, dead. His white robes were stained red with blood, both his own and what he had taken.

Alistair lay on the Pralia apparatus as he bled out, feeling the energy build higher and higher, emitting more and more heat and light as it reacted with the Glathaous Core. Alistair's Life Ynia surged into the apparatus and was converted into Natural Ynia before being reconverted back into Life Ynia by the Glathaous Core. The conversion cycle rose until the Ynia breached an unstable level.

Suddenly, there was a loud gush like rushing water, and an explosion of light lit up the turret tower, visible from miles around as the PRIMAL Pralia apparatus gave a last majestic surge, blasting Alistair back onto the floor before finally going dark and taking its light from Byrant's forces.

With Lenocius dead, the magical bonds he had used to bind his opponents to the wall now failed, and they fell, landing lightly on their feet, struggling to process the fight that they had witnessed.

"Cal!" Claere cried, running first to Alistair's supine form as he lay dying on the floor. Lifting his head off the floor, she examined his wounds. His skin was burned lightly red from the failure of the Pralia apparatus. He was covered in small nicks and scratches, and a long, shallow cut ran across his torso, but the most grievous wound was the last inflicted. His central blood vessels had been severed and now bled profusely from both sides. His lower ribcage had also been shattered by the injury, and examining it, Claere saw the dimming light of the Glathaous Core.

The core had a small crack in the base above the wound, and the light that had shone so brightly moments earlier was now dwindling and flickering. Life Ynia was no longer passing into Alistair; it had bypassed him in its mad rush to eruption.

The rest of the companions stood around Alistair, unsure of what to do. Their mission was complete, but they had no idea what to do next. Lauren knelt beside Claere, and together they began to wearily cast their healing magic, only to be stopped by a weak, bloodied hand.

"Leave it …" Alistair murmured, the shock of his wounds bringing him back from the brink of madness. "This is … the way it should be. He's dead, and now, it's my turn."

"Calunoth … or … or Alistair. Who are you?" Claere asked, tears forming in her beautiful red-and-blue eyes.

"I am Alistair Glathaous. I conspired with Lenocius to procure the Glathaous Core for him. In exchange, my family, my people would be safe from Byrant. We would have protection … and wouldn't have to send anyone to war." Alistair spoke slowly and with great difficultly, blood wheezing out of his mouth with every word. "He came to Glathaous and convinced me there was no way for us to win this war. I … I just wanted to protect myself … and them."

"Why did you lie to us?" Luca demanded. "We're your friends. We could have helped you!"

"When you found me … I was confused. I couldn't remember much. Then when it started coming back to me, all I knew was … was I had failed. They were dead. All of them. And it was my fault. Alistair Glathaous was at fault. To get to Lenocius, I … couldn't be Alistair anymore. I'm sorry," Alistair whispered softly, his voice growing weaker with every word. "I, and two of Lenocius' men from PRIMAL, killed the guards at the gates ... and opened them while everyone was at the feast." A coughing spasm racked his body as he seized for his last desperate breaths. "The rest of PRIMAL ... was supposed to have ... taken over the castle ... seized the core, and left, without harming anyone they didn't need to. They ... they couldn't have done it without me ... I killed Calunoth Leiron. He died guarding the gate after stabbing me through the heart. I fell from the gatehouse and was rescued by Aaron. He ... and my father ... implanted the core in me and carried me to safety in the woods. Everyone died in the explosion ... so ... so there was no one left to find out ... that I was lying."

"Everything you've said to us. Everything we've done! Was it all a joke to you? A lie?!" Lauren cried out.

"I'm sorry. Truly I am. I ... I just thought I had no other way. I've been living as a dead man since that day ... living on borrowed time. But now, I must pay that debt. I will not ask for forgiveness ... because I would not expect it myself, but ... thank you. All of you ... for walking this path ... with a wretch like me." Alistair's breathing slowed as the bodily damage done manifested itself. Alistair Glathaous cast his gaze to the ceiling, ready to die.

"No." Bleiz's stern voice broke through the pain in the room. "You have much to answer for before your god, Alistair Glathaous, but you have much to answer for before your king first. Claere, Lauren, keep him alive," Bleiz ordered the two healers before addressing the barely conscious Alistair.

"Alistair Glathaous, under my authority as Knight Captain of the Wilds, I hereby place you under arrest for high treason, subterfuge, and murder. You will face trial for your actions and your deceptions. As a personal favor to you, as someone who has saved my life on many occasions, I will see to it that you are given a fair trial. There is nothing more I can do for you." Bleiz turned around, bringing the helmet of his visor down.

***

The shattering of the Pralia Core in the Central Tower had sent a wave of light bursting through the skies that had commanded the attention of all the combatants fighting in the streets below. With that radiant arc of light dissipating into the sky, the energy that had powered the insurrectionists' advanced weapons and defenses disappeared, leaving them dim and useless against the oncoming tide.

While the royalist forces had been held at bay throughout the city, with multiple contested nodes of the city seeing battles of attrition between the royalists and the insurrectionists, the loss of their technological advantage pushed the insurrectionists from being outnumbered to outmatched. The superior training and tactics of the offending Knights were too much for Byrant's forces, who were being pushed further and further back into the city, unable to stem the rush of the oncoming attack.

The battle came to a head late in the evening when Guardian Artair personally led a battalion of Wings Knights into the city square. As the streets channeled all the retreating forces back into the square, Byrant and his surviving Guardian, Van, attempted to fortify the square even as they found themselves surrounded on all sides.

Artair and his men broke through the hastily erected barricades and charged the fallen duke's convoy, Guardian facing Guardian in single combat as the remaining royalist forces pushed toward the square.

Van was a hero of Southern Renderive. A farmer's son, who had by auspicious business come into a vast fortune, he was the idol of the people of Byrantia. During a series of enemy raids on his southern farmlands, he had defended his lands with naught but a rusted pitchfork. He had rallied the local men and driven off the invaders, winning the respect of his people. He had become a Guardian after sacrificing his own fortune to help rebuild in the aftermath of the Sieth Incursion, devoting all his efforts to offering justice and peace to the least fortunate among the Southern Renderiveans.

A fierce warrior and scholar, he was the emblem of Byrant's movement, and even the bravest of Knights were hesitant to engage him in combat. Van now wielded a trident, emblematic of the pitchfork by which he had made his name, and stood as the last man standing between the royalist forces and Duke Byrant. Artair alone approached him.

The square fell silent as all the combatants paused in their struggles to watch on as the two legends of Renderive fought each other to the death. Artair was stronger; Van was faster. Artair had a longer reach. Van was more dextrous. But in the end, there could only be one winner. Van whipped his weapon around, taking advantage of the long haft of the trident and sending the sharp points whistling across Artair's face, cutting clean through his right eye.

An attack such as that would have ended most men on the spot, but Artair was a stronger man by far. With a mighty roar, and fighting through the agony of losing his eye, he slashed his mighty blade upward with one hand, forcing Van to raise his trident as he braced for the oncoming blow.

With two hands on his mighty greatsword, Artair brought his blade down heavily on the trident, cleaving it in two and sending the pieces, and their owner, crashing to the ground. Van the Hero had been slain by Artair the Beast.

Duke Byrant had lost. He knew there was no way for his forces to achieve victory. The Pralia technology had failed. His talismanic Guardian had fallen. There was to be no victory for him on the field of battle. He knew what he had to do.

The duke charged Guardian Artair, who was injured and panting from his bout with Van but still incredibly dangerous. Using his shield to block the oncoming greatsword, Byrant went to stab the Guardian through the chest, determined to die on his own terms. But he was fighting a foe who made no such mistakes. Artair shifted, unable to dodge out of the way entirely, but deflecting the oncoming blade into his right shoulder. Then with a might twist, he slashed his blade horizontally through the rebel king before him, parting his head from his body and sending his dream spiraling into the pages of history.

With their talisman dead, there armies routed, and Duke Byrant lying dead on the cobbled stones of the city, the resistance quickly crumbled, and the highest-ranking surviving member of the insurrectionist forces ordered his remaining soldiers to lay down their arms and fly the white flag over the towers of Byrant Castle.

With the battle over, a pall of silence fell over the battlefield as storm clouds rolled across the city. Heaven's gaze was shielded from the sight of the battle, and the gently falling rain worked to wash away the ugly scars of death from the streets of the fallen city.

Chapter 28

Trial of the Traitor

    Over a month had passed since the conclusion of the Rising War, as it had come to be known, and the crisp fall air had given way to the winds of winter as dark nights swept across the country. Following the victory at Byrantia, King Greshaun had withdrawn most of his army to reinforce Caern Porth and Asta's Gate. Upon hearing of the incoming reinforcements, and with winter settling in quickly, the Legrangian forces outside Caern Porth had retreated.

    Although the attack had been brief and harsh, the move by the Legrangians was viewed as an act of war. They had decided to press their advantage against a country wracked and divided by an ongoing civil war. However, the war had not lasted as long as the Legrangians had anticipated, and they had been unable to effectively marshal their forces to march in earnest upon Renderive. As such, they had retreated back beyond the Sieth River to the fortress Regigaard, where they were reported to be awaiting the amassing of the army to attack again in the spring.

    With the borders secured, King Greshaun had left the ruins of Byrantia under the stewardship of the Guardian Artair, returning with the remainder of his army to Deirive. Although the war had been brief, it had been devastating to the Renderivean forces. With each combatant a native of Renderive, the losses had been catastrophic and left Renderive vulnerable to the inevitable attack from the north that would come in the spring.

    Alistair had heard about the events of the world from what whisperings he could hear from his locked tower room in the royal palace. After the death of Lenocius, Lauren and Claere had managed to heal the traitor's terrible wounds thanks to Alexander, who had poured Natural Ynia into the Glathaous Core to stem the loss of Life Ynia as he had lain dying. Their work had been nothing short of miraculous but had still left an ugly scar across Alistair's torso. The scarring matched the wound Calunoth Leiron had inflicted upon him at the gates of Glathaous Castle in his last act of defiance.

    Given the nature of his crime, and the reputation he had previously held among the men, Alistair's identity had been hidden, and by order of King Greshaun, he had been smuggled across the plains, manacled, and hooded. Rumors of the events that had transpired in the tower had spread across the country. Calunoth Leiron was being widely acknowledged as one of the heroes of Byrantia, whose group had slain the Guardian Relgar, along with Artair, who had thrown down the deposed duke. As those stories gave great hope and inspiration to the common folk who needed their heroes now more than ever, the king had insisted Calunoth's true identity be hidden as a strictly guarded secret until such time that proper measures could be taken against the disgraced noble.

In the two weeks since his return to Deirive, Alistair had been well tended to, but a prisoner regardless as he awaited his trial. His companions had returned separately after swearing oaths of secrecy to the king and handing him over to a contingent of the Royal Guards to be delivered back to Deirive. Alistair had not seen any of his companions since the conclusion of the battle. Alone in the tower, he had spent the nights in a sleepless dream where his demons still reigned supreme. Even after avenging his family by killing Lenocius, he could find no respite from his pain. He should have died at Glathaous. And then he should have died at Byrantia. He had cheated death twice in a perversion to the natural order of the world. Alone and friendless with the madness beckoning, all he could do was wait for the eternal sleep that would be granted him at the conclusion of his trial.

There wasn't long to wait now. He was set to be judged by the king himself at dawn. He would be given a chance to speak in his own defense. And then King Greshaun would decide his fate. And that would be the end of Alistair Glathaous. Perhaps, in an act of righteousness, the name, Calunoth Leiron, would live on as that of a hero, inspired by events months after his death. Maybe that was the justice that Calunoth deserved. Of all the lives he had taken, the one who had looked so similar to him, almost like a brother, was still the one that took center stage in his nightmares. That man had been better than him in every measurable way and had been cast down honorably in pursuit of his duty.

How different would the world be had he survived and I had died? Would he have pursued Lenocius? Would he have overcome the creatures of the Caerwyn Bogs and thwarted PRIMAL's efforts? Would he have killed Reil as I did? Would he have risen above me? Or would he have fallen to the madness sooner? Alistair wondered pensively.

His musings were interrupted by a faint knock on the door, startling Alistair out of his reverie. He looked at the door, confused. It was not yet dawn, and the summons was not supposed to arrive for hours yet.

The guard who stood vigil over Alistair's room pushed open the heavy wooden door, and a tall, weak figure walked slowly into the room, leaning heavily on a staff he carried in his left hand. The figure perceived him with weary green eyes before he went to sit in a chair in the corner. It took Alistair several moments to realize who the man was.

"Valthor! What's happened to you?" Alistair asked the Guardian. His dark-brown hair had turned a dull shade of white. His handsome, strong features had hollowed out and become gaunt. His powerful stride had been reduced to a heavy-handed gait. He wore no armor, only a flowing green robe.

"Didn't you see? I thought it was a hell of way to go out," Valthor replied, smiling weakly.

"I know you and the council brought down the meteor that destroyed the barrier, but I didn't know you'd been injured like this!"

"This isn't an injury, Cal. This is a cost. The cost of violating the laws of nature and calling on the wrath of heaven when the forces of earth are at war," Valthor answered. "To complete the spell, I had to channel an abhorrent amount of Ynia through my body. You see the result. My body has been almost completely destroyed. But I'm alive. Just. And that's far more than I should expect given my actions. Three of the seven Grand Council members died casting that spell. Another is as useless as me. This war has taken a heavy toll on the kingdom."

"I'm sorry," Alistair said, genuinely sorry to see the once invincible Guardian reduced to such a state. "And you shouldn't call me 'Cal' anymore, Valthor. My name is Alistair."

"Are you sure?" Valthor replied, his piercing gaze meeting Alistair's.

Alistair crossed his arms, confused. "What do you mean? Of course, I'm sure. Alistair is the name I was born with. It's the name I lived with most of my life. And now it's the name I'll die with."

"That wasn't what I meant," Valthor replied. "You told me on the hill before the battle that you'd already died once. So, Alistair Glathaous has already died once. Are you Alistair Glathaous, or are you

373

Calunoth Leiron? Very few people have the opportunity to remake themselves as you did. Who now will go to stand trial?"

Alistair was silent for several long moments until at last Valthor gave an exasperated sigh. "I know you *were* Alistair Glathaous. My question is, who are you now?"

The question hit Alistair with the weight of destiny. Who was he? What was he? Could a person truly be remade? And at what cost?

"I … I don't know," Alistair admitted. "I'm not the same coward Lenocius consorted with. But I'm still a murderer and a traitor. I don't know what I am beyond that."

Valthor looked at him with his inscrutable, piercing eyes before rising heavily from the chair.

"Well, I suggest you figure out the answer to that question before you stand trial. Or maybe someone else will have to do it for you. As your official commanding officer, Bleiz was supposed to supervise the trial. I was your commanding officer for a while too, however, and he has granted me the right to stand in his place." Valthor turned to leave. "Think hard before you come to judgment, Hero of Byrantia." With that, he knocked on the door, and the guard outside opened it for him. Halfway out, he stopped and looked at Alistair over his shoulder. "By the way, there's someone else coming to see you after me. Maybe she'll give you a push in the right direction." Then the door slammed shut behind him, and Alistair was left alone in the room once more.

The isolation was not prolonged. After being alone for the past two weeks, Alistair was ill-prepared to receive two visitors in the hours before his trial, but he rose regardless when he heard a gentle knocking at the door, and his heart skipped a beat when a wash of raven hair swayed into the room.

Claere strode into the room wearing the unique steel-inlaid leather armor that marked her as a Sihleon priestess, her long hair tied back. She exuded the same cool, calm, collected air as always. Of everyone on the planet, she was both the first and the last person Alistair wanted to see. Her eyes held their usual steel, but a veil of concern was present deep within her red-and-blue eyes.

"Claere, why did you come to see me?" Alistair asked the priestess, his heart pounding more than a forsaken man's should.

"I wanted to hear you what you had to say for yourself, now that you've had time to think," Claere answered softly.

"Why didn't you just wait for the trial then? You'll hear enough about me there to know my fate," Alistair replied bitterly.

Then Claere did something he didn't expect. He had expected a harsh reprisal, or a blistering interrogation, or merely a dismissive sneer from the superb priestess. But he received none of those. Instead, Claere strode over and put her finger on his lips.

"Because I don't want to hear prepared answers and judgments from people who don't know you. I want to know what you're thinking, what you've decided, Calunoth," she replied quietly.

"Calunoth …" Alistair's voice stumbled, almost breaking. "Valthor called me that too. Why do you use that name? It belongs to a man far better than I."

"Because I do not believe it is the name of an evil man. I believe it is the name of a man who suffered horrendous loss, who gave in at the worst moment of weakness. And a man who rose from his own ashes to reclaim his honor. Whatever you were before, I have only ever known the man I call Calunoth Leiron. It is a name that suits the person you are now better than the name of the traitor who betrayed his people." Claere somehow edged even closer to him. She was so close now. Closer than they had ever been. Alistair smelled the juniper and floral notes in her hair in a wave of overwhelming sentimentality.

"Claere," Alistair was gradually becoming aware of a strange watery sensation in his eyes. "I can't be that person. I'm not strong enough. I gave in to my fear before. I can't guarantee I won't do it again. And if I did, I might end up hurting you. Or Luca, or Bleiz, or Lauren, or Alex, or all of you."

"You've done a pretty good job of being that person so far," Claere reminded him. "And if you do end up hurting me, well, I guess I'll just have to slap some sense into you. I'm still a lot stronger than you are, you know?" A radiant, albeit small, smile graced her face.

"Why don't you hate me?' Alistair asked her, overwhelmed by her faith.

"I hate Alistair Glathaous. He's a traitor, and a coward, and a loser who should be dead and buried," Claere replied. "But I don't think that's who you are anymore. At least, not to me."

"But it *is* the name that I carry. And the lies I've told. How can you, of all people, have any faith left in me?" Alistair asked.

"Well, it's because …" Claere's voice trailed off, and her cheeks turned a becoming pink. "It's because I don't believe that the past should own us. We're all sinners in one way or another. To err is to be human. You have acknowledged your failures and now go to face judgment for them. I wish more people could do the same. The world would be a better place for it."

The sun was rising in the eastern sky, spilling light into the dark room of the tower, but all Alistair could see was the light reflected in Claere's eyes and her hope for him that he had himself forsaken. He gravitated toward her until his forehead touched hers, and his senses were overwhelmed with the scent of juniper. "Whatever happens to you Cal," Claere whispered, "I forgive you." Alistair touched his nose towards the priestesses, growing ever closer, his mind awash with affection.

Then a heavy knock sounded, and the moment passed. The door swung open. Alistair took a step away from Claere as it did so. It was the captain of the Royal Guards, Amderg, who beckoned for Alistair to come with him.

"Come with me, Master Glathaous. The king awaits you."

Alistair felt the priestess's sturdy hand tightly squeeze his own, just briefly. "I'll come with you. We've received permission to attend the trial," she whispered.

Alistair's thoughts were muddled. He had spent the last two weeks convinced that there was only one price to pay for his deceit. Were Valthor and Claere telling him otherwise?

The walk to the throne room was the longest of Alistair's life. Claere walked behind him, her hand on his shoulder as Amderg guided him, his arms manacled, into the room. Deirive's throne room was exactly as Alistair remembered it. Unlike the rest of the country, Deirive had escaped the Rising War mostly unscathed. The stained glass behind the marble throne tinted the light of the rising sun, bathing King Greshaun in brilliant hues as the light filtered in around him.

The room was not crowded. Alistair had expected a public trial and a public execution soon afterward. This was not to be the case. The room held only a handful of inhabitants. Valthor sat to the right of the throne. He would have been standing were it not for his condition. The left wall was lined with his former companions, Bleiz and Luca in full regalia, Alexander and Lauren wearing their best robes. Alistair could not look them in the eye. There were no other eyes in the room.

Amderg brought Alistair before the throne, bowed to the king, then departed. Claere removed her hand, then went to stand beside her friends. King Aiden Greshaun sat pensively on his throne, his fist propping up his head as he pondered the fallen noble before him.

Valthor broke the silence, reciting the rights of law accorded to Alistair in his trial before asking him to submit himself formally to judgment, which Alistair did so.

"What is the charge?" King Greshaun spoke wearily as though the sight of Alistair brought a heavy burden to his heart.

"Alistair Glathaous is charged with conspiring to steal top-secret research and technology from the Lord Isaac Glathaous, and his actions resulted in the destruction of Glathaous Castle. He is also charged with the first-degree murder of Calunoth Leiron and of continuous subterfuge employed thereafter by taking the name of the aforementioned Calunoth while retaining possession of the Glathaous Core, Isaac Glathaous' legacy." Valthor read from a script that had been prepared beforehand. Ordinarily, Bleiz would have read the charge, but this was far from an ordinary case.

"You have heard the charges laid against you by the Crown, Alistair Glathaous. How do you plead: guilty or not guilty?" the king asked from his throne.

Alistair was silent for a long moment, considering everything that had happened to him, his family, his home, and his friends. His closest advisors had tried to steer him away from his responsibility, but there could be no escape from his own guilt without it.

"Guilty, Your Highness." Alistair spoke quietly but confidently.

King Greshaun considered him carefully before responding. "Do you have anything to say in your own defense?"

"No, Your Highness. I have hurt far too many people already. I must pay the price for my failures," Alistair replied.

"And what do you think that price is, Alistair, son of Isaac?" King Greshaun asked.

"The price is my life. I am at peace with my fate. It is the only way to redemption," Alistair responded.

The king was quiet for a long time. He would make the final decision, but he had to ensure he made the right one. This was a most extraordinary case. "Alistair, using the name of Calunoth Leiron, you fled Glathaous, purged the Caerwyn Bogs of its magical ire, uncovered the secrets of the organization, PRIMAL, helped secure the city of

Commerel during a coup, galvanized the Galgrenons to stay out of the war, and single-handedly slew the Second Minister of Sihleo—an avowed enemy of the state—and paved the way for our victory in the Rising War. Why have you not raised these sterling actions in your defense?" King Greshaun questioned of the noble.

The defendant responded with carefully chosen words. "My actions set me on the path to redemption but do not complete it. I am responsible for my father's death and the destruction of my home for no other reason than my own cowardice. I have not slept properly since that night. I do not believe I will ever sleep properly again. I've been living on borrowed time. I must pay the price demanded of me by the dead," Alistair said.

"And why do you believe the dead demand your head in compensation?" the king asked.

Alistair was quiet for several long moments before responding. "Because that would be justice. That would be the right way for me to die."

King Greshaun let out a heavy sigh and leaned back in his chair. "I believe your pain has given you wisdom beyond your years, Alistair. But it has not yet made it to your shrouded heart," he said slowly. "If you are committed to your judgment, then I will grant it to you. Alistair Glathaous, for the crime of high treason, I hereby sentence you to death. Let word be sent out to the streets that Alistair Glathaous has been executed for his crimes against the Crown. Alistair, while serving as Calunoth, you were the best version of yourself and distinguished yourself against many foes. Therefore, I will grant you back your honor, in death."

King Greshaun murmured a few words to Valthor, who withdrew a pointed dagger from the folds of his green robes. Rising from his seat, he went to Alistair, the dagger outstretched. However, his condition proved to be better than him, and Valthor stumbled down the steps of the dais, only saved from collapsing onto the ground with a curse by the quick-thinking Bleiz. Wiping blood from his mouth after a coughing fit, Valthor passed the dagger to Bleiz, who helped him back to his seat. Bleiz then brought the dagger to Alistair, holding it out for him to take. Refusing to look into his eyes, Alistair grasped the handle, unsure of what he was supposed to do. The knife was deceptively light.

King Greshaun's voice rang throughout the room. "In return for your service, I offer you the opportunity to die on your own terms, rather than be hanged in the public square. May Sentential guide you, Alistair Glathaous."

Alistair looked up at his companions, finally meeting their gaze. He saw anguish in Lauren's eyes, pity in Alexander's, tears in Luca's, anger in Bleiz's, and pain in Claere's. Unable to bear their gaze, he knelt before the king and positioned the dagger below his core, aiming for the arteries that had been severed by Lenocius less than thirty dawns ago. His hands were steady. He would at last be free of his guilt, his anger, his pain. Thoughts of raven hair swung desperately into his mind, and he fought the urge to give voice to them. He would no longer cause pain to those he loved.

Alistair Glathaous gave out a last deep breath and then thrust the ceremonial dagger deep into his abdomen. And then he waited for the pain to come. Then he waited to die.

But death did not come.

Opening his eyes, Alistair looked down at the dagger he had stabbed himself with. To his astonishment, the metal had folded in on itself. The dagger was collapsible! Nothing more than a stage prop. Alistair's resignation of his own death gave way to confusion, and he looked at the throne for guidance.

"And so my sentence is passed, and the debt is paid. Let it be known to all that Alistair Glathaous died by his own hand on this day." King Greshaun's stern face had given way to a relaxed smile. "Rise, Calunoth Leiron, and know my judgment. You will carry the weight of the Glathaous Massacre in your heart until you find your own redemption. However, you will not find it in death, but in life. Take on the name now, forever, of the person who you have become, and strive always to be worthy of it, so that eventually, you will find that which death cannot grant."

"Is this ... is this really the way it must be?" Alistair asked the king.

"Yes. You carry the hope of our nation in your chest. You are the Hero of Byrantia, and Renderive needs you to be that. There are rumors of a schism within the Church of the One. The Legrangian Army is massing to march across the Sieth again. And the heart of PRIMAL, I can now reveal to you, did not die with Lenocius. Your punishment for your crime is that you must spend your life redeeming yourself for it. Forgiveness will not await in the cold embrace of death. There is too much yet I expect from you in this life. This is way it must be." King Greshaun finished passing his final judgment. "Now, you have received forgiveness from your king, but not yet from your god, nor from your companions. I think you'd better get on that, don't you?"

"Of course, Your Majesty, and ... and thank you." Calunoth bowed deeply before the king, who dismissed him.

The king rose and left. Amderg came and released Calunoth from the manacles that had now been rendered moot. Free now, and unsure of what to do with that freedom just yet, Calunoth turned and left the throne room, part of him waiting to be called back or for a guard to come rushing over with the manacles again.

But no one followed him. He reached the doors unscathed and disappeared into the throne room's antechamber. There, Calunoth sat, dazed and overwhelmed by what had occurred. He was interrupted by a surprisingly crushing hug from Lauren, who wrapped her arms tightly around him.

The rest of his companions followed, with varying degrees of exclamations. Luca punched him squarely in the stomach, knocking him to the floor, before helping him up with his steady hand, smiling wryly. Calunoth felt sure Bleiz would have met him similarily, but he was spared a second winding by Valthor's appearance from the throne room, moving as fast as his shattered body would allow him to. The Guardian stopped before him and clasped Calunoth's shoulder, providing them both support.

"Valthor, did you know the king would judge Cal in this manner?" Bleiz asked the Guardian.

"It was my idea, actually," Valthor replied, his demeanor more serious than usual. "You haven't been pardoned, Cal. You understand that, don't you?" He turned his gaze to Calunoth.

Calunoth nodded slowly in response. He gazed at the companions that had brought him all this way, from the ruins of Glathaous to driving his sword through Lenocius to standing trial for his sins. Bleiz, the captain. Luca, the would-be hero. Claere, the priestess. Lauren, the healer. Alexander, the aspiring archmage. They had all fought by his side as he had fought to fuel his rage and to cast down the foe that had tempted him to his most base nature. After all he had seen and heard from them, he now realized what Claere and Valthor had been trying to tell him.

"My death would only compound my guilt. I would be running away again and disgracing the name I took to seek justice," Calunoth spoke slowly.

Valthor continued the thought. "And only in living can you recover the honor you lost in death. You have been given a life sentence, rather than the death penalty. I trust you will make good use of it."

"I understand, and I'll spend the rest of my life justifying the trust you and King Greshaun have placed in me," Calunoth responded.

"It might not be a very long life," Valthor remarked, returning to his humorous nature. "This idea came about for political reasons as much as for justice. We couldn't very well let the world know that Alistair Glathaous was still kicking about. We also couldn't let the Hero of Byrantia be executed in the streets. The people know you as the Hero of Byrantia and the bearer of the Glathaous Core. You're going to have to prove yourself a few more times yet."

"Indeed," Claere interceded. "Lenocius led a large arm of PRIMAL, but he wasn't the head. More branches have been discovered in Sihleo, and they're fostering unrest between the Politik and the Church of the One."

"And the Legrangian Empire is waiting just over the river to march into Renderive in the spring. And by all reports, they have technology similar to what PRIMAL used at Byrantia. Indeed, we've cut the head off of the hydra, but I fear there are many more that will take its place," Alexander added with a shake of his head.

"So, now that this trial business is over, we have work to do," Bleiz concluded, crossing his arms. "Can we trust you'll stand by our side permanently now, Calunoth?"

"Absolutely. If you need me to fight, I'll fight. If you need me to study, I'll study. If you need me to cut trees down in the forest, then I'll do that too. I won't let this opportunity go to waste," Calunoth replied, his eyes burning with a new resolute passion.

And in his heart, Calunoth knew this to be true. By chance or fate, he had been given a second chance at life. And he had no intention of wasting it. Turning to the door, his head held high, he led his companions out of the castle. The demons that had haunted his soul no longer stifled his mind. But he knew they would always be there in the shadows, waiting for him to slip up and claim him, as they had Alistair, and tempt him back into darkness. But so long as the light of the Glathaous Core burned in his chest, he would be safe from the demons in the dark.

Alistair Glathaous had lost his life to the demons. Calunoth Leiron could finally let his life begin.

End of Book II

Author's Note and Acknowledgments

Well, that's it. This is the first novel I've completed in full. It has been an incredibly journey from start to finish getting this book to print, especially in the middle of a pandemic. No story can be told alone, and I would like to acknowledge a few individuals who have helped me along the way.

The first is my editor, Bobbi Beatty, who did a great job making sure that all 150,000 + words were grammatically correct, among her other editorial contributions. The second is my cover artist, Zoe Webster, who realized my vision of the cover without letting me screw it up with my unartistic ideas. My third thank you goes to Angela de Leon and Helen Hughes for taking the time to read the unfinished manuscript before publication. I would also like to thank my family and friends for supporting me throughout the development of this novel.

Lastly, but most importantly, I want to thank you for reading my novel. It is a humbling honor that anyone would deign to read the work that I have produced. I have worked incredibly hard to make this novel as entertaining and engaging as possible, and I hope you feel that you got your money's worth.

Shadows of Redemption is just one story. There is so much more to explore in this world, and I would love to continue Calunoth's story, but I need your help to do so. I am currently a small-time novelist writing for the enjoyment of my fans and I lack the means to make writing my full-time occupation at this moment. If you enjoyed Shadows of Redemption and want to see the story continue, you can help make that happen. Tell your friends about the book, share the story, and if you can't share it, leave a five-star review on Amazon. It's a small task, but it makes a world of difference, and I truly appreciate every single reader who's taken a chance on this, my debut novel. Thank you again for taking this journey with me, and I hope to have the privilege of sharing more of Calunoth's tale with you in the future.

Printed in Great Britain
by Amazon